DIVING IN

Resort to Love #2

GRETCHEN GALWAY

Eton Field

DIVING IN

Chapter 1

As she watched the love of her life stick his tongue into another woman's mouth, Nicki Fitch realized she'd made a terrible mistake.

She'd walked into her friend's kitchen for coffee, not sexual humiliation.

"Oh, Lucy," Miles moaned. Eyes closed, he leaned against the kitchen table, lifting a petite redhead off the floor to insert his tongue deeper into her mouth. The woman, engrossed with the oral probe, didn't see Nicki either. "Lucy, Lucy, Lucy."

This isn't happening. Her chest tightening, Nicki stared at Miles's handsome head under the ten delicate, womanly fingers clutching it.

Why was he in Betty's apartment? They shouldn't even know each other. And why was he kissing somebody? He'd just been through a serious breakup. Nicki had been working up the courage to—

"Oh, Miles," the redhead gasped. The vintage table banged against the wall. The pair kissed for so long Nicki wondered if the woman had SCUBA tanks hidden under all that hair.

How *could* he? He should still be depressed from his last girlfriend throwing soda cans at his head when he asked her to marry him. She, Nicki—his *friend*—had comforted him. They'd talked late into the night over Panang beef. Joked about being hopeless with the opposite sex. Reaffirmed the importance of real, lasting friendship based on mutual respect, common interests, and laughing at the same jokes. Usually she had to rely on her seventh graders to appreciate—however reluctantly—her compulsive joke-telling, but Miles *always* appreciated her bad jokes, the badder the better.

"Oh, Lucy," Miles repeated. Each of his massive hands spanned a well-rounded butt cheek to lift her higher.

I think I have the wrong idea of what badder and better is. Nicki sagged against the kitchen doorway.

When was the last time a guy kissed *her* like that? She was thirty, so—she counted back through the years—one, two, three…

Never. Yeah, never was about right.

"Oh my God, not again," Betty said behind her. "If I want to see heterosexual courtship, I'll watch a nature show on TV."

Miles didn't move, but the redhead broke the suction. "Sorry, Betty." She patted him on the shoulder to release her, and when that had no effect, she pinched his nipple through his UC Berkeley T-shirt.

With a yelp, he loosened his grip and turned to the door. "Hey there, Betty." Then he saw Nicki, and his smile fell.

This is it. A skateboarding thirteen-year-old did a back flip in her abdominal cavity. *This is the moment he realizes he loves me, hopes I love him, that we've just needed to be mature enough to admit we're both ready to get serious, settle down, give up on shallow, frivolous sexual relationships, and devote our lives to the deeper bond between us.*

His face broke into a grin. "Hey, Nicki! What are you doing here?"

She couldn't believe it. No sign of discomfort, guilt, or regret. Not even a tiny bit.

Still smiling, he moved away from the table, rising to his full six and a half feet. The woman in his arms plopped to the floor next to him, the top of her blazing copper head reaching only as high as his pinched nipple. Long strands of her red hair, still attached to Miles's stubbly jaw, stretched between them like telephone wires spanning a mountainous countryside.

Since when did he like petite women? His previous girlfriend had been tall. Nicki had hoped that since she, too, was tall—and on the broad side—maybe… someday…

"I'm here to see Betty," Nicki said, her tongue dry and clumsy. "She's a friend of mine."

"You guys know each other?" Betty asked, one black eyebrow arching into her green bangs.

Nicki taught history at a local junior high. "School connection," she said, swallowing. "He runs the youth center. Some of my students go th—"

Miles put his index finger over her lips and turned back to the redhead.

"I've been meaning to introduce you." He took Lucy's hand and pulled her over, looking as excited as a talk show host reuniting two loving sisters tragically separated by decades of war. "Luce, this is a teacher friend of mine, Nicki Fitch. Nicki, this is my fiancée—I know, I know, don't laugh, it's true—Lucy Hathcoat."

Nicki's lungs deflated. *Fiancée?*

The redhead leaned in to offer her hand to Nicki, but her pretty green eyes were sharp, observant. "Nice to meet you. What do you teach?"

It took Nicki a second to look her over. Her black T-shirt hugged her small curves and her skinny black jeans were skin-tight. She had a vision of that old *Grease* movie where the goody-goody fifties girl shows up in skin-tight black leather.

If I dressed like that, would things be different? All those dinners, drinks, movies—and my plans for us in the future—but I never made a move.

Playing it safe.

Always so damn safe.

Lucy's handshake was firm, strong, and warm. Nicki barely managed to return the pressure. "Seventh grade," she said. "I teach seventh grade. History."

"She's the most popular teacher in school," Miles said. "Practically a legend."

Students and parents loved her, that was true, but it was entirely different from the kind of love that got you naked.

"Wow, you must be really grounded," Lucy said. "I barely survived junior high the first time around. I can't imagine going back. I'd probably use it as an excuse to get even."

"Even for what?" Miles's broad, friendly face wrinkled with confusion.

Lucy rolled her eyes at him. "I bet you were big and popular. Never had anyone pick on you."

A grin split his face. "I'd sit on anyone who tried."

"That didn't work for me," Lucy said.

"I don't know." He slung a hand down her back and lowered his voice. "I get nice when you sit on me." He bent down and nuzzled her neck.

Nicki's hands started to sweat. *I need to get out of here.*

Flushed, Lucy dragged her gaze away from Miles and rolled her eyes apologetically at Nicki. "Sorry." She pushed Miles away. "We're being really annoying."

"Don't worry about Nicki." Miles shot Nicki a grin. "She's still relieved I chucked my ex."

Don't worry about Nicki, Nicki thought, lost in his handsome face. Obviously, *he* never had. She forced her lips into a smile. "Your ex is the one who chucked you, remember?"

"And I have the scar to show it." He rubbed his forehead. "Can of Red Bull, right here. Violently unstable, that one. I've learned to go for the calm and logical types." His melting gaze drifted back to Lucy.

"I have to get out of here," Nicki said. *Damn, did I say that out loud?* "I mean, I've only got a minute."

Betty sighed. "Don't get scared off. Lucy just came by to say hi, but Miles had to follow her here and try to get in her pants, which is kind of getting old, but whatever," she said. "We can talk about your next Phobic Phoebe post in the other room. I'm not sure I want you writing about so much hetero angst on my site."

Nicki flinched. She'd been writing a weekly post for Betty's popular blog, *Betty Me than You,* for over a year as Phoebe and often had to remind her to keep it secret. But coming out as a lesbian in high school had made Betty militant about being open, very open, about everything. Way, way too open. There was no TMI with Betty, one reason her blog was such a hit.

"You're Phobic Phoebe?" Lucy asked. "Really?"

"Don't tell anyone," Betty said helpfully. "It's a secret."

"I love your posts," Lucy said. "Love them."

Oh, God. The redhead was a fan. It was going to get worse.

Miles looked confused. "Who's Phobic Phoebe?"

Eyes twinkling, Lucy said to Nicki, "I loved the one you wrote about overcoming a fear of public speaking. I'm impressed, I've never been able to do that. I'd never guess you were a teacher."

Nicki smiled weakly. She didn't want to talk about the blog. One conversation would lead to another, and soon everyone would make the connection…

"You can survive almost anything if you put your mind to it," Nicki muttered.

Miles stepped forward and jabbed her shoulder. "You never told me you were a writer."

Forcing a laugh, Nicki shoved her hands in her jeans pockets. "It's nothing. Just a fun hobby."

"Phobic Phoebe, huh?" He grinned. "You write about all those fears of yours? That's excellent. I'll have to check it out."

He knew all about her crazy anxieties—water, bridges, heights, elevators—but that wasn't what she was hiding.

"I'm so glad to meet you. You're so funny," Lucy said, laughing. "I love it when you write about that guy you've got a thing for, the way you describe his ass, how he manages to be cute even though he's totally enormous—" She cut herself off. After a long moment, her gaze darted to her six-five, two-fifty boyfriend.

Nicki could almost hear the wheels under the red hair grinding to the painful, humiliating conclusion.

"Holy shit," Betty said. "Miles is Thor, isn't he? He has to be."

Nicki broke out into a cold sweat. *I'll never be able to look at him again.*

Betty sighed. "You should've told me. I could've told Lucy to leave his big butt at home."

Lucy whipped the phone out of her pocket like a cop in a shootout. "Look at the time." She put a hand on Miles's arm and took a step toward the door. "Miles, I think we'd better get going."

He didn't move. "I want to hear more about Thor."

This is the part in the movie where I come up with an outrageous lie to save my ego and get ensnared in some long, dreary, embarrassing misunderstanding that only drags out the inevitable. Nicki dropped her head, frowned at her faded black sneakers, and studied the vinyl kitchen floor for signs of a sinkhole.

Belatedly, Betty got sensitive. "Forget it. Thor's blond. Couldn't be you."

"You write about me for Betty's blog?" He sounded incredulous. "What do you say?"

Nicki would have to shovel some grade-A bullshit to get out of this one with her head high. She lifted her head and met his gaze.

Sinkhole or bullshit, sinkhole or bullshit…

"I write about how much I love you," Nicki said.

His eyes rounded.

She put a hand over her heart. "I love you, Miles. I thought you loved me too."

The cheap rental refrigerator hummed in the silence.

"Got you," Nicki said, reaching forward to punch his arm. "Relax, you big oaf. I was just kidding."

He released an audible breath. "Really?"

She snorted.

"You scared the hell out of me," he said.

"Come on, Miles. I'd rather French kiss a llama."

"I'm not Thor?"

"You? Thor's an invincible, immortal god. You, my friend, are an aging college dropout with a bad back." Nicki managed a convincing laugh, and after a couple of seconds, she watched the terror drain out of Miles's face. Finally, he laughed with her.

"Have you set a date?" she asked.

"Sometime next summer." He gave his fiancée a devilish grin that made Nicki want to die.

"How nice for you." Her voice sounded far away. She hoped she looked more normal than she felt.

"Neither one of us wants a big ceremony, but we'll have some kind of party." Looking lovesick again, he pulled Lucy against him. Eventually, finally, the happy couple said their good-byes.

"Well, that was awkward," Betty said as she dead-bolted the door after them.

Wiping the sweat off her upper lip, Nicki collapsed on the arm of the couch. She felt like a deer that had almost been flattened by a truck, but at the last minute had leaped onto the hood, and now clung for dear—so to speak—life, trying to catch her breath as the wind whistled through her antlers.

Except she was a female deer. She wouldn't have antlers.

Typical. She couldn't even get femininity right as an imaginary quadruped.

"The sad thing is," Betty continued, "I think he would've jumped on you in a second if you'd ever made a move. You guys were practically dating."

Nicki thought of all the coffees they'd shared, movies they'd seen, dinners they'd eaten; all the times she'd almost said something to him before panicking.

"I never had the guts," Nicki said, standing. Her fears had always held her back; and now she'd lost Miles, the best guy she'd ever met, because she'd been too damn *nervous*.

"I'm not straight, but I know guys," Betty said. "He would've had sex with you at least once if you'd let him know you were interested."

"God, what if you're right?" Nicki muttered, going to the window. She saw the giant man and his tiny companion kissing against the door of a compact sedan. They didn't look as if they were afraid of being seen, of denting the steel, of a passing car striking them. They didn't look afraid of anything. They were too happy.

I'm going to learn how to be like that, Nicki thought. *If it kills me.*

Ignoring his father's third text message of the day, Ansel Jury-

Jarski popped open the paint can and inhaled the scent of fresh wet latex.

Dad probably wanted to know why he'd taken over twenty thousand dollars out of the family accounts in the past month.

Twice.

Shaking his head, Ansel lifted the paint can. He wasn't ready to explain. In a few days, the restaurant would be painted, the kitchen set up, the sign bolted over the door, and the menu printed. Then he'd call his father, email a few pictures, maybe invite him for the opening. When everything was ready. When *Ansel* was ready.

With the grace of a professional, he poured the paint into the roller tray. Not a single drop spilled on the pages of the *San Francisco Chronicle* he'd laid out along the wall of the dining room. Who knew unemployed playboys could perform real labor?

Grinning, he replaced the lid on the paint can and turned to his twin sister, Rachel, who was helping him. "You're not the only one skilled in the painterly arts." So she'd studied art in Europe. Big deal.

She flashed him a colorful thumb that was as well coated as a chocolate-dipped ice cream cone at Dairy Queen. "I knew you could do it."

Jordan, his best friend and owner of the new restaurant, frowned at the glowing paint tray. "I appreciate your help setting up, guys, but…orange?"

"It's not orange. It's Coral Daze," Rachel said.

"It's orange," Jordan replied.

"Haven't you ever heard of color theory?" Ansel asked. "Warm color sparks the appetite. It'll subconsciously spur your many patrons to order lots of items from the menu, drink to excess, and then post glowing reviews online."

"You think?" Jordan asked.

"If it doesn't work," Ansel assured him, "we'll hire somebody to redo it in another color."

"I'm paying you back for all this," Jordan said.

"Sure," Ansel said. "Whatever."

"I will."

"Feed me when I visit, that'll be enough." Ansel wasn't joking; Jordan had magical powers in the kitchen. If anyone in San Francisco should be running his own restaurant, it was Jordan Boyd, and that was saying something. Someday, Ansel would tease him that he deserved the credit because he'd contributed a little money and painted the walls orange. For now, he had to twist his old college roommate's arm just to consider taking a dime.

"I've got a spreadsheet," Jordan said. "I'm calculating the interest I'll owe you."

Embarrassed, Ansel ran the new fuzzy roller over the palm of his left hand. It felt so soft that he regretted the need to dunk it in paint. "Come on. It's pocket change."

"Fifty grand?" Jordan turned to Rachel. "Must be nice to be rich."

When Ansel and Rachel were in third grade, their last living grandmother had died. The quiet old lady's secret investments in a few local startups (in Menlo Park, Palo Alto, and Sunnyvale, California) had led to their mother's shocking inheritance of ten million dollars. Their family's life had changed overnight.

"It has its moments." Rachel turned to the front of the restaurant. "What do you think about adding a mural over the doorway?"

"You're already doing enough," Jordan said. "Both of you."

Ansel joined her, following her gaze overhead. "I think you should. It's kind of boring."

"Even with the orange paint?" Jordan asked weakly.

"It needs something more," Rachel said.

"Maybe," Jordan said.

"You're a chef, not an artist," Ansel said. "Trust Rachel."

Jordan waved in resignation. "All right. I'm going back to the kitchen where I belong. Do what you need to do." He started to walk away.

"You'll love it," Rachel said.

Ansel called after him, "You don't have a problem with unicorns, right?"

With his hand on the kitchen door, Jordan turned, his mouth stretched open in horror. Rachel covered a laugh with her hand.

"Or rainbows?" Ansel added.

Jordan looked relieved, as if he'd decided they were kidding. "I love you, man, and I couldn't do any of this without you. If you want to paint rainbows and unicorns on the walls of my restaurant, go ahead." He grinned, patting his chest. "I'll just paint over it when you move on to your next charity case."

"You're not *charity*."

"I won't be after I pay you back." Jordan disappeared into the kitchen, the double doors slapping behind him.

"People are so stupid about money," Ansel said.

"It's because they don't have enough of it," Rachel said.

"Rich people are worse. Look at Dad."

"What's he done now?" Rachel asked.

"Nothing." He returned to the paint tray and picked up the roller. "Just the usual. Unimpressed with my lifestyle."

"Mom says he's going through a midlife crisis," Rachel offered.

"Since we were born? No, this is between him and me. Nothing I've ever done was good enough for him." He looked around the unfinished space, imagining a crowd of people, the rumble of conversation, the smell of fantastic food. "But this restaurant will be different. Jordan—well, you know. His food's unbelievable. The restaurant will take off. Even Kevin Jarski will be impressed."

Rachel looked uncomfortable. "I hope you're not doing all of this for Dad. He's just not the type to—"

His phone rang in his pocket. Thinking about the ignored text messages, his stomach tightened. He took it out and stared at his father's handsome face on the screen as it rang a second time. "Speak of the devil," he muttered.

"It'll be worse if you put him off," Rachel said softly.

"I hope Mom calls you next," Ansel said, pushing the button of doom. His sister was right; he'd run out of time. With a deep breath, he lifted the phone to his ear. "Hello?"

"Hey, Ansel, what's up?" His father sounded easygoing, with the accent of the Southern Californian surfers he'd grown up with, but his voice was purely an accident of geography— Kevin Jarski hadn't been mellow a day in his life.

"Hi, Dad."

Rachel took the roller out of his hand and tiptoed away. She knew better than to be around the two men of their nuclear family when they had a conversation, even over the phone.

"So," his father said. "How're ya doing?"

"I'm fine." Ansel stood taller, bracing for the inevitable.

"Twenty-three grand," his father said.

"Yes."

"Then, a few weeks later, twenty-seven."

Ansel looked out to the narrow street. More of an alley, really, and too far from the trendy neighborhoods for the rent to be outrageous. He wished he'd been able to give Jordan more money so he could open in North Beach or Pacific Heights, closer to where the *rich* hungry people lived, but Jordan had refused. "I'd wanted to make it an even fifty," he said into the phone.

"What'd you spend it on?" his father asked. "Or should I

say, who?"

Annoyed at his shaky hands, Ansel straightened his shoulders and lowered his voice. He wouldn't let his father make him feel like a child. "Actually, I'm helping Jordan start a restaurant."

"Jordan…"

How could his father not remember? "*Jordan*. You know, my roommate for three years? In college?"

"Forgive my memory," his father said. "Your college years weren't exactly in a row. And there were so many of them."

Ansel clenched his teeth. He'd never been happy in school. He'd been terrible at it, never turning assignments in on time, always distracted by more interesting things. School was where he'd discovered how powerful a few dollars could be; how, with his help, the guy down the hall could travel to Peru for that archeological dig over the summer; or how the two women in his history class could devote an entire year to a political campaign they believed in.

Part of him hoped his father would see the restaurant as an impressive, practical enterprise. One that could make money. "Jordan's a great chef. He just needed a little start-up funding."

"Will you be sticking around to help him run the place?"

Ansel swallowed. This was the awkward part. Jordan didn't want any long-term help. He'd refused it. He insisted on being the man in charge, the captain of his ship, the only cook in the kitchen. "No. I—"

"Just prefer writing the checks," his father finished.

Ansel imagined his father sitting at the computer, managing the family investments; because of him, the Jury-Jarskis never ran out of funds, no matter how quickly the rest of them spent it.

"I like helping people who don't have the same privileges I have," Ansel said. "Isn't that what you and Mom taught us to do?"

When Belinda Jury had inherited the ten million from her mother, she'd immediately formed a foundation to help people. She was especially active in Central America, never resting, always traveling, fundraising, working.

"You're doing the easiest thing in the world," his father said. "Spending somebody else's money."

"Does Mom know you feel this way about being generous?"

His father was silent for a moment. "Your mother is a saint. Giving money to friends is hardly the same as feeding orphans in developing countries, is it?"

Ansel put a fist over his mouth and stared at his feet. He noticed a streak of orange paint on his favorite sneakers. *It's just Dad*, he told himself. *Just being his usual grouchy self. Don't let him get to you.*

Rachel came up beside him. "You okay?"

He met his twin's concerned gaze, stuck out his tongue to lighten the mood, and said into the phone, "Rachel's here. We're painting the restaurant."

"She's an artist, not a contractor."

"She's doing a mural," Ansel said.

"I hope Jacob appreciates what he's getting from her," his father said. "She's got a gallery in Seattle already interested in scheduling a show, you know."

"It's Jordan, not Jacob," Ansel said, but he flashed Rachel a genuine smile. "Gallery in Seattle?"

She flushed. "We'll see."

He punched her lightly on the shoulder. "I know a great caterer up there. Let me know when your opening is." He'd helped a friend set up her business a few years ago, and it seemed to be doing well.

"It's a pipe dream," Rachel said, walking back to her paint tray.

"It'll happen," Ansel said. He heard his father clear his

throat, so turned his attention back to him. "Anything else, Dad?" Of course his father wasn't impressed yet; he hadn't seen—or tasted—what Jordan was capable of. Next month, when the restaurant opened, or in a few months after that, when it was fully established, he'd bring his father there to see it in person. Then he'd understand. This was bigger and more serious than anything he'd done before. "We're kind of busy. The paint's drying out."

"You can't keep doing this, Ansel. Fifty thousand dollars is a lot of money."

His parents never liked to spend money on themselves, even with millions in the bank. He knew that reasonably pointing out the minuscule percentage of fifty thousand out of the entire bonanza that was the family treasure chest would not impress his father's sense of financial modesty.

"Jordan's a great chef," Ansel said. "This restaurant is going to be awesome."

"Good for him."

"He's keeping it small to start, but I bet you, within ten years, his place is going to be famous." Ansel looked around the tiny space, not smelling the latex paint but conjuring up the aroma of garlic, Asian spices, searing meat, roasting vegetables, wonderful things. "No—five years."

"If it is, it'll be because of the work *he* puts into it, not you. It'll be because he stuck with something, kept his nose down, saw it through."

"I agree," Ansel said, his voice low.

"When are *you* going to show that kind of commitment to something?"

Ansel held his breath. He wished he hadn't said anything. He wished he hadn't answered the phone.

"Ansel?" his father prompted.

He swallowed. "I told you, I'm—"

"Or to someone?" His father's heavy sigh buffeted his ear.

"I had two kids by the time I was your age."

He and Rachel had been born a few weeks before their father's thirtieth birthday. "Barely," Ansel said with a forced laugh, "and we were twins. Doesn't really count."

"Oh, you count. That's why I have to do this. I should've done it years ago."

Ansel's bad feeling got worse. "Dad, I really should be going. I've got four walls and three doors to paint before—"

"I'm cutting you off."

Ansel stopped breathing.

"Did you hear me?" his father asked.

Hot burning shame washed over him. It was a few seconds before he could speak. "I assume you're talking financially? Or are you chucking me out of the family altogether?"

"Don't be hurt. I don't enjoy doing this."

The tightening in his throat disgusted him. "I'm not hurt," Ansel said. He shouldn't have been surprised. The things he could've done over the years with that money instead of giving it away, the luxuries and trips he could've indulged in, but no—nothing he did was ever good enough for Kevin Jarski. "I'm bummed you don't seem to care about the same things I care about." There, that was honest. He wasn't going to lie, or beg, or get angry.

"Who could keep up with what you care about? I don't have the slightest idea, between the dog walkers, the restaurants, the hopeless tech startups—and all those messed-up girlfriends of yours, one after the other, none of them sticking around for more than a year." His father sighed again. "And those were just the women I knew about. I can't imagine how many there were between the *serious* ones you introduced to us."

Ansel could hear the air quotes over the phone. "I haven't found the right person yet. I'm still in my twenties—"

"Barely," his father said, throwing Ansel's own word back

at him. "In nine months you'll turn thirty and realize what a waste you're making of your life. It's much harder when you're older to get serious about something important."

Ansel raised his voice, letting the anger pour out of him. "I'm not wasting my life." Rachel put down the roller and came over to stand next to him. Always nice to have a twin to ride shotgun in a crisis. "I'm good at starting things," he continued. "That's what I do. I help people launch businesses, go after their dreams."

Rachel squeezed his arm.

"That's a copout, Ansel," his father said. "You're patting yourself on the back, but the truth is you leave all the hard work to other people."

"I'm not patting myself on the back. I'm explaining how I'm not a total waste of a human being."

"Of course you're not. You have loads of potential." His father cleared his throat. "I know it doesn't look that way right now, but I'm doing this because I love you. I know you can do better."

"Thanks, Dad. Nothing is more comforting than hearing you say that," Ansel said bitterly. "Just tell me, how much money do I have to make before you believe I'm living up to my potential? When I pay back the fifty thousand? Or do I need seven figures to prove myself, like Grandma Jury did?"

"It's not about money," his father said, his voice rising, as if Ansel's reminder about getting *his* money from his mother-in-law had hit home. "It's about commitment. To a person, a cause, a craft—like Rachel is with art. It's not about the almighty dollar."

"Let me talk to him," Rachel said, reaching for the phone. She hated when they argued.

Heart pounding, Ansel shook his head and moved out of reach. If it wasn't about the almighty dollar, then why was it such a big deal he'd never made enough of them? "I think it is.

I think you're ashamed of how important money is to you. I think you still feel guilty for ever telling us we were rich." He ran a hand through his hair, recently buzzed short at Supercuts. The cut had exposed a shocking amount of prematurely —obviously it was premature, he was still twenty-nine, wasn't he?—gray hair mixed in with the black. "You think it spoiled us."

"Not your sister," his father said. "Just you. It spoiled *you*."

Ansel's heart seemed to stop beating. He lowered the phone, waiting for normal functioning to return. After a full five seconds, still unsure he was all right, he returned the cell to his ear. "Well. I'm glad to know where I stand."

His father's voice softened. "It wouldn't be fair to spring this on you without a grace period, so you can have a few months to draw from your favorite account, what's left of it, but absolutely, after your birthday, no more. That'll be it. The flow of cash is being diverted."

"I don't need it. I don't want it."

"Don't be like that," his father said. "You'll need something to get started. And if you have long-term plans that lead somewhere, like graduate school, then of course we can talk about the money again."

"I need to go now."

"Ansel—"

"Good-bye."

His father sighed. "Give my love to Rachel. Now *that* girl knows what she's doing."

Ansel had to hang up on him. It was that or drop his phone into the paint can.

He thought he *had* known what he was doing.

Hand shaking, he picked up the roller and began to blindly paint the walls.

Maybe the problem was that it wasn't enough.

And never would be.

Chapter 2

The following May, eight months after letting her heart get crushed under the boot of Miles and Lucy's happiness, Nicki was still a work in progress.

The senior stylists at an exclusive salon had cut and colored her hair. The oversized hoodies and faded jeans had gone into a bin at Goodwill. An employee at Nordstrom's, after measuring her in a cavernous dressing room scented with lavender, had fit her into five new bras that cost a week's salary but felt like heaven, and now her breasts floated like astronauts.

To top it off, she'd had LASIK eye surgery and no longer wore the glasses she'd had since she was five. Glasses were a lot cooler than they used to be, but she wanted the transformation to be as comprehensive as possible.

Yet, even after all that, as beautiful as she ever was going to get, she was still alone.

Weren't makeovers supposed to change lives? In movies, the newly beautiful woman had fresh confidence and attracted men like bees on shit. Honey. Either way, it wasn't happening. The biggest compliment she'd received after her transformation was from Kennedy Madison, the prettiest thirteen-year-old in class, who told her, enthusiastically, that she looked younger than Kennedy's mom did. Given that Nicki had just turned thirty, and Kennedy's mom was pushing fifty, this didn't have the intended impact.

Regardless of her appearance, she was still Ms. Fitch, seventh-grade history teacher and director of today's mummification.

"Ms. Fitch! Noah wants to be the dead guy," one of her students shouted from the front of her classroom where he sprawled on his back over three desks shoved together. "You said I could be the pharaoh."

Nicki plugged in the stereo for the eerie music she'd be playing in a minute. "Noah, if Carl wants to have his brains sucked out of his nose, wouldn't you like to help?" When she turned out the overhead lights, thirty-two thirteen-year-olds burst into giggling and whispers. "Let the mummification begin," she intoned into the semidarkness.

The kids didn't care if her breasts floated like helium balloons under her trendy blouse; it was Egypt Day, the biggest day of the year. The tradition she'd created six years earlier was already legendary. When her former students visited her, they often mentioned the mummification demo as the highlight of seventh grade.

Two girls and one boy, white sheets wrapped around their T-shirts and jeans, paraded to the front of the classroom. They gathered around Carl, who laid face-up on a folding table, bug-eyed and open-mouthed. Carl, who had told her he hated school, had spent six hours drawing an extra map of the Nile to earn the role of important dead guy.

Other students flicked on the battery-operated candles and aimed video cameras while parents, those who could get away from work or other children, lined up along the back wall to watch the show.

Furtively, pretending to take a picture with her phone, Nicki checked her email.

She couldn't help herself. Today she'd find out who won Rachel Jury-Jarski's Hawaiian condo for the summer. Maui, all summer, for free. A chance to break out of her comfort zone. On an island in the Pacific, she'd have no choice but to grow and change.

"Stop laughing," the priest told the dead pharaoh, pulling Nicki's attention back to the classroom. "You're dead."

"Ava," Nicki prompted.

The middle girl, snickering over the body, held up a wire. "First we remove the brain." She pretended to shove the wire up the dead body's nose, and ignoring the impossible thrashing of the corpse, hooked a plastic brain under the table, pulled it up, and chucked it across the room. "We throw that in the garbage."

While the room burst into laughter, Nicki checked Rachel's Facebook page.

They hadn't seen each other in a year or two, but back in college they'd been fairly close, and they had connected online. Thank God, because when Rachel announced last week that she was giving away the condo to the friend who posted the best joke on her page, Nicki was *there*.

But still no news. It was already eleven. Rachel had promised to announce the winner today. The wait was killing her.

"The other organs are preserved for the afterlife," Carl said, holding up a jar. "The heart is the most important. They believed it was responsible for thinking, feeling, the soul, all that crap."

Lined up along the back wall, the parents laughed.

It is *crap*, Nicki thought. It had been months since she'd seen Miles with his fiancée, but she felt the pain of that moment in her chest, not her cranium.

She needed to get away. Far away, for more than a weekend, to reinvent herself. Away from her job, her students, her friends, her family—everything that kept her frozen as she was.

"After we stuff the body with spices, we have to wait for everything to dry out," Carl said. "The whole process takes seventy days. Only rich and important people can afford it."

Nicki nodded, scrolled over to the camera app on her phone, and snapped a picture. Transformation was expensive. She started to peek at her email again before making herself shove the phone in her pocket.

She had to focus on the show. The kids were pretending to stuff and anoint the body now, and Noah stumbled over his lines about amulets and perfumes while Ava tried to wrap the body in white streamers Nicki had picked up at the party store.

"It's a wrap!" Nicki declared when they descended into hopeless silliness, clapping to let the parents know the show was over. She nodded to Mackenzie to turn on the lights, and soon the kids were all taking their bows, posing for parents, and throwing the removed organs around the room.

Just as she was shaking hands with the stars and congratulating their parents, her phone vibrated in her pocket.

Her fingers twitched, aching to pull it out, but she really couldn't. Not yet. A few minutes to get rid of the parents, a few more until the period ended, and then she'd have a break.

"I just wanted you to know how much Noah loves your class," a dad said to her. He was a handsome guy in a geeky, outdoorsy kind of way, just the sort of man Nicki thought would be perfect for her; but obviously he preferred Noah's mom, who was pretty with fake eyelashes and teeth as white as the streamers dangling from the mummy's narrow shoulders.

"Thank you," Nicki said. "That's great to hear. He did a great job."

The phone vibrated again.

"I don't know how you manage it," another mom said.

Fisting her hands to resist the temptation in her pocket, Nicki smiled and tried to concentrate on the woman's face. She bore a strong resemblance to the giggling corpse—sandy hair, little nose, big lips. Holding out her hand, Nicki said, "Carl jumped at the chance to participate. He did a great job."

"I don't hear that very often," the mom said. "You're the only teacher he likes."

It was hard to think of a diplomatic reply without insulting the other teachers, many of whom were her friends. "He's a pleasure to have in class." Nicki glanced at the clock. "All right, class, hug a random parent and let them get out of here. Time to clean up the body parts and have some lunch."

The parents meandered out of the room in an agonizingly slow fashion, obviously not like their children who, even allegedly liking her class, bolted out the door every day as if candy bars and dollar bills were falling from the sky.

Five and a half minutes later, when the last student was gone, Nicki threw down the tangled rubber intestines she'd just picked up and whipped out her phone, heart racing.

Email. From Rachel.

Her finger trembled over the screen. Rachel might just be apologizing for choosing somebody else—

She read the email. Very short. Just a few words…

Yes.

She'd won. Rachel was giving her the Jury-Jarski Hawaiian condo for the summer.

Her legs weakened. She reached out to a desk and sank into a chair, waves of anxiety washing over her. "I'm going to Maui," she whispered.

She'd have to fly, drive, and God only knew what else.

She sank forward until her forehead pressed against hard, scratched Formica. When the phone in her hand vibrated, she lifted her head to read the screen, expecting Rachel, but it was Betty's name on the screen.

"I see you won that contest," Betty said.

"How'd you find that out?"

"Are you kidding? When you told me about that contest, I friended her on Facebook, too. She just posted her regrets to us losers."

"I'm going to Hawaii," Nicki said in a daze.

"Yeah, yeah, don't rub it in."

The thought of the airplane made her hands clammy. "I can't go."

"You can write about it for the blog," Betty said.

"I can't go."

"Fine. I'll take your place."

Nicki snapped out of it. "Am I nuts?" She stood up from the desk. "Don't answer that. I don't care if I pass out on the plane. I'm going to Hawaii."

Betty sighed. "You won't pass out. At least not on the plane. That's one of your minor phobias, right?"

Nicki thought of all that water that usually surrounded islands. Feeling anxiety cramps coming on, she rubbed her stomach. "Right."

"You'll do fine." But then Betty's voice suddenly rose in alarm. "But you'll miss Lucy and Miles's wedding!"

Nicki bent to pick up the white streamers off the floor before her next class. "I know."

With a sigh, Betty said, "I suppose it's a decent excuse, being outside of the continental United States."

"Promise me you'll never tell Miles the truth about Thor. Not even at the wedding. That's when you'll be most tempted."

"Too late to worry about that, babe. I'm sure he ran home and read the whole blog. You didn't disguise him very well. You even mentioned the little scar over his left eyebrow."

Nicki flinched. "I hope he believes I'm over him," she said. "Whenever I see him, I always act extra thrilled for him and his miniature redhead."

"Watch it. Lucy's one of my best friends."

"Sorry. Even though she ruined my chance at happiness in this life, I'm sure she's very nice."

"She didn't ruin anything." Betty lowered her voice. "You'll be fine after you have a *real* vacation, you know what I mean?"

"There's a spa at the resort, but I don't know how much I can afford," Nicki said.

"What I'm talking about should be free."

Nicki wound the streamers into a ball and set them on her desk. "Ah."

"It's about time Phobic Phoebe finally had sex," Betty continued.

"Phobic Phoebe keeps that part of her life private."

"Because it's imaginary."

A student stuck his head into the classroom. "Hi, Ms. Fitch!

"Hey there, David," Nicki said. "Ready to have your internal organs sucked out?" His class was at the end of the day, but he was already wearing a plaid sheet around his shoulders.

"Yuck," Betty said in her ear.

"I've got to go," Nicki told her.

"Reconsider the sex thing. Not for the blog. For you."

Nicki suspected Betty just wanted the page hits. Since David was still lingering in the doorway, she turned away, cupping the phone to her cheek. "I've got other plans for this summer, and it's got nothing to do with men."

"Oh, no. You've gone gay." Betty pretended to weep. "I blame myself. If only—"

"If only I hadn't answered the phone," Nicki said, hanging up. She stared off into space, imagining white beaches, warm sun, and blue water stretching north, south, east, and west.

Everywhere. Surrounding her.

Her hands trembled.

With rough movements, she arranged the props for the

next mummification. She was going to get over this. Having a fling on a tropical beach was what normal people did. *She* needed to learn how to walk on that beach without going batshit crazy. She'd have eight gloriously solitary, empty weeks she could devote to self-improvement.

Me, myself, and I.

Glorious.

Chapter 3

nsel never got tired of their family's condo in Maui.

The sun was hot on his bare torso, making him feel like an organic free-range chicken breast too close to the broiler. He'd be hurting later, but he couldn't resist all the warm, tropical goodness.

Poor Rachel. Stuck in London with her paintbrushes, unable to enjoy her yearly allotment of Hawaiian paradise.

With a contented sigh, he put his feet up on the railing overlooking the glimmering blue ocean and wiggled his toes. Hawaii looked good, it felt good, it even smelled good. If he had to get old and responsible, this was the place to do it.

As he reached for his smoothie, still frothy from its spin in the blender, he saw his phone blinking with a message. He hesitated—why ruin a perfect moment?—but then forced himself to read a text from his old friend and new business partner, Brand Henry Warren.

Agent's ready to show unit in Kīhei, Brand wrote. *Check it out tomorrow. Take pix.*

Ansel groaned into his smoothie before adding the appointment to his calendar.

Offices. Retail space. Boring but practical. He had only a little money left over from the days before Dad turned off the tap, but it was a good time to buy, safe, blah, blah, blah.

He took another sip.

Investing in commercial property didn't turn him on like starting up restaurants, used bookstores, mobile dog groomers, or for-profit senior-citizen walking tours, but it was more likely to give him the independence he needed. Dad thought he was a useless sponge? *Watch me thrive without you, grouchy guy.*

Having grown up in the San Francisco Bay Area, he'd thought about investing his paltry nest egg in high tech, but he just didn't have the head for it. Those people were crazy with their virtual machines and "open source" whatevers, their Scala and Python and Gnu, always rambling on as if regular people had any idea what they were talking about.

Food, books, dogs, old people—he could get excited about those kinds of things. Normal, real things. They made you happy.

He inhaled the scent of the sea, closed his eyes.

Office buildings don't make you happy, a voice inside him said.

He brought the bowls of chips and salsa over to his lap, took a few bites, and chewed without tasting, reminding himself that office buildings brought in steady income. He wasn't doing this for his father's approval. That was both optional and unattainable.

A dollop of salsa fell on his bare chest. Tomato juice trickled down his abs and pooled inside his belly button.

Smooth, very smooth, he thought, mopping it up with his T-shirt, which then tipped the entire bowl of salsa into his crotch. As he jerked back, chips flew across the patio.

He clambered to his feet, chunks of tomato and onion avalanching down his legs, and tried to reclaim some of his lunch before it blew off his balcony to the unfortunate people who lived below him.

Man, he was covered with it. Tortilla chip shrapnel clung to his belly like sprinkles on a cupcake. The fly of his khaki shorts looked like his dick had been blown off.

He strode inside to wash up, not realizing until he was halfway across the living room that a good-looking woman in a huge floppy sunhat was standing in the front doorway with a suitcase, gaping at him as if *he* were the intruder.

"Oh, no," she said.

He froze, wondering how a tourist could've gotten into the wrong unit, before he remembered he hadn't told his sister he'd be stealing her time at the condo for a few weeks. He thought he'd be safe, since she was in London.

Guess not.

"Hi." He cleared his throat, brushing crumbs off his stomach. "Friend of Rachel's?"

She nodded slowly.

"She loaned you the condo?"

The woman nodded again. She was very tall, powerfully built with broad shoulders, and wore a dress that showed off her legs.

Wow. Those were *legs*.

"I'm her brother. Her twin brother," he said, recovering himself. He'd thought the Pacific was beautiful, but her long legs were a miracle. They practically reached her ears. "Don't mind me."

She obviously did mind. Still not moving in or out of the doorway, her horrified gaze raked over him.

He looked down at his crotch. The gore looked even worse out of the sun. "Had a little accident. Not as bad as it looks." He grinned at her while his mind raced through salvage plans.

He couldn't move out. He'd promised Brand he could handle the deal in person—only because he had free lodging at the condo. He couldn't afford to stay on the island for a month, not anymore, not yet. Maui prices would eat up the last serious money he had.

She looked harmless; big but shy. He'd have to convince her to share the condo with him. "Come on in. Did you just fly—?"

She spun on her heel and fled out the door.

HE DIDN'T RECOGNIZE ME, Nicki thought. Relief warred with outrage. *The bastard!*

Breaking into a jog, she rolled the suitcase down the hall and around the corner to the sunny bank of elevators, where she paused. She'd rather jump out the window than get into one of those dangling death traps right now.

Ansel Jury-Jarski was supposed to be thousands of miles away. Rachel had promised.

Spinning around, she found the stairwell, yanked open the door, and stumbled across the landing. After a demoralizing drive from the airport, in which she got lost six times on the small island, she'd given in to her phobias and taken the stairs instead of the elevator to the fifth-floor condo. Now she had a blister swelling on her right palm, and the straps of her kitten-heeled sandals felt like razor blades.

She put a hand on the wall of the stairwell for support, sucking in shallow breaths. Did she look that different from when she was eighteen? Sure, she was wearing a dress and no glasses, and her hair was a little brighter than it had been then —perhaps three shades brighter—and that dorm room had been dark, not to mention they'd been lying down, which is of course how one thing had led to another...

But she'd just told him she was a friend of Rachel's. That should've rung a little bell in that thick, handsome skull of his. The most memorable night—well, early morning—of her entire college career, and he didn't even have the decency to remember it?

God, what a disaster. And that disaster was standing smack dab in the middle of paradise, pooping all over it.

She pushed the suitcase over the top stair and followed it down. Paying for a room was going to bankrupt her; even one night in a place like the condo she'd just glimpsed—*oh, it was gorgeous*, she thought with a stabbing pain between the eyes— cost as much as a month's rent in Berkeley. And the change fees with the airline for the flight home were no lower than the cost of a brand-new ticket.

She needed this vacation. But how could she stay? Picturing Ansel's dumb, cheerful face, she kicked her suitcase and watched it tumble down the stairs and flop on the landing of the floor below.

The door banged open behind her.

"Wait!" Ansel jogged down the stairs two at a time. Stopping at her side, he raked his eyes over her before settling on her hands. "Where are you going?"

She wobbled down the stairs and picked up her suitcase handle to continue, as irritated with her hot cheeks as she was with her trembling.

"Hello?" he asked.

She released her suitcase and wiped her sweaty palm on her hip, stopping herself when she remembered her new dress was dry-clean only. Keeping her chin down, not saying anything because he might recognize her voice, she moved down the stairs.

"Good-bye," she muttered. Might as well be polite, even if he didn't deserve it.

"No, wait." He leaped down to the landing. The impact of his feet hitting the floor reverberated against the walls. "What's the matter?"

"I'll stay somewhere else. It's okay." She just wanted him to leave her alone.

"It's not okay. Rachel gave it to you, right?"

She gritted her teeth and nodded without meeting his eyes.

"Then it's yours. I didn't know you were coming."

He was looking right at her under a shaft of sunlight coming through a skylight at the top of the stairwell, and still no hint he recognized her. Being rich and handsome carried him through life, apparently. No need to remember the little people.

Her breathing steadied. Little? Right. Carefully she lifted her head, stood up to her full five-foot-eleven-and-fifteen-sixteenths, and met his gaze straight on. "You're not staying?"

His smile dazzled. "Just here briefly on business."

Those gorgeous gray eyes of his were oblivious. No flicker of curiosity, familiarity, or unease, just the easy, good-natured charm she remembered. A guy who'd never met a person he didn't like.

Or one he'd remember, apparently.

She should be relieved. She *was* relieved. Now she didn't have to worry about running into him someday and seeing him get uncomfortable—or worse—at the sight of her. He'd probably crawled into bed with lots of girls in college.

Fabulous.

She moved her suitcase to her other hand.

No. This sucked the big one. The exact type of guy she was trying to get away from had contaminated her tropical sanctuary. The proto-guy, the one who'd set the stage for all the others. The first one to be totally, completely oblivious to her. She couldn't possibly turn into a sexy butterfly with that nasty caterpillar crawling all over her leaf.

"We can talk in the condo," said the caterpillar. "My sister would kill me if you went off and paid for a hotel room in Maui just because I scared you away."

Her pride, buried deep, burrowed to the surface. "You didn't scare me. You…" *You pissed me off.* "You surprised me, that's all. It's your home, not mine."

"It's not a home, it's a vacation timeshare that belongs to my parents, and they insist it be occupied at all times because they feel guilty about owning it. When I leave soon, it'll be all yours, and they'll be happy." He reached out and peeled the suitcase out from her hand. "You must be tired. Where'd you fly from?"

"San Francisco," she said slowly.

With her suitcase as hostage, he turned and climbed the stairs. "Cool," he said. "Me too. You kept in touch with Rachel after she moved to London?"

"We go way back." She heard herself say it and cringed. No reason to trigger his memories if she didn't have to. With a glance at her throbbing feet—the shoes were killing her—she followed him from a safe distance. He didn't *scare* her. God forbid. Elevators and airplanes and water, sure, but not some selfish rich boy from the distant past. "A few years."

He led her up the stairs, over the landing, and down the hall to the condo. "There!" he said, pushing the door open. He parked her suitcase near an entrance closet. "Make yourself at home. I have to change into something less disgusting."

The view of the azure waters of the Pacific through the panoramic windows captured her attention. She lived less than a mile from the Pacific—or the Bay—back in Berkeley, but nothing she'd ever seen in real life could compare to this. The ribbon of pale sand stretching to either side below, the ocean of blue all around, another island in the distance. The sliding door to the balcony was open, letting in a warm, sweet-smelling breeze that brushed her bare legs.

Why the hell was she wearing these torture devices on her feet? She bent down and unbuckled the expensive sandals that were clearly designed by a misogynistic, sadistic, greedy, sociopathic asshole.

"Looks like you and my sister share the same taste in shoes," Ansel said, coming back into the living room. "Makes me glad I'm not a woman."

She looked up and caught her breath. *Damn it, me too.* He'd changed into a gray polo shirt and a fresh pair of black cargo shorts, all very casual, but breathtaking. He still had loads of boyish charm, though his dark hair was prematurely salt-and-peppered. It didn't make him look old but even cuter, like a wolf cub. "There's a first aid kit in your bathroom. Help yourself."

She hobbled over to her suitcase and set the adorably cruel shoes on top. "Thanks." Maybe her feet just needed practice. All the shoes they'd known until now had been well-padded and roomy. With time, and calluses like oyster shells, she'd break them in.

"You didn't tell me your name," he said, striding into the kitchen.

Sure I did, right when I pulled off my T-shirt and you licked my nipples.

She could use her full name, Nicola, but it would get back to Rachel eventually, and she'd have to explain. "Nicki Fitch," she said softly, bracing herself for his memory to belatedly fire up.

His easy smile didn't falter. "Well, Nicki, how about a drink? I make a mean smoothie." He pointed a thumb over his shoulder at the refrigerator. It was an open floor plan, with the sink overlooking the breakfast counter, the living room, and the ocean view. Anyone standing in the kitchen had a full view of the common areas.

She strolled across the room to the balcony. The sound of children laughing in the pool drifted up to her. "Just water," she said, letting out her tension in a long, slow breath. "Thanks."

"I probably should've told Rachel I'd be here this week," he said.

She turned. It was only Sunday. "This *week*?"

He came over and handed her a wet, icy glass. "And maybe next, but that's tentative. Don't worry, you'll hardly see me. I'm here to buy an office building. Very exciting."

She had to look away from him in dismay.

Two weeks? Maybe longer?

She turned her gaze to the interior of the condo. Big, but not as huge as she'd expected rich people to buy for themselves. The living room held a pair of sofas, a few easy chairs, and a kitchen table. Rachel had said there were two bedrooms. The wraparound balcony overlooking the ocean was the dominant feature, but Ansel's towel, a laptop, two tiny speakers on long black cables, and the spilled salsa littered the area.

His things were all over the living room, too—swim trunks hanging from one chair, a wet towel on another, his laptop, books, notebooks, a camera, gear for snorkeling draped over the tables and floors.

She'd wanted solitude. All of her plans depended upon it. But from what she could see, he *lived* here. He hadn't just flown in for the night or even a few days. He'd brought more shit than *she* had, and she was a woman with lots of clothes—and shoes—and was staying all summer.

She pivoted to face him. "It doesn't look like you're only here on business."

Putting his hands on his hips, he stared back. One corner of his mouth curled up, exposing the slightly uneven canine incisor her tongue still remembered. "That depends what the business is, now, doesn't it?"

Sexual awareness shot through her. The way he could look at her as though she were naked and yet not see her at all…

Her muscles tensed for flight before she told herself to get a grip.

It was a test. Earlier than she'd expected, but a necessary one. Ansel was funny, charming, and sexy, and she'd had a little thing for him a long time ago—okay, a huge thing—and this was her chance to practice her new defenses. She wasn't eighteen and stupid anymore. She was thirty—tough, wise, and mysterious behind her fortress of cool. That kind of woman wouldn't overreact to a cute little rich boy getting too close; if he were sleeping in the other bedroom, what was it to her? She'd be out at the beach. Snorkeling. Surfing. Getting over that water phobia thing.

"Are you sure you don't mind?" she asked.

Smiling with obvious relief, he clasped his hands together. "Of course not. Let me show you your room." He went over and lifted her suitcase with the shoes resting on top. "Is this all you've got?"

At that moment, the question struck her as rather profound. Wasn't what he saw enough?

"Just that," she said coldly.

His smile faltered, making her regret her tone, but he recovered quickly, picked up the bag, and cheerfully strode off to their right. She turned to follow.

"Were you up early to catch your flight?" he asked, pushing his way into a spacious, sunny room decorated in pale green and ivory.

Thank God, it was clean and tidy, with no sign of his things anywhere.

"Yeah, I'm pretty wiped out."

After he set her suitcase near the closet, he moved around the four-poster bed, slid apart the floor-to-ceiling glass doors that let in a balmy breeze.

Then he came back and paused next to the bed. "Here on vacation?"

She noticed a slight sunburn on his cheeks under black-

and-gray stubble. Heart pounding, she made herself busy with the suitcase. "Yes."

"How long?"

"About two months."

"That's great," he said. "By yourself?"

"Yes." On one hand, she hated the rudeness in her voice, but how else could she let him know she wasn't here to make friends? She had enough friends. More than enough attractive male friends.

"Right. Well," he said, moving toward the door, "let me know if you need anything."

"I'm sure I'll be fine. Thanks."

He paused in the doorway and turned. "One more thing," he said, rubbing the back of his neck.

She suppressed a groan. A decade earlier, she'd wasted two years fantasizing about him staying in her bedroom; now she had to clench her hands together to stop herself from shoving him out of it.

But it was his family's condo, not hers, and he was being generous about sharing it. "Yes?"

"Have we met before?" he asked.

Chapter 4

*A*nsel knew he'd seen her somewhere. He'd noticed the slightly hurt, irritated way she looked at him. They'd probably met at some point over the years, and she was annoyed he didn't remember.

"We have, haven't we?" he asked. "I'm terrible with faces. Please don't take it personally."

Her eyes, which had widened momentarily, slowly shrank to normal. "It was a long time ago." She turned away, giving him the chance to admire her from the rear. Her dress stuck to the small of her back, hitching up the skirt a little over her generous bottom. His gaze drifted lower. He'd happily be shorter than every woman on the planet if he got to look at legs like that every day. He wondered if she was over six feet. He was a few inches below it, so he didn't have the perspective to guess accurately.

"Well, I'm sorry," he said.

She glanced over her shoulder. "No big deal." Perhaps because she'd seen him staring, she tugged her dress down. "I'm just really tired."

"Sure. I'm leaving now."

"Thanks—"

He pulled the door shut, saying just before it closed, "See you around."

Then he went to the living room and spent a hurried twenty minutes cleaning up all his crap.

If it were a year earlier, he would've gotten another place. He knew a few fully furnished units were vacant right now even on the same floor as this one. The woman would have had the solitude she obviously wanted.

However, as he hooked his snorkeling fins over a coat hanger in the front closet, he wondered if he might have stayed even if he could've afforded another place. Something about her irritated, impatient face brought out the devil in him. Rachel had a few friends that always got on his nerves. Several of them, in his opinion, clung to her for her money; Rachel was too generous, handing over her goodies to the slightest of acquaintances.

At least this friend was a woman, not some dude who took *everything* Rachel had to offer.

A lot of woman.

He picked up his swim trunks and shook out the sand into the wastebasket. He wasn't cleaning up for her; he was cleaning up for himself. He was a responsible working adult and had business to attend to. It had nothing to do with her sexy legs that were longer than he was.

After he'd removed all of his things from sight, he went out on the balcony, munched on scattered chips, and waited for his phone to power on.

Yes, he was working. He had important emails, phone calls, texts, everything. He was going to make money for once, not just spend it.

He peered down at the pool and watched a waiter carrying a tray heavy with colorful drinks, weaving through recliners, umbrellas, tables, and prone, glistening bodies. How the hell did he carry all that without dropping it? One little kid makes a sudden move and *bam*! Game over, man.

That was work. Hauling garbage and smiling at the ungrateful public was work. What he was doing was like web surfing with a credit card. Even now, after losing access to the family piggy bank, he knew he had it easy. He had an education, connections, and the knowledge of what was possible. Even for a man without any talent or brains, like himself.

The sound of the sliding door around the corner caught his attention. The condo had a wraparound balcony, and the second bedroom faced the courtyard and the north. It got most of the wind and not nearly as much of the ocean view, which is why he hadn't taken it for himself.

He listened to Nicki come out to the balcony, slide the door again behind her, and drag a chair, maybe a table, into position.

Would she try to butter him up now that she'd recovered from the surprise of finding him there at the condo? He knew it wasn't his good looks that made women throw themselves at him. And Rachel would never tell anyone, even a friend, that his father had cut him off from the family fortune. Twins kept secrets better than anyone did.

He idled over to the corner, casually glancing to the right, not too ashamed of himself for wanting to see if she was sunbathing. He liked her type. Tall and strong, a classic figure, the type to be carved out of marble and draped in a toga—bare-breasted, of course. At this point, his imagination transformed her into flesh, a dream come to life.

Ah. Wearing shorts and a tank top, she faced away from him, though the fact that she was juggling distracted him from admiring her body for more than a split second.

She was *juggling*.

Not just lazy, inept juggling, either, but deft. Perfect. The beanbags rose and fell in a steady rhythm, all following the same trajectory. Her exposed shoulders flexed in the sunlight, already shining with sweat. The legs he'd admired earlier bent in a slight squat, displaying well-rounded but athletic thighs and calves.

The beanbags flew higher.

He watched her juggle for a full thirty seconds before saying, honestly impressed, "You're amazing."

One by one, she snatched them out of the air and spun on him. "Damn it," she said. Flushed, she jerked the sliding door open and escaped into her bedroom with the door banging behind her.

He frowned at the tinted glass. "You're welcome." Maybe her parents were circus performers; maybe it was a trendy upper-arm toning exercise. He didn't care; she was rude. He went back to his wing of the balcony, got his phone and the last tortilla chip wedged in the padded seat of the recliner, and plopped down to work.

He sent a text to the real estate agent about an office space in Kihei: *9am tomorrow is perfect.* He sent another text to Brand, his friend and partner. *Relax, I'll bring my camera. And I've got two contractors bidding on windows tomorrow.* Then he spent twenty minutes comparing two properties in Kahului near the airport. Square footage, lease terms, zoning. If there was anything more sedating than zoning, he didn't know what it possibly could be. Learning about organic dog shampoos was more interesting.

Finally, when his neck began to ache, and the yawns were coming only seconds apart, he leaned back and closed his eyes.

He couldn't shake the vision of the naked, juggling goddess.

This was going to be a problem. He hadn't had a girlfriend in almost a year, and stress always made him horny, his body's way of demanding he deal with excess tension.

He sat up and went back to work. He couldn't afford to get distracted.

No matter how much he wanted to be.

———

FIRST THING IN THE MORNING, Nicki put on one of her new outfits: a white sundress, a silk scarf, and jeweled thong sandals. Dressing in such feminine clothes, after years of baggy athletic wear, made her feel like a character in one of her theatrical productions at school.

She kept waiting for the day she got used to it. She wasn't a man; there was no reason to feel like she was in drag. Just because she was tall and weighed more than average and had the shoulders of a linebacker. And could bench press a water buffalo.

No reason. She grabbed her makeup bag and set up near the mirror by the dresser, and while she was swiping fresh powder over her nose, telling herself she was awesome and beautiful, she heard the front door open and close.

Ansel. He'd finally gone out.

She cringed, remembering the look on his face when he'd found her juggling. She shouldn't be embarrassed; it wasn't as if he'd found her surfing porn and playing with herself, but still. He was a handsome guy. And she was a goofy chick who juggled—except the goofy part was supposed to be trapped inside the Old Nicki, not lingering around the fun, fashionable, pretty one.

Unfortunately, she needed the juggling to help her deal with stress. Some people had yoga; she had beanbags. From now on, she'd make sure she indulged in a juggle only when he was out.

She put on eyeliner, lip gloss, and blush, telling the familiar voice that told her she looked ridiculous to shut up. Then she left her room, made herself a quick breakfast with the supplies she'd bought at the store downstairs the night before, and spent a few minutes exploring the condo. She resisted the temptation to peek into Ansel's room before going out herself. She didn't want any unnecessary exposure to his attractive male essence. He was a slob, but he was a sexy slob, damn it.

Once again, she avoided the elevator, juggling imaginary beanbags in her mind as she passed the doors, to take the stairs down to the ground level. One day at a time.

The resort was a long, sprawling property along the coast consisting of several high-rise towers, swimming pools in various shapes, an elongated golf course, intertwining bike and jogging paths, two spas, a high-end shopping center, and an underground parking garage. It was so unlike her usual no-frills wilderness camping spot, she felt guilty for liking it so much. Some people owned their condos, others rented them out, but most paid for their rooms by the night from the resort itself.

When she reached the main floor, she paused to inhale the thick, sweet scent of gardenias growing in pots along the wide tiled foyer and took out her phone to call Betty. "I made it," she told her, wiping the sweat off her upper lip.

"Did Phobic Phoebe need the Valium I gave her for the plane?" Betty asked.

"Of course not. I'm not that bad."

Betty exhaled a soft snort of disbelief. "You hyperventilate on escalators."

"Maybe if escalators went to Hawaii, I wouldn't have a problem."

"I guess."

"Plus," Nicki admitted, "there was this amazing juice in tiny little glass bottles a woman on the plane gave me. It burned my throat at first before I got used to it."

"Aha," Betty said, laughing. "But how did you get to the hotel if you were wasted? Was there a shuttle?"

Nicki helped herself to a cup of citrus-infused water on a table near the elevators and felt the tension inside her ease almost as much as if she were throwing beanbags in the air.

This. This is why she'd come. She could become whomever she wanted in this beautiful, dreamy place.

"I sobered up and rented a car," Nicki said. "No problem."

"Really?"

Nicki decided not to tell her about getting lost and crying in a gas station's bathroom. Week after week, she'd spilled her guts for Betty's blog, every little fear and failure—but what if it merely reinforced the weaknesses of her character? To remake herself she had to change *everything*, not just her clothes but also her conversation. No longer would she tell stories, laughing at herself for being neurotic, obsessive, and ridiculous. Self-deprecation was for losers.

"I'm a perfectly good driver," she told Betty coolly.

"You're okay, but you know how you are, all freaked out and sweaty about it, especially if you're somewhere new."

"I'm not that way anymore."

"Uh-huh," Betty said.

Nicki sipped the fruity water and walked down the path past the spongy green lawn to the beach. Everything in the resort pointed to the sea, nudging your gaze and your body to the sand, the waves, the wind.

But before she went to feel the sea with her bare feet, she had to tell Betty about Ansel. Not in an emotional way as if she were, after all these years, vulnerable, but matter-of-fact, lightly, amused. The way she imagined Miles's redhead would say it.

Oh, Miles, Miles, Miles...

No, not like that. More like, "You won't believe what I found at the condo," Nicki began, forcing a laugh.

Betty perked up. "Drugs?"

The water caught in Nicki's throat. Coughing, she said,

"No. Her brother is here on business for a week or so. I have to share the place with him."

"Holy crap."

"It's no big deal."

"Wasn't this the guy you got to third base with in high school?"

"College."

"I thought it was your first time fooling around," Betty said.

"It was."

"Jeez, I was gay and even I had a guy put his hand down my pants in high school," Betty said.

"And look where that got you. Now you're a bitter, promiscuous lesbian."

Betty snorted. "I'm not bitter."

"Neither am I. I've moved on. I barely recognized him."

"You keep lying to me," Betty said. "You must totally be freaking out."

Nicki opened her mouth to protest, but being fake went against thirty years of living honestly. "I'm fine," she said weakly.

"Write about it for the blog, and I'll expense the airfare. He'll be like Thor II."

"When hell freezes over," Nicki replied. "I'm never writing about the men in my life again. I still have nightmares about Miles Girard."

"Do you wake up all hot and sweaty?"

"If you keep insulting your most popular unpaid contributor, she might decide to stop contributing."

After a melodramatic sigh, Betty said, "All right, you won't write about him, even though it would be great material and the perfect opportunity for you to work through your issues."

"You're so full of shit. You just want the page hits."

Betty laughed. "He's there a week, you said?"

Beyond the resort, the sand sank sharply into the rough

surf. Nicki sat on a bench near an open public shower for people to wash off the salt water. "Maybe longer. Of course I have to stay. I'm not giving this up, no way. But, oh, if you'd seen him…"

"You showed me a picture once."

"I did not."

"Isn't he the guy in your bathroom cabinet?" Betty asked.

"What the hell were you doing looking in my bathroom cabinet?"

"Looking for condoms."

Nicki nearly dropped the phone. "What?"

"Kidding. I needed a tampon. Is he still cute?"

"Oh, yeah." Nicki's thoughts turned to salt-and-pepper hair, a naughty grin, that compact, athletic build.

"Any chance you might—"

"Still be an idiot?" Nicki cut her off.

"Practice your new persona on him?"

"No." Then, "No way."

"Hold on," Betty said, her voice rising. "What did he do when he saw you? Was he totally embarrassed?"

Nicki couldn't bring herself to say anything.

"No, he wouldn't be, I suppose," Betty went on. "Probably smiled and asked for seconds. Did you wear that dress?"

"I did."

"And?"

"I sweated like a pig in it," Nicki replied.

"I'm sure he was too busy looking at your breasts to notice a few sweat stains."

"God, listen to you. It wasn't like that at all."

"I bet it was. You looked hot in that getup."

"He was very polite, no drama. We agreed to share the condo and went our separate ways." Nicki got up and returned to the walkway to find a recycling bin for her cup. "Besides, I don't have any boobs."

"They look like perfect little mouthfuls to me."

"You're just saying that to gross me out, and I don't appreciate it."

Betty laughed. "Don't let him know you still have a thing for him."

"I don't."

"Every time you look at him, remember how you felt when he never asked his sister who you were, or if he could see you again."

"I shouldn't have told you anything. Ever." Nicki tilted her head back to lose herself in the sky. A bank of clouds hovered over the inland hills, casting dark green shadows and reminding her a little of the fog that rolled into the Bay Area.

But only a little. The soft warm moisture in the air, the volcanic peaks of the land, the sweet-smelling flowers everywhere, even on the people, reminded her of where she was. "I'm going to say good-bye now. I'm about to hit the beach."

"You didn't follow him there, did you?"

"Yeah," Nicki said. "And I don't want him to get out of sight, so I've gotta run."

"You're kidding, right?"

"Can't talk. I've got to get my fins on so I can chase him underwater."

"Now I know you're kidding," Betty said. "I hope you go into the water at least once while you're there, though. You can't go to Hawaii and not go swimming."

Nicki reached the western boundary of the resort, where manicured sod and tidy gardens ended at pale sand. The beach was surprisingly narrow and steep at that spot, the crashing waves only thirty yards in front of her, where a dozen people of all ages and physiques were jumping, surfing, paddling, floating. The sight of a grown man with huge muscles being thrown up against the shore, arms flailing, tumbling and powerless as if he weighed no more than a tennis ball, made her freeze where she stood.

Betty's voice broke her daze. "Nicki? Promise me you'll go into the water once while you're there."

Nicki looked back at the resort complex. The water in the wading pool closest to her barely reached the belly buttons of the toddlers splashing in it. "I promise."

"You'll love it. Once you get over your fear, you'll love it."

Nicki took off her shoes to feel the hot sand under her bare feet. "It's not only fear. It's common sense. I never learned how to swim."

"So learn."

"Stop nagging and get your own life, Mom," Nicki said. Oh, the sand felt good. Why wasn't the sand back home ever hot and soft like this? The last time she'd been to a beach near San Francisco, she'd had to wear hiking boots and wool underwear.

When Betty finally let her off the phone, Nicki turned and marched back to the resort, eyes fixed on the baby pool. Her pulse raced.

There was absolutely no reason the sight of ten inches of water should make her mouth go dry, her breath shallow, or her knees tremble. No reason. She wasn't a three-year-old staring up at the sun from underneath six feet of shimmering pool water; she was an athletic, healthy, adult woman.

Why should that one little incident twenty-seven years ago still haunt her? She hadn't been afraid at the time—in fact, she'd been thrilled to be swimming, proving she wasn't a baby anymore—when a nearby grandmother, fully dressed, had jumped in and rescued her from the tile bottom of the City of El Cerrito's pool that afternoon in late August.

But then, apparently, she'd refused to go near the water again. Screamed throughout every swim lesson her mother had ever signed her up for. Eventually, understandably, everyone had given up on her.

And so had she, until now. Just the thought of getting in the water made her fall apart. She stopped and wiped the sweat off her forehead.

All of her stupid anxieties had flared up since that afternoon with Miles and his fiancée in Betty's kitchen, and were getting worse. It was as if getting passed by in love—again—had resurrected every latent fear in her psyche. She'd written a lot of Phobic Phoebe from memory, as a joke, reliving her adolescence. But now…now she jumped at the sight of her own shadow.

Gritting her teeth, she marched to the pool. It was a pinprick of turquoise, the rest of the world disappearing into the shadows of her peripheral vision.

Woodenly, without taking her eyes off the pool, she leaned down to unbuckle her right shoe, her left, and then kicked them off.

Chapter 5

*A*nsel hit the upload button on his laptop one last time before closing the screen with a weary sigh.

He'd taken more pictures of the office building in Kihei than a lonely, unemployed photographer would of his firstborn child. Only six hours as a real estate investor, and he'd already overdone it. Hundreds of pictures of drywall and gray carpeting.

He smiled, unplugging his phone from his laptop and walking out to the condo balcony, savoring the daydream of Brand making himself study each boring, soul-crushing image because he was too perfect not to. They'd need a roomful of computers to store those high-resolution suckers. Luckily, they were about to be the proud landlords of their own climate-controlled office building.

The sun felt good on his face. He'd been in his room for hours with the shades drawn, going over the pictures and researching the property. He sank into the chaise, took out his phone, and called Brand.

"How was it?" Brand asked without saying hello.

"Great. What do you think about solar?"

Brand groaned. "Focus, Ansel. Focus. Just the building."

"I mean solar panels for the property. On the roof. There's this thing here, this fiery ball of gas in the sky, and it's really bright and hot," he said. "You've lived in San Francisco so long you probably don't remember what I'm talking about."

"Money pit," Brand said.

"Not in the long run."

"You wanted me to tell you when you were being stupid," Brand said. "Here you go."

"Hey, it's not stupid to save money on energy. The woman I found to bid on the windows is thinking about moving into solar. We had lunch, and she told me all about the industry here—"

"Ah. You had lunch with somebody. She talked to you about her life's dream, and you were putty in her hands," Brand said. "This is how you ended up with that organic dog food business."

And a dog training one. But Brand didn't have to know about that. "I'll show you the numbers. Even within five years, solar makes sense."

"It's more money up-front. Harder, longer to make a profit. I believe you said you wanted to pile up a mountain of moolah as soon as possible. Those were your words."

"Not right away…"

"Stick to the plan. Just once, why don't you experience the thrill of having a business give *you* money?" Brand asked. "You might like it."

"Check out the photos. I'll send you the spreadsheet."

"Just trying to help you meet the goals we set up on our plan," Brand said.

"Appreciate it. It's all cool," Ansel said. "Just keep an open mind. We'll talk soon. Bye." He stabbed the phone with his index finger. Just below him, the resort's beachfront restaurant and its broad, flat roof were baking in the sun. The palm fronds over the bar wouldn't be good for solar panels, but the rest of the building would be perfect.

He'd talk to the resort management company about it. Some of the newer resorts were much more ecologically aware than this one; it made good advertising and, hell, why not pay attention to the bigger global picture?

He shoved his feet into his flip-flops, grabbed his wallet, phone, and keys, and left the condo to find somebody in the facility's management. He'd get a few names and make an appointment if necessary. When he stepped off the elevator and strode through the foyer, out of habit he glanced across the courtyard to scan the ocean for signs of whales, though the humpbacks wouldn't return in numbers until the late fall.

Had Nicki had ever been out on a whale watch? he wondered. He never got tired of seeing those tails pop up out of the water. If she'd never been to Hawaii before, probably not. It was a shame she'd come in the summer; she'd miss the show.

Don't think about her, he reminded himself. *Solar panels and commercial property. Interest rates. Zoning.*

But then he saw her sitting on the edge of the wading pool at the end of the courtyard, and he came to a sudden halt, all serious thought leaving his head like air out of a whale's blowhole.

She was staring down into the water, leaning forward with her hands under the surface. Her dress was hitched up above her knees, exposing her upper thighs.

Ansel stared. Had she dropped something? Her expression was intense, almost urgent. He took a step forward to ask her if she needed help.

But then she looked up and saw him, and her face broke into a blinding smile.

He froze again, surprised by the way his heart swelled to see her so happy. "Did you find it?" he managed to ask, finally breaking his paralysis to approach her.

"Find it?" she asked, still smiling.

He stopped about three feet away next to her and stared into the shallow water. "I thought you'd lost something."

"Only my marbles."

"Ah," he said, not understanding but willing to play along. "Did you find them in there?" He slid out of his sandals and sat down on the ledge next to her. A fake grotto and a low wall that opened up into a small waterfall several yards away surrounded the pool.

She looked at her feet. "A few of them." She kicked the water with her legs, distracting him again.

"Need help finding the rest?" The words came out before he could stop himself. An attractive woman always triggered his charm reflex.

"I just need a vacation," she said, sighing. "But thanks."

They sat in silence for a few long seconds, during which he wondered if he should get up and leave her alone with her marbles and long legs, but there wasn't any point in being unfriendly.

So he stayed. He stretched out his hairy, short man legs in the warm water next to hers. "It would be pathetic of me to say I know what you mean, given how little work I've ever had to do, but I'd like to think I do know what you mean anyway." He leaned back on his hands and glanced at her. Her profile was strong, with a high forehead and a long nose; it suited the rest of her. "What do you need a vacation from?"

She stood up in the pool, holding her skirt aside with one hand; the water lapped at her shins. She stared at her feet with that oddly intense expression again.

He waited. "Nicki?"

"It's a nice pool," she said, sighing louder this time.

"One of many. The one near the second tower goes around in a loop."

"I like this one."

"It's very nice." He wouldn't pry. If she didn't have a job, who was he to judge or sympathize? "I was about to try to find somebody around here who might be interested in solar panels. Reducing the carbon footprint of the resort, you know?"

Nodding vaguely, she pulled her skirt up to her hips, exposing the tantalizing red bottom of a swimsuit, and strode away from the edge. She splashed through the pool and stopped in the middle about twenty feet away from him. She spun around.

"Check it out," she said, breaking out that blinding smile again. "I'm swimming!"

He must think I'm nuts, she thought, flexing her toes on the rough tile bottom, *but I don't care*. She was in the water! Only a few of her internal organs had shut down from fear; the rest were plugging along just fine, desensitized by the afternoon's slow-mo exposure to wet, baby-blue, chlorinated pool water. It had taken her two hours to go from the deck to her spot in the middle of the pool, and now look at her. She was still breathing on her own. No ambulances had been called.

Progress!

Her triumph faded when she saw the look on Ansel's face. He didn't look like he thought she was crazy; he looked like he thought she was *hot*. One side of his mouth curled up in a grin, his posture leaned forward, his eyes shone bright and eager.

Fresh terror struck her.

No. Not Ansel Jury-Jarski, not now. What was the matter with him? Didn't he see she was the incumbent mayor of Crazytown?

"What are you doing for dinner?" he asked.

"I'm not hungry," she said.

"I meant later." His lopsided smile tilted another few

degrees. "I was thinking about cooking something up at the condo. Easier to cook for two." He jerked his head at the tower behind them.

"Thanks, but no. No thank you." She couldn't think of any excuse, so she just stared at him from her spot in the middle of the pool.

He didn't look offended. "Sure, no problem." He got to his feet. "I promised you privacy, and I meant it. I'll leave you alone now."

She bit back an apology. "Thank you."

"Don't worry about it." He waved and slipped his feet into his sandals. "I'll see you later. Or not. Whichever you prefer." He flashed the grin at her again as he walked away and disappeared behind the fake boulders of the landscaping.

He was flirting with her. She'd noticed him checking out her body. Free-range professional models flocked to Maui, yet he wanted to look at *her*?

The worst thing was, she'd been laughing and smiling in return as if he were just any other guy.

She marched through the water and sat on the edge of the pool with decade-old, horribly good memories washing over her.

It had been late, and they'd been sitting around in her room with six or seven other people in the semi-darkness, drinking and eating, sharing stories about sexual fantasies or experiences that were true, false, in-between, inhibitions melting away the way they did sometimes those first years in college; most of them were still too young to be jaded or careful.

Ansel was just visiting his sister. He'd brought a fondue set. It had been a big joke; they were all going to eat fondue in Rachel's room, even though it barely held four people standing up, let alone the two dozen hungry college students excited to dunk random stuff into melted cheese instead of studying.

But Rachel's roommate had kicked them out. Nicki, though she had a human biology midterm at nine the next morning and was already in her pajamas, immediately flung open her own door. The crowd filed in, and the sound of laughter and the smell of melting cheese attracted the entire floor and the one above them. Two hours later, everyone was full and half-asleep, drunk, happy, sad, and naturally thinking about sex. Some paired up and disappeared into their own rooms. One couple started right there and were encouraged for a few minutes before disgust prevailed and they were evicted. The rest of them began talking. A trio of aromatherapy candles was the only light in the room, inviting confidences. A few people, two men and a woman, said they were gay. One guy said he wanted to be a psychiatrist, then got drunk and told everyone to shut up.

And then they were all gone, and it was just Nicki and Ansel.

She remembered it all like a movie she'd seen in the theater, owned on video, shared copies with her friends, watched too many times, and now despised.

They hadn't actually had sex. Sometimes she wondered if that made it all that much worse. Not only had Ansel forgotten her, he hadn't even mustered the enthusiasm to finish the job. Right when she'd worked up the courage to unzip the fly of his jeans to feel him—to feel any man was new, but *him*, oh my God—he jumped back, fell out of her bed, and half-ran, half-crawled into the hallway, never to be seen again.

Next she heard, he'd gone back to UC Davis, his school at the time, though he dropped out soon after for a while.

Nicki, who never saw him in person again, kept that damn fondue pot for six years. To this day, the smell of melting cheese made her want to vomit.

And he didn't even remember her.

It's a test, she told herself. *If he were a different guy, I might be tempted to go for it.*

Thank goodness she wasn't tempted.

She sank into the water, arms spread out along the edge, and lifted her face to the sun.

He liked her. She could see the like all over his face.

Remember the cheese, she told herself. *Just remember the damn cheese.*

Chapter 6

---

*A*nsel walked away from Nicki at the pool, intending to return after he finished his errand about the solar panels. Grinning, he savored the memory of her standing in the water like a goddess, all that shining feminine skin on display.

He'd been too obvious, too fast, so she'd put up her walls, but he'd felt something spark between them. He'd just been so charmed by the look on her face that he'd forgotten how to be subtle.

As he paused to read the resort map near the foyer, looking for the business offices, his phone rang.

To his surprise, it was Rachel, not Brand. He hesitated. He wasn't supposed to be in Maui, but he didn't usually lie to his twin and didn't relish starting now.

But Nicki might've talked to her. He should answer, reassure her he wasn't staying long and that he hadn't made any unsavory moves on her friend yet. Well, he'd leave off the 'yet' part.

He lifted the phone to his ear. "Hi, Rachel."

"I have huge news, but you have to promise not to give me a hard time."

He stifled a groan. She'd been in London since Christmas. After her gallery opening in Seattle had been a hit, she'd followed friends to London, hoping for more success there.

"Don't start," Rachel said. "You're already being difficult."

"What did I say?"

"You made a noise," she said.

"I tried not to."

"Try harder." Rachel cleared her throat. "Ready? Here it comes."

He sat on a low wall surrounding the koi pond. Three little girls in ascending height order and matching black hair were on the opposite side, peering down into the water. "Okay. Hit me."

"I'm getting married."

He laughed. "Right."

"I am."

To his dismay, she sounded like she believed it. "You're not old enough."

"I'm two minutes older than you, bro," she said. "Two minutes closer to thirty."

"Thirty is the new eighteen."

"Maybe for you. Your sperm has decades of babies ahead. I'm the one with ovaries."

Turning away from the pond, Ansel propped his elbows on his knees and dropped his head into his hands. "I hate it when you talk about your reproductive organs."

"Aren't you even going to ask me what his name is?"

"It doesn't matter," he muttered. "You're not getting married."

"I knew you'd be annoying. You always thought you'd be the one to get married first."

"I did?"

"Maybe you will. Seeing anyone lately? My wedding is in January. Can you beat that?"

"Very funny."

"It would fix things with Dad. He'd have to admit you're not the little kid he thinks you are." Her tone changed, became warmer. "Seriously, that's the solution to all of your problems. You should settle down. It'll make you happy, it'll make Mom and Dad happy, and it'll make *me* happy."

"Even my imaginary wife?"

"She exists somewhere. You just haven't met her yet. Or you have, just don't realize it yet."

"You're not really engaged," he said, sighing in relief. "You only said that because you wanted to talk about me. Well, sorry. I'm not going to marry some poor woman to make Dad—or even you—happy."

Rachel let out a frustrated breath into the phone. "You dork, I'm really, really engaged. You know how this stuff works with us," she added. "Where I go, you go."

He smiled to himself, knowing how far from London he was at the moment. "Not always," he said. "So, how long have you known this guy?"

"Long enough."

He chewed on a thumbnail, hearing the defensiveness in her voice. "Does Romeo have a name?"

"Of course." She paused. "Oliver Alcock."

His head flew up. "You're shitting me." He glanced guiltily at the children watching the fish, then stood and walked out of earshot.

"He's English," she said.

"Sure he is."

She frowned. "What do you mean? I met him in London. He was born here."

"He can't be *all* English, though."

"I suppose he might be Welsh or Scottish or something."

"It's obvious what he is, Rache." He paused for a full two seconds. "All cock."

She let out an exasperated exhalation. "I give up."

"I'm surprised you didn't notice, though," he went on, unable to hold his laughter any longer. "Or are you waiting until after the wedding before you go that far?"

"I'm sending the invitation to your place in San Francisco. And if you don't send back the RSVP envelope, I won't let you in the church." Then she hung up.

Feeling a little guilty, but still chuckling, he walked into the springy lawn of the courtyard. He waited a minute before calling her back.

"Sorry I was a dick," he said. "So to speak. Not one-hundred-percent dick, of course—"

"I've got you all figured out."

"I'm so glad," he said.

"You're jealous."

He snorted. "Of Oliver Allpenis?"

"You're making fun of his name just because your life is empty."

"It isn't…"

"You're worried about turning thirty. You're ready to find your own soul mate."

"Maybe your dude has a cousin." He put his hands on his hips. "Vanessa Vagina, perhaps."

"You always make jokes when you're hiding your feelings."

"Okay, last year I might have said something about wanting to settle down, but I'm over it. I've got more on my plate now. Serious stuff. Mom and Dad were already retired by the time they turned thirty. I'm just getting started."

"You're lonely."

"That's irrelevant. I'm not going to date anyone seriously until I've got my first mother lode in the bank."

"You're being stupid," Rachel said. "And so's Dad. There's

no reason for you to try to get rich when the family has more than we know what to do with. Mom would never agree with what Dad's doing. All you have to do is talk to her—"

"Never. This is between me and Dad." He shook his head. "No, scratch that. It's between me and myself. It has nothing to do with him. I need to do this for myself."

"Then get a regular job. You know people. You don't have expensive taste—you don't need a fortune. Become a dog-walker, or work in Jordan's restaurant—you don't need to be rich to be in love."

He ran his hand through his hair. "We had it so good," he said. "I want my own kids to have the same great childhood."

"Oh, Ansel, you're just as ready to settle down as I am," she said. "Let me help. I have tons of friends all over the world. There has to be somebody who we could both tolerate."

"That's so romantic of you."

"A woman." She smiled. "I'll find you a woman. Then you can bring her to my wedding and enjoy yourself."

"No. Congratulations on your impending nuptials with Lord Phallis-on-Trent. Leave my love life alone, and I promise I won't say another word about it."

"But I know so many great women…"

"You want me to show up at your wedding, you stop talking about setting me up. Got it?"

"But…"

"I'm serious, Rachel. No."

"Not even a teacher? She's totally cool. Funny, smart, cute—"

"No."

"Fine, fine," she said. "Whatever you want. I'd never do anything you didn't want me to."

"Except get married," he said before hanging up.

<hr>

Nicki managed to avoid him for three days. As promised, he didn't intrude. They ate their meals separately, nodded at each other from a distance, kept to themselves.

She thought she was doing pretty well until she talked to Betty on Thursday afternoon. Apparently, her achievement in the wading pool wasn't as impressive as she thought.

"I'm sure it meant a lot to you," Betty said, "but it doesn't really translate to the blog. People could relate to you lusting after the unattainable Thor, but I'm afraid this just makes you look kind of insane."

Nicki was sitting on the balcony eating a peanut butter and pineapple sandwich, her main source of nutrients. Maui was painfully expensive. "Thanks."

"Just looking out for you," Betty said.

"Since when?"

"Fine. I'm looking out for the blog. People like to laugh when they read Phoebe, not get uncomfortable."

Nicki peeled the crust off her sandwich and ate it separately. "It's hard not to share the joy."

"Look, it's just the wading pool. When are you going to the beach? People actually drown there all the time. I looked it up. People don't realize how dangerous it is. They put their back to the waves and whoops, bye-bye," Betty said. "You should go there."

"I'd rather have sex on the registration desk with a bellhop."

Betty whistled. "That would work. I bet that's your subconscious talking. Have someone in mind?"

"I'll write about whatever I want," Nicki said. "If you don't like it because you think it's too much of a bummer, you can delete it."

"Just go to the beach. Even if you don't go in because you're freaking out, write about that. Most people never get to go to Hawaii."

Nicki shoved the last of her sandwich in her mouth. "You know, Betty, you'd have a lot more influence over my writing if you paid me."

"That's so mercenary," Betty said. "You should be ashamed of yourself."

"I'll work my way up to the beach, but it's not going to happen today."

"Just jump in and get it over with," Betty said. "You freak out, you recover, you're done."

"And then I can never do it again, because the trauma has been reinforced. I'm going to do this my way. You don't like it, fire me."

"Take it easy, Nemo. I'm your biggest fan. Just trying to help."

After they hung up, Nicki decided to go for another swim. She wasn't going to flood herself with her fears, but she could accelerate the desensitization a bit. Two swims a day in the baby pool instead of one wouldn't hurt. Not fatally.

She gathered her towel, hat, sunglasses, lotion, book, magnesium supplements, bottle of iced "Calming Caress" herbal tea, and phone loaded with relaxing hypnosis sessions she'd downloaded from a psychotherapist in Scotland. Just his accent was enough to take the edge off. *You aaah the kind of pairsin who is caaahhhm and confident...*

Earbuds in place, mellow Scotsman chanting in her ears, she returned to the pool.

HEAD HIGH, legs bare, sunglasses disguising her worried eyes, Nicki strutted past umbrellas and palm trees, fragrant gardens, bubbling spas, and bodies, bodies, bodies. She wasn't the only one with rocky nips under her bikini.

She snapped a hot-pink blossom off a planter in the court-yard and stuck it in her hair, humming a recent hit single with the immortal words *Get me some* repeated for five minutes to a techno beat. When she reached the first of the hot tubs, she dropped her cover-up to her feet like a woman in a moisturizer commercial.

She'd waded across the baby pool every day since Monday, and now the blasting panic was more of a dull, distant buzz. She was ready to tackle the hot tub. It wasn't really a pool. More like a very wet sofa.

Telling herself it was all for fun, great material for the blog, no big deal, she stepped into the bubbles, still wearing her glasses so she could check out the other people.

Men were everywhere at the resort. Young men, youngish men, not-so-youngish men. All of them were new, and none of them was Ansel. She scanned the area twice to be sure.

Or Miles. Since when was this all about Ansel? He was an old problem. She was here to deal with the current, real prob-lem, which was how a wonderful guy, who was Miles, a man who devoted his life to children just as she had, a man with charm and maturity, the one she knew would've made her happier than anyone else, never considered her as anything other than a coworker or friend.

Ansel was ancient history. She didn't need to forget him. That *other* guy was the problem.

Ah, the water felt good. No surge of panic, though her nerves did jump at the shock of scalding water. Instead of hunching her shoulders, slipping under the surface, waiting for them to relax into their usual flaccid, placid selves, she arched her back and tilted her face up to the sun.

The guy across from her noticed. He was almost as big as Miles, built like an action figure. Rivulets of water ran down his pecs—and his own erect nipples—and she decided he either came from a sunny location back home or had been in

Hawaii for a while, because although his hair was lighter than hers, his skin was perfectly bronzed.

Under the tufts of hair. He was kind of like a blond gorilla.

From her peripheral vision, she watched him stare at her breasts. It took every hot, steaming drop of her willpower not to cross her arms over her chest and dive under the water. If she weren't terrified of drowning, she might have.

"Hey, baby, come here," he said.

All the breath—which apparently she'd been holding for the last six minutes, because it came out in a tight, stale *whoosh* —burst out of her. Under her erect nipples, her heart pounded against her ribs. "What?" she whispered.

"I saw a turtle, Daddy!" A little girl jumped fearlessly into the spa and splashed over to the big man. "In the ocean! Come see!"

Smiling broadly, the man lifted the little girl up in the air. A snorkeling mask hung around her neck, and a single flipper clung to her tiny left foot. She was very young, maybe four, but she wore a spongy rubber wet suit from neck to knee that fit her perfectly.

"It probably swam away by now, honey, don't you think?" he asked her.

"No, I told him to wait. He likes me. Come on, come on!"

The man turned away from the little girl to gaze above Nicki's head. "She told him to wait," he said, grinning.

A woman who'd been blessed by God's airbrushers strode around the spa and squatted down behind the man and the little girl. She wore a black-and-neon-orange athletic bikini with the crotch coverage of, approximately, her clitoris.

It seemed the blond gorilla had all the hair in the family. Not even a single razor bump was visible. My God, didn't that hurt?

All at once, the sporty trio glanced up at her. Nicki quickly smiled at the little girl. "Cute," she said. *Not you,* she added silently to the woman, who'd caught her staring at her shaved labia.

The woman smiled tightly. The man didn't look at her. "She wants to go back in," the woman said.

"I told him I'd be right back," the girl said.

"Well, we don't want to be rude." The man stood, slinging the girl over his shoulders, and stepped out of the pool, water streaking down his hairy legs like balls in a pachinko machine.

The woman rose and they walked toward the ocean. No doubt the turtle was glancing at his watch.

When she'd stopped hyperventilating, Nicki climbed out to try the baby pool again.

ANSEL LOOKED at the pizza on the counter, then at the clock on the microwave. It was past eight. Shouldn't she be back from swimming by now? He'd seen her go out hours ago, though she hadn't noticed him sitting in the living room.

It had been three days since she'd refused his invitation to dinner, long enough, he hoped, that she'd share a pizza with him. The delivery guy had just delivered it, and it was getting cold.

He went to the door and put on his shoes. The hotels and resorts along the beach all looked the same to newcomers; maybe she was lost.

Imagining her gratitude when he rescued her, he was a little disappointed to find her floating on her back in the wading pool within two hundred yards of the condo tower, exactly where she'd stood the other day, laughing about swimming.

He stopped and considered going back inside without bothering her, but then he saw the scowl on her face. She was glaring at the sky and breathing heavily.

"Nicki?" he asked. The pool was as big as a soccer field, but the western half of it, near the hot tubs, was only a foot or two deep. This late on a Thursday night, she had it to herself. Ansel scanned the deck chairs. Mostly to herself. A couple of guys near the bar watched her, drinking silently. Floating like a pale mermaid in a bikini, her long hair splayed out on the surface around her face, lit up from all sides by the pool lighting and tiki torches, she was quite a sight.

He couldn't resist a moment to savor the view. Sundresses were nice, but bikinis were a gift from the divine. He called out again, louder this time, "Nicki?"

With a start, her butt hit the bottom of the pool. Rolling to her side, she pushed herself up with her arms and sat up, showing just how shallow the water was. It barely reached her navel. "What's the matter?"

"Are you all right?"

"Why wouldn't I be all right?"

He hesitated. "It's getting late."

"Late for what?"

Now he felt stupid. "Never mind," he said, turning. "Sorry. See you around."

He heard splashing and looked back to see her striding out of the pool to a pile of towels. After a moment she wrapped herself up in her robe and came over to him, her shoes, towel, and tote bag crushed together in a mess in her arms. "I guess I lost track of time," she said. "Swimming is so relaxing, don't you think?"

"You didn't look relaxed."

"Sure I did."

"Not really. You looked kind of angry. I thought one of those guys might've been bugging you."

"What guys?"

"The drunk jerks ogling you from the bar."

Her eyes went wide. She glanced back. "There was ogling?"

He shook his head and tried not to laugh. He didn't understand her at all, which he liked. "There's a pizza upstairs if you're hungry. No pressure."

"Pizza?"

"Hungry?"

"A little." She sighed. "Very, actually. What time is it?"

"After eight. I was getting worried."

She frowned, rubbing her hair with a towel. "About what?"

"Nothing. How about that pizza?" He took a step toward the condo tower.

"You were worried about *me*?"

"What can I say, I'm a worrier," he replied. "But you seem to be okay."

"I'm fantastic." She followed him into the building and then jogged past the elevator to open the door to the stairwell.

He raised an eyebrow. "Ah, you're one of those."

"One of what?"

"Fitness type. You really think one elevator ride is going to ruin you?"

She rolled her eyes. "You have no idea." She hiked up the stairs, leaving little puddles in her wake.

He admired her flexing thighs below the hem of the towel, following a few steps behind, and said nothing.

"Actually," she said in a funny voice when they reached the third floor, "I'm afraid of elevators. That's why I take the stairs."

"No kidding?"

"I had a panic attack in the rental car, too."

"There was an elevator in the rental car?" he asked. "I need to shop around more."

"Ha-ha. No, I'm afraid of driving."

"Sensible of you. Leading cause of accidental death. Anything else?"

She gave him a challenging look and turned to face him completely. "Lots," she said. "It took me an hour to stop hyperventilating in the baby pool."

An unusually wise instinct prevented him from laughing. Her words were funny, but her eyes were serious. "You were doing great. Good for you."

She shot him a wry smile. "You've probably never been scared in your life."

"I'm afraid of heights a little bit."

"Yeah?"

"When I got to the top of Half Dome, I got this weird tingling feeling in my stomach."

Her eyes narrowed. "But you climbed up there yourself?"

"I had friends with me."

"Were you carried up in a straightjacket? Because that's what I'd need. And a few bottles of prescription medication."

"I think one of the guys was on something, but I don't think he had a prescription for it." He was relieved when she laughed.

"Actually, drugs don't help me," she said. "I've tried."

"Maybe you're not trying hard enough," he said. At her worried face, he said, "Just kidding. I don't use anything either."

"Well, I was talking about medicine. Too many side effects. So I have to go through life constantly teetering on the edge of a nervous breakdown." She leaned closer. "I'm a nutjob, Ansel. Batshit crazy. Keep that in mind."

He looked her over, grinning. "I like crazy."

She scowled. "You don't mean that."

"You don't know me."

After a pause, she said, "Rachel has told me about you."

"She'd be the first to tell you—" He cut himself off and stared at her.

Rachel would be the first to tell you how much I like fixer-uppers. She always teased him for having strange taste. His last girlfriend had just married her bankruptcy attorney. Ansel had introduced them to each other.

"Tell me what?" Nicki asked, eyeing him.

He'd been too distracted earlier to see the obvious. Although he hadn't told Rachel he was coming to Hawaii, she could've heard about it through a mutual friend. Not their parents, of course, since he wasn't going to tell them anything about his professional plans—until he was a success, anyway.

"Nothing," he said, dropping the charm. Rachel had planned this, and he'd walked right into it. It didn't help that stress made him horny. And she was his dream woman, right there in the wet, dripping flesh.

Must. Stop. Flirting. Immediately. He'd dish out the pizza and make a run for it.

"I hope you like pineapple on your pizza," he said, passing Nicki on the stairs. He kept a few steps ahead of her the entire way to the condo, saying nothing more.

When she came into the kitchen after hanging up her towel, he handed her a plate to let her serve herself. Then he had to bite his tongue to stop himself from offering her a drink, Parmesan cheese, red pepper, napkins, or his charming company.

"It's hard to get a decent pizza around here, so don't get too excited. And it's been sitting out on the table for over thirty minutes," he said instead. "If you're afraid of food poisoning, you might not want to eat it."

"No such luck. None of my phobias makes me afraid to eat something that's bad for me." She lifted a piece as big as her left thigh directly to her mouth. "What do I owe you?"

"For what?"

"For what? This. I'm not a total leech." She got down a glass from the cupboard, filled it with water from the dispenser on the refrigerator door.

"Forget it."

"That's not going to work. You'll be here two weeks, you think?"

"About that."

"So we'll keep all our receipts, add them up at the end, and pay each other back the difference. That way we don't have to worry about buying two bottles of ketchup, two boxes of cereal, that sort of thing." She caught him staring. "Haven't you ever gone on vacation with friends?"

"Sure." But he always paid for everything. Why wouldn't he?

"So don't you think this is easier than carving out separate shelves in the fridge, afraid to eat a banana in case you didn't pay for it?"

"You're afraid of eating bananas, too?"

She made a face. "Terrified."

"You don't have to pay me for the pizza. I don't have the receipt. And I ate more than half of it anyway."

"That's not how it works. We just split it and relax. I'm sure I can eat my share, don't worry about that." She shoved a pizza crust in her mouth, her cheeks bulging as she reached for the resort notepad and pen by the phone. "About how much was it? We'll jot down an estimate."

"I have no idea."

"Twenty?" She frowned. "No, I bet it's more here. Just a loaf of bread in the store downstairs was more than five. Thirty?"

He'd given the delivery guy a fifty and refused the change. People got the happiest looks on their faces just to get a few extra bucks. He'd have a steady income soon enough. "That's about right."

She scribbled, tore off the note, stuck it to the fridge. "There. Don't forget to save a receipt next time." She eyed the other fresh pineapple he'd bought. "Did you use a credit card for the groceries? Because you could just look up the total online. I can make a spreadsheet, we both update it as we go, compare the accounts, settle later."

He stared at her. "I'm not going to fill out a report just because I bought a few groceries." Doing work for life was bad enough; turning life into work wasn't going to happen.

"It's not a report," she said. "It's just a list to keep track."

"We don't need to keep track. Help yourself to whatever you like."

"Don't be silly. Rachel's letting me stay here for free. I can't let you buy my food, too."

"Yes, you can."

"No—" She put her plate down. "Forget it. I'll get my own groceries tomorrow."

"You don't have to buy your own groceries."

"I'm not a charity case."

"I don't make guests pay for their food." He marched over to the pizza box, offhandedly offering her another slice, which she refused, before he pushed it into the refrigerator. "Especially when they're between jobs."

"Is that what you're worried about? Well, you can rest easy. I'm a teacher. This is my summer vacation."

"Teacher," he said. "Like, for kids?"

"Seventh grade."

"Oh," he said. Not unemployed, not a socialite; a teacher. Sexy *and* smart.

Watch out, Ansel. She pushes all of your buttons.

"Try to control your awe," Nicki said. "Now will you let us share the expenses?"

"No. I know what teachers make. I'm surprised you can afford shoes." He poured himself a glass of water and strode out of the kitchen toward his bedroom. He wouldn't call Rachel to chew her out; he wouldn't give her the satisfaction. Now that he knew she'd set him up, he'd be on guard. He wasn't an eighteen-year-old kid anymore, jumping in bed with any girl remotely willing to join him.

"I'm going to pay you back anyway," she called after him.

He turned and waved as he walked away. "I hope you enjoyed the pizza." Losing the battle to ignore her completely, he added, "Tomorrow I'll get us Hawaiian barbecue."

Chapter 7

"You told him *everything*?" Betty asked her the next morning.

Nicki walked along the boardwalk, cooling down from a five-mile run as she talked into her earphone mic. Clouds blocked the sun, threatening rain, but the beach was still crowded. "No, just about my anxiety."

"Oh, God. You panicked. You were trying to scare him away."

"Of course I want to scare him away. It wasn't panic at all," Nicki said. "It was cold and calculated. I'm working on other things right now. I need to focus."

"I thought you got over the swimming thing in the baby pool." Betty's tone turned grudging. "Your column this morning was pretty good, by the way. Phoebe got sixty-two percent of my entire website's traffic the hour after it posted."

"Not bad for an unpaid basket case."

"I don't get it," Betty said. "I start a blog for punk lesbians, and a straight, sexually repressed schoolteacher gets all the love. What's with that?"

"Maybe I make people feel good about themselves in comparison."

"That must be it." Betty took a bite of something crunchy; the sound of her chewing crackled in Nicki's ears. "Maybe I should develop a phobia. Penises have always freaked me out. Does that count?"

"I think you have your next post right there." Nicki smiled at the thought of the graphic Betty would come up with for that one. Animated, no doubt.

"The next thing I want to post is you getting laid. Just because you're straight doesn't mean my readers can't appreciate a good romance." Betty took another bite of her noisy snack. "You said he's short, right? I bet he's good in bed. He has to overcompensate."

"I didn't say he's short."

"Is he taller than you?"

"I'm six feet tall," Nicki said.

"And he's not?"

"The average guy isn't."

"And the average woman is a size fourteen," Betty said. "Doesn't mean she's skinny."

"*I* wear a fourteen," Nicki said.

"You're an Amazon, he's a shrimp," Betty said. "Recipe for hot sex, I'm telling you. It breaks the rules. Forbidden fruit is always a turn-on."

"Which one of us is the fruit?" Nicki asked.

"Hopefully not him. You know he's straight, right?"

Nicki had heard about his exploits over the years from Rachel. "Either that or he's trying really, really hard."

"Is the family religious?"

"No."

"Then he's probably safe. He'll have sex with you if you express a little interest," Betty said. "Trust me."

"I don't want him to have sex with me."

"Yeah, you do. You just don't want to get hurt."

Wedging her water bottle into its pouch on her hip belt, Nicki watched a pair of snorkelers across the beach walk into the water. "I'm going to swim in the ocean. That's my next thing. I'll even write about it. That's what you want, remember?"

"Sex is way better. Listen, the way to sleep around without getting hurt is to do it more often," Betty said. "Take it from me. Practice makes perfect."

"Bet, I love you, but you're a slut. I'm never going to be like you."

"You couldn't even if you tried. You wasted too much time in your twenties," Betty said. "Fine. At least find somebody who's got a sex drive. That last guy you were with had less testosterone than I do."

Her last boyfriend, another teacher, had been a nice guy but definitely bland in bed. "This trip is about me, myself, and I. It's about learning I don't need anyone to complete me, sexually or otherwise." She bent over to smell a gardenia blossom growing in a hotel display garden. "I've got to go. I'm almost back to my resort."

"What are you going to do if your oversharing didn't scare the love shrimp away?" Betty asked.

"I'm sure I told him enough to do the trick. It always does," Nicki said, thinking of Miles.

"But what if it didn't? Do you have the intestinal fortitude to turn him down if he hits on you?"

"He won't," Nicki said. "Trust me."

WHEN SHE WOKE LATE the next morning, Nicki heard Ansel moving around the kitchen.

Instead of putting on a silk robe or showering, she rolled

out of bed as is, her hair like Jennifer Aniston on one side and an overgrown juniper hedge on the other, her eyes puffy with sleep, and walked out into the living room. There was more than one way to scare him off.

The smell drifting over the breakfast counter from the kitchen made her stomach grumble. She stopped wondering how he'd react to her fright wig and scanned the kitchen for what smelled so good.

"Sorry I didn't get the barbecue yesterday." He held a mixing bowl in the crook of his elbow and had a spoon in his hand. "I got caught up in some business appointments. You wouldn't believe how complicated it is to buy an ugly little office building."

"You don't have to apologize." The last thing she wanted was for him to think she cared or noticed anything he did. Yawning, she climbed up on the barstool behind the breakfast counter across from him. "I was busy myself."

He looked up from the bowl he was stirring, his expression guarded. "Talk to Rachel lately?"

She pulled a banana off the hook on the counter. "Just to leave a message thanking her for everything."

"Did you mention me?" He glanced up from the mixing bowl, strands of black and gray hair falling into his eyes.

She'd decided not to. If she had, she might've given away how annoyed she was about him being there, which would've been tacky. Whining to a friend who'd loaned you a luxury condo in Maui just didn't seem cool. "I thought you might rather I didn't," she said.

His gaze sharpened. "Yeah?"

"Since you're not supposed to be here," she continued carefully, wondering why he looked edgy.

"I'm not?" Flushing, he turned his attention back to the bowl and stirred more vigorously.

"That's what you said."

He put down the bowl to pour her a cup of coffee before turning around to get a pair of plates out of the cupboard. "Yeah. I did, didn't I?"

Grateful for the coffee, Nicki didn't ask him to elaborate. She stretched out a leg to reach the floor. "Well. Got to take a shower and get going." She waved the banana at him and edged away.

"Wait, I just put the eggs in the water to poach." He held up a pan with golden rolls—brioche, maybe—split in half, and the aroma of full-fat dairy and tarragon wafted over to her. "Lobster eggs Benedict. Do you smell that?" He thrust the pan closer to her.

Her stomach growled. "Wow."

"I listened at your door to make sure you were here. I was about to wake you up."

"Listened?" Reluctantly, she reclaimed the barstool. The sound of her delicate feminine slumber could knock a vase off a shelf. She lifted the coffee to her lips. "I'm surprised you had to even walk to the door."

"Snoring's sexy," he said without any hint of mockery.

Sexy? Yeah, right. Maybe if she'd fallen asleep that night in college, he never would've left.

He lifted out the eggs, frowning at his phone propped up on the kitchen counter. "Shoot, I forgot to warm up the plates. I'm supposed to keep these warm while I scoop out the lobster."

"That looks and smells amazing. Really."

He shook his head. "The eggs are getting cold."

"Can I help?"

"No, only one captain of this ship, thanks." He glanced at her. "How's the coffee?"

"Great." She took a long gulp. "Excellent."

"That is local. Unlike the New England crustacean here." After a few minutes of jogging around the kitchen, he arranged the eggs over the rolls and lobster, topped it with sauce, and sprinkled a pinch of chives over the plates. Frowning at his creations, he asked, not looking at her, "Are you hungry?"

"Give me that plate or I'll kill you." She held out a hand for a second, then withdrew. "Sorry. We should set the table."

"No time. It's already cold." He set the plate and a fork in front of her and crossed his arms over his chest.

Unable to resist licking her lips, she picked up her fork. "Aren't you going to join me?"

"Sure." He held his fork in one hand and stared at her.

Uncomfortable but starving, she lifted a bite to her mouth and tasted rich, savory perfection, which made it easy to take another bite, and another and another, ignoring the serious look on his face as he watched her.

"You're a great cook," she said over a mouthful of butter-soaked brioche.

Only then did he shovel forkfuls into his mouth. He ate it as if it were no better than instant oatmeal warmed up in a motel room's microwave. "Glad you like it," he mumbled.

"It's incredible," she said, but after a minute, she got tired of his lack of reaction and settled in to enjoy it in silence. Too soon, her plate was clean, and she lifted her coffee to wash it down. He'd already finished and had begun washing up. She frowned at his back. His broad, handsome shoulders.

Christ, she was drifting again. She climbed down from the stool and carried her dishes to the sink. "Let me clean up," she said, bumping him with the empty mug.

"Give it a rest. You want to pay and you want to clean, but you can't. Like it or not, this is *mi casa.*"

"But…" She stopped. Even with the meal over, he was still tense. His usual smile was missing. Not a good time to argue. She nudged her plate into his hands under the running water. "Thanks. It was delicious."

"You're welcome."

She hesitated. Did something happen to him yesterday? Was it anything to do with her?

No. She wouldn't let herself obsess about a man again. He had his own life and it had nothing to do with her. Without another word, she walked back to her room to get ready for the day. She was working up the guts to sign up for an official swim lesson; she'd just read on a sign downstairs that the resort had people on staff who taught at one of the pools.

Before she got in the shower, she picked up her phone to check her usual haunts online.

Ah, she thought. *That's what his problem is.*

The *Countdown to Thirty* on Rachel's Facebook page had reached zero.

Happy Birthday, Rachel! Nicki typed out to her, adding her message at the bottom of dozens of others in earlier time zones. While she turned up the hot water, she tried to understand Ansel's problem with something as silly as a birthday. Every second of every day you were getting older and so was everybody else; today was no different from yesterday or tomorrow. In the scheme of the universe…

She propped one foot on the edge of the tub and lathered up for the daily shave. Wearing swimsuits meant maintenance she usually let slide back home. It was a sunny morning, and she'd been looking forward to getting in the water again, which was a miracle. The blog already had a fun discussion going about Phoebe's courageous aquatic journey; she could elaborate on it for next week's post and save herself the exhausting effort of coming up with a new topic.

But…

Standing under the spray, she thought about Ansel's melancholy face at breakfast. It bothered her that he might spend his birthday alone, obviously feeling so down.

He may have decimated her self-confidence when she was young and vulnerable, but thirty could be an intimidating number—and he'd made her lobster eggs Benedict—and maybe she could try to cheer him up a little. It wouldn't kill her to take a day off from her self-improvement journey, spend time with him. He hadn't made any passes, and she could easily brush him off if he did, which he wouldn't, and she didn't expect him to, and she could handle that. Unlike Ansel, she liked getting older, precisely because it had thickened her hide.

After drying herself off and brushing her teeth, she faced a dilemma. If she was going to hang out with him today, should she put on makeup or go natural? Wear sophisticated resort fashion or old shorts and a T-shirt? She wiped the fog off the mirror and stared at herself.

Who the hell was she, anyway?

She was a thirty-year-old single schoolteacher on vacation. She was funny, smart, caring, and…

She leaned closer, poking her face. And she had a zit on her chin so big it deserved its own tourists. They could drive up it in the middle of the night to watch the sunrise.

Well, even the old Nicki would wear makeup during bad-skin days. Mascara and eyeliner did wonders to distract away from facial volcanoes.

She went split personality with the outfit, wearing an old favorite T-shirt with new capris, and she went out to find him before she changed her mind.

Leaning on the balcony railing, staring off into space, he didn't hear her approach. She hesitated and glanced over him toward the pool before saying, "Happy birthday."

He jerked and turned around. If he noticed the geological wonder on her epidermis, his eyes didn't betray it. "Thanks. Rachel reminded you?"

She nodded. "I'm surprised you two wouldn't be together today."

"We usually are but… we're on the opposite sides of the earth this year."

"You chose to come here, though," she said.

"And she chose to move to England and paint little pictures."

"Good thing you're so supportive." She joined him at the railing. "Where are your parents?"

"Central America," he muttered.

"They don't love you either?"

His mouth tightened, fighting a smile. "Apparently not."

"You sure are grumpy. I'm usually in a *fabulous* mood on my birthday."

"Congratulations."

"I eat whatever I want, that's number one. And I always take a vacation day. That's easy, because it's in late December and school's out anyway. And no matter how much she nags, I don't let my mother take me to the mall."

"Don't all women like shopping?" he asked.

"Not the day after Christmas."

"Ah."

She nodded. "So you should snap out of it and have a nice day."

"You should leave me alone and have a nice day."

"What are your plans?" she asked.

With a groan, he hung his head.

"I mean for the day," she clarified. "Not your life."

"What's the difference?"

She frowned at his profile and thought of a different tack. His resistance only made her more determined. "I told you about my little driving phobia, right?"

Straightening, he glanced at her. "Car elevators are especially problematic, I believe you said."

The gold flecks in his gray eyes stunned her stupid for a moment. He had such gorgeous eyes. "Yeah," she whispered.

He waited. "And?"

"And…" She turned away. "I'd really like to do that drive through the rainforest."

"Hana?"

"It sounds so beautiful."

"It is. You have to do it while you're here."

She wasn't exaggerating the sigh that came out of her. "I'm dreading it."

"There are a lot of sharp turns, but the traffic makes it slow," he said. "You're from California. Haven't you driven Highway 1 up the coast?"

"It almost killed me."

"Well, it's nowhere near as terrifying as that, so you'll be fine." His tone became cautious. "Were you thinking of doing that today?"

"No, I was thinking of doing that yesterday. I just couldn't get up the guts." She glanced at him, batted her drag queen eyelashes, and grinned.

His lips twitched. "I thought you were trying to overcome your fears. If I drove you, wouldn't that be a waste of a perfect opportunity?"

"Baby steps, Ansel," she said. "Baby steps."

"We'd have to leave soon. It's a long drive."

"I'm ready right now."

He held her gaze, and she felt a moment of fear; her knees got wobbly when he looked at her like that.

But it was worse when he shook his head and said, "I'm sorry, Nicki. I wouldn't be good company today. How about a rain check?"

Her smile froze. "The offer's only good today."

"Then it really is my loss." He flinched. "I'm really sorry."

It took her a second to breathe. "Hey, don't apologize, I was trying to cheer *you* up," she said, unwilling to come within a million miles of his pity. Punching him lightly in the shoulder, she moved away from the balcony to go inside. "I've got a swimming phobia to overcome." Burying any embarrassment about being rejected, she hurried to her room and put on her bikini, the designer cover-up, a new floral headband to keep the hair out of her eyes, another layer of waterproof mascara, more waterproof eyeliner, bright red sandals—she looked around for something else to decorate herself with—and a scarf. It was Hawaii, but the scarf was silky and girly, and she could cover her face with it if she needed to hide suddenly. Such were the backup plans of a coward. Whatever it took.

She fled the condo, shouting a good-bye, and ran for the stairs with her towel flopping behind her and one strap unbuckled on her shoe.

Rain check. Sorry. *Ugh.*

Chapter 8

*A*nsel heard the door slam. He hung his head, sagged against the balcony railing.

A pretty girl invited him to spend the day with him on his birthday, and he told her to get lost?

Am I nuts?

Is this what old age did to a man? So what if his sister had tried to set them up; going for a drive wasn't a marriage proposal.

He spun on his heel and ran inside to get his jeans and hiking sandals, a couple of family rain ponchos, and a cooler filled with bottled water, a pineapple—

Okay, maybe not a pineapple; too messy. He'd buy them a picnic on the road.

He was already in the hallway when he remembered she was wearing only a swimsuit and a robe. Although it was a little presumptuous—a lot presumptuous—he jogged back into the condo to her bedroom and grabbed the clothes she'd left on the bed. Thank God he didn't have to look inside any drawers; though he did of course have to get her underwear and bra, which meant touching them, but he was quick and deliberately didn't hold them up and imagine taking them off her. Because that would be something a dirty old man would do.

Better to actually *do* it.

No, that would be worse. He'd just take her up on the drive. Because this was his birthday, and he didn't want to be alone.

He caught up to her just as she was kicking off her shoes at the side of the pool. When she started to take off the robe, he galloped over and grabbed her by the shoulders.

She gaped at him. "What is it?"

"I was stupid. Let's do it," he said, smiling. "I would love to spend the day with you."

Her expression wasn't as thrilled as he'd hoped. "I was just getting in the water."

"It's a long drive there and back, all day, really. We should go now."

Her eyes narrowed. "What changed your mind?"

"As soon as you left, I realized I wasn't going to get a better offer," he said, meaning it as a self-deprecating joke but, seeing the flash of anger in her eyes, he realized he'd screwed up.

"Maybe you should give it a few minutes to an hour," she said, "give yourself time to rake in a better one."

"That's not what I meant." He rubbed his hand over his mouth. "I mean, I could never get a better offer than to spend my birthday in the most beautiful place on earth with a beautiful woman."

She looked at the sky, pressing her lips together. Out of all proportion to the situation, his heart skipped a beat as he waited.

"Because it's your birthday," she said finally, "I'll give you another chance."

He let out a breath. "Thank you."

"But I'm swimming first." She frowned at him. "You can wait upstairs."

"It's a long drive. We should leave as early as we can," he said. "We wouldn't want to get stuck out there in the dark."

Her eyes widened. "Right. I'll go up and change, meet you down here as fast as I can."

He readjusted the bag with her clothes in it on his shoulder. Maybe it would be better to admit he'd touched her underwear after they were on the road. "I'll meet you at the front circle in the car."

Fifteen minutes later, he was behind the wheel of his family's first-generation hybrid with Nicki at his side in a faded blue T-shirt and cropped jeans, heading south. He was in agony, wondering when she'd ask him where her clothes had gone. The Hana Highway was on the opposite corner of the island, hours away, often choked with tourist traffic, and he had a moment's hesitation about spending his entire thirtieth birthday stuck in a car instead of...

Well, that was just it. Would he rather be drinking alone at the condo, staring at himself naked in the mirror, flexing his muscles to feel young and vigorous?

No, that was so *last* year.

"Ansel?"

They'd been driving for about thirty minutes, but because of the traffic, they still hadn't left the western coastline. Soon they'd turn left and head north toward the airport before they could go east into the rainforest, a vastly different microclimate from the arid, sunny west. "Yes?"

"Did you get my clothes? The ones I had on earlier?"

What could she do, jump out of the car? "Yeah," he said. "Sorry. I was trying to be helpful."

"You didn't say anything."

"Thought it might creep you out," he said.

"It did kinda."

Braking for the row of slow-moving cars ahead, he

shrugged. "I didn't want you to have any excuses about coming."

"And you think handing me my panties, which you found in my bedroom and I'd already worn, would persuade me?"

He pointed at a fruit stand on the other side of the road. "That guy sells sugar cane. Should I stop? Have you ever chewed on sugar cane?"

"In the future, I'd appreciate it if you didn't touch any of my things," she said.

He felt his face get hot. "Gotcha. Sorry."

She craned around to look at the fruit stand disappearing behind them. "Maybe we could stop on the way back."

"Deal." He eased his foot off the gas, letting out a slow breath of relief.

He'd turned her down, clumsily changed his mind, then touched her underwear without her permission.

She was incredibly nice to forgive him.

He glanced at her.

And beautiful, too.

He turned his gaze back to the road, heart pounding, wondering if he'd developed a driving phobia of his own.

I'm way over my head with this one.

NICKI ENJOYED the beginning of the drive more than she wanted. Having apparently shaken off his earlier depression, Ansel was a cheerful, talkative companion who pointed out rainbows and volcanos and encouraged her to come back in the spring for whale watching. He told her about a woman starting a solar business here on Maui, and how he was thinking about investing in her new company, which led him to tell her about a friend with a restaurant in San Francisco, and then about a dog-walking business in the East Bay.

It was a little weird he hadn't told her about getting her clothes, but he'd obviously been dreadfully embarrassed about it. It was a treat to see confident, cheerful Ansel lose his cool when she'd confronted him. He'd blushed so red, she'd nearly burst out laughing.

When they passed the road to Kihei, where he said he was buying an office building, the car fell quiet. He didn't say another word until about twenty minutes later, when, as they were passing the airport in Kahului, he pulled into a strip mall and parked in front of a surf shop.

"What do you think?" he asked.

"I don't know that I'm ready for surfing just yet," Nicki said. "I think I need to master the hotel pool first."

Ansel pointed to the row of new buildings in the neighboring lot. "My business partner wants us to buy one of those next. After we close the deal we're working on now."

She peered over at the small calligraphed sign on the wall. "Medical offices?"

He bent over to rest his forehead on the steering wheel. "Dental," he muttered into the plastic.

"Sounds practical," she said. "Everyone has teeth."

"If they go to the dentist."

"Exactly. Very motivating," she replied. "But you don't want to buy it?"

"Look at it." He rolled his head back, yawned. "I'm falling into a coma just looking at it."

"So don't buy it."

"I have to."

"No, you don't," she said. "Why should you have to do what your friend wants?"

"Because I twisted his arm to work with me, and if I'm difficult…"

"Yeah?"

He shot her a sad puppy look. "He'll dump me."

She hesitated. He was only sort of kidding. "But aren't you the one with the cash?"

Shaking his head, he played with the buttons on the aftermarket GPS attached to the window with a suction cup. "You don't understand."

"All right, explain. What's so great about this guy?"

He sighed. "Brand Henry Warren, Jr. is really, really good at making money."

"So?"

"So I want to make money too. To date, I've only shown an aptitude for spending it."

For the first time since she'd arrived in Hawaii, she studied him dispassionately, as she would if she'd never seen him before. His well-worn sandals were high quality but old. His khaki shorts were pale from many washings, and his San Francisco Giant's T-shirt was a popular commodity garment sold across the Bay Area. Even the car was at least eight years old, not the type a swinging playboy would choose; zero to sixty… eventually.

"It looks like you only spend money on other people, not yourself," she said. "Your friend's restaurant, those other businesses…"

"Don't remind me. Brand is trying to break me of that habit."

"I don't like the sound of *Brand*," she said. "Even his name is corporate. He'll name his kids 'Proctor' and 'Gamble.'"

"It's easy to give money to friends. I'm trying to learn how to find successful businesses. It'll be better for everyone in the long run," he said. "They can hire employees, support their families, and contribute to the tax base of their community."

She made a retching sound. "Let me guess. Brand told you that?"

"Bank commercial. But it was very touching." He restarted the car and maneuvered the city streets of Kahului, past the airport, then out along the country highway. Both of them slipped into silence. When they reached Paia, a small artsy town on the coast that reminded her of gourmet ghettos around San Francisco, he pulled over and they went into a cute little place to order a picnic lunch, along with a line of two dozen other tourists, and then they were on their way again. So far, she agreed the drive was pretty, but she wasn't sure she would enjoy six more hours of the same, even with Ansel's company.

Especially with his company.

Soon the forest thickened, the air grew moist, cooler, and the long highway behind them became narrow and twisted.

"Here we are," Ansel said. "The famous Hana Highway." Braking, he drove off the road and parked in a turnout of gravel under a lush overhang of flora. The movie set of *Jurassic Park*, ferns and humid air and chirping exotic birds, surrounded them. Then, to her surprise, he got out of the car, walked around, and opened her door, smiling.

Her heart had understood what he was doing before her mind processed it. Pounding wildly, it bounced off her lungs, restricting airflow. "No," she said, gazing up at him.

"Your turn." He opened the door wider and held out a hand.

"You didn't warn me."

"You would've said no."

Licking her lips, she glanced around in a panic. "Maybe I've never driven a hybrid before."

"It's not a spaceship. I think you can figure it out."

She had to close her eyes and focus on breathing. He was trying to be helpful, but the surprise made it worse. If she'd had a few hours to get used to the idea, she wouldn't be suffocating right now.

Deep breath.

Just a car.

She could do it.

His eyes softened. "Hey, Nicki, I'm sorry. Never mind. I was just kidding." He started to close the door.

"No!" She thrust her leg out. "I'll do it."

"No, really, it's a crazy drive. Windy one-lane bridges, traffic, distracting views…"

Seatbelt unbuckled, lungs pumping, she climbed out of the car, hand gripping the metal roof, slick with mist, and swatted away the tendrils of panic rising up from her toes. "I'm thirty years old. I've been driving a car half my life in urban California. I'm capable, sensible, and totally fucking insane because I'm about to puke." Folding over, she braced her hands on her knees.

"I'll drive," she heard him say from a foggy distance. "It's okay. Can I get you anything?"

"A spine," she said through her teeth, straightening. She drew lush rainforest air into her lungs, which reminded her where she was, how lucky she was to be there. A tree with peeling red-and-purple bark over a lime-green trunk rose up in front of her, straight as a redwood. She focused her attention on it to calm herself. "What is that?"

He turned. "Painted bark eucalyptus. Pretty cool, isn't it?"

She saw now that the river of rental cars was slowing down to stare at them, not just at the trees. Faces peered out at her from the windows. "Fantastic." She took a clumsy step, then another, until she was walking behind the trunk of the car and reaching for the driver's-side door. "But we're making a traffic jam. Let's go."

After hesitating only a moment, he flashed a smile and jumped into the passenger seat. "Hybrids have a few quirks you need to learn…"

She took hold of the wheel with the iron grip of a cliff-hanging villain in an action flick, signaled, and eased out into the row of slow-moving cars. "I have the same car at home."

His eyes widened. "But you said you'd never driven one before."

"I said, 'maybe I haven't.' But I have."

"Sneaky," he said. "Some might even call that lying."

"Some people are a pain in the ass."

He laughed. "You're doing great."

"Don't patronize me, old man."

"Damn, you're grouchy."

"Quit your blabbing," she said. "I need to concentrate."

Out of the corner of her eye, she saw him grinning at her.

Chapter 9

*W*ithin ten minutes, her anxiety had faded to a sour memory, the way an early morning nightmare weakens by breakfast time. If it had been an unfamiliar car, perhaps she wouldn't have managed it so well, but it was the same year, even the same common slate-blue as hers back in Berkeley, and she had to focus only on the wiggly road and the brake lights on the rented silver compact twenty feet ahead. Her pulse slowed to normal levels, and although she couldn't spare any energy to appreciate the view, she managed to maintain consciousness.

When the traffic came to a stop, her nerves calmed, and she became aware of Ansel's gaze on her. He wasn't saying anything, just watching.

Was he struggling to place her face? Or was he just wondering why she was so screwed up?

She wished that night had never happened. In the days and months afterward, she'd been secretly happy to have had as much fun as they did, even if she'd wanted so much more. The taste of his skin, the feel of his tongue in her mouth, the smell of his body on her sheets the next day—she nurtured them as the most delicious memories she'd had from college.

Now she'd give them up in exchange for meeting him fresh and spending the day with him as a stranger in this beautiful, magical place. She was glad she hadn't reminded him about that night in college. They'd been kids, still teenagers, what did it matter now?

"Try to find a parking spot along the side of the road," he said. "There, behind that one. There's a waterfall here you'd like."

"Are there other ones ahead?"

"Oh, yeah," he said. "A bunch. Bigger and better ones. But this one is nice, too."

She wasn't ready to stop; she could feel the old fear lurking under her skin, waiting to take over if she let it. "I'm going to keep driving if you don't mind. Stopping now would break my mojo."

He reached into the backseat for the bag from the deli. "No problem. Mojo onward." He pulled out a package and unfolded it. "Banana bread?"

The traffic was creeping onto a one-lane bridge ahead of them. She shook her head, eyes locked on the road and not on the rushing white water beneath it.

"It's really good. Best in Maui." He waved it under her nose.

"Do you want to die on your birthday?"

He withdrew his hand and took a bite. "There are worse ways to go," he said with his mouth full. "Damn, this is good. You sure?" He pushed it at her again.

The traffic forced her to stop in the middle of the narrow bridge. She heard the roar of water tumbling beneath them and imagined it was the old stone itself collapsing. Surely the original engineers hadn't anticipated this level of congestion when they designed the bridge, or it would be two lanes. One day the overburdened structure would crack and tumble into the rapids, and the media would broadcast the disaster across the globe: Tragedy in the Tropics!

That day could easily be today. It would happen to some poor people, why not them?

"It's still warm," he continued, pushing the bread against her cheek. "Feel it."

The sweat on her hands made the wheel slippery. "I hate you," she whispered.

He drew back. Folding the wrapper back around the bread, he said, his voice wounded, "Just trying to help you relax."

"I'm sorry," she said. "I wasn't talking to you." Traffic started moving again. She eased her foot off the brake, sighing as she pulled the car up to solid ground. The rapids and the bridge were behind them.

It was the *fear* she hated. The senseless, irrational anxiety.

She released one hand at a time to wipe her hands on her pants so she didn't lose control of the car. The wheel was as slippery as a well-lubed erection.

No, no, no. She was not thinking about penises.

"What's so funny?" Ansel asked.

"Nothing."

"You have to tell me. You were freaked out a second ago, but now you're smiling."

She glanced at him—no, not his crotch, oh damn, how could she not look down there just for a second?—and imagined his penis as the primary control device of their energy-efficient automobile.

Punchy laughter bubbled out of her. Unfortunately, anxiety and hysterical laughter were old friends.

"What?" he said.

That night in the dorm, it was when she'd reached down his pants that he'd jumped up and ran away. How inconvenient that would be if it was your only way to steer a car.

"What?" he repeated, more loudly.

She swallowed her laughter, sucked in a breath. "Nothing. Really, it's nothing. Just—nothing."

Making a sour face, he crossed his arms over his chest. "Not fair of you to keep it to yourself."

"Really," she said.

"Long, boring drive, my birthday—you have an obligation to share any and all entertainment."

If she didn't think of something, he wouldn't drop it. "I'm just glad to be over that bridge."

He looked skeptical. After a second he said, "Seriously?"

"Very, very glad," she said. "Got an adrenaline rush."

After a minute he said, "Why not let me drive? I really don't mind. There are tons of other bridges ahead."

"I have to do this. If I give up now, I might never do it."

"But you don't have to do it," he said. "It's supposed to be fun."

The urge to laugh drained out of her. She checked all her mirrors, wiped her hands again, braked to give the car ahead of them extra room. "It's no fun being afraid," she said quietly.

He seemed to accept that. She thought he'd dropped it until, after five minutes of driving through the trees and across another narrow bridge, which was blessedly short, he asked, "Are you afraid of all bridges?"

"I'm not afraid of bridges."

"Weren't you just having a panic attack?" he asked.

"I'm not afraid of bridges."

He jerked his thumb. "Then what was that back there? An allergy?"

"I'm afraid of the *water* under the bridge," she said. "There's a big difference."

"It's all just water under the bridge," he said, then, "Sorry," when she glared at him.

"I'm going to keep driving now," she said.

"Okay."

"And you're going to be quiet."

He slumped in his seat, crossing his arms over his chest.

"Thank you," she said, accelerating a little.

The road snaked through the rainforest, a beautiful, calming wonder of the world. As her anxiety ebbed, her guilt surfaced. She hated herself for snapping at him, losing her manners, being a freak—but this place was so beautiful, even those feelings waned, and she lowered the window all the way and breathed the pseudo-prehistoric loveliness deep into her lungs. Even when she had to cross bridges over rushing rapids, she kept her head. It was just too gorgeous to live trapped inside her own neurosis for long.

"We might want to stop at this place ahead." Ansel pointed at the cluster of parked cars at a sharp bend in the road. "We can hike up and see the waterfall. It's a big one, if I'm remembering it right."

But the other cars had taken all the spaces on the side of the road, and because so many other cars had stopped, the road ahead was clear. She found herself driving on. Rain spattered the windshield, but it was light, barely enough to merit using the wipers. "We can stop at the next one."

"Are you afraid if you stop you won't be able to start up again?"

She didn't look at him. "Maybe a little."

"You're doing great."

It should've felt patronizing, but somehow, coming from him, it didn't. "Thanks." She let out her breath. "Sorry to snap at you earlier."

"I'm used to it. Twin sister, you know."

"Well, I'll try harder to behave."

Another hour passed in slow, winding silence through the trees. Her anxiety fluctuated with the challenge of the turns, the bridges, the traffic, but she had conquered the worst of her phobia, at least for the day. She had the lifting, cheerful sensation of personal accomplishment.

"You ever going to eat this banana bread?" He unwrapped it in his lap, not pushing it at her, just admiring the golden slices. "I'm not sure I can wait any longer."

"You were waiting for me?"

"Like I'm going to snarf down the treats while you're slaying your dragons," he said. "How's that going, by the way? You look good."

She smiled. "I think the dragon's sleeping."

"Hungry?"

Nodding, she braked and pulled the car onto the shoulder behind several other parked cars. "Is this a good place?"

He frowned out the window. "I think so. Might not be a waterfall, just a tree or flowers or something. I'm not sure I've stopped here before."

"I like trees and flowers."

"I've pretty much only got eyes for lunch," he said.

But when she glanced over, it was her he was looking at. His gray eyes, heavy-lidded and intelligent, were watching her with an intensity that startled her. Heart lurching, she engaged the parking brake and busied herself with getting out of the car without getting run over. A row of sedans with only several feet between each bumper rolled past at about six miles an hour. By the time she climbed out and walked over to the shoulder, he had their picnic lunch under one arm and his attention on the sky.

With eye contact broken, the butterflies in her stomach folded their wings.

He wasn't starved for anything but lunch. She was imagining things.

"Would you rather eat in the car?" he asked. "It's about to rain."

"It's been drizzling for a while." She pulled her hood up. "I read in the guidebook it's often like that here."

"Pretty much."

"I don't mind eating my sandwich under an umbrella," she said. "Do you?"

"Nope. Only takes me a second anyway. Rachel says I have the table manners of a shop vac."

Smiling, she got the umbrellas out of the trunk and tiptoed down the muddy path to where she could leap over a ditch to reach the trail into the forest, letting him follow. The rain was only a light mist, barely enough to merit pulling up her hood, but it protected her from sharing lingering glances with the birthday boy.

She stepped off the side of the path to let a family of six pass, the youngest one in a baby sling on Dad's chest, the rest of them in flip-flops. They were heading back to the road.

"The hike is harder than it looks," the mother said to Nicki as she passed. Wearing a transparent plastic poncho over shorts and a tank top, she carried a small dark-haired boy on one hip.

"Did you see a waterfall?" Nicki asked.

"We had to turn back when it started raining," the woman said. "But there's supposed to be one."

Nicki stopped under a large canopy of branches, watching the drizzle turn to rain. When the family had passed, she caught Ansel's gaze and pointed up.

"I thought you said you didn't mind the rain," he said.

"It's really coming down now."

He raised an eyebrow. "Afraid of water even when it's just in the sky?"

"Hey."

"Just asking, just asking." His face broke into a grin.

When the rain stopped soon after, they hiked for five minutes up a rocky, fern-lined trail along a small creek as the trees dripped on them from above. To her credit, she wondered only every few minutes if he was staring at her butt. The rest of the time, she knew he was.

Two other groups passed them on their way down, one couple in high-end weather gear sufficient for a climb up Everest, the other family more like the previous one, in shorts and sandals and plastic-bag ponchos.

And then they were alone at the base of a glassy pool, fed from above by a ribbon of water snaking down a mossy wall of stone.

"It's so beautiful," she whispered.

"Some things only get better with time." He let out a long, exaggerated sigh. "Lucky them."

She elbowed him lightly in the ribs. "Better old than dead."

Another sigh. "I'm not so sure. Some men don't age well."

"I think you're doing okay."

He tilted his head, eyes dancing. "You do?"

His nearness, the flirting, the gorgeous surroundings—it was too much. "You're just a big baby," she said, rolling her eyes.

The humor drained out of his face. He looked away. "Yeah." He forced a laugh. "Too true. Should we take a picture?" Pulling his phone out of his pocket, he held it up to the waterfall and fiddled with the controls.

"Hey," she said. "I was just kidding."

"No, it's true. But I'm working on it. Just this morning I decided it was time to throw away the Pull-Ups." He pointed at a cluster of rocks at the base of the cliff. "Stand over there and I'll take a picture for your... whatever. You have a boyfriend?"

She'd really hurt his feelings. He wasn't afraid of getting older; he was afraid he wasn't. "No." She met his gaze and held it a second too long.

"Give the camera some skin, post it online, and you will." With a big phony grin, he grabbed her shoulder and gave her a gentle push toward the waterfall. "Guys love a wet woman."

Well, she *would* need photos of the trip for the blog—her face cropped off, of course. She made her way around the pool's edge to the cliff face and turned, clasping her hands in front of her in a traditional pose.

"Are you kidding me? You might as well be in Iowa. Get closer," he said.

She looked down at her feet, then at the pool. "I'm not getting in there."

"Of course not, but you can stand on the rocks. Those," he said, pointing, "right there."

"They're in the middle of the lake."

"It's not a lake, it's a puddle, and they're like four inches away."

"More like four feet."

"You've got awesome long legs," he said. "That won't be a problem for you."

Damn it, she was blushing. Awesome? "What if I slip?"

"You've got tread on those sandals. You'll be fine."

She frowned at the rocks, the waterfall, him. It would be a much better picture if she were closer. Who knew if she'd be able to come back and find somebody else, a stranger, to take one?

Rocks in rainforest pools at the base of waterfalls were going to be slippery. Signaling for him to wait, she walked off into the forest to find a fallen branch to use as support, just in case, but she couldn't find anything longer than a few feet long and returned to the pool empty-handed.

Giving up on her courage, he had the phone up to his face. "Say cheese."

What the hell. "Hold on!" Front teeth grinding into her bottom lip, she leaped over the water. Her right foot landed at an angle and she lurched sideways, arms windmilling, but her left found a flat stone and she braced her weight, turned, and waved triumphantly at him.

"Damn! I thought you were going in," he said from behind his phone. "That would've been an awesome shot. Oh well, guess this will do. Hold still, will you? You're blurry."

She put her hands on her hips, grinning. Water surrounded her. Birds chirped in the trees. The mist from the falls shimmered in faint rainbows. Her heart swelled with tropical, exotic happiness.

And then, while she was still absorbing the world in a blissful daze, Ansel jogged over and leaped across the water to join her.

"No!" she gasped, jerking sideways. Her right foot slipped.

From midair, he saw her panic and shortened his stride to abort the leap. With comical resignation on his face, he went directly into the water, two feet shy of anything solid, and disappeared under the surface.

"Ansel!" she screamed. Squatting down, she reached her hand out, but he was too far; she could barely reach the water from up on the rocks. Without thinking, she stepped closer, submerging her feet in cold water, wondering how the hell deep it was for him to disappear like that. "Ansel!"

A hand shot out and clutched her ankle. She screamed—until she saw his laughing face come out of the water. That made her so angry she jerked her leg free and kicked him in the shoulder.

Well, she meant to kick him in the shoulder. She may have clipped him in the side of the head.

He went under again and didn't come up.

"Ansel! Shit! God damn it! Get up!" She squatted down and pawed at the surface like a St. Bernard after an avalanche. "Fuck!"

He sat up, rubbing his ear. "First you kick me, then you swear at me like a frat boy on meth. You use that language in class, Miss Fitch?"

He was sitting up. Sitting. The water only reached his neck.

Because of the waves from the waterfall and the returning sun's reflection, she hadn't seen the sandy bottom under his skinny, annoying ass until now. "I hope you drown." She jumped over him and landed on shore, her feet wet, her heart pounding, furious.

He rose to his feet and wiped his face. The water hit him mid-thigh. "Unlikely. But I might need a new phone."

She was already striding away down the path, knowing her anger was out of proportion to the offense, but not caring. It was hard enough to be afraid of every goddamn ordinary thing in the world, but to have people mock you for it—

She tripped over a gnarled root and flung her arms out for balance so she could walk faster. Her feet slid off the front of her wet sandals, poking into the mud and bringing it back inside the sole of her shoe where it blended with the soggy leather. She reached out and swatted a leafy branch out of her way.

Was he even following her? Was he even sorry?

Twenty feet down the path, the red fury coloring her world faded and she stopped, licked her lips, forced a deep breath into her lungs, and closed her eyes to count to ten backward in Japanese, a calming technique that worked because she imagined her elementary school judo sensei. He was one of the first people to teach her a few tricks for managing the craziness.

She was fine. Nothing bad had happened. Ansel was just fooling around, no harm intended, none done.

In fact, he'd been great. He'd seen her freak out when he'd tried to join her on the rocks and had chosen to go into the water fully dressed, with his phone, without hesitating.

So what if he'd teased her a little? Wasn't she always so proud about her sense of humor, funny Ms. Fitch who told jokes and played *The Simpsons* during lunch on Fridays?

He came up behind her. "Nicki, I'm sorry…"

"It's fine, really. Ignore me. I'm fine." She smiled but

couldn't look at him; the sudden emotion was making her eyes burn.

"I didn't mean to scare you. My feet went out from under me and I sank to the bottom…"

"It was funny." She turned, smiling brightly. "How's your phone?"

"Are you crying? Jesus. I'm such a dick."

"This is my problem, okay? Not yours. You're fine."

But he was moving closer. Wet hair dripped onto his face, emphasizing his high cheekbones, the deep gray eyes.

He lifted a hand and brushed his thumb along her cheek.

With her emotions already out of control, she couldn't resist leaning into his touch.

He edged closer and lifted a second hand to her face, his eyelids falling as his gaze dropped to her mouth. "I really am sorry," he said softly.

"Don't be…"

His voice dropped. "No, I mean for this." And then he kissed her.

OF COURSE he had to kiss her. From the moment she'd admitted she had a Prius back home and slid behind the wheel like a sacrificial warrior, he'd known it was hopeless; he'd have to try.

When he'd been under the surface and heard her screaming profanity—muffled by the water—it had taken all of his self-control not to pull her in with him and have his way with her right there in the water she hated.

He wasn't a vain guy, but he saw the way she looked at him every now and then. He knew the type of woman who wasn't into him at all, and Nicki Fitch wasn't one of them. She was into him a little bit. If he were smooth, she'd be into him plenty.

And why not? They were adults, happily isolated together in Hawaii, and the warm climate was conducive to undressing.

He caressed the back of her neck, admitting to himself that his feelings ran deeper than that. She felt real, she felt important, she felt...

Better under him than he'd imagined. Her soft lips parted for him just as he tilted her face to fit against his. Shivering with lust and his soaked clothes, he ran his hand down her back, pulled her against his hips, and stroked the curve of her bottom before sliding his fingertips back up along her curves to her neck and jaw. He held her face there between his palms and focused on kissing her.

She tasted sweet and salty, like lip gloss and tears. It bothered him that little everyday things made her suffer, or that he could've contributed to any of it, however unintentional.

He licked her bottom lip and felt her tongue slide out to meet his. What had started as a fun impulse flared into hot, serious need; he deepened the kiss, forgot about her cute neuroses, and ran a hand down her body, pushing aside her jacket to touch her breast through her thin, damp T-shirt. She gasped into his mouth, arched into him.

Since he'd been shockingly young he'd been a breast man, and he'd often joked, if he were a woman, he'd never get anything done because he'd stay home all day fondling himself. Therefore, when a woman let him kiss him, a woman he'd seen all week in a bikini, a woman with just the kind of breasts he loved—a woman's breasts, with nipples, right there on her chest—he couldn't help himself.

And Nicki didn't seem to mind. Emboldened, he tugged up the hem of her shirt and felt the satiny bra fabric over her hardening nipple, then the nipple itself as he glided his hand under it from above, turned on further by the little moan she made in the back of her throat.

She was perfect. She felt perfect, she tasted perfect, she sounded perfect, she smelled perfect. God help him, he loved women. It had been much too long. The surge of raw lust he felt shocked him, and he wished he'd chosen a better spot than a tourist-infested rainforest for his first move. Somebody was bound to appear on the trail any second.

Time to get back on the road. With him driving, they could get back to the condo in under three hours. Maybe even closer to two.

Aware of his own trembling, he caressed her breast back into the bra, withdrew his hand, pulled the shirt down over her, and returned his hand to her face. Her eyes were dark, seductive, watching him hungrily. Unable to resist, he leaned into her again, mouth open, and she rose up to kiss him with gratifying enthusiasm.

It was when she did something wild with her tongue along his top teeth, sucking and tickling, that he remembered.

Like an anvil on a cartoon coyote's noggin, the ten-year-old memory slammed down on him.

Food, pillows, candles, beer, secrets, friends, girls in the dark.
Girl.

The others had left, but he'd stayed, totally into the cute one in the dark corner of the room who kept making jokes, even after they'd started fooling around. He'd never had so much fun in his entire life, laughing and feeling her up, French kissing, groping, giggling, gasping, falling a little in love until he'd realized he was drunk out of his mind and so was she and had the decency to leave.

He tensed and drew back, still holding her face, eyes closed, between his palms. "Mickey," he said roughly.

It was as if he'd slapped her. Eyes popping open, she stiffened, staring, mouth still parted. Then she pushed free and pivoted away from him.

"I remember you now," he said.

She walked away from him down the muddy path, arms out for balance. An elderly Asian couple, hand in hand, appeared in front of her, hiking up to the waterfall with a grinning black Lab on a leash pulling them along. Mickey—Nicki —whoever she was—greeted them with a loud, cheerful hello as she left the path to pass them. Once the couple was between them, she broke into a jog.

Ansel watched her in a frustrated, confused daze. Was she going to run all the way home? Steal the car and leave him on the Hana Highway with a broken, waterlogged cell phone and a half-erect dick?

"Hi," the woman with short hair said, smiling at him.

"Hi," her companion said.

They were side by side, taking their time, savoring life under their six-foot-wide golfing umbrella. Even the dog moved as though he had bad joints, slow and deliberate, and the three of them blocked the path completely.

Ansel nodded his hellos and moved into the ferns to let them pass before bolting after Nicki. She still had the keys, after all. Phobia or no, she could take off without him; she probably was more afraid of him than of driving. What had been a shock to him couldn't have been to her; she must've known who he was before she ever landed in Hawaii. Rachel had found out he was in the condo, then set him up with Nicki.

He stumbled over a clod of earth. As he recovered, a new thought struck him: would Nicki *ever* have told him she was that girl in college?

He caught up to her just as she climbed into the driver's seat. "Wait!" He ran along the shoulder and threw himself against the hood of the car just in case she was going to peel out and leave him—on his birthday, damn it—and then he pulled the passenger door open and jumped in, soaking wet, breath heaving, and put on his seat belt.

"Want to drive?" she asked. Her voice was low, flat.

"What?"

Without looking at him, she held up her hands. They shook like a laundry basket on top of a college dorm's coin-op washer during the spin cycle.

Memories of his university days were fresh in his mind just then.

"You want me to drive?" he asked, sucking in another breath.

"Yes. If you would." She looked at him, chin raised. "Please."

"Fine." He pushed open the door. "Hope you don't mind if I head back home." *Home*, he thought. As if they were a happy family.

She shook her head and got out. He walked around the back, she walked around the front, and in a minute, they were both seated again and on the road to Kahului.

$\mathscr{N}$icki pulled the suitcase out of the closet. Her new jeweled sandals caught on the wheels, dragging along the carpet like the security boot on an inner city grocery cart. She jerked harder, stumbled, and fell to one knee with her heart pounding.

It had felt so… sweet. Not just hot, but warm, soft, and familiar. For two years in college, she'd had recurring hot dreams about him; now she'd start having them again.

Damn it. Obviously she couldn't resist the guy; one peck on the lips, and she'd practically flung herself on her back in the mud. *Way to go, Nick. That's exactly why you came to Hawaii, so you could humiliate yourself again.*

She lifted the suitcase onto the bed, swiping the hair out of her eyes. It had dried in frizzy waves around her face. She probably looked like a crazed witch. All she needed was a cauldron and a few animal parts. She certainly felt like doing black magic, anything to make herself forget what had happened, or to wipe the shock off that handsome face.

He'd barely spoken during the drive back to the condo. Shivering behind the wheel in his wet clothes, he'd stared straight ahead, jaw clenched, stopping once only for gas. While she'd been trying to recover from the rush of blood to her reproductive organs, he'd seemed irritated and put out. As though it were *her* fault he hadn't remembered her.

She dragged her poppy-pink fingernail along the zipper. Expensive polish chipped off the edge.

It wasn't entirely his fault, either. She'd never sought him out after that night, just waited for him to come to her and act smitten and romantic. If she'd really wanted him, she should've gone to him. Used Rachel to track him down, at least for his phone number. But she'd been a coward. Giving *him* all the power.

She stared at her empty suitcase. Then up at the ocean glimmering out the window. Her feet had touched sand, but not salt water, not even once.

Why should *she* be the one to leave?

It was late, almost dark. She had time to run to the beach for a minute. She shoved her feet into the sandals and grabbed a towel before she froze.

Was putting her toes in shallow water right before she ran away the sort of courageous act she'd had in mind when she started this trip?

A knock broke her daze. "We need to talk," Ansel said through the door.

She threw the towel on the bed. If he had the nerve to act irritated again, she'd shove him off the balcony. But his voice was polite. Not warm, but neutral.

"I thought we could go for a walk," he added.

Letting out a breath, she checked herself in the mirror. Frizzy hair, flaking mascara, mountainous zit, stress rash on her neck.

Perfect. She headed for the door.

What had triggered his memory at the waterfall? Was it stupid to hope she was such a great kisser that her skills had haunted him all these years? Back in eighth grade, prompted by some yellowed, coverless paperback a friend had given her at summer camp, she'd practiced for hours making out with the inside of her arm. She shuddered to think of it, grateful she didn't have siblings or YouTube to worry about back then. Some humiliations were too big to be lived down. Kissing a rich, good-looking guy in Hawaii was nothing compared to that.

She pulled open the door. "Hi."

For a moment, they stared at each other. She didn't know about him, but the feel of his mouth under hers was fresh in her mind. He broke his gaze to glance over her shoulder. "You're packing."

The plea to stay didn't come. She gave him another second before she stiffened her spine and said, "No. Just getting out my clothes for tomorrow."

Was that relief on his face? Or discomfort? "Well," he said, glancing away. "The wind has died down. We could walk to Kaanapali."

Nothing like a stroll along a tropical beach at sunset to kill the sexual tension. "We can talk here." She maneuvered around him and down the hall to the kitchen, where she busied herself pouring a glass of water and putting a few plates and a handful of silverware in the dishwasher.

"First question," he said, taking the stool behind the breakfast counter and clasping his hands together like a judge. "What's your name? Mickey or Nicki?"

She spun to look at him. "Where did you hear my name was Mickey?"

"That's what you said. How could I forget?"

She gulped down some water. "That is an excellent question. How *could* you forget?"

"You said Mickey. I totally remember thinking, 'Why not Minnie?'"

"And I remember thinking, 'I wonder if he's going to run out of the room like a bat out of hell.'"

"It was college. We were drunk. We barely knew each other —obviously—and we fooled around. Once. Neither one of us made any promises. I left before anything really happened, if I remember correctly." Slight unease crept into his expression.

She took another drink and swallowed slowly to buy a few seconds to calm down. Did she really want him to know how much that night had meant to her at the time?

"Okay, exactly." She inhaled deeply over her pounding heart and managed to smile. "That's exactly why I decided not to remind you of it. Why dig up ancient history? Especially since you'd forgotten it. It was embarrassing, okay? Besides, if I weren't friends with Rachel, I probably wouldn't have recognized you. That was over ten years ago. Neither of us was even remotely sober."

"*I* certainly wasn't," he said.

Was he suggesting she'd taken advantage of him? It was almost funny, given her complete lack of experience with men or alcohol at the time. Or now. "It was just too awkward to bring it up. I wish you'd never recognized me."

"Did you know I'd be here?"

Her voice rose an octave. "What?"

"Rachel's been talking about setting me up."

"I would never be a part of anything like that." She shoved her glass into the top rack of the dishwasher.

"Why not? We had fun once," he said. "And neither one of us is getting any younger. Maybe you didn't like turning thirty any more than I did."

She shook her head. "No, no, no."

"Even if it wasn't your idea, I wouldn't put it past Rachel."

"Of course it wasn't my idea. I wouldn't have come if I'd known there was any chance you'd be here."

"Of course there was a chance. It's my condo."

"Your *parents'*. She said they have a bunch of these all over the world."

Eyes widening with triumph, he pointed at her. "She lied. They don't. My parents have way too much liberal guilt."

"She didn't know you'd be here," she said through her teeth. "She set it up *weeks* ago."

"You never know," he said. "She *is* my twin. Maybe she used her mind control powers on me. Made me think coming here was all my idea."

"This is possible in your world?" She flung up her hands. "Maybe you should stop wearing tinfoil hats to bed to break her transmissions into your brainwaves."

"You share a uterus with anyone?"

She sighed. "No."

"Then you have no idea. One day they'll research it and prove what I already know." He leaned forward. "Somehow, this is my sister's doing."

"I won it in a raffle."

"Were international monitors there during the draw?" he asked. "Because unless an ex-president was watching, I'm assuming she stuffed the ballot box."

"Believe what you want. I had nothing to do with it."

He shrugged. "Maybe, maybe not."

"I didn't." Was he going to make her say the obvious? "You walked out on me. I made Rachel promise me there was no chance you'd be here. When I saw you, I ran. I stayed because I wanted the condo, not you."

He drew back and stared.

"Maybe now you believe me," she muttered.

He ran a hand through his hair. "I thought you said it was no big deal."

"It wasn't. Now it's a mess."

"Driving to Hana wasn't my idea," he said.

"It was your birthday!" She took out a fresh glass from the

cupboard, shoved it under the fridge's water dispenser, and jabbed the button. "You were moping around, alone, depressed. I felt sorry for you."

"Is that why you kissed me, too?"

Her hand froze, holding the glass midway to her mouth. He was throwing her a lifeline; why not take it?

But man, it was his birthday. She knew what it felt like to be pitied, and even Ansel didn't deserve that. "You're a good kisser. It was hard not to respond."

His eyebrows rose on his forehead. After a long moment, he ducked his head, looking as if he might be chewing on a grin. "Why, thank you."

"You're welcome."

Then he sighed, all humor disappearing. "Maybe I'm the one who should apologize." He cleared his throat. "Yeah. Of course I should. It's not your fault Rachel tried to play us. And I have a bad habit of hitting on every woman who crosses my path."

Ouch. She smiled tightly. "Exactly. That's why I didn't want to cross it again."

He flinched. "I can believe that. For what it's worth, I'm trying to change. I thought I had." He held out a hand. "Friends?"

Holding her fake smile in place, she moved her glass to her left hand to shake quickly, not paying any attention to how nice it felt to touch him again, even for a moment.

"Friends," she said.

"You were right," Nicki told Betty the next morning. She sat with her phone in a café near the beach, drinking six sugar packets dissolved into a cup of hibiscus tea. The tea was for the vitamins. "He's just like pizza. I'm never afraid of things that are really bad for me."

"Oh, you're afraid," Betty replied.

"I finished the blog post for next week already."

Betty perked up. "You wrote about him?"

"No way. It was about bridges."

"Bridges," Betty said, sinking back into a monotone. "How exciting."

"Welcome to my world," Nicki said. "Let me read it to you…"

"Don't bother. I'll see it next week."

"Why wait? Listen up." Nicki took a gulp of her tea. "Poor Phoebe declares that if she were the one designing bridges, every bridge would have a backup bridge underneath it, and there would be foam insulation between each layer just like the cream filling in an Oreo."

"You've written about bridges before."

"Totally different kind of bridges. This isn't the Bay Bridge we're talking about. These are like stone walkways over waterfalls. Honestly, you have the sensitivity of frozen green beans."

"You won't write just one sentence about getting a little tongue?"

Nicki hung up on her and added another sugar packet to her tea. She wouldn't obsess over Ansel. He'd kissed her, she'd kissed him back, they'd talked about it, now they were friends. End of story. Hopefully now he would stop following her around, cooking her meals, and touching her face with his lips.

What a relief *that* would be.

She kicked back the dregs of beige, grainy syrup at the bottom of her cup. Time to get back to the business of phobia reduction. Before she went back to California, she was going to swim in the ocean, even if it killed her. Hopefully it wouldn't. If there was one thing the kiss had done for her, it was to put her anxiety in perspective. Drowning just didn't seem like such a big deal anymore.

The morning was warm, humid, and lovely. She left the café, sucking in the scent of gardenias and freshly mown grass, and marched to the activity kiosk between the wading pool and the bar. The guy inside was playing a game on his phone as she approached.

"Hi, this is kind of embarrassing," she said quickly, before she lost her nerve. "I need to learn how to swim well enough to go into the ocean, as quickly as possible. I never learned. Crazy, huh?"

"Not crazy at all." The guy put down his phone and stood. He was thirty-something, had a dimple on his chin, and was taller than she was. "It's very common. I meet people like you all the time."

She scanned her body for any reaction to his obvious hotness, hoping to diversify; no luck. "I don't want to do SCUBA or anything fancy. Just learn enough so I don't drown."

He brushed a strand of dark hair out of his long-lashed blue eyes. "To be sure of that, you might consider wearing a life jacket."

"I can do that?"

He smiled. "Absolutely. I rent them right here."

How funny she'd never thought of that. "Great, but..." She straightened her spine. "I need some help getting used to being in the water without freaking out. It's not just about drowning. Plus, I'd rather not float away, you know? Even if I can breathe."

"Sure," he said.

"Do you ever do that kind of thing? Just a quick intro for a newbie?"

He paused for a split second. "Of course." He flashed

another smile. "The resort doesn't have a specific class for just that, so I'd do it off the books. No charge."

"Are you sure?"

He leaned over, bracing his elbows on the brochures spread out on the narrow counter. "You'd be doing me a favor. I get bored sitting here all by myself." His eyes met hers and held her gaze.

He was flirting, but she didn't care. Unlike so many things, he seemed harmless enough. "Thank you."

He straightened and strode out of the kiosk, gesturing at the pool. It was smaller and deeper than the splash pool, rimmed with a waterfall at one end. Much deeper. "Why don't you get in," he said. "Put your feet in the water while I get some floats."

"Here?" She squinted through the glimmering surface to see the drain at the bottom of the pool. The round metal cover looked tiny, as if from a great distance. This pool was really deep. Anglerfish could live down there.

"Don't worry. We'll work from the edge."

I'm used to living on the edge, she thought.

She took off her swim cover-up, folded it, and set it on a chair with her shoes before walking over to the pool. Walking around in a bikini was like greeting the world in your skimpiest underwear. Under the Hawaiian midday sun, every lump, mole, and hair was as visible as her mom's embroidery under a 150-watt craft light with a magnifying-glass attachment.

She sat down and slowly put her feet in the water. The slight chill in the water didn't bother her at all; it was the threat of the vast, hungry space pulling her down. Chest tightening, she scowled at the tile bottom. *It's right there. That's as far as you can go.*

Her handsome swim instructor rejoined her with long foam noodles in pastel colors under his arms. "I'm Lawrence, but everyone calls me Law." He regarded her for a moment. "You okay?"

"How deep is this pool?"

"Ten feet at the deep end."

When she sank, she'd have four feet over her head to stare up into. "Huh."

"If you're afraid, we can start out in the wading pool. It's a lot warmer, too. The resort has been having issues with the pool heaters lately."

She couldn't give in so soon. Giving herself to fate, she shoved herself off the safety of the cement into the abyss. Before she sank, she twisted around and clutched the edge. "This is better," she gasped, kicking frantically to fight off the anglerfish, sharks, spiraling whirlpools, black holes, doom.

"Excellent. Fantastic." Throwing in the noodles, Law jumped feet-first into the water, slicing through the surface. He wore a sleek white swim shirt and turquoise board shorts, practically a snowmobile suit compared to her skimpy attire, yet he gasped as he bobbed back up, obviously freezing.

Poor guy. Lacking body fat wasn't always a good thing. "Cold?" she asked.

"Never get used to it."

"Bad luck for a SCUBA instructor." She kept talking to distract herself from the bottomless well that was yawning open for her shivering, mortal flesh.

"I wear a wet suit for dives. Feel stupid doing that here." He smiled, grabbed a pair of pink noodles off the side, and swam to her. "I'll get used to it in a second. You okay?"

She unclamped one hand to wave a few fingers. "Fine."

"Fantastic." Smiling, he bumped her with a noodle. He had very nice teeth.

Teeth made her think of sharks, which made her think of her bare feet all alone down there in the deep, which made her pull her knees up to her chest and huddle against the wall with her face in the water, scanning for predators.

Then she remembered she was afraid of putting her face in the water so jerked it out again.

"Perfect," he said. "You've had lessons before?"

She blinked at him. Her mom talked about taking her to the Y for the last time when she was seven, but it hadn't gone well. "Not that I remember."

"I like to start just like that," Law said. "Face in the water. Then your whole head. Like this." He sucked in a breath, went under, bobbed back up, went under again. He repeated this several times, finally staying up to smile at her some more. "Your turn."

He sure was peppy. She thought she could go underwater as long as she could hold on to the ledge, so she sucked in a deep breath and went under, decided she was going to die, popped back up. No, not dead. Before she could talk herself out of it, she went under again, wondering if she'd remembered to put her parents down as the recipient of her retirement plan or if she'd left it all to UNICEF, as she'd considered last year during the famine in…

Law pulled her back up. "Terrific! You're already staying under for five seconds. I usually save that for my second lesson." His teeth flashed. "You didn't even take off your sunglasses."

She was too afraid to release even one hand from the ledge. "They're waterproof."

He laughed as though this were the funniest joke he'd ever heard. "Totally. Ready to try it again?"

Clinging to the tiles, her finger joints seized up like a muddy bike chain. She gritted her teeth, all of her willpower directed at loosening up, letting go, trying again. The war between mind and body, anxiety and reality, made her limbs shake.

"Whoa, you're shivering." Law touched her shoulder, which broke the spell, one fear vanquishing another.

"I am a little cold," she said huskily, and he moved closer.

Uh-oh.

"Maybe we should take a break in the hot tub," he said. His gaze flickered downward over her body. "Warm you up."

Death by anglerfish forgotten, Nicki gazed through her blurry, dripping sunglasses into his eyes. Was she misinterpreting again? She glanced up to look for toddlers in flippers or women's Olympic volleyball champions.

"Hi," Ansel said. He was reclining in a deck chair right behind them at the edge of the pool, a straw sunhat and dark glasses covering his face, a paper basket filled with something fried in his lap. "Having fun?"

Chapter 11

icki gaped at him. "What are you doing here?"

Saving you, Ansel thought, watching her kick the water behind her. She looked pretty good, considering just a few days ago she could barely get into the baby pool. Busy overcoming her fear of the water, she wouldn't have her defenses up for other threats, like those from philandering swim instructors. He'd seen Law working his magic at the pool for years.

Now Law was splashing away from Nicki to gather the noodles. He didn't look as cheerful as he had a second ago, which pleased Ansel. "Here for the SCUBA, dude?" Law asked.

"No thanks, *dude*." Ansel shoved a coconut prawn as big as his fist into his mouth. "Are you?"

Nicki removed her sunglasses and gave Ansel a worried look. "Law's giving me a swim lesson."

But to Ansel's satisfaction, the aging horndog—he had to be pushing forty by now—was already climbing out of the pool, introducing himself to an older couple who were reading the sandwich board by the kiosk. After a moment, he turned back to Nicki. "Sorry, but these folks signed up at the front desk for my noon class. Did you want to join in? You're making totally great progress."

"Not right now, but thanks," Nicki said. "Maybe I'll catch you tomorrow." She shot a narrow-eyed look at Ansel.

He took another bite and wiped his fingers on a napkin. "Pretty good coconut prawns. You should try them."

She braced her hands on the pool and hauled herself up. He meant to avert his eyes, not just out of courtesy to her, but also out of compassion for his own raging testosterone, and failed. Dripping, shiny, and majestic, she strode toward him to claim her towel on the chair next to his. She dried off quickly and pulled a swim cover-up over her head.

He held up the basket of prawns, squinting at her over his sunglasses. "Help yourself. I saved the receipt."

"No thanks," she muttered, walking away.

He jumped up to follow. "How about lunch?" he asked. "You can buy. You owe me for the pizza, remember?"

The bright sun lit the side of her face, exaggerating her high cheekbones. Mickey. All these years, he'd thought her name was Mickey.

"What are you doing?" she asked.

His sister would've killed him if he hadn't saved her teacher friend from Lawless Lansing. When he'd seen them in the water together, he'd sprung into rescue mode. "Too much, too soon?"

"Friends, remember? We're friends."

"You said friends pay each other back for meals."

"You don't play fair." She took one of his prawns and popped it into her mouth. As she chewed, her scowl melted. "Wow, that's good."

He pointed at the restaurant. "You up for more?"

Her pink tongue darted out and licked her lips, making Ansel clench his teeth.

"Know any place cheaper?" she asked.

"Nope. I don't have to worry about money," he said. "Because I'm rich." He shrugged inwardly. Close enough.

"Yeah, well, I'm not."

He sighed. "Sorry about that."

"Forget it. I'll order something small," she said. "Come on."

There was already a line forming at the entrance to the restaurant; families, well-dressed retired couples, twenty-somethings in bathing suits. When Nicki started to walk to the end of the queue, behind two teenage girls wearing bikini tops and cutoffs, he grabbed her arm and squeezed.

He brought her over to the hostess, who smiled at him and waved them inside. Within ninety seconds, Ansel and Nicki sat at the best table in the house—small but set aside from the others in a shaded corner of the patio overlooking the water. Live ukulele music blended with the rhythmic sound of the waves across the pale sand.

"Ex-girlfriend?" Nicki asked him, watching the hostess walk away.

"One of Rachel's surfer friends from the old days," he replied.

"And you never had a thing with her? Not even close?"

Her skepticism annoyed him. "I don't have a 'thing' with every woman I know."

"You only try to?"

"There is no try, only do," he said.

Just then the waiter showed up to present the daily specials, and when he was done, he handed them each large menus on papyrus-like scrolls tied with twine, clasped his empty hands together in front of him, and asked if they were ready to order a drink. It was the type of restaurant where they only hired wait staff with total recall, as if the sight of a notepad would ruin diners' appetites.

"We'll start right away with another order of coconut prawns," Ansel said. The devil in him took over. "And a lava flow for each of us, though make mine a virgin."

He could tell by the distress on Nicki's face that she was dying to argue. "Mine, too," she said through her teeth. "Do those come in small?"

The waiter shook his head. "Sorry, just the one size."

When the waiter left them, she unfurled the menu like a medieval scribe.

Poor Mickey, he thought, scanning the prices. There wasn't anything on the menu under ten bucks.

Which he'd known, of course, when he brought her there. "I'm thinking lobster," he said. "I bet they do a better job with it than I do. My eggs Benedict was a little disappointing."

"Lobster again?"

"It's a little pricey, though maybe that's the caviar glaze that jacks it up. That's okay, right? We'll just split everything fifty-fifty and call it even."

She narrowed her eyes. "Get whatever you're used to, rich boy."

"But… you don't mind?"

"I won't eat for the rest of the week to make up for it," she said, "but I could stand to lose a few pounds, don't you think?"

He laughed. Funny woman.

But when the waiter returned with their drinks, Ansel ordered the lobster—for two—and then, putting his hand over hers, asked for the dessert tray to wheel by as soon as possible. "Don't worry. I'll pay my half."

"You better eat every bite," she said. "No doggy bags."

Grinning, he toasted her with his drink. "To swimming."

She smacked her glass against his, sending white foam over his knuckles. "To swim instructors."

Smile souring, he said, "Rachel calls him Lawless. Want to guess why?"

"Lawless the pool boy," she said, nodding. "I like the sound of that."

"That 'boy' is older than me."

"Ooh, that old?" She slurped her drink, smiling at him so hard her eyes disappeared.

"He's been working here since Rachel and I were *kids*," Ansel went on. "Doesn't that weird you out a little bit?"

She shrugged. "What weirds me out is that you followed me out to the pool to spy on me." She plucked the drink umbrella out of the pineapple. "Even after yesterday."

He bit one of the prawns he'd brought into the restaurant with him, smiling around the fried tail sticking out of his mouth. "I'm a mystery, aren't I?"

Her gaze lingered over him before dropping to her glass. She plucked out a wedge of pineapple. "Just wondering why. Is your life that empty?"

"Of course not," he said. "I'm actually very busy at the moment."

"Could've fooled me."

"It's Sunday. Even a working man gets a day off."

The waiter arrived, set the fresh order of prawns on the table, and refilled their water glasses before striding off again. He wore a belted sarong low on his hips, low enough to make Ansel uncomfortable.

Not Nicki, apparently. He noticed she didn't take her eyes off the young man's butt until it disappeared behind the bar.

"Like the view?" Ansel asked.

She jerked her head around to face the Pacific. "It's beautiful."

"You're kind of flushed. Feeling okay?"

"I'm sunburned."

"So, pool boys, waiters..." He dipped a prawn in chili-cucumber sauce. "Don't forget about the valet guys. They're the best-looking dudes in the whole place."

"I'm surprised you'd notice that."

"I'm surprised you didn't."

"Well, when I arrived, I was a total basket case. As usual." She made a spiraling motion around her ear with her index finger. "After the flight and the drive, I barely managed to check in at the front desk for the key, let alone have the mental balance to check out the staff's bodies."

She was still trying to scare him away. Was that why he suddenly found her so fascinating? He rubbed his chest. "Shame you missed them. If I had to go gay, the resort entrance wouldn't be a bad place to start looking."

She choked on a prawn. "Glad you have a contingency plan."

"What's your preference—light, dark, big, small?" he asked. "As one friend to another."

"Maybe we shouldn't be friends after all. When did you say you were leaving?"

He scanned the restaurant. "I'm not picky—talking about women now, you understand. Guys will have sex with anybody, as I'm sure you've noticed, but women, well, you're different. You're much more judgmental."

"No, we're not."

He beamed. "Great. Then you'll sleep with me?"

She set the glass on the table and turned away in her chair. "I don't believe you."

"See? You're picky. But any guy here would have sex with you in a second," he said, looking around. "Or with any of the women here." He added that so she'd relax. Like one friend with another.

She rolled her eyes, sucked strawberry lava up her straw.

"It's true," he continued. "If men were really in charge, everyone would be at it like bonobo monkeys all day long. Did you know they have sex like we say hello? It's sort of their handshake."

"I get the feeling you've given this entertaining speech before," she said.

"Nope. It's an original."

She shook her head. "I don't know if I should be offended for men or for women. Both of your generalizations are insulting."

"You should be offended for men. Women are normal. Men are the pigs."

"I thought they were bonobo monkeys."

"Right," he said.

"I think you're just trying to get a rise out of me."

He wasn't quite sure what he was trying to get, but it was a lot better than nothing. "Maybe."

"Because you're bored," she said.

"I told you, I'm very busy. How could I be bored?"

"Easy. Ever work retail?"

"Nope, never worked retail." He captured the waiter's attention and ordered a fruit cocktail, a bottle of Pellegrino, and an iced coffee.

"Thirsty?" she asked through her teeth.

"I couldn't make up my mind, so I ordered them all." He patted her hand. "And I wanted to get enough to share."

"You really don't want to take any of my money, do you?" she asked. "Even if it's fair."

He set his untouched cocktail aside. "I've never had a real job." He leaned forward, lowering his voice. "How fair is that?"

After eating another prawn, she licked her fingers and leaned back in her chair. "I hope the lobster you're paying for gets here soon," she said with a sigh. "Swimming really builds up an appetite."

Ansel's grin widened. "Imagine how hungry you'll get if you ever let go of the wall of the pool."

"You have no idea how hard that was for me."

"I apologize." He poured out two glasses of the water,

handed her one, and added, "Seriously. I figured you'd rather not be patronized."

"Thank you."

He held up the water in a toast. "Here's to personal growth."

She paused before tapping her glass against his. "Got any growth of your own in mind?"

"You could say I've got a few dragons of my own to slay."

"Oh yeah?"

"I'm tired of being a slacker," he said. "It's time for me to grow up and join the real world."

"Hate to break it to you," she said, "but this ain't it."

"I'm only here on business. As soon as that's finished, I've got work back in San Francisco. The work of a real estate tycoon is dreary and infinite."

"Sounds like you're looking forward to it."

He sighed. "Yeah."

"Why do it if you don't like it?"

He shrugged. "Have to make my fortune somehow."

"Why? Was there some kind of—" She reached over for a bread stick. "Never mind."

"Some kind of what?"

"Nothing. It's none of my business."

"Go ahead. Ask."

But maybe she didn't want to hear about all that; he already had a platonic female friend to listen to that kind of thing. Which reminded him it was Sunday, the day he usually checked in with Diane. He took out his phone and set it on the table. Given their routine, she'd be annoyed if he didn't pick up.

"Did your family have some kind of financial disaster?" Nicki asked. "Because if so, you shouldn't be ordering long-distance seafood in exotic tourist locales."

He smiled, shook his head. "Nope. The Jury-Jarski fortune is intact."

"So why do anything at all?" She held out her hands. "Just enjoy it."

"This has nothing to do with them. This is about me." He poked his straw into the strawberries at the bottom of his glass. She was right about not spending money, but he wanted her to have a little fun. More than she had yesterday, more than she had that night in college when he'd bailed on her without an explanation.

"Are you worried you might fail?"

His head shot up. "Excuse me?"

"Sorry. Not my business."

"It'll be fine. Maybe."

"It will. What do you have to lose?"

"Right. Exactly." He smiled brightly. "It's not like my parents wouldn't pick me up again if I totally flopped. Poor little Ansel screwed up again, oh well. I could go bankrupt and fly home first class on Mom and Dad's Amex card." Well, he could have in the old days.

No, he could still do it. It would take a phone call, maybe an apology, but even his father would extend a hand if he really needed it.

The thought galled him. He wasn't entirely convinced he wouldn't have to do it someday.

The waiter arrived, setting plates of grilled chicken over wilted greens with fresh fruit on the table.

Nicki gaped at the chicken. "When did you change the order?"

"It's kind of a little joke of mine," he said. "A standing joke."

She sank back into her seat. "Very funny."

"Rachel was going through a locavore phase last year. When I ordered the lobster, she argued with me for fifteen minutes, so now I order it every time I'm out with her." He speared a glistening slice of papaya with his fork. "Given our, ah, little conversation the other night about splitting costs down the middle, no matter what, I couldn't resist a sequel."

"Great."

"Have you had the papaya? Really good." He closed his eyes and chewed.

"I'm still going to let you pay," she said.

"But the chicken salad's the cheapest entree on the menu," he said with mock outrage.

"Yeah, well, I was looking forward to lobster."

He laughed. Warning bells chimed in his head, but he pressed on. "We'll go somewhere else. You can order it with Yorkshire cream, Russian caviar, Chilean sea bass, Japanese sake, you name it." He leaned closer. "How about tonight?"

———————————————

Chapter 12

———————————————

The chicken caught in her throat. She had to force it down with a mouthful of mineral water. "You're asking me out? After what happened yesterday?"

"I thought we'd settled that."

What game was he playing?

It didn't matter, as long as she remembered it was a game. He was just having fun because he'd been overcompensated at birth and was chronically bored with the lack of any challenge.

She lifted her fork. "Why does Rachel call him Lawless?"

Ansel looked at his watch. "You held out longer than I expected."

"Just making conversation."

He shrugged. "It's not what you think."

"He doesn't sleep around?"

"Of course he does," he said. "But it's not actually illegal. He's not, like, going for the fifteen-year-olds or anything."

Trying to look intrigued, she looked in the direction of the pool. "Did Rachel sleep with him recently?"

"Recently?"

"Unless it's like some regular deal they have going, I

wouldn't want to get involved."

"But if it's a 'regular deal' it's okay?"

She propped her elbow on the table and played with her hair. "If it's just some fun little tradition that doesn't mean anything, yeah. I won't be messing anything up." She gave him a dainty shrug. "If I take advantage of whatever he's offering."

"Except my good impression of you."

"Ooooh, Mr. Slut-Shamer," she said. "Nice to meet you." She slid a cherry tomato between her lips.

His voice dropped. "If you're trying to scare me again, it's not working."

As they stared at each other over the table, his phone vibrated.

"I'm really sorry," he said, "but I have to take this call. Just for a second. Sorry."

Nicki shrugged as if she couldn't care less and went back to eating. It was pretty good, but it wasn't lobster.

"Hi, Diane," he said, holding the phone up to his face.

She made an internal note in thick black pen, highlighted with fluorescent yellow: *He's video chatting with another woman while he's having lunch with me.*

"Can we talk later?" he continued. "I'm in a restaurant. Like in an hour? What is it there, eight, nine o'clock?"

Nicki reached over and stole his pineapple slice. Diane. And he'd been expecting her call.

"No," Ansel continued, "I'm here with a friend of Rachel's."

Nicki could feel the woman's jealousy from across however many thousands of miles their digital video traveled. She started shoveling in mouthfuls of vegetables and protein as fast as she could; they might be leaving any minute if Diane was as bossy as the tone of her voice implied.

Ansel smiled at his friend. "Sure, here she is." He aimed the phone at Nicki like a vampire hunter with a silver cross.

She flinched appropriately, resisting the urge to pull up her hands in front of her face. Instead, she sat up taller and nodded at the beautiful brunette on the screen.

Diane wore a blouse her mother would've approved of, had the perfectly bobbed hairdo of a senator's wife, and sat in a dim office.

"Hi," Nicki said, wishing Ansel would shove the phone up his ass.

Smiling without parting her lips, Diane looked her over. "Nice day at the pool?"

Nicki nodded. This kind of woman made her nervous. Not just beautiful but composed, self-assured, mature. *She*'d never tell a knock-knock joke in the throes of passion the way Nicki had with her first real boyfriend.

Knock knock.

Who's there?

You don't remember?

Nicki never did understand why you weren't supposed to laugh in bed.

"I was just in the pool, yes," Nicki said.

"Lucky you," Diane said.

"Not really," Nicki replied.

Ansel retracted the phone and said, "About an hour, okay? Call me from home. Remember? Where you're supposed to sleep?" With a relaxed smile, he hung up, put the phone away, and went back to eating, not looking up at Nicki. "She works too much. Young executive type."

Whatever charge had been humming between them was now gone. They finished the meal, Ansel signed the tab—not even teasing about it—and they walked out into the resort courtyard. The line was just as long as when they'd entered. She thought she recognized some of the same faces, still waiting.

"I'm going to go back to the pool." She was glad that

woman had called. It was just the jolt in the spine she needed. "Thanks for lunch."

"Wait, hold on. Are you going swimming again? I could spot you."

"I haven't decided yet. But I wouldn't want to mess up your schedule. You've got to call your girlfriend back."

"Diane's not my girlfriend. We're just really close."

"It's none of my business."

He tapped her shoulder, rolling his eyes. "Don't make that face. It's true."

"I'm not making a face."

"Everyone thinks that just because Diane and I had a thing a long time ago, and neither one of us got gay or married, we can't really be just friends."

She slipped on her sunglasses. Any man who put his phone on the restaurant table to take a call from one woman—who wasn't a relative or a coworker—while he was having lunch with another one, had feelings that went beyond friendship. "It's none of my business."

"Oh, come on. Don't be that way." He put a hand on her shoulder, the second time he'd touched her; yes, she was counting.

"Last night you said you were trying to change." She turned and began walking away. "I think you need to try a little harder."

BETTY CALLED her again that night.

"Are you hitting on me?" Nicki asked, chewing on a Swedish fish. The red, sticky, gelatinous candy clung to her teeth like bright, artificially-colored barnacles. "Because we already talked to each other today, and I'm starting to feel uncomfortable."

"You should be so lucky," Betty replied, then sighed. "It's pathetic of me, but I was wondering what happened with the love shrimp today."

Sprawled in bed, with her freshly painted nails drying under the ceiling fan whirring overhead, Nicki told her about her day.

Betty sprang into action. "First thing in the morning, you're letting Lawless know you're hot and ready for him."

"He did seem to catch a chill easily. Maybe that's how I'll turn him on, by talking about my body heat." Nicki had decided to stop arguing with Betty about her little fantasies.

"Whatever works," Betty said. "But don't tell him you're a schoolteacher. He can't be the sharpest tool in the shed, so you shouldn't intimidate him. Tell him you're a flight attendant. Dudes love that, right? Sexist bastards."

"Wasn't your last girlfriend a flight attendant?"

Betty chuckled. "She certainly knew how to put my tray in the upright position."

"You have a tray?"

"It's a strap-on."

Groaning, Nicki popped another candy fish into her mouth. She had a pile of them off to one side, lined up like sardines in a can. "Does Jaynette get jealous when you talk about your conquests?"

The line went quiet.

"Betty?" Nicki asked. "You still there?"

Pause. "Yeah."

Nicki's supportive friend radar went off. "Is everything okay between you two?" Jaynette the yoga instructor had stolen Betty's heart the summer before.

"I told her when we met that I was a free spirit. I mean, duh, look at me."

"The green hair should've tipped her off," Nicki agreed.

"I know, right?"

"So she *is* jealous?"

Betty sighed. "It's so annoying."

Nicki tried to remember if she'd ever met a girlfriend of Betty's who lasted more than a few weeks. One of her friends was an on-again, off-again type, but that was more about convenience than true connection. "When's the last time you were in a serious relationship?"

"When's the last time *you* were in a serious relationship?" Betty retorted.

"Guess I hit a nerve."

"Marriage equality is great for some people," Betty said, "but for lone wolves such as myself, it's a pain in the ass."

"Uh-oh. Jaynette wants commitment?"

Betty fell silent again. "No," she mumbled finally.

"But you're upset she doesn't want to share?" Nicki wasn't quite sure what the problem was. "You've been single for a really long time. I'm sure it's hard to get close enough to somebody who tries to put limits on you."

"That's not it."

Nicki held the phone up to her ear with her shoulder so she could juggle the last three candies. It wasn't like Betty to be evasive; she didn't know what methods to use to pry the truth out of her. "Where is she right now?" she asked to buy some time.

"Out." Betty's voice was sour, resentful, hurt.

"Oh," Nicki said softly, finally understanding. She let the candies scatter over the bed. "She's not jealous. *You* are."

"I told her when we met that I never get exclusive. Now she's holding me to it. How can I complain? How can I change the rules in the middle of the game?"

"Does she know how you feel?"

"Pfft," Betty said. "I'm not going to tell her that. It would be manipulative and unfair. I've been on the other end of that way too many times to do it to somebody else."

"It's the truth. You can't avoid it forever."

"If I tell her now…"

Nicki wiggled her red-tipped toes, kicked the empty candy wrapper to the floor. "You think she'll dump you. Because that's what *you* would do."

Betty made a pained, breathy noise, like a sleepy person stubbing her toe in the dark. "Jesus," she said.

"It's what you *did* do," Nicki continued. "More than once."

"Way to make me feel better, Nick."

"But I'm right, aren't I?"

"Karma's a bitch. That's the truth."

"You need to talk to her about how you feel," Nicki said.

"Oh, great idea. I'll send her a text message this second telling her I've never loved anyone the way I love her, that she completes me, that she's the wind in my sails," Betty said. "And she'll read it while she's in bed with somebody else."

"Or you could, you know, talk to her alone later."

"Yeah. Whatever."

"Now you're just feeling sorry for yourself."

"No, I deserve to have my heart crushed like a bug," Betty said before adding in a more typically robust tone, "What do you say you change out the bridge phobia post with something about Lawless? Is there a place you can hide and snap a good shot of him?"

"I'm not doing that."

"We can crop out his face. Nobody really cares about that anyway. Is he hairy? We've got a thread going right now in the forums about the tyranny of body hair removal."

"I don't know. He wears a swim shirt and board shorts— Never mind. I'm not going to expose some random guy on your blog, give me a break. You get thousands of hits a day."

"He'd never know," Betty said. "Unless he's secretly a left-wing lesbian, he'll never know."

"The blog's demographics are much more diverse than

that, like it or not."

"Don't remind me," Betty said. "It's your fault. Phobic Phoebe attracts wishy-washy heterosexual chicks."

Nicki prodded her sleeping laptop. "I'd be happy to skip next week's post this week if you'd like. We seem to argue a lot more than we used to."

"No! You can't skip anything! You promised me two years ago you'd be reliable. If I stop delivering what I've promised, Phobic Phoebe and the rest, the blog will never survive, it'll become just another abandoned, dead, dated—"

"Chill," Nicki said. "Of course I'll write it. If you lay off the heavy-handed editorial."

Betty exhaled loudly. "Promise. I'm launching new Phoebe merchandise next week, and I can't afford to lose any momentum. Wait until you see the new stress balls."

"Mail me a pair."

"To Hawaii? No way. Too expensive."

"You are so cheap," Nicki said.

"*You* try making a living from blogging. I'm lucky I can eat."

Nicki snorted. "You make more money doing part-time programming jobs every few months than I do working all year."

"All year, my ass," Betty said. "You are in Hawaii, aren't you? Anyway, I don't get benefits. I have to think of the future. What if I want to start a family someday?"

Not believing what she'd heard, Nicki raised the volume on her phone. "Excuse me?"

"I better go before my ovaries get too hopeful and pop out an egg," Betty said. "Love makes you crazy. I'm walking proof. You're lucky to be out of it."

"Yeah. Real lucky." Unbidden, it was Ansel's face, not Miles's, that flashed before her eyes.

No, not him. In a panic, she dug out her favorite fantasy

about Miles, the one when she climbed him like Mt. Everest, and waited for the wave of unrequited longing to wash over her.

"You still there?" Betty asked.

"Not really." She'd lost it completely. Even in her favorite fantasy about Miles, she was picturing Ansel; and he was laughing.

She said good-bye to her unhappy friend and quasi-boss, then dragged the computer onto her lap and began to type. Ahead of schedule, but she needed a place to vent.

Smelling blood in the water, the sharks came for me immediately, she wrote.

PERHAPS BECAUSE OF his distracting relationship with his roommate, Ansel forgot to mute his phone when he went to bed, which allowed Brand to wake him in the middle of the night to complain about his pictures of the office building in Kihei.

"My God, you went to the wrong one!" Brand shouted in his ear.

Ansel squinted at his phone: 4:24 a.m. "Time change, buddy, remember? Curvature of the earth and all that?"

"You were in the ocean-side building. We want the inland one. There are two properties. *Two.*"

Ansel sighed, rubbed his eyes. He'd left the shades open to watch the moonlight on the water as he fell asleep. Unfortunately, that had been less than an hour earlier. Sleep wasn't always easy for him. "It's taken you this long to look at the pictures?"

"I've been busy."

"You missed my birthday."

"Oh, shit. Sorry. Thirty, right?"

"Yup."

Brand cleared his throat. "Is that why you took pictures of the wrong building? You're having a crisis?"

"I'm not buying a building right across from the beach that doesn't face the ocean."

"It's not for tourists," Brand said. "It's for accountants, lawyers, small business types."

"Who need the view even more. And who live in Maui for a reason."

"It costs too much," Brand said. "Just to have a few windows that glimpse some water they see every day anyway."

Ansel slipped lower under the sheets, closed his eyes. He could still fall asleep again if he hung up now. "Mmm," he said, his thumb rubbing the screen to make the unhappy man go away.

"I've already emailed Jenny and explained the mistake."

Damn it. Ansel fumbled with his phone. He'd locked the screen somehow and Brand was still talking. "There was no mistake."

"We'd have to charge twice the rent."

"You're exaggerating." Drifting back into his dream, Ansel tried to remember his password to unlock his phone and make the loud man go away.

"I've run the numbers," Brand continued. "We'd never find tenants in this economy at the higher rents."

Finally, Ansel saw the glowing red button that would solve his immediate problem. "You worry too much," he said as he tapped it, already half-asleep.

Silence. A belated birthday present.

Ah, that was better.

But he'd forgotten to mute it, and the wind chimes he used as a ringtone knocked him awake again. In his stupor, he'd left the phone wedged between the pillow and his ear.

"Jenny will meet you there at nine," Brand said. "At the right one."

"Actually, it's on the left," Ansel muttered. And then, "Fine," just to make him be quiet.

He slept until Brand called him a third time. Now the sun was up, making Ansel squint around him at the white sheets, pale walls, golden dawn sky. It was like waking up in heaven. "I told you I'd meet her at nine," Ansel said, pulling a pillow over his face.

"It's 8:12," Brand said. "Better get moving."

"Crap."

"You wanted to be a businessman."

"Yeah," Ansel said. "Not your minion."

"Listen, *partner*. Jenny Kapule is probably already there waiting for you. She's been really patient with us so far, don't punish her."

Ansel thought about the flash of joy in the real estate agent's eyes when he'd told her they'd be making an offer on the expensive property instead of the discounted, hill-facing one. "I won't," Ansel said with a smile, rolling out of bed.

He cleaned up and rushed out of the condo without seeing his housemate, reaching Kihei with a minute to spare. In the parking lot between the two buildings, he reassured Jenny they were only going to look at the other structure to rule it out, and that, yes, they still wanted to proceed with the oceanfront one.

Jenny looked hopeful but unsure. Recently married with a baby on the way, she was as eager to close the deal as he was. "But Mr. Warren..."

"Needs to see a few good photos to clarify the situation."

He returned to the condo two hours later with three dozen unflattering shots that would look even more convincing after he touched them up a little on his computer. Bad lighting, inopportune close-ups, slightly excessive percentage of shots taken of a water stain below a (since repaired) window.

Brand would have to agree with him now. Being a businessman could be fun after all.

He was opening the first photo on his computer when his mother called. He'd assigned an operatic ringtone to Melinda Jury that suited her tireless and powerful personality. It gave him a second to prepare before answering the phone.

"Hi, Mom."

"You didn't call me back. Don't forget—your birthdays have more to do with me than you. And thirty! That's a big deal."

He moved the phone an inch further from his ear. "You said in your message not to call you back."

"Did I?" She laughed. From the heart, like she did everything. "I didn't mean it. Rachel knew not to believe me. Did she tell you she's getting married?"

"That's what she told me."

"We all deal with mortality in our own ways," his mother said.

Ansel groaned. "Even my mother thinks thirty is over the hill."

"There's always another hill to climb, no matter how many birthdays you have," she replied.

"Sounds exhausting." But he smiled. He loved his mom. Everyone did.

"She's still in London, you know. Your sister."

"I know," he said.

"And where are you? In the old days, I wouldn't have to ask that unless you were the one calling me, which apparently doesn't happen anymore."

"You told me not to call you back," he repeated, smiling. "You know I'm the obedient one."

"I didn't mean never. You could've called me yesterday, for instance. From wherever you are. Which is where, kiddo?"

He stood and went out to the balcony. "Maui. Didn't Rachel mention it?" He was still convinced she'd set him up.

Possibly successfully. He couldn't get Nicki out of his head.

"Maybe she did, I don't remember. I can't keep up with you two," his mother said. "Have you seen that friend of yours with the coconut business? That shampoo of his was wonderful."

He'd almost forgotten about that. A few years ago, he'd introduced one of his friends to another, and Primal Pedro's Products from Paradise was born. "Actually, I'm here on business of my own."

"How wonderful. Your father would love to hear about that."

Turning his back on the ocean, Ansel leaned against the balcony. The sun was hot on the back of his neck—too hot, like a dragon breathing on him.

She'd never hinted at the argument with his father; she never asked about his finances; he didn't know if she knew he wasn't taking money from the family coffers anymore.

If she really didn't know—and he didn't think she did, because she would've called a family meeting by now with a professional mediator that would've gone on until everyone was hugging each other—he wanted to keep it that way. Someday, perhaps as he handed her a new yacht (she could donate it to Greenpeace) he could casually mention he'd paid for it with his own millions.

He went back inside. "Brand and I are partnering up to buy some investment property. There's an office building in Kihei, right on the ocean, pretty cool."

"An office building on the beach?"

"A cube with a view," he said.

She laughed. "I love it! Good for you. You're always up to something interesting. If only I could hear about it from you instead of from Rachel. And no, I'm not going to get on the Internet and chase after you like a lovesick stranger. If I want pictures and stories about your life, I'll make you give them to me directly."

He sat at his desk, smiling at the photos of the building he had up on his screen. "Are you guys still in Costa Rica?" His mother was the founder of an environmental education foundation and personally escorted tours of low-income American city kids through the rainforest three times a year.

"Just flew back yesterday. We're home." They'd kept the small house in Menlo Park where he'd grown up—though the booming tech economy over the last three decades had made the three-bedroom, 1954 stucco box worth more than a two-hundred-acre thoroughbred horse farm anywhere else. "I'm actually calling for a reason," his mother added, her voice dropping an octave.

Here it comes, he thought, sitting taller. Dad *had* told her, and she was going to make it better.

But Ansel wasn't going to let her. He was on his own, and though he wasn't half the man his mother was—he admired her more than he could say—he wasn't going to let her rescue him. He'd do all right. Eventually. "Yes?" he asked.

"That restaurant of Jordan's," she said brightly. "Where the heck is it? I can't remember the name, and I'm determined to check it out. I know people. I can help."

"Mom, he's already doing pretty well on his own." Against all the odds, he was.

"Then I'll eat there because I'm hungry. Come on, spill."

So he told her all about it until she was satisfied: the name of the restaurant, the address, the hours, the best items on the menu, where to find a parking spot, the color of the walls, Rachel's mural.

"Email that to me and CC your father. He needs a distraction from his birthday coming up. Turning sixty has made him mental. This will be his project."

"I don't think that's going to work. He doesn't even remember Jordan."

His mother let out a quick sigh. "Of course he does. He

just doesn't want to admit how much he cares about you. I'm getting him in therapy, I swear to God." Then her voice returned to its usual boom. "I'm proud of you, Ansel. Have a rewarding time in Maui. Are you alone?"

The sudden topic shift knocked him off balance. But you couldn't lie to Mel about anything. She'd know, she'd be hurt, she'd remind him to be a better person. "Rachel gave the condo to a friend of hers. I'm kind of butting in. The woman has been nice enough to let me stay."

"Is she there with her family? Did you offer to take the sofa bed?" His mother believed in high-density housing.

"She's alone, so I'm in one bedroom, she's in the other."

"Then nothing goes to waste," his mother said.

"That's what we figured. I didn't tell Rachel, though, in case she got upset."

"Why should she care? She's in London. You're putting the toilet seat down and washing your own dishes, right?"

"My mother raised me right."

"She sure did. What's the woman's name?"

"Nicki."

"Nicki what? This isn't preschool, Ansel."

"Nicki Fitch. Sorry, I don't know her middle name."

"And what does she do?"

"She teaches junior high in the East Bay somewhere. History, I think." There was no point playing dumb. His reluctance to talk would be like blood in the water for her. "She was friends with Rachel in college." He waited for the interrogation to resume. His father wasn't the only one who tired of his serial monogamy, and surely Rachel had already mentioned to their mother about her plot to set him up? The two of them were always in cahoots with one scheme or another.

"Glad it worked out," she said, sounding like she was yawning.

He waited. Really? That was it? No further cross-examination?

"I'll say hello to Jordan for you," she continued.

Ansel frowned at the blank wall. Maybe Rachel hadn't set it up. Their mother had many talents, but being sneaky wasn't one of them.

"Will I have to lie about liking the food?" she asked.

"No. Jordan's a genius."

"Good. That makes my life a lot easier."

"Since when do you like it easy? If you liked it easy, you'd be sitting here in Maui with me."

"Maybe you should've invited me."

He laughed. "You wouldn't've come. You're too busy saving the world."

"I'd find a way," she said. "How about this. Next time, let's talk because you called me. Doesn't that sound nice?"

"I'm writing it on my calendar this second."

"Well, I'm sure you will as soon as you hang up with me," she said.

He laughed. "I'll talk to you before Dad's birthday. Promise." The big day was in July.

"You'll talk to me *on* Dad's birthday," she said. "In person. I'm throwing him a surprise party."

Ansel hung his head. "You just can't believe him when he says he hated the last one?"

"I don't care. Something needs to snap him out of this funk he's in. You don't really mind, do you? It's a short flight from there to San Francisco."

It was too soon. He wasn't ready. Not just the money, but his whole life. He needed more time. Facing his father with everyone, his family and associates, gathered like that, on his birthday—he'd ask questions, want to be proud.

And he wouldn't be.

"We'll have to see, Mom." He rubbed his neck, suddenly throbbing with tension. "I'll let you know."

$\mathcal{A}$fter skipping the pool on Monday to ride a rented bike along the boardwalk, Nicki returned to tackle her water demons on Tuesday with a pair of new goggles she'd bought in the resort store.

Law was sitting bare-chested at the edge of the deep pool with his feet in the water. He smiled brightly when he saw her. "I was afraid you wouldn't come back."

"Here I am." She kicked off her sandals under a deck chair. "I'm serious this time. I want to pay for the lessons and make it official. Do I sign up at the front desk?"

He climbed to his feet. "Sorry about the other day. I can write you up here. Bill it to the room?"

"Sure." She followed him to his little hut, where he handed her a clipboard of forms to fill out.

She scanned the form. The prices noted on the lesson agreement were almost as disturbing as the fine print of the liability waiver. *Shouldn*'t it be his fault if she, you know, *did* sink to her doom while he was giving her a lesson? What else was she paying for but his expertise in the basic chore of keeping her alive?

She looked up at his face. He was watching her, the laugh lines around his blue eyes faintly engaged in their sexy creasing action.

Dropping her gaze to the sheet, she underlined the relevant passage. "It says you don't care if I drown. See? Right here."

He leaned forward to look where her ballpoint pen had scratched a trough into the paper. "It says that?"

"Haven't you ever read this before?"

"You know how it is. It's just so the resort doesn't get sued. I wouldn't worry about it."

"So you *do* care if I drown?"

"You're not going to drown." He walked out of his hut and stood next to her, leaning close. "Trust me. I've been doing this a long time."

"So I heard," she muttered.

"You did great the other day." He nudged her shoulder with his. "Beautiful job. Beautiful." He looked into her eyes.

Just then, Ansel popped out from behind the eight-foot display of foam noodles, hooked an arm around her waist, and kissed her cheek so hard she lost her balance.

"Hi honey," he said loudly. "Where'd you go? I rolled over and you were gone."

She had to grab him to stop herself from falling over. "What are you doing here?"

"I was going to ask you the same thing." He gave her a wounded look.

She tried to pull free, but his grip was surprisingly strong. She gritted her teeth. "I'm learning how to swim."

With the sigh of the long-suffering, Ansel pulled her closer. "Is that what you're calling it now?"

Torn between kneeing Ansel in the crotch and putting her arms around his neck, she turned to Law. "This guy is crazy. Ignore him."

"I'm crazy, all right," Ansel said. "Crazy for loving you."

Law was already back in the hut, reaching up to arrange the display along the back wall of designer sunglasses for sale. She watched his cowardly but muscular buttocks.

"Guess he's a lover, not a fighter," Ansel whispered in her ear.

"I'm not." She dug her elbow into his ribs and strode away. That was the second time Lawless had bailed ship; she'd find somebody else.

Ansel chased after her, speaking in a low voice at her shoulder. "You should thank me, you know. Old Lawrence has slept with half the women who've ever stayed here." He took her elbow and squeezed it. "There isn't enough chlorine in the world to sanitize that dude's equipment."

She snatched her arm away. Her heart was beating too fast. "I only wanted a swim lesson," she said, brushing the hair out of her eyes. "Thanks for screwing it up."

"I'd be a better teacher. Seriously. I'm also free." He gestured over the fake boulders. "There's a great pool over there that's empty."

"Why are you doing this? Aren't you busy?"

"I'm between appointments. Look, I couldn't let you give that guy actual money."

"I'm not going to sleep with you."

His eyes widened. "Of course not." He crossed his arms over his chest. "Rule number one of water safety, maintain consciousness."

She snorted. He was wearing a black T-shirt, gray shorts, and black flip-flops. Even his towel was colorless. So much of him, though, like his laughing mouth and sunburned cheeks, blazed with life and color.

She couldn't stop looking at him. "Why do you always dress like an undertaker?"

"Since when do undertakers wear board shorts?"

Every reason to avoid him—there had to be loads of them

—went out of her head. Why would she pay for a guy like Law when she could have Ansel Jury-Jarski for free?

"Let me get my shoes," she said.

After she slipped them on, he led her out of the fake grotto, past the baby pool and two more spas, to a round pool with a slide at one end. Before she could avert her eyes—or get them into sharp focus—he pulled his shirt over his head and strode over to the water, his shorts low on his hips, a hint of two dimples above the waistband on either side of his spine.

Don't look, she chanted silently.

He turned just then and saw her staring. Grinning, he put his hands on his hips. "Not bad for an old man, huh?" He looked past her to where they'd been. "But you do seem to have a thing for geezers."

"Be quiet. All I ever wanted was a swim lesson." She put her bag on a deck chair, slid her feet out of the sandals again, and hesitating only a second, tore off her cover-up. "Now I'm going to drown. It's all your fault."

"Blame the victim," he said. "No, seriously. If you do drown, it's your own darn fault. Why the heck didn't you ever learn before now? Too crazy?"

This time, she did laugh. She liked that he wasn't afraid to call it what it was. "Basically." She walked over to the pool and squatted at the edge, tilting her knees so he didn't see she wasn't as well shaved as the Olympic volleyball mom; although, her generous thighs didn't allow a clear view of that area anyway.

"Why so determined now?"

"It's past time, that's all."

He looked at the sky. "I can relate to that." A bird peeped nearby. He sat next to her and put his feet in the water. "How are you feeling right now?"

The sun was too low to reflect off the water, giving her an

unimpeded view of the pool bottom. Another deep one. Did anglerfish need such a large habitat?

Her heart was beating harder and faster than normal, but it wasn't because of the water. She'd broken through the worst of the irrational anxiety the first day just by getting in. Now just the rational fear of drowning remained. She didn't have gills or flippers or skill.

The racing pulse was because his body was inches from hers, and his dark gaze was watching closely.

Jumping in might actually be a welcome escape. She held her breath, expecting cold water, twisting around to grab the edge. "Fine," she said through her teeth. When she realized the water wasn't cold at all, she relaxed her jaw. "Why's this one so warm?"

"Kiddie pee." He slid in next to her.

She wasn't sure if he was kidding, or if she cared. It felt good.

Okay, she cared. "Seriously," she said, lifting her chin above the surface.

"They do water therapy in here." He dunked his head. "Gets way too hot in the afternoon, but it's nice in the morning. So, what do you think? You willing to let me help you a little bit?"

She relaxed into the water but didn't want to let go of the edge. "You didn't bring a noodle."

"*Au contraire.*"

She rolled her eyes. "It's not big enough."

"Give me a minute."

She put her face in the water. How could she have a panic attack when she was laughing?

"Now that you're blowing bubbles, put your hands on my shoulders," he said. "I'll pull you to the other side while you practice."

She lifted her nose out of the water, skeptical, but he'd

turned his back to her and was treading water a couple of feet away, waiting.

She had to let go of the edge. Just once, before she died, she wanted to see a sea turtle on the other side of a mask—not a TV screen.

Rejecting the comfort of solid concrete, she reached out her right hand and clasped his shoulder, flinching at how much she enjoyed the feel of his bare skin under her fingers before she took a deep breath and grabbed onto his other side with her left.

"Hold on, here we go!" He started to move. His muscles flexed under her palms like an elite stallion. Practicing her bubbles, she put her face closer to the water and checked out his ass.

This really isn't so bad at all, she thought, watching him propel them through the water. The water was warm, she was getting warmer, and he was *hot.*

God help her.

Too soon, they reached the other side. Her body floated closer to his, her knees bumping his thighs, but she didn't let go, assuming they'd do another lap. Putting a hand on the edge, he turned and met her gaze over his shoulder. His smile wasn't quite as cocky as before. "You doing all right?"

Nodding, she stared at the water droplets clinging to his eyelashes.

His voice lowered. "Want another go?"

"Yeah."

"Yeah," he repeated. His gaze dropped to her chest before he closed his eyes and took a deep breath. "Hold on tight. I'll go faster this time."

He pushed away from the ledge with her in tow, and he seemed to reach out wider with his arms and kick harder with his legs, though she was preoccupied with the feel of his biceps.

Somehow she'd slipped her hands lower. He hadn't seemed this muscular when he was dry.

They got to the other side again, but he didn't pause, just pivoted in the water and kept going. She pretended to work on her technique—face in, face out, kick, kick, kick—while she thought about the different kinds of fears a person could have, how some of those might be reasonable, given her limitations, but how they could steal away some of the greatest pleasures in life.

This time when they reached the edge, he held on with both hands and didn't turn around. She didn't let go of his arms, and without him pulling her along the surface, her feet sank, and soon her body extended along his, lengthwise, floating vertically in the water, skin to skin.

"I've got that noodle for you now," he said.

She stayed where she was.

Okay, you'd better let go, or he'll get the wrong idea, she told herself.

Any minute now…

Finally, she splashed away from him. For a full second, powered by the engine of her pounding heart, she swam unassisted. Water filled her mouth, open from all the panting she'd been doing.

She folded her arms over the concrete edge and rested her forehead between them, more impressed than afraid of the raw need flowing through her. It defied thought. It was a thing separate from her mind, a living force without words or memory. All it wanted was to be satisfied.

Ansel moved closer, stopping about two feet away. "Sorry. Bad timing. Are you all right?"

She nodded into her folded arms. Never in her life had she felt the urge to launch herself upon another human being the way she did at that moment.

"I was a jerk." He touched her shoulder briefly, so lightly

she wouldn't have felt it if her nerves weren't already on red alert. "You're doing this amazing thing that scares the heck out of you, and I had to go and make a dick joke. Do you need help getting out? I won't make a pass, swear to God."

He thought she was freaking out about the water? She lifted her head and gave him a small smile. "I'm great. That was great." Knowing she wouldn't have the strength to gracefully get out of the water with just her arms, she hand-walked around the edge of the pool and climbed out at the stairs. Her knees wobbled but she felt good. The breeze against her wet skin didn't bother her at all. She felt like she could fly.

"I'll get us some towels." He climbed out of the pool and jogged off to a hut near the bathrooms. Naturally, she watched him go, watched him while he waited in line and talked to the attendant, watched him stride back with the stack of white terrycloth in his arms. "Here. You're shivering."

She took the towel from him and unfurled it to wrap around her shoulders. The longing she'd had for him years ago, like how she felt for Miles, was a soft, weak wanting compared to this raging hunger burning her now.

"Thanks for the lesson," she said, hearing the huskiness in her own voice. "You're a much better teacher than Law."

He stopped rubbing the towel through his hair. "Yeah?"

"Someday I'd like to go out on one of those chartered boats and snorkel around the reefs. I've never seen a sea turtle."

"This is the place for sea turtles if that's what you want," he said.

Far more terrifying creatures than big, cute turtles lived in the ocean, ones that even scared brave people, ones that could even kill you. She swallowed. "That's what I want."

It seemed impossible that having this hunger satisfied could be a bad thing. The alternative was starvation.

She had some thinking to do.

THIS TIME BRAND woke Ansel up at 5:12 a.m.

He'd have to get an app that shut down the volume on his phone every night because he could never remember to do it. At least he'd fallen asleep before midnight.

"What now?" Ansel asked, pulling the sheet over his face.

"You photoshopped the pictures."

Ansel worked up some mock outrage. "What?"

"Did you really think I wouldn't notice?"

"I hardly did anything. I just made it look more like real life than I was able to capture on camera," Ansel said.

"If I didn't have a meeting in Chicago today, I'd be on the first plane to Kahului."

"This is how we're different. If I had a meeting in Chicago, I'd be sure to be on the first plane to Kahului."

"Chicago's a fantastic town. Have you ever been there?"

"I saw the weather report. Ninety-eight—Fahrenheit, humidity, and percentage of people who'd rather be in Hawaii. No thanks."

"Do you even remember why I'm going there?" Brand asked.

Ansel groaned into his pillow. What kind of friend grilled you in bed in the middle of the night? That's what girlfriends were for.

"It's a restaurant supply convention," Brand answered. "Ring any bells?"

"Restaurants have bells now?"

"Ansel, I swear to God..."

The genuine anger in Brand's voice snapped Ansel fully awake. "The CDA! You're going to the CDA." Creative Dining America had an annual convention in Chicago every summer. "I thought you hated the idea of investing in restaurants."

"You've already sunk fifty grand in Jordan's hole-in-the-wall, might as well try to recoup a little of it."

"I told you," Ansel said. "That was a gift, not an investment. My money. Get it out of your head that it has anything to do with you."

The line went quiet for a second. "Talking as your financially savvy friend here, Anse, not your partner. You throw too much of your money away on lost causes."

"Jordan would kick your ass if he heard you call him a lost cause."

"That's why I'm telling you, not him," Brand said. "Asian fusion peaked ages ago."

"He's doing great. That's just what he has to call it so people aren't scared away. Running a restaurant is all he's ever wanted out of life. He'll figure it out."

"With a little help," Brand said, "maybe he will. I've got six hours of workshops lined up to get some ideas. Dinner with a few bright guys. I'm taking a lot of notes."

Ansel imagined uptight Brand walking into Jordan's kitchen. "Better bring a bodyguard if you're going to tell him how to run his restaurant. Even without his knives, he's scary."

"You'll talk to him. Leave me out of it."

"I'm trying to," Ansel said.

"And tell Jenny we're buying the hill-facing property."

"Now who's throwing money away?"

"I'm serious," Brand said.

"You're always serious."

"Rule number one about getting rich," Brand said. "You have to take in more money than you give out. Basic math."

"I'm not going to buy that crappy building, Brand."

"And I'm not going to sign on the other one."

Ansel stopped himself from saying he'd do it himself; he needed Brand's money and his MBA expertise. "Give it a few days to look over the pictures again." He yawned loudly. "I'm going back to sleep. Talk to you later." This time he remembered to turn off the phone completely.

But he couldn't fall back asleep.

Did he throw money away on lost causes? The investments Brand had the biggest problem with were the ones Ansel enjoyed the most. When he met people who just needed a few thousand bucks or maybe a little more to pursue their dream instead of slaving away in a cubicle or cash register, how could he not want to help? Money was—or had been—like his mutant superpower—nothing he deserved, just something he'd inherited. He couldn't resist using it any more than that girl with the kiss of death.

Great, he thought, pounding the pillow. What a wonderful analogy for a venture capitalist. Everything he touched turned to stone.

Giving up trying to go back to sleep, he put on shorts and a T-shirt for a run. The resort had a path that led up to the golf course. Nice view of the ocean, the mountains.

The condo was quiet. No surprise; it wasn't even six yet.

He banged the cupboard door as he removed a water bottle then went ahead and used the ice-crushing feature on the refrigerator's water dispenser.

Still no sound from her room.

He took out his phone, synced it with the stereo, and turned on his running music. As it blasted out its one-hundred-eighty techno beats per minute, he said, "Whoops," waited a few seconds, then turned it off.

And waited, listening.

A door opened. Nicki came out, squinting at him with her hair mussed and a splotchy left cheek, where, just seconds ago, it must've been pressed against a pillow. "What the hell's going on?"

"Sorry! So sorry." He flinched, actual guilt poking him. He screwed the cap on his water bottle and shoved it into the hip pouch he carried with his phone. "I'm going for a run. Go back to sleep. So sorry I bothered you."

"I thought there were contractors remodeling the kitchen or something."

"Nope. Just me. Sorry."

She ran a hand over her hair, grimaced, and looked around. "What time is it?"

"Early."

"So it's morning, not night?"

"About six."

She sighed. "Oh. That's not bad. I thought it might be the middle of the night."

"I'm sorry," he repeated again, even though he was enjoying their chat. She had a cute chin. Six feet tall with a cute chin. He had a good view of it from his position a few inches below her.

"You said you were going for a run?"

He nodded.

"I didn't know you ran," she said. "I run."

He tried to keep his voice casual, indifferent, unsuspicious. "Want to come?"

"I wouldn't want to make you wait. You look ready to go. I'll need a minute."

"I'm still trying to get some good tunes on my phone. That's how I woke you up, being stupid with it." He waved it at her. "Go ahead and get ready. I'll probably be here a little while."

Probably.

"Great. That's great. I was getting tired of running alone," she said, returning to her room.

Tired of running alone.

Smiling, he put his phone away.

———————————————

Chapter 14

———————————————

*J*ogging always relaxed Nicki. Nothing like authentic agony to put the imaginary variety in perspective. She was too tall and heavy to be fast, but she'd loved running since she was a teenager and got out every other day, no matter what.

They started their run along the golf course, dodging early morning tourists, bikes, strollers, people on their way to work and those already there, trimming the hedges, adjusting the sprinklers, maintaining the unnatural grass. From there they joined up with the paved path along the beach to Kaanapali. The dawn sky was lavender.

"Am I going too slow?" he asked.

Perhaps because he adjusted his stride to hers, their pace matched, and only a few times did she have to run harder or slower to stay at his side. "Not at all."

"Am I going too fast?" He turned to her with his hand on his chest, tongue wagging out of his mouth. "Please say yes."

She laughed and slowed to a walk. "You're right. I could use a break."

He bent over, hands braced on his knees. "I'm more of"—he gasped—"an intervals runner. Lots and lots of them."

"Got it."

"Sometimes I have an interval that involves coffee and a muffin." His hair, damp with sweat, flopped over his eyes.

It was a good feeling, being good at something. All week she'd been a sad combo pack of phobias and lust, but now she was on her own turf. "Keep moving your legs. It's not good to stop."

Nodding, he started walking, only to trip over a twisted wad of fuchsia vinyl on the path. He picked it up and shook out a long, partially deflated pool toy. "Just what I needed. A watercraft." Balling it up, he strode over to a waste can next to a tourist kiosk outside of the hotel they were passing. As he was throwing the litter away, his phone chimed. He took it out, glanced at the screen, and put it back in his pocket.

Nicki took the opportunity to take one of the flyers in a display, not getting close enough to the kiosk to let the guy setting up behind the counter lasso her into booking an excursion.

"I don't mind if you want to take a call," she said.

"It's just Diane. I'll call her back."

"I really don't mind."

"I'll really call her back," he replied.

She looked over the brochure as she continued with Ansel along the path. Maybe she'd just imagined the other woman's jealousy. It wouldn't be the first time she'd projected her own feelings onto another.

"Snorkel tour?" he asked, peeking over her shoulder.

She nodded.

"Check it out." He pointed. "It says it's appropriate even for those not familiar with the water."

She looked up at the vast blue sea. "Sure, but what if you're familiar in a *bad* way? Like how you know *The Exorcist* by heart after seeing it on TV late at night twenty years ago and now you still get the creeps whenever you see a priest?"

"You'll do fine."

She studied the boat departure times. Early. Weather dependent. To various spots that promised fish and coral, turtles, even an eel. The pictures were stunning. Aerial shots of geological wonders, turquoise water, and everyday people splashing around with fins, cameras, and snorkels. Even little children.

Before she flew home, she'd do it. If there were any priests on the tour, she'd pass; otherwise, she was going to snorkel in the ocean and see a damn fish somewhere other than on her plate. Afterward—and she'd pay the ransom to get photo evidence of the thing, whatever it was—she'd retire to her well-padded suburban apartment, her loving students, and live out the rest of her life knowing she'd done it, and might—if climate change, for instance, made it necessary—do it again.

The tickets were expensive. It was all so expensive. Inhaling the breeze off the shore, she scanned the horizon for whales. A clerk at the resort store, where she'd bought a five-dollar bottle of water, had told her she should come back in March to see the mating season. Boats went out just to watch the whales.

She tried to imagine how she would feel if she were one of the massive creatures, just trying to have a little sexy time while humans floated around giggling and pointing. It would be like if aliens were bobbing about in the sky overhead with their high-tech monitoring devices, just hoping she and one of the human males would get interesting with each other so they could snap a recording and bring it to their home planet as a souvenir. They, too, would prefer to come in the spring, when the most action took place.

The brochure had color photos on both sides. Apparently, she'd have to get on a boat that didn't look much bigger than a Fiat and had been designed for a much thinner generation of

Americans; and then, once she propelled herself onto the boat, she'd have to stay there until it left the dock, ideally without physical restraints.

That was just the boat. Getting into the water—the kind with living things that were familiar with the water in a totally non-*Exorcist* sort of way—would entail overcoming at least five more steps on the fear scale. One, there was the danger of the waves, riptide, and all the understandable risks of drowning. Two, marine organisms, benign. Three, marine organisms, hostile. Four, lingering body image issues that would be brought to the surface, so to speak, by taking off her clothes in a crowd. And five…

Five was the killer.

Ansel.

Would it be easier with his company… or without?

"Ready to run some more?" she asked. She needed to work off some tension.

He bent over, coughing like a dying man, then straightened, hand over his heart. "I was born ready," he choked out. "Boy, I sure do love running." He pounded his chest.

"Is Rachel your next of kin? In case you don't make it?"

"You'd think someone with your problems would be more sensitive," he said.

She laughed.

It was after eight when they staggered up the stairs to the condo. Actually, Ansel staggered; Nicki jogged ahead of him and gloated. She'd figured out on the return run that he was faking his infirmity.

"Go ahead." He tripped on the stairs. "I'll be… fine."

"Geezers have to take it easy," she said. "You should've taken the elevator."

"I would have, but my companion has a disorder."

"You wouldn't like me when I'm freaking," she said.

"I bet I would," he said, in such a low voice, she hoped she hadn't imagined it.

Feeling good, she ducked into her bathroom for a shower. And a more aggressive shave. She could see from the lines of sunburned pink flesh on her thighs—and above—that she had overestimated what percentage of her private parts were private.

Stupid bikinis. If she were a stronger swimmer, she'd wear shorts like a boy; but added drag was the last thing she wanted. She lathered up again. If razor-burned pubes were the price for buoyancy, she'd pay it.

After she got dressed, she wrote a quick post for the blog about Satan and water sports, then called Betty to see how she was doing.

"You got twice the hits last night," Betty said, then sighed. "Just like Jaynette at the café the other night."

"Still haven't talked to her?"

"I did." Betty's voice rose to an unfamiliar pitch. "I told her it had been great, but it was time for me to move on."

"No! She wasn't willing to stop seeing other people?"

"I didn't ask."

"Betty."

"What? It would've been manipulative. I don't do ultimatums. I tell all my girlfriends, 'If you make an ultimatum, I'm out of here.'"

Nicki juggled two beanbags with one hand while she rolled her eyes. "You aren't even kidding."

"Children of immigrants know what it's like to love freedom."

"Yeah, you're very patriotic," Nicki said. "How'd she take it?"

"She laughed."

"You're lying," Nicki said.

"No, she thought I was joking. And then we sort of dropped it. We're going to the movies in an hour."

"You're more messed up than I am," Nicki said.

"Says the woman who wishes bridges were made out of Oreos as a security measure."

"I'm going snorkeling." Nicki needed to reestablish the high ground.

"I'll need proof."

"I don't care if you believe me or not."

"You're right," Betty said. "Half the time I think you're making up Phobic Phoebe's freak-outs just to make a good story, which is totally fine with me, by the way. And oh, I sent the stress balls. So don't say I never pay you."

"I hope you sent a case."

"There's a male genitalia joke in there somewhere, but I'm too gay to think of it," Betty said.

"I really am going to go snorkeling. I'm going to take a charter tour. Maybe next week."

"That's great, seriously. I've always wanted to go on one of those. Don't drown, okay? I want to hear how it went."

"For you, okay. I won't drown," Nicki said.

"Excellent. We done here?"

"Tell Jaynette after the movie how you feel about her."

Betty hung up with a grunt.

Nicki threw the phone on the bed and looked at herself in the mirror, frowning at her body in the lightweight sea-green dress she'd put on after her shower. In her continuing efforts to triumph over anxiety, she'd chosen a dress that reminded her of mermaids—the color, the shimmery material, the low-cut neckline.

She thought she looked pretty good.

Before she could listen to her brain's reminders about being in Hawaii for me, myself, and I—and not he, himself, and that nice butt of his—she strode out of her room until she found him, butt and all. He was on the balcony, drinking water and staring off at the ocean. Palm trees fluttered in the distant breeze.

She took a moment to stare. He wasn't the oversized specimen of manhood that Miles was, but he had a compact, muscular, sculptural perfection, strong but not perfect, just a man, a real human being.

"Hey," she said, stepping out on the balcony and closing the glass door behind her. Her heart began to pound.

He turned and saw her. "Oh, my."

She should've worn something else. The hot stare thing was unnerving. Plus she'd just seen how his hair was mussed. Her fingers itched to smooth down the cowlick over his left eyebrow. And her tongue wanted to make a matching one over his right.

Her hands plucked at her dress. "You seem to have recovered from the run," she said.

He grinned. "I am feeling pretty good at the moment." His gaze slid over her head to toe. She held herself still, let him look. "What else are you up to today?" he asked.

"I have to swim," she said. "Otherwise the phobia builds up again. I thought I'd spend an hour in the pool where you, you know..." She trailed off when all she could think of was *dragged me around*. It sounded dirty.

He lowered his voice. "Taught you a lesson?"

Oh, he made it sound dirty, too. She leaned against the balcony railing. "Yes. But I don't want company this time. You might turn into too much of a crutch. I need to know I can do this on my own. While the bucket's relatively empty."

"Bucket?"

"I had a therapist once. That was her word." She might as well dump it all on him; she'd already admitted most of it. "All of us have a fear bucket. Every time you're afraid of something, the emotion goes into the bucket so you can ignore it and carry on normally. If the bucket gets full, you freak out. That's the fear spilling over."

"Sounds messy," he said.

"You have no idea." She took a cookie from a plate on the table and took a huge bite. "So, basically, I have a really small bucket."

His eyes flickered downward. "Oh, I wouldn't say that."

"Hey, watch it." She wiped the crumbs off her hands. "I have to empty my bucket often or it fills up, the lid gets screwed on top, and so do I."

"Can you get, like, a trough? Or a drain pan?" He was studying her, probably for signs of distress, but she liked the jokes. Hell, she made them herself.

"She didn't say. Totally wedded to her buckets. Maybe her family was in the bucket business."

"How do you empty the bucket?" he asked.

"I have to do what I'm afraid of. If I avoid it too long, it becomes a *thing*. If I do it frequently, it fades. It doesn't even go into the bucket at all." She sat on a mesh chair. "Until two years ago, I thought I'd outgrown all of this—the phobias, the anxiety, the panic. I thought I was cured."

"But then, when you were jumping out of an airplane with a Special Forces team, you were like, 'Darn it, I forgot! I'm afraid of heights!'"

"Close. Pool party at the principal's house. All my coworkers, a few former students, the superintendent, their spouses, everyone." She sank into the chaise. "I couldn't even join them on the patio. I'd been worrying about it all week—mistake number one—and then I started worrying about panicking—mistake number two."

He sat next to her. "Mistake number one was counting your mistakes. That's never a good idea."

"They called an ambulance. I had a minute where I stopped breathing, and they figured it was an emergency." She sat up tall. "Just like my malfunctioning body. Full flight-or-fight mode. It had nothing to do with reality. It came from here." She pressed her knuckles into her diaphragm and then tapped her fingers on her temple.

They sat in silence for a long moment until he said, "*Wan tago King al Canowithy?*"

His transition was so abrupt that her brain took a minute to process his words into English. *Want to go hiking on a volcano with me?* She frowned at him. "Excuse me?"

"Haleakala. No water. Just rocks, native plants, and panoramic views." He looked up at the sky. "If we got going now, we'd have time to hike into the crater. You've proven your cardiovascular prowess."

So tempting. She'd planned on hiking later in the summer as a reward for mastering the water; maps of the high country were already loaded on her phone. She'd get to spend some time in her comfort zone, returning to her hiking boots and cargo pants, savoring a dusty trail without wearing makeup or sundresses, not caring about looking like a girl or appealing to men.

It was too soon—and besides, he didn't belong in her comfort zone. He lived in the big, red-hot, danger, danger, danger zone.

"Thank you, that sounds great," she said, getting up to her feet, "but I can't. I have to stay here near the water until I get over the fear." She didn't look at him.

"Without the crutch guy."

"I'm just going in the pool. Two steps forward, one step back."

"Steps? See, this is where you need my help," he said. "They're called *strokes*. If you try walking around on the bottom of the deep pool, you'll drown. Clearly you're not ready to swim solo."

This was the moment, the chance to ask for a real favor. "If you really want to help, how about going on a snorkel tour with me? Next week, maybe Monday? That'll give me enough time to practice." She swallowed. "And get used to the idea."

He smiled slowly, then nodded. "I'd love to."

"Before then, though, I was hoping you could recommend a beach that has fewer waves than the ones around here. The pool just isn't enough preparation. My guidebook lists some north of here that might be what I'm looking for, but I'm not sure." Inside her head she crossed off each request with a mental checkmark, bracing herself for the last one she was about to make. "And it would probably be best if I brought a lifeguard with me."

He nodded again. "I agree."

"Great." Her heart was beating so hard he could probably see it under the thin fabric of her dress, as if she were in an animated cartoon. "How about tomorrow?"

NICKI PARKED her car in the lot and eyed the sky. It was windy, with half of the sky filled with dark clouds, the other half a clear, sunny blue.

"Thanks for inviting me," Ansel said.

Nicki nodded, more afraid of the beach than the way her body thrummed like a sitar whenever he was within fifty feet of her, which, given how she trembled when her toes hit sand, was saying a lot. "Thanks for coming." She got out of the car, realized she'd forgotten the keys in the ignition, got the keys, stepped out again, and dropped her phone on the asphalt.

"There's no hurry," Ansel said.

Counting backward in Japanese wasn't going to be enough. Clenching her teeth, she retrieved her beach bag from the backseat and pivoted away from Ansel as she dug her beanbags out from the bottom. "I just need a minute," she said. "Do you mind?"

"No, I think it's cool."

"I mean," she said, "do you mind not watching?"

"Why, are you going to strip?"

She shot him a look from under her eyebrows.

"Sorry." He leaned against the car with his back to her and crossed his arms over his chest.

Meditation hadn't been invented by calm people; it never would've occurred to them. It took someone like Phobic Phoebe to develop revolutionary stress reduction techniques.

She inhaled a calming breath and let the beauty of gravity and physics take over. Just a minute or two to lose herself in the rhythm. Back in high school, she'd done talent shows in full clown makeup.

God. What could be sexier than that? No fucking wonder she'd been a virgin when she'd met Ansel in college.

Capturing the beanbags, she turned, already better after only sixty-four rounds. Ansel bowed his head over his phone.

Nice of him to give her the privacy she'd asked for. "Okay, I'm ready. Let's get this drowning started." She sang that in the same tune as the pop song.

"Great attitude." He shoved his phone in a cargo pocket and pointed at the small harbor on the other side of the hotel's lawn. "There's your watery grave right there."

"I like it. Show it to my parents when they come to mourn."

"Seriously, though, don't worry," he said, taking her arm. They each had a towel around their necks. "I'll be sure to tell them you perished bravely."

She laughed—not as deeply as she'd prefer—and strode ahead of him. The average age of the children playing along the wide, curved shore was less than her shoe size. After meeting the turtle-befriending infant in the wet suit, however, she no longer underestimated the small ones. They were born to the water as she'd never been.

The sand slowed her death march to the water. Her rubber flip-flops, old ones from before her fashion transformation, slid out from under her heels. "No time like the present," she said, kicking them off. She dropped the bag, flung the towel on top of it, and tore off her T-shirt. That, too, was an old favorite. If she still had her childhood blankie, she would've brought that, too. Every little thing helped.

"Tell me what you want me to do," Ansel said. He'd taken off his own shirt and stood there, hands clasped behind his back, wearing only a pair of gray-and-black striped swim trunks.

Since she'd never been the type to get turned on just by the look of a man's bare chest, she was surprised the way her pulse, already accelerated, hiccupped into warp speed.

"Do?" she asked. The white surf—the existence of it in the previously blue, glassy bay—caught her attention. "Don't do anything unless I ask. Or if I'm flailing around after my third breath. You know, as I'm going under."

"Got it."

She strode down the slope to the flat sand at the water's edge. "I'm not afraid to get my feet wet," she said, feeling the pressure build inside her chest as if a balloon were inflating with all the air she needed to exhale. "It's…it's… knowing I'm going in all the way."

"Makes sense."

She imagined herself wading up to her knees, how soothing the soft water would feel lapping against her skin. Visualization worked sometimes, sometimes not. This felt like a not. Although the air temperature was warm enough to melt butter, her hands were cold and getting colder.

Two tiny boys in flippers ran past, their knees bobbing up almost to their chins with each stride until a lump in the sand took the taller one down, and his body landed like a fly swatter smacking the kitchen counter. Knowing children, Nicki waited out the stunned silence until, sure enough, he began howling.

It was cute until the wave came in and got him. He tumbled away, fins and fingers spinning.

The hungry, merciless ocean had swallowed the boy whole.

Nicki galloped into the water to lift the boy, still crying, up into her arms. A minute later a bald guy with a goatee joined them, smiling like it was nothing, and took the tot from her.

"You're fine, Nate, you're fine," he said, lifting him aboard his bald head like a baseball cap, holding out his hands so he flew like a snorkeling superhero above him.

With his sudden change in perspective, and his dad's round skull pressing into his stomach, the boy laughed as his dad hauled him away.

Nicki, unimpressed with the parenting, stood up to her waist in the water, glaring after him. Although the waves were, she had to admit, much smaller now that she was measuring them against herself instead of a two-year-old.

"I'm having visions of *Baywatch*," Ansel said, wading over to her.

She crossed her arms over her chest. "That guy should take better care of his child."

"He was right there."

"People drown all the time in Hawaii. It's much more dangerous than it looks."

"If you hadn't been in his way, the guy would've got to his kid before you did."

She stepped down deeper into the water. It covered her chest—her vital organs—and waves brushed her chin. On sensory overload, panic and pleasure at war, it took her a moment to notice the sharp pain in her foot. Something sharp had poked her left heel during her daring rescue. She paddled her arms to get back into shallow water where she could lift her foot and inspect the damage. "It's still dangerous. See? I'm bleeding."

Christ, now the sharks can smell me.

"Nicki," Ansel said. "The kids were wearing life jackets."

"So? You've never heard of PTSD? Survival isn't the only goal, you know. Some scars never heal."

He raised his eyebrows. "Is that what happened to you?"

"Are you going to help me or what?" She waded over to him. "Turn around and take me for a ride."

He laughed. "Oh, yeah, baby."

"Focus, Hasselhoff. Give me those big shoulders to hold on to."

"Yes, ma'am," he said, grinning, doing as she said.

The shoulders were even nicer than she remembered. The thrill of true adventure heightened her senses, making each muscle feel firmer, bigger. "Go back and forth," she said, sliding her hands out to grasp the roundness of his biceps. "Please."

"Don't worry about being polite," he said. "I can take a little dominating."

After two minutes of bobbing up and down the shore at chest-level, she had to admit that the perilous surf… wasn't. Only right at the shore were there any waves at all. Where they swam, the surface was as smooth as the pool. "I like this place," she said.

"You haven't seen the best part."

She knew what he was talking about. Most of the action in the bay was under the surface. All around them, colorful pipes stuck out of the water as people of all ages looked at the life below.

Like the other day, however, her emotions had shifted away from cold, tight fear to hot, tight lust. She kicked the water behind her to keep herself from wrapping her legs around his waist, rubbing her chest along his shoulder blades, nibbling the tendon at the base of his skull where the hair curled up at his nape like black-and-silver parentheses.

Her mouth moved closer. "I'm ready," she said in his ear, "for the, uh, mask, snorkel, all that."

Rotating around in her arms, he captured her hands and slowly removed them from his shoulders while he looked into her eyes. The current pushed them into each other, hip to hip, thigh to thigh.

Then he let go of one of her hands and pivoted toward the sand, pulling her with him until the water was only waist-deep, where he released her. "Great. Why don't you take a break and get the gear?"

Ansel watched Nicki stride like a goddess, muscular thighs and round bottom pumping, away, away, away from him.

He should've been the one to retrieve their gear, but if he'd gotten out of the water just then, he'd get arrested for indecent exposure, even taking into account the shrinking effects of chilly water.

He'd been too tired, too tempted, to say no yesterday when she'd invited him. He was never any good at saying no, even when he wasn't infatuated with the woman asking.

Infatuation. That's what it was. He couldn't give her what she deserved. Look at her, eyeing the water like a firing squad with its rifles drawn. That kind of vulnerability wasn't something a guy could screw around with, no matter how his heart expanded like a marshmallow in the microwave to see her rush in to save a stranger's kid.

She stood in the white surf, waving the fins, snorkels, and masks at him while he stared. "You doing this or not?" she called.

Such a good question. Anatomy in remission, he strode

over to her and took his stuff from her. "It's easier to get the fins on in the water." He waded back in, donning his mask and snorkel, and bent over to put them on. Distracted by the sight of her jogging back to the towel for the life jacket she'd rented that morning, he dropped one fin and had to wait for it to bob to the surface. By the time he'd recaptured it and shoved his foot inside, she was wading out to him encased in a bright green vest, her mask pressing her cheeks down toward her jaw, the snorkel jutting out like a chubby antenna.

She was the most beautiful space alien he'd ever seen. "You'll have to wade out on your own. The flippers make me clumsy," he said. Or maybe that was just his emotions.

"No problem," she said. "No problem. I got this." She closed her eyes and her chest swelled, straining the black buckles on her vest.

"You've totally got this," he said.

She jogged into the surf like a shopper on Black Friday. "Show me a fish or show me death!"

"Choices, choices," he said, reaching out to her. She came into range, laughing, cheeks bulging under the rubber band of the mask, and he wondered what she would do if he kissed her.

No, you selfish dork. For once in your life, show some self-restraint.

He turned to give her his back. "Hold on like you were before, but this time put your face in the water."

When he didn't feel her nice soft hands stroking him as he'd expected, he looked over his shoulder. Bent over at the waist, she'd stuck her face in the water without him. Then her posture stiffened and she began flapping at the water. Her anxiety had infected him, making him worry that, although she was standing in four feet of calm water, she was in grave danger.

She lifted her head out of the water and cried, the snorkel still between her lips, "Fif!" She pounded the water with her open palms. "Fif! I faw fif!"

He pretended not to understand. "Excuse me?"

She spat out the snorkel and pointed, grinning wildly. "I saw fish!"

"Are you serious? Here? I thought they'd caught them all by now." He shook his head. "We need to tell somebody."

She put her snorkel back in her mouth and twirled her fingers in the air at him. "Wef go, funny guy."

Laughing, he turned, and this time, to his deep satisfaction, she grabbed his shoulders and pushed him into the sea, where they saw lots and lots of *fif*.

Not once did he infect her triumph with a cheap come-on; not even an hour later when she came out of the water, beautiful and dripping like Aphrodite in that painting; not even when she smiled at him as they got into the car, and his knees went weak.

Later that night in bed, staring at the moonlight on the ceiling, he realized if he'd ever had a better day, he couldn't remember it.

Which is why he shouldn't have been so surprised about what happened next.

Chapter 15

At 5:46 a.m. Monday morning, Nicki stepped out into the hallway wearing a huge floppy sunhat. She was juggling three beanbags in one hand while she closed the door behind her with the other.

Ansel stood in the hallway, watching her and smiling. Her circus skills continued to amaze him. "I want to see you do that on the boat," he said.

"You just might." She got the beanbags going higher in the air for a few cycles before catching them and striding down the hall. "Let's go before I wig out."

He hurried after her. "You won't," he said. "I'm too good of an instructor."

They'd had one more outing to the beach together—though she'd said she spent hours at the pool without him with a resort instructor, a female one this time. Ansel would've joined her, but he had to meet with the solar panel people and the resort manager, and interview a few property managers on the island to oversee the office building after the deal closed. He was wearing down Brand's resistance to the oceanfront building, but Mr. MBA had concerns, as usual, that Ansel was struggling to address. He'd been looking forward to a day off.

At the door to the stairs, Nicki hesitated. Then she marched over to the elevator buttons with her sword arm extended. "I've been avoiding this stupid thing too long."

"Don't you think you should fight one dragon at a time?" he asked.

She pushed the button with her thumb gently, as if it were a baby's nose. "Shh."

They waited in silence for the car to arrive. The lights over the door blinked at the third floor, then the fourth, another pause…

She lifted the beanbags, kneading them between her fingers. He could hear her taking deep breaths, see her ribcage expanding with them.

Finally the car arrived; the doors slid apart with a beep. She stood frozen, so he put out a hand to hold it until she was ready or decided she wasn't, but then she rushed forward and waved him in after her. "No problem," she said. "Piece of cake."

He watched her carefully during the descent, especially when they stopped several times to take on more passengers, but she seemed giddy now, greeting an elderly couple with a bright hello, asking a small girl already wearing a full snorkel mask about her plans, high-fiving her when she said she was going on a boat, too.

On the ground floor, Nicki held the door for everyone to get off first, even Ansel, then walked with him to the valet guys at the front of the resort with a wild smile on her face.

"Are you all right?" he asked her.

"Totally. Just had to break through. It's not the ride, it's the getting on. Can't explain it."

"Maybe it's that moment of decision when you give something else all that power over you."

Smiling at him sideways, she adjusted the bag on her shoulder. "Maybe."

Since he'd called the valet guys already, the car waited for them at the curb. They climbed in with their gear, two coffees he'd made for the journey, and headed south along the coast to Maalaea Harbor. It wasn't quite thirty miles, but to be safe, they were allowing an hour for the drive.

He doubted Nicki ever felt safe.

"Did you bring a sweatshirt?" she asked him. "I read you can get cold, especially after you've been in the water."

He tapped his chest under his long-sleeved T-shirt. "This is fine."

"It's okay if you get cold. I mean, just let me know, because I brought an extra. Sweatshirt. It's a men's, too, extra-large."

He glanced at her. She was nibbling a thumbnail. "I'll be fine," he said, resisting the urge to reassure her, which might be patronizing.

"I'm really looking forward to this." She clutched her knees.

"I can tell."

They drove in silence for a little less than an hour, slowed by the typical traffic. They parked in the harbor lot and went in search of their tour company's dock amid the other tourists. She strode ahead of him a step or two, as if slowing down would break her courage; he couldn't help himself from admiring her long legs. He looked forward to seeing her take off her shorts.

Take it easy, he told himself, dragging his gaze to the open sea. He felt responsible for her. Like a teacher. Or a therapist. A trusted friend. None of those people would slide his hand down her back until he found round, firm ass and pull her hard against his—

Nicki smacked him on the shoulder with her beach bag. "There's our boat!"

"There it is," he agreed.

They gathered with three dozen other people waiting in the morning chill. He looked around curiously, never having gone on a tour with so many people, realizing his parents must've paid extra for the small excursions he'd enjoyed over the years.

Finally the herd lunged forward. "Welcome aboard," a very tan, freckled, middle-aged guy said to them, taking their tickets at the top of the gangplank. "Find a seat. Help yourself to breakfast."

The ship had two decks and an inside seating area and didn't look nearly big enough for the three dozen bodies climbing aboard.

At the back of the line, he and Nicki elbowed their way into an inside corner of the crowded boat, forced to stand near a counter filled with doughnuts, fruit, and coffee, since the bench seats were already filled with teenagers and children, retired people, couples, everyone but them.

After a long wait, the boat finally left the dock. Ansel stuck an arm through the crowd grazing at the breakfast counter, plucked a slice of pineapple off a tray, and offered it to her.

"No," she said. "Thanks."

"Bagel?"

She shook her head and stared out the blurry window. He could see the whites of her eyes all the way around the pupils, like a doll.

Her anxiety was contagious. He found himself clenching his teeth at each rock of the boat, gripping the windowsill to hold himself steady, hoping the ride out to Molokini wouldn't be too long or too rough.

"It looks beautiful in pictures," she said.

"It is." He smiled, trying to lighten up. "You'll love it. And don't worry about drowning—there are so many tourists there that you can just grab on to one of them if you feel yourself going under."

"I'll grab you, okay?"

His nerves shifted from fear to lust. Blood returned to his extremities, including his favorite one. Annoyed with himself, he said, "Whatever you need," and patted her quickly on the shoulder.

A brief smile flashed on her face. She had sexy lips. He liked watching them move. So many emotions in one person, like an overflowing grocery bag.

Or a bucket.

The boat pitched and rolled in the surf, knocking people into one another, although Nicki was holding on to the side of the boat so tightly she barely moved. He regretted not getting ahead of the crowd so she could've had a seat. Noticing a mesh bag filled with towels sprawling between two different groups on the bench seating, he sashayed over and asked, already lifting the bag from the seat, "Mind if I move this?" He set it underneath and waved Nicki over.

She shook her head.

"Come on," he said.

"You take it," she said. "I'm fine."

A woman who seemed to be one of the family's grandmas, with jet black hair and a neon pink T-shirt, scowled at him as he sat next to her. He gave her a huge smile. "Isn't this fun?" he asked.

Her frown deepened, so he stared cheerfully ahead at Nicki, who was biting back a smile, watching them. For all her worries, she sure seemed happy, always quick to laugh. Testing her, he stuck out his tongue. Sure enough, she smiled and crossed her eyes.

The boat lurched, making one girl scream and a man spill coffee over the bagel tray. Nicki pivoted to grab the door frame to the front deck, her smile fading.

Ansel called out to her. "Come on! Save your energy."

Without a word, she wobbled over to him and took his seat

when he got up. After another few minutes of violent pitching, she looked up at him. "Thanks."

"No problem." He lost his balance and fell against Grouchy Grandma. "Sorry," he said, retrieving her white baseball cap from the floor where he'd knocked it and handing it over with his most charming grin.

Grandma clamped a hand on his shoulder, hauled herself up, and staggered over to where a younger man with the same warm expression sat at the end of the row. After a jab in the arm, the young relative got the hint and stood up. Then, when the man walked away to stand on the open deck, Ansel decided Grandma's old seat was fair game and plopped down into it.

"My mom would spank me," he said. "Taking an old lady's seat. I feel kind of guilty."

"How do you think I feel? Those poor towels have to sit on the floor because of me."

He leaned against her. "Next time let me book the tour. I know this guy with a catamaran. It's awesome."

Awkward silence stretched between them. What was he implying—next week? Next year?

A voice crackled unintelligibly over the speakers. Broken sentences tricked through about wind and waves, an apology, something about turtles. People groaned and looked at each other.

"What's going on?" Nicki asked, clamping a hand on his thigh.

He was wearing shorts. Her touch sent shivers up his leg. He closed his eyes, clenching his teeth.

"We're not going to Molokini?" a boy asked.

The man next to him put an arm around his shoulders. "Too windy today. He's taking us to Turtle Town instead."

The boy's mouth opened in outrage. "Can he do that?"

"Guess so," his dad said. "Safety first."

"That's stupid," the boy said.

"I agree," Nicki said, releasing Ansel's thigh to stand up.

"Going to complain to the captain?" he asked her, sucking in a breath. *Just a few more inches*, he'd been thinking.

"Getting a doughnut." She went over, surprisingly steady on her feet, and got a chocolate glaze, a rainbow sprinkle, and a glass of orange juice, then returned without spilling a drop. "I'm going to drown my sorrows in carbohydrates."

"As long as you're drowning," he said.

She handed him the chocolate one. "Sorry about my choice of boat."

"Don't worry about me," he said. "I'm cool. This happens. They'll find somewhere else."

Since turning around, the boat had steadied, and people got up from their seats to wander out to the decks. Nicki and Ansel stayed where they were until the crew, a young man and two women, one young and one older—all with impossibly perfect bodies—came around with the gear they rented out for an extra fee.

Within five minutes, Nicki held a wet suit, a life jacket, and a boogie board with a round plastic window in the middle of it.

"This thing looks tiny," she said, holding up the black neoprene suit.

The older woman, who introduced herself as Spike, turned around. "You'll actually be more comfortable in the water when it's tight."

Nicki glanced at the tanned, athletic fiftyish woman with the washboard abs, then at Ansel, and widened her eyes. "Is there a bathroom on board where I can try it on?"

"Yeah, but it's small. You won't be able to move around in there," the woman said, returning Nicki's credit card with a receipt. "Better just to try it here. Let me know if you can't squeeze into it. We might have a men's suit that would fit you."

When the woman was out on the front deck, Nicki wriggled out of her sweatshirt. "Is it wrong to hate her?"

"Yes."

She sighed. "How can something wrong feel so right?" In one sudden movement, she pulled her sundress over her head, uncovering a simple black bikini, like an athlete would wear, that he hadn't seen before. It should've been boring, but he stared like an idiot. Her hips, her thighs, her breasts and waist and arms, all of her, was right there under a thin layer of stretchy fabric.

He swallowed. "I don't know," he said under his breath, ducking his head. He stared at his hands so she could try it on without him staring, a mercy to himself as much as to her.

After a minute she said, "Forget it," and he looked up just as she flung the wet suit aside. "I'll feel like a mummy in that thing. I need to be able to move. And besides, it's kind of gross, all wet and slimy. God knows what's living in that fabric. Not that I'm a germaphobe."

"You're young," he said.

"Still time, you mean?"

"Exactly," he said. "Besides, with the vest, a wet suit is overkill."

Nicki pointed at him. "Don't mention death."

"Sorry."

She put the life vest on, which would help him keep his gaze above her neck. The legs, though—man, they killed him.

Death again. Her mood was contagious.

The boat stopped near a cluster of other boats, some much smaller, and dropped anchor. Within five minutes, the people were jumping out with their flippers and snorkels, laughing and shouting to one another. Nicki stood at the outskirts of the crowd queuing for the ladder down into the water, her lips in a hard line.

"I wish I could give you a drink," Ansel said.

She turned suddenly, blinking at him as if she'd just

remembered he was there. Her gaze dropped to his mouth and she said something too quiet to hear.

"Excuse me?" he asked, heart pounding. He leaned closer.

"Kiss me," she said. "For good luck."

Heat exploded inside him. *Oh, my pleasure.*

No, no, no. She was too vulnerable. He'd never be able to stop. He'd promised he wouldn't hit on her.

But she'd asked.

"Sure," he said, stretching his face into a smile, as if it was all a joke, just fun, nothing really. He moved his face to within an inch of hers, close enough to smell her sunscreen. At the last second, he dropped the smile and brushed his lips across hers.

Blood roaring in his ears, he turned away, grabbed the railing of the ladder, and dunked his mask in the freshwater bucket they kept on hand for rinsing. "I'll get in first so you can grab on to me if you want to." He didn't look back at her, just plunged into the water he hoped would cool him down.

Chapter 16

 icki had felt a little stupid for asking for the kiss, but if anything was going to distract her from the suffo-cating tension closing her throat, it would be the feel of his lips. Preemptive mouth-to-mouth resuscitation.

It did help. She had a dumb smile on her face as she watched him jump into the water with the others, his swim trunks slung low enough for her to check out the dimples again. He didn't seem so scary when all she looked at was his butt.

She tested the buckles on her life vest and waddled to the ladder.

"We'll be right here," the captain said. "You'll be fine."

"I'll be fine," Nicki said, lifting a flipper over the edge. The life jacket flattened her breasts. All this gear just to get into the water. To be fair, it had taken eons of evolution to get her ancestors out of the sea, so perhaps it made sense.

People in the water began shouting at each other, waving, splashing around, then disappearing under the surface.

"Turtle," the captain guessed.

"Oh, good," Nicki said, sitting on the top rung of the ladder.

"Would you like the board?" he asked. "You can look through the window."

Facing the Membrane of Terror, she barely heard him. *Just push through. There's a turtle.*

She didn't give a rat's ass about turtles. But Ansel was down there, swimming close to the boat, though the current kept pushing him away. She couldn't see his face under the mask, snorkel, and waves, but she knew he had to be smiling that goofy grin of his. Her life had so many drama queens in it—students, fellow teachers, herself—it was great to be with an easygoing, fun-loving person who knew how to enjoy life.

She crept down another rung, felt cold water fill her flippers, chill her toes. Not cold like San Francisco cold, but cold enough. Everyone else was floating facedown or submerged under the surface. The crew member otherwise known as Spike was busy setting up something called Snuba for a couple in their sixties who kept groping each other over the neoprene. Honeymooners, apparently.

She turned around to climb down another two rungs. The boat bobbed up, down, up—and then a wave caught her thighs, and she just let go and let God.

Or Neptune. Whatever.

Well, good news. She wasn't dead. The life jacket kept her face out of the water, although she was on her back, facing the sky.

No turtles. Nice birds, though.

"How you doing, Nicki?" the captain called out. She'd told him she was a new swimmer and might need a little extra attention, like an airlift.

"Great!" Floating on her back, she decided she was having fun, lots of fun, so much fun.

"The fish are the other way," Ansel said, paddling closer. "Turn over."

"I love swimming." She couldn't move. How long could she float before something ate her? Perhaps she'd focused too much on drowning as the sole danger. Now her mind raced through the other threats in the sea—vast and ancient, big and small. There were sharks, sure, but what about eels? Weren't there tiny stinging things than could put you into cardiac arrest?

Oddly, the sensation of living creatures below her in the mighty depths wasn't so bad. It was the water itself that terrified her.

She continued to float on her back. How far would she get if she didn't move? The waves seemed to be pushing her away from the boat, parallel to the shoreline, which was just close enough to recognize the hair color of the people on the beach. Was it like flying around the moon and some kind of rebound would bring her back? Or would her remains float to one of the continents along the Pacific Rim?

Ansel put a hand on her arm, brought his face close to hers. "I can pull you back to the boat."

"Not from Seattle," she said, watching the gulls. She wondered if some birds had malfunctioning brain chemistry that made them afraid of flying. Lifting her head, she scanned the distant beach for little white blobs pacing the sand, imagining one of them was just like her, fretting about his problem, comfortable eating bugs on the beach but knowing there were better snacks if he could just fly like the other birds...

"I'll pull you in. Hold on to my shoulder if you can." Ansel's grip on her arm tightened, waves rolled over them.

"No, I'm fine." She peeled his fingers off. "I was just getting used to the water. I'm totally fine." Kicking herself upright, she blew the water out of the snorkel, sucked in a breath, and plopped her face in.

Cloudy green water sparkling with yellow fish. Coral about

five feet below her. The sandy bottom around the coral, only about ten feet deep, maybe less. In the distance, the bodies of her fellow tourists, most of them kicking below the water, bubbles rising from their snorkels.

She lifted her face out of the water, spat out the mouthpiece, and smiled at Ansel, who was treading water, watching her.

"What's the matter?" She had to shout over the sound of the wind, the water in her ears.

Finally, he smiled. "Nothing. Can you see anything? The water's a little cloudy."

"I'm fine. I can totally see those little yellow fish." She replaced her snorkel, breathed, reminded herself she was encased in a life vest, and put her face in the water again. The other people were swimming down to the coral, where she assumed most of the action was. Even without fear, she couldn't go any deeper without better swimming skills.

She lifted her face back out and said to Ansel, "Go ahead —go down there. I'll watch you."

"I've seen it before. Don't worry about it."

"I want you to. Please? You can tell me what's going on. What are those people looking at over there?" She pointed to the southeast. "Look under the water. Everyone's clustered around something."

"It's probably a turtle."

"Go find out. I'll stay near the boat."

He glanced behind them. "You're not near the boat anymore. The wind has picked up."

Perhaps it was only adrenaline, but she wasn't worried. "I'm fine! I've broken through the membrane, you know?" She laughed. "Be my eyes and ears. I'm stuck up here on the surface. Please."

"You're sure?"

They had drifted about halfway between the largest group

of snorkelers and the boat. Now that she had time to adjust, she could admit the water here was no deeper than the pool she'd been in all week. She could see faces on the beach, so it couldn't be very far. "Yes! Find out what they're looking at and come back and describe it to me."

He looked around. "We're getting kind of far from the boat."

"You can rescue me when you come back," she said. "The sooner you go, the less rescuing you'll have to do."

His gray eyes smiled behind his mask. "Okay. If you're sure. Only for a minute." He swam closer and patted her life jacket before emptying out his snorkel, shoving it in his mouth, and diving down.

Two teenage boys were only a few body lengths away, shouting to each other as they came up for breath. She watched them, splashing and racing, diving down, popping back up, impressed by their energy and reckless happiness. It was only June but she already missed her students back home. These boys would've been in her class two or three years earlier; they weren't much older than freshmen. She was always amazed how big they got within a year or two of leaving her class. The little boys turned into men. On the outside, anyway.

While Nicki practiced her kicking and paddling to stay within range of the boat, one of the boys swam away to join the larger group, leaving the second one alone under the water. She put her face in to look for him, finding him directly below her, kicking his way deeper. Finally, he shot back up to the surface for air only two feet away from where she floated.

"Jake, did you see—"

He cut himself off when he saw it was her, not the other boy, in the water next to him. He was panting for breath, his shoulders low in the water. He didn't look energetic anymore.

"What did you see?" she asked him, knowing from experience that a teenage boy wouldn't admit if he were having trouble.

"Eel. Where"—he took a breath—"my cousin. Was here."

Shoving the thought of eels out of her mind—they hid under coral, far, far, far from the surface, right?—she kicked closer to him and pointed. "He swam that way. Should we join him?"

He shoved the mask up on his forehead and squinted, looking behind her. "Where's the boat?"

She twisted around. "That's it."

His eyes widened. "That can't be it." He began blinking quickly. "It's too far."

It *was* getting far. The waves seemed higher, the boat rocking more from side to side—or whatever boat people called that. Aft to Starbucks? "The captain sees us. He's on the deck. Hold on to me. I'll wave to him and somebody can help—"

"No!" The boy took the mask and snorkel off his head completely. "I just need to breathe. I can swim. I'm fine. I just need to breathe."

She'd recognized a kindred spirit immediately, and now she saw the fearful tyrant in his mind, so much like hers, taking over. "Of course you're fine. You just need to catch your breath."

To her horror, he hurled the mask and snorkel over her head. "Stupid thing. Can't breathe." The whites of his eyes matched his protective swim shirt.

"Float on your back and catch your breath," she said, trying to reach for the snorkel, but it was gone.

"I don't float. I sink!" He tilted his head back, gulped air.

She could feel his panic rising as if it were her own—her own throat closing, her own limbs freezing. Waving at the boat, she called as loudly as she could, "Help! We"—she corrected herself—"I need help!"

"No!" The boy grabbed her shoulders. He was bigger than Ansel, but with a baby face, blue-lipped and terrified. "I just can't breathe! Stupid snorkel! I knew it was a bad one! Jake got the good one! Jake! Jake!" He sank up to his lips. Water flooded his mouth.

She had that feeling that her brain was recording every detail of everything that happened, giving her a moment that would haunt her for the rest of her life. "I float. You take this." She unbuckled the top buckle of the vest.

"No! I don't need it!" His voice cracked. "Jake!" He punched the water and let himself float away from her, too far for him to hold on to her and the life vest.

She unfastened the next buckle. She would float. She'd been floating in the pool all week. She just had to keep calm, take deep breaths, and wait for the crew or Ansel to come for them.

They were now twice as far from the boat as they'd been when the boy had thrown his snorkel, and the gap was growing, accelerating.

"What's your name?" She kicked and joined him. Before she could change her mind, she wriggled out of the vest and held it between them as she loosened the straps. If he had any trouble getting it on, it might set him off, push him further into panic.

He was openly crying now, no longer staring at the boat but at the sky, letting the current take him.

Her body felt naked without the vest. "Hey, you're doing great. You just need to breathe… Jake? Did you say your name is Jake?"

"Jared," he gasped.

"Hey, Jared. I'm Nicki. Please hold this for me for a second." Putting a hand on his shoulder, trying not to dig her nails into his skin in her haste, she moved the vest against his chest where he'd have to grab it.

"I don't need anything!" Jared pounded the water with his fist, but he had his arm on the floating vest. "Leave me alone! Jake!"

I can float, I can float, she told herself. Being too close to Jared was fueling his panic by making him feel trapped. And if he lashed out at her or grabbed her shoulders again, now that she didn't have the life vest...

Better to float away.

Chapter 17

Ansel kicked up to the surface and scanned the horizon, surprised by how far he'd traveled from the boat. Several other vessels had arrived, some tied together, and dropped anchor. The humans, fins, and plastic snorkels breaking the surface around him messed with his sense of direction. Nicki had to be right on the other side of the raft that had just dropped anchor next to him.

Deciding it had been three minutes, the longest he felt comfortable leaving her, he started swimming around the raft and the tourists already jumping into the water next to him. The crew on their tour seemed competent, but with such a mob, all the boats, the churning water, the increasing wind, he didn't trust them to be lifeguards.

Narrowly avoiding a hairy knee to the face from a guy fiddling with a waterproof camera, he swam freestyle around the raft, kicking hard. He hadn't gone far, but he still didn't see Nicki's yellow life vest.

Ever since they'd arrived at the slip and seen the size of the boat and number of other passengers, he'd had a bad feeling. She should've had a small private charter with a relaxed, attentive crew, or at least a tour that went to a quieter spot with a lower profile than Turtle Town. It even sounded like a carnival ride. *Buy a ticket and hold on to your fins!*

The vest she got on the boat was yellow and black, like a radioactive bee, and should be easy to spot. He found their boat, scanned the space between it and the shore, his view blocked again by a trio of young women who came up for air, shouting to each other about not seeing anything good, until finally he spotted a glimpse of neon yellow about fifty yards to his left. Man, how'd she get so far away already?

His crawl stroke wouldn't win him any gold medals, but he was strong enough to plow through the waves at a steady clip, especially with fins and a snorkel.

Halfway to the bee, he lifted his head to wave, then saw with dismay it wasn't Nicki but a teenage kid. In between the boy and the boat, he lifted his mask, treading water, to see better. Where'd she go?

The boat wasn't far. Maybe she'd gone back. He hoped she hadn't; she'd be mad at herself if she'd given up so quickly.

He didn't see another jacket like hers anywhere, but the raft tour blocked a lot of his view. Deciding his best bet was to return to the boat, he swam there, slicing the water even harder now, angry with himself for losing sight of her.

He put a hand on the bottom rung of the ladder, looking up at the captain, who was frowning at the water, binoculars in hand.

Ansel was breathing hard. "Is anything the matter?"

The captain didn't seem to hear him.

Ansel climbed up the ladder, struggling to maneuver the rungs without taking off the flippers. "Did my friend come back to the boat? The woman in the life jacket?"

But the captain was talking to the crew member named Spike and pointing at the boy with the yellow vest, who was kicking like a shark was after him, seeming to have lost his snorkel and mask. The kid looked worried, probably afraid he'd get in trouble with whoever had brought him.

"You all right?" the captain shouted. Then, to Spike, "You'd better swim out there. See if he needs help."

Spike already had an orange flotation belt in her hand and dove directly from the deck into the water, slicing into the water like a pale, elongated dolphin. Ansel could believe *she* just might have a handful of gold medals tucked away somewhere.

He peered over the edge of the boat into the cabin, up at the top deck, not seeing Nicki anywhere and furious that he didn't. "We need to find my friend right now," he told the captain. "She can't swim."

The captain's attention snapped from the boy to Ansel. "I gave one lady a vest."

"That's her."

"Now that kid's wearing it." The captain pointed. "Was he with her?"

"No, listen to me. She can't swim." Ansel shoved a towel out of his way and flopped onto the deck. "She's wearing a life jacket."

"No, that's the only yellow one we've got. The rest are orange." The captain held up the binoculars to his face and rotated in a semicircle, scanning the area.

"Give me those." Ansel grabbed the binoculars, feeling nauseated.

"Be my guest." The captain held up his hands.

"We've got to find her." Ansel tried not to shout, but the man was half-comatose. "She's wearing a black bikini." Under the life vest. Which she was wearing because she couldn't swim, damn it. Where was she?

The captain held out a hand for Spike and hauled her aboard. "This man's trying to find somebody, a woman who started out in the yellow vest. Says she can't swim."

"Can't swim at all?" Spike asked.

"Only a little," Ansel said. "And she's terrified of the water."

The boy's head appeared as he pitched the vest over the top rung of the ladder. "She made me take it. I was fine, but she made me take it."

"She must've had a reason," Ansel snapped, grabbing the boy's hand to pull him up. First he'd get the story, then he'd kill him. No, it would take too much time. "Where'd you last see her?"

"I don't know? Out there?" Ansel belatedly noticed the boy's lips were blue, and saw the horror in his red-rimmed young eyes. He was just a kid, barely a teenager. He stumbled into the boat and collapsed onto a bench, shivering.

Ansel jumped up on another bench to look again through the binoculars. His hands shook; the boat lurched beneath him.

"She must have some skill," the captain said, joining him. "To give up her jacket."

"She can't swim. She's phobic. She's out there and you aren't…" Ansel bit down on his lip so hard he tasted blood. He didn't swear. It was a quirk of his from college that began as a bet and became a way of life. But now, ten years' worth of foul curses swamped him like seawater in a drowning man's mouth. "You aren't doing anything."

"I think I see somebody. There. Is that her?" The captain got close to Ansel and pointed downwind.

Squeezing the binoculars so hard they creaked, Ansel stared hard. He saw a body in the water facedown, the orange tip of a snorkel sticking up. A woman's body.

Nicki's body.

He shoved the binoculars at the captain, yanked the yellow vest out of Spike's hands, crammed the snorkel into his mouth, and dropped over the edge into the water before windmilling through the water as fast as he could with the vest under one arm. His breathing through the tube was louder than the waves crashing around his head.

It seemed to take forever, like he must've headed in the wrong direction, but he had her position fixed now with a landmark behind her, and she was getting larger.

Her figure was utterly still. As if—

Finally he reached her, hyperventilating and shaking and cold. Maybe he should've brought two life jackets. "Nicki!" he choked out. "Nicki!"

As a wave smacked him in the face, she lifted a hand out of the water, flapped it at him, and put it back down. As she went limp again, spit and seawater flew out of her snorkel like a humpback's blowhole.

Treading water, trembling so badly he lost his hold on the vest for a moment, he finally found her hand and shoved it through the armhole. Only then did she lift her face out of the water, reach back to push her other arm through, and flopped back onto her back to buckle it as the waves pulled them apart.

She was smiling.

"What—why—" He couldn't speak. A torrent of profanity was all he could come up with. He swam after her and hooked his fingers around the waist straps to tug her toward the boat.

"Is the boy okay?" She spoke around the snorkel mouthpiece. Now that she wore the life vest, she was more animated, kicking and paddling along with him. She looked fine, sounded fine.

"Yeah." He put his own snorkel back in his mouth and blew out the water.

Smiling broadly, she spoke around her own mouthpiece. "He wore himself out. I gave him my life jacket."

"Yeah." Ansel kicked harder, scowling at the boat through the fogged plastic of his mask. His heart banged in his chest, angry and tired.

Spike reached them with another life belt strapped to her wrist. "Everything all right?"

"Great!" Nicki said.

It is not great, Ansel thought as he swam. He'd known she was crazy but this was *crazy* crazy. He was in love with an insane person.

He choked and closed his eyes.

Oh, God help him.

Chapter 18

"**I**s he okay?" Spike asked.

Ansel was floating with his eyes closed, his body numb.

"I'm getting my second wind," he heard Nicki say. "I can help kick if you pull him."

He twisted his head around. "I'm fime." He spit out the snorkel. "*Fine.* You're the one…" He snapped out of his paralysis and poured his frustration into dragging Nicki back to the boat. Spike took her other hand, and the three of them kicked upwind together to the boat. Half of the other tourists had climbed out of the water and were hanging around the decks, wrapped in their towels and sweatshirts as they drank coffee and laughed, nibbled doughnuts, oblivious to Ansel's hell.

He waited in the water while Nicki climbed up the ladder. He refused to look at her long legs, her sexy anything. He refused to love her.

She could've died. Willingly. For no reason, no good reason, the crazy, adorable nutjob…

"Oh my Lord, is this her?" a woman in her late forties in a turquoise robe pointed at Nicki. She rushed forward and held her arm, unfurling a towel. "I will never forgive myself." The boy stood behind her, arms crossed over his chest, slumped over to about half his full height, staring at a puddle under his long skinny feet.

Holding her fins in one hand, Nicki hopped gracefully onto the deck and glanced back at Ansel with a grin as the woman wrapped the towel around her shoulders. She still wore the vest. Ansel climbed up to join her, vowing if she tried to take it off, he'd drown her himself.

"I can't thank you enough." The woman glanced back at the boy for a moment. Leaning closer to Nicki, she lowered her voice. "Jared would thank you but he's… still a little shell-shocked."

Ansel maneuvered past the two women, eyeing the boy, fingers twitching to throw him overboard if he made the slightest snotty move—an eye roll, a snicker, a sneer.

But he looked too miserable for any of that. He backed up until the backs of his legs hit the bench, where he sank down in a crumpled ball under his hoodie.

Bright-eyed and glowing, Nicki patted the woman's turquoise arm. "I had the time of my life," she said. Then she went over to Jared and punched him lightly in the shoulder. "Thanks for bringing the jacket back to the boat for me. It was really cramping my style."

Ansel stared. Style? Cramp? *Thanks?*

Spike put a towel around Ansel's shoulders. "You're shaking."

The captain pushed a cup of steaming coffee into his hands. "Maybe you should sit down."

Before he could argue, they herded Ansel into the inside cabin and plunked him on a bench. The captain whacked him on the arm. "Drink it. We've had enough drama today."

Ansel lifted the coffee but didn't drink, just inhaled the steam. "What is the name of this boat of yours?"

"The Blue Magoo," the captain said with a smile.

Ansel nodded, storing it away in his memory for the future. Buying it and dropping it into a volcano might make him feel better.

Nicki hurried over and put the back of her hand against his cheek. "Are you okay? What happened?" She was like Florence Nightingale in a bikini. "Your skin is freezing. Is that coffee? Drink it. You don't want to get hypothermia."

He couldn't believe it. She was worried about *him?*

Nicki put a motherly arm around his shoulders and guided the cup to his lips. "Thanks for the rescue, by the way."

He gulped the coffee and savored the scalding pain on his tongue and throat. Anger simmered deep within him, the stewed remains of his fear. She had no idea how badly she'd scared him. He barely understood it himself.

"You're welcome." He stood up and handed her the half-empty cup. "I need to use the bathroom."

He left her there without another word.

———

Flying as high as a hippie on Telegraph Avenue in 1968, Nicki strode down the gangplank to the dock, smiling, swinging her arms, and humming a tune as she watched Jared walk ahead with his mother.

She knew he felt humiliated, and she really did empathize, but he was alive and Nicki was cured and she couldn't regret any of it.

Yeah, she knew it was temporary. And she still couldn't swim very well. But she'd faced a nightmare and not only survived but had risen above it.

She refused to think about what would've happened if Ansel hadn't come for her. Of course he was going to look for her—that's why she'd brought him along. She knew the crew would be too busy to watch her every second.

But even if he hadn't found her, she would've survived. She hadn't wanted to wear herself out, but when she was doing the dead lady's float, she'd steadily kicked her legs, moving the fins enough to keep her relatively close to shore and the other snorkelers—but not too close. She'd been bracing herself for a rough landing on the beach, worried she might hit the reef on her way in, which would be bad both for her and the coral. But then he'd found her.

First thing she'd do back at the resort is get in the pool. Strike while the fear remained submerged, so to speak. Drown it. Drown it until it was dead, dead, dead. Then take more lessons. She'd join a swim team back home. Compete on weekends.

It felt great to be triumphant.

"Slow down," Ansel said behind her. "Please." His voice was clipped. He'd disappeared into the bathroom for so long, she'd wondered if he'd been seasick.

"Sorry." She waited, hugging her damp towel to her chest, smiling warmly at him—though his gaze was fixed on the dock.

When he looked up and saw her, his scowl deepened. Rather belatedly, she realized he was angry with her. She'd thought he'd been worried about her, then cold and maybe seasick, but angry? At her?

"What's the matter?" she asked, dropping the smile.

He jogged ahead, reaching out for her bag as he passed her. "You got everything from the boat?"

"Ansel."

"Cap'n Crunch's floating piece of shit?"

"Ansel?"

"Sorry." He slung her bag over his shoulder. He was walking so far ahead of her that she let him go on without her, watching his rigid back disappear behind an RV parked in the lot next to the harbor.

Now she was angry, too, and she didn't even know why. She reached the car—he was already behind the wheel—and took a moment to dry her hair with her towel. Maybe it had nothing to do with her. Something had happened, he wasn't feeling well, he'd explain over lunch.

She got into the car and he floored it, as much of a floor as the old hybrid had in it.

"You're angry," she said.

"You want to drive?"

"I'd love to. I'm having a great day."

"Because you're invincible, is that it?" He adjusted his rearview mirror. "Hold on, some of these curves are pretty tight."

"What's the matter with you?"

The car screeched around a turn in the road; the foaming sea lapped the rocks directly below her. Her stomach lurched, but she closed her eyes and didn't make a sound. She'd kill him later, when he wasn't in command of the vehicle she was strapped inside.

He slowed, exhaling through his nose like a bull. "Sorry." The car took the next turn and the one after that at a crawling pace that created a line of three cars behind them, and after a silence stretched out between them, he flicked on the radio.

She watched him from the corner of her eye. They were traveling south, away from the condo. "Where are we going?"

"Near Wailea. Not far."

She knew that from reading the tour guides. "Why?"

"You said you wanted to see more of the island."

"When did I say that?"

He turned off the radio. Turned it back on, then off. "I thought you did. Don't you?"

"I suppose. Yes, of course."

He didn't answer, just turned the radio back on. It was mostly static.

She turned to the window. The Pacific was much better company.

After about thirty minutes of poor radio reception and awkward silence, he turned off the highway onto a street lined with coconut palms and brightly colored gardens. They snaked past a rolling manicured lawn to park behind a fountain shaped like a clawed hand, right between a Tesla and a Ferrari. The ocean was just below them to the left, past a luxury metropolis of bungalows.

Eager to escape the pressure cooker, she got out of the car and walked around to the back to get her bag and towel. Other people of modest means were walking through the garden toward a path at the end of the parking lot, on their way, she assumed, to the public beach. She wasn't dying to get back in the water, but she didn't mind sunbathing, people watching, reading, and reliving her morning triumph.

She pulled on the hatch but found it locked. She knocked on the metal and waited for him to pop it open, but he didn't move; it still wouldn't budge. She knocked again.

Eventually it clicked open, and he got out to join her. "I hope you're hungry," he mumbled. "I made us reservations for lunch."

She slung her bag over her shoulder. That sounded formal. She was wearing a wet swimsuit and a dress more like a large washcloth than anything suitable for a place that took reservations.

"Where?"

He scowled. "Here."

"I'm not dressed for this kind of place."

"Didn't you bring a change of clothes?"

She had noticed he'd already changed into khakis and a gray polo shirt on the boat. She'd worried he'd been sick on his other clothes; now she didn't care. "Yes, but I'm not going to strip in the parking lot. And I need a shower."

He bit his lip, turned away. Then he said, "Fine. I'll get us a room."

"*What?*"

"Relax. I'll wait in the bar. Hang out here. I'll be right back." He strode away before she could stop him.

Get them a room?

She was more confused than angry, but definitely angry. What the hell was the matter with him? Ex-girlfriend on the boat? The captain beat him at poker?

She took a deep breath and sat on the edge of the fountain, hugging her bag in her lap and letting the sweet aroma of tropical flowers and her coconut sunscreen calm her down. Working with hormonal teenagers every day had taught her how to deflect other people's irrational emotions. Just because Ansel was upset about something didn't mean she had to follow him off an emotional cliff.

Clearly, she should've left him behind. She'd rescued a kid when she could barely swim. She was in a damn good mood. Damn it.

Ansel reappeared, the scowl still fixed on his face. "All right, here's the key. It should be one of those over there." He pointed at the cabanas overlooking the beach.

Walking out of one of the tastefully arched doorways was a man in a tux and a woman in the type of fashionable getup Nicki had only seen on the covers of periodicals displayed in the checkout aisle at the supermarket. The dress had lots of feathers—and holes—yet the effect was stunning.

"Got all your stuff?" Ansel asked.

She didn't answer him, mesmerized by the couple moving toward them. Then she gasped. The woman was the star of a TV show she used to watch.

Nicki leaned toward Ansel, lowering her voice to a whisper. "You got one of those? But that must've cost a fortune."

"I'm rich, remember? I like an excuse to throw my money around." He thrust the plastic key card at her, not meeting her eyes.

She couldn't take much more of this. "What happened on the boat?"

"Nothing happened on the boat."

She got up, adjusting her bag on her shoulder, and walked to the car. "I want to go home."

"What?"

She opened the door and got in.

"You can't! I just spent two thousand bucks on this lunch!"

"Then you're an idiot." She slammed the door.

Jesus. Two thousand dollars? Her heart pounded in her ears. Hands shaking, she put on her seat belt.

He walked away from the car, arms rigid at his side, then spun around, marched to her door, and yanked it open. "I am an idiot," he said.

Suspecting he was being sarcastic, she said nothing.

"I'm angry because I'm an idiot," he continued.

"I have no idea what you're talking about."

"Will you please get out of the car?"

"I can't believe you spent two grand so I could take a shower," she said.

He held out the key, head bowed. "It's nonrefundable," he muttered.

Unbelievable.

She sighed. She was curious to see it. He could mope in the bar, whatever; she didn't care. She snatched the card in its little white envelope, then read the number noted in a curly metallic script before striding past the Tesla to find cabana 7.

The lawn was as springy as a birthday cake. She was tempted to bend over and taste it.

He caught up with her as she stormed around one of the unit's private patios looking for the number. "It's down there," he said, pointing at the one at the end under a trio of palm trees that leaned into each other like gossiping girlfriends.

"I see it."

He was right behind her when she walked through the courtyard and unlocked the door. The ocean was over her shoulder, the beach only ten steps away. A white hammock stretched between the palms, bright orange pillows and a red throw blanket arranged at one end. When she stepped inside the cabana, a pitcher of fruit juice and a wooden bowl filled with cut tropical fruit greeted them on a hall table.

What a waste.

She turned to him. "I thought you were going to sit in the bar."

Kicking the door behind him, he picked up the pitcher and began to pour. "I was afraid you wouldn't be able to find it."

"I'm not helpless. I rescued a kid in the *ocean* and I can't even *swim*. I think I can manage to find a stupid little bar in a stupid little resort."

"You—you—" He slammed the pitcher down. "You didn't rescue anybody."

"Like hell I didn't. You should've seen that kid. He was going under."

"The only person who was in danger of going under was you. If it weren't for me…"

She flung her bag on the floor. *This* was it. *This* was why he was mad. "I would've floated up on the beach."

"You didn't know that," he said. "You should've called for help."

"We were too far," she said. "And I didn't want to embarrass him."

"So you gave him your life jacket?"

"Yes!"

"You—you—" He held up his hands, staring at her as if he wanted to throttle her. "I should go to the bar."

"Go ahead!"

"Good luck guessing which one." But instead of leaving, he moved closer. His voice dropped. "You scared the hell out of me."

That was it. She'd been so busy being proud of herself, it had never occurred to her he might worry. "I was fine."

"You were lucky."

"I was practicing how to float for days, Ansel. You didn't have to worry."

Shaking his head, he took her by the shoulders. "I don't usually drink, but I will today." His unblinking gaze fell to her mouth.

Her breathing, already shallow, stopped altogether.

He slid a hand up over her shoulder, behind her neck. "I haven't had a drink since the night I met you." His other hand found the small of her back and pulled her against him. He lowered his mouth to hers. "Mickey," he said.

Chapter 19

This isn't love, he told himself as he kissed her. *This is the same thing it always is.*

He ran his tongue along the seam of her lips and heard her groan.

Nothing wrong with that.

All the anger that had been raging in him changed direction, feeling the opportunity to explode here into nothingness with her in his arms, under his mouth and hands.

Of course he'd been scared out there in the ocean. In the heat of the moment, he'd called it something else.

She snaked her arms around his neck. "Ansel," she whispered into his ear. Her hot breath triggered another cascade of desire.

He'd been dreaming about this since he saw her juggling, or even before that, when she ran down the stairwell with her suitcases.

And over a decade before that, when he'd had to walk away from a little fun before it got out of hand. He'd told her he didn't have a condom. She hadn't seemed to care. If he hadn't already had a close call in high school, he wouldn't have cared either.

Christ, she felt good. He deepened the kiss, pushed her against the wall. She bit his lip. He ran a hand up her ribs and cupped her breast, hard, demanding, remembering how he could've lost her.

"Nicki, damn it," he moaned. He could still see her motionless body facedown in the water, far from the boat, floating away from him.

"At least you got my name right this time," she whispered in his ear, slipping a hand under his shorts.

Oh my God. "Minnie?"

Her fingers wrapped around him and squeezed. "This seemed to bother you last time," she said.

"Not the word," he choked out.

She withdrew her hand. "If you're going to freak out and run away again, you better tell me now."

He slid his hand up her throat to cup her face. "Didn't have a condom last time," he said, tasting her, smelling her. "Don't have that problem today."

"You didn't… that's why… but we didn't have to go all the way, I didn't think we—"

"We would have. I couldn't stay. Even if I managed to keep it up long enough, and even if I was eighteen, I was so drunk…"

She stepped back. "I wish you'd told me."

"I did." The thought of having to leave her right then made him press her harder against the wall. Maybe she'd try to rescue some other kid and finish the drowning she'd started this morning. Getting her in bed could be a very limited-time offer.

"I'm thinking about taking a shower first," she said.

He dipped a finger into the V of her swim cover-up along the soft, warm flesh. She was still wearing her swimsuit. "Later," he mumbled. Taking her mouth in his, he untied the soft drawstring at her neck and shoved the soft fabric over her shoulders.

"I don't mind taking a shower," she said. "Really."

He pressed his palms against her breasts, driving his tongue into her mouth as he slipped down the fabric to expose her nipples. He leaned back to look at them, dark pink and hard. "Not"—he licked the left one—"necessary." Then the right.

He sucked. Hard.

Moaning, she arched her back. Her skin was salty and sweet, the best thing he'd ever tasted. He ran his hands up her arms to stretch her out along the wall to lick her everywhere.

But in his haste, he bumped the water pitcher; it crashed to the floor, jolting both of them back to reality for a split second.

"Bed?" she asked, panting.

"Hope so." He grabbed her hand and pulled her around the corner. The bedroom was tiny, barely more than an alcove. Floor-to-ceiling windows overlooking the beach dominated the space, making the low bed look like a raft in their own private ocean.

"This isn't going to work." He hooked an arm around her waist and tried to turn her back toward the main room.

"What's the matter?"

"There are people right out there," he said.

"The windows are tinted," she said. "And the bed is low. Nobody can see."

"Look at those kids," he said. "The light could hit the window at a certain angle, right when—I can't relax, thinking we'd be giving those babies a show."

She squinted at the window. "I don't see any kids. But I do see something else." Breaking away from him, she reached up and pulled down a sleek modern blind, then two more, turning the beach outside, and any inhabitants, into unfocused silhouette.

"Can you relax now?" she asked, turning to him. Her

breasts swelled over the cups of her bikini, where he'd bared them.

His voice fell to a growl. "No."

She shimmied out of the cover-up, which had fallen to her hips. Then she wriggled out of the bikini top, flinging that off, too.

"How about now?" She put a hand on her hip.

He had his arms around her before she finished the question. "I'm still mad at you, you know," he said as he fell backward onto the bed, pulling her on top of him. He held her face between his hands. "You could've drowned."

Collapsing against him, she brushed the hair away from between their lips and kissed him. Hot, molten need engulfed him.

In his fantasies about making love to her, she'd been sweet and passive—not because that was his preference, but because he'd assumed, given the phobia thing, she'd be skittish in bed.

Boy, was he wrong.

While he was trying to ease his tongue into her mouth, she lifted the hem of his shirt up to his armpits, dragged her nails across his chest, and pinched his nipple until he broke the suction, giving her the opportunity to push the shirt over his chin and face.

He groaned in shocked pleasure, then rolled her aside so he could tear off the shirt altogether.

"You're beautiful," she said, shaking her head, watching him. She dug her heels into the bed, lifting her pelvis in the air, and pulled off the bottom of her swimsuit with one hand while she clasped the back of his neck with the other. "Kiss me."

She wasn't what he expected, but she was everything he wanted.

God help him.

MAYBE SHE WAS GOING to embarrass herself. Maybe this was the last time she would have her hands on Ansel's bare chest, kissing her way along his collarbone to taste the thrumming pulse in this throat. Maybe she'd be heartbroken again and spend a few months crying into her juggling beanbags.

She didn't care. He felt so good. Warm and strong, smelling like seawater and sweat. She moved her tongue over his nipple and licked it until it hardened, smiling at the way he went rigid beneath her.

Oh, God, to be in the game again. She'd been on the sidelines too long, watching, waiting, wanting. He wasn't her soul mate, but it wasn't his soul she wanted right now.

"Take off your pants," she said. "It'll be easier if you do it."

Smiling, he stretched his arms over his head. "Since when is the good stuff ever easy?"

She didn't feel like laughing, so she bit down on his nipple.

"That's the way you want to play, is it?" he growled, grabbing her shoulders.

To her surprise, she found herself on her back with the full length of him pinning her to the bed. He still had his shorts on. The fabric was rough against her bare thighs, her pelvis, her stomach.

She spread her legs, wrapped them around his hips, and caught his mouth in a kiss as she thrust upward.

His tongue tangled with hers as he groaned and fumbled with his fly. "God, Nicki," he gasped. "I want you. I want you so much."

She reached down and caught the waistband with her thumbs, slid the material, with his boxers, over his hips. Then she caught his ass in both hands and squeezed, driving another cry out of him.

He wasn't smiling anymore, which she appreciated. His eyes were wild, his mouth frantically searching hers for another deep, hot kiss as he writhed out of the shorts and kicked them to the floor.

Now when she bucked up to him, his nakedness met hers, hard to soft, and she closed her eyes to feel more, to block out the blue hazy view around them, to forget about the future.

He slid his hand between her legs and stroked her until she was incapable of remembering her name, let alone next week. Just as she was on the verge of falling over the cliff, he touched her face.

"Now, Nicki?"

Chest heaving, she blinked up at him. Then she glanced down. He'd put the condom on. Nodding, she reached for him as she arched up to him. "God, yes."

He stroked her with the head of his penis, teasing her.

"Now?"

"God!" she cried.

"You're so beautiful." He thrust into her. "You are so beautiful, Nicki. Nicki."

When she fell, she brought him with her.

<hr>

THEY SLEPT for a ridiculously long time. When Nicki opened her eyes and saw the sun setting behind the curve of Ansel's shoulder, she lifted her head with a start.

What time was it?

He must've felt her jerk awake, because he opened his eyes and stared back at her. "You okay?"

They weren't touching. Perhaps because it was hot in the sunny sex alcove; perhaps because after the second time, they'd both needed to sleep more than they'd needed to cuddle. He slept facing her from one side of the bed; she woke on her stomach, using her arms as a pillow, at the other.

The magic's gone, isn't it? she asked herself. The air between them was thick, not at all like it had been an hour—four hours —earlier.

They'd slept too long, and now things were weird. Just as she'd expected.

He smiled. "Hi, beautiful."

A nervous giggle threatened to break out of her throat. She bit her lip. "Hi."

Grin deepening, he lifted himself up on to his elbow and leaned closer. Beads of sweat dotted his upper lip. "Are you as hot as I am?"

She raised an eyebrow. "You need more proof?"

He sprung up and came over to her on his hands and knees. "I always need more proof." Then he wiped his upper lip with the back of his hand. "Maybe a little later, though. Seriously, I'm cooked. If you poked me with a fork, my juices would run clear. I need another shower."

They'd shared one before falling asleep. She lifted a hand to her head to see how badly her hair had dried. She felt tufts flying parallel to her shoulders, as if an arrow had impaled her skull. "Oh, my."

He kissed her quickly on the lips, leaped over her to the floor, and strode out of the room, his butt as bare as her own. Were all of those marks on his back really her doing?

When the naked man show was over, she sat up, patting her hair down, and looked around for her clothes.

Right. She hadn't worn any, just the swimsuit. She got up, flinching a little when she sat up. It was like riding a bicycle: you didn't forget how, but that first ride of the summer was a doozy.

She limped out into the main room. Her bag sat in a puddle of water by the front door, the fallen pitcher beside it. Trying not to get her feet wet, she bent over to clean up the mess, glad the pitcher was plastic, not glass, and shook out her bag. It, unfortunately, was cotton, and had absorbed much of the water.

No help for that. She pulled on the underwear first, which was synthetic, so would dry quickly; but her T-shirt and capris were as damp as a kitchen sponge.

The fading sunlight was turning the walls of the cabana a dark reddish-orange. The decor was a blend of 1950s Elvis and generic luxury hotel: garish Hawaiian print pillows over hand-crafted leather furniture. The Jury-Jarskis' place was much more her speed, and she wanted to return to it.

Because of her wet clothes, she arranged the colorful pillows in a pile on the leather couch and perched on them as if she weren't nervous, not at all worried about whatever happened next, that she was confident and sophisticated because she had urgent, hot, uncommitted sex all the time.

By the time he came out of the shower, her back ached from holding herself in her oh-so-casual position.

"How about dinner?" he asked, leaning against the door frame. "I'm starving, aren't you?"

"I could eat a moose."

"Not native to the islands."

"Neither was the lobster," she said. "But I get your point. Would you mind heading back to the condo?"

His smile faltered. "You want to go back?"

"Is that a problem?"

"Of course not. I just figured…" He looked around, shook his head. "Sure. Whatever you think. Did you want to go now?"

Now she'd made things awkward. She crossed her legs, which, on her tower of pillows, used all of her core abdominal muscles. "No hurry."

"It's okay. We can go now. I shouldn't have assumed, you know…"

She stood up. "It's because my clothes are wet." She patted

her thighs and plucked at her T-shirt. "We knocked the pitcher over them."

"I believe that was my doing." He walked over and stroked the damp spot over her left nipple. "You could take them off. They'll be dry by morning." The corner of his mouth curved up.

This wasn't how it was supposed to go. She'd prepared herself for chilly regret, not this.

The back of her throat constricted, reducing her airflow. Lungs that had, minutes ago, been pumping normally, turned into a matching pair of bricks in her ribcage. She began to shake.

No, not now. She wouldn't let herself panic now, not here.

"Sure, good idea," she said, reaching for the bottom hem of her T-shirt. "We'll have…" Her tongue caught on her teeth. She couldn't inhale deeply enough to force words out. *Sex. We'll have sex again.*

Nnnggghh.

"You're shivering." He grabbed a pink-and-yellow floral throw blanket and wrapped it around her shoulders, forcing her arms and her shirt back down. "We'll get you into fresh clothes back at the condo. We can pick up something to eat on the way."

No, she wanted to say. *Let's stay here. Let's enjoy the moment.*

Instead, she said, "That sounds great," and the panic ebbed out to low tide.

Chapter 20

The valet who took their car at the front of the resort was a tall, future movie star kind of guy who made Ansel—not jealous, just curious—study Nicki's face for signs of lust.

Nothing. She walked past Mr. Box Office into the resort without a glance.

Well, at least it wasn't personal. For the last hour, as they'd driven back up the coast, eating chicken katsu and rice out of takeout containers in the car, he'd kept quiet to allow her a chance to explain. She was polite, even friendly, but the sex kitten of the tropics was gone. He started to wonder if he'd lied to himself about how good it had been, perhaps to justify taking it so far when he'd meant to keep it platonic.

He jogged through the resort doors to catch up to her near the elevators. The way she stood there, glaring at the glowing buttons, made him ask, "Would you rather take the stairs?"

Shaking her head, she hugged her tote bag to her chest. When the doors opened, she marched aboard, nearly steam-rolling a middle-aged man in a tight Hawaiian shirt clutching three mai tais against his chest.

"Excuse me," she said, giving the guy the phoniest smile Ansel had ever seen. She even sounded like somebody else, dumb and bubbly. When the car arrived at their floor, she twinkled at the drink guy as she sashayed out into the hall. But as soon as the doors shut, she returned to her rigid-limb march, which she maintained until they were inside the condo.

What was going on?

He dropped his bag on a barstool. "Nicki?"

She stood in the middle of the living room, staring out. The shades were drawn, the doors were closed, and the sun was long gone; they could've been in a motel in Bakersfield. "I'm not feeling well," she said. Then she turned to face him. "Would it be weird—well, of course it is, this is me we're talking about—but would you mind if I slept in my own bed tonight? Alone?"

"No, no," he began, trying to be reasonable, but then he couldn't stand it anymore. "Is it because I called you Mickey?"

A smile flashed across her face. "No. It's not you. I'm just not feeling well."

She did look kind of queasy. "Could've been the katsu. I'm feeling a little sick myself."

"I think... I don't want to guess. I might make things worse." She crossed her arms over her chest. "Let's talk in the morning, okay?"

He walked over to kiss her good night but faltered when he was a few inches away. A woman didn't clench her jaw when she felt like kissing. "It was a big day," he said. "What with the near drowning and hot sex."

"Maybe that's it. I'm so sorry to be like this." Then *she* was the one to lean over and kiss him. On the lips, but lightly. Quickly. And no tongue.

To hell with it. He caught her around the waist and gave her a proper kiss. She stiffened beneath him, but then she thawed. For a moment he thought everything was better, that this was the same woman he'd met in college, that afternoon, and his dreams; and then she was pulling away.

"Sorry," she said, closing her eyes. "I'll make us breakfast, okay?"

"I'm not hungry. How about in the morning?"

That earned a small laugh. "Deal."

He wanted to kiss her again. She felt soft, strong, and real in his arms, even better than the afternoon in bed.

But then a chime rang out from the door, and she took another big step back, completing her escape, and he was left standing alone in his own personal space.

The bell rang again.

"We should get that," she said.

"It's probably the drunk guy next door getting confused again." Reluctantly, he walked away from her to look out the door's peephole.

But it wasn't the drunk guy.

Diane?

***

ANSEL OPENED THE DOOR A CRACK, assuming he just needed a better look.

No. It really was Diane. She stood in the hallway with a giant white flower in her hair, big as a baby's head.

She was his best friend, and he loved her, but her timing was terrible. "What are you doing here?" he asked, opening the door the rest of the way.

"Hello to you, too." She swatted him on the arm with her briefcase. "Where the hell have you been?"

"What?"

She wriggled past him into the condo. "You're like my grandmother, never answering her phone. Did you forget to recharge it or something? Don't tell me you got another number and didn't tell me, because then I'll have to kill you." She strode into the kitchen and set her purse on the counter. "Hi, Nicki. Diane Gambau." She held out her hand. "Nice to see you again."

After a short pause, Nicki took her hand. "Hi."

The three stared at each other.

"You should've seen the look on your face when you opened the door," Diane said to him.

"It's that flower," he said, reaching out to poke it. "That sucker must weigh two pounds."

Diane tilted her head and stuck her tongue out at him. "I bought it in the gift shop downstairs while I was waiting. And waiting. And waiting."

"Ansel agreed to come with me on one of those boat tours, to go snorkeling," Nicki said without looking at him. "I'd never done anything like that before."

"Then we drove down to Wailea," he added. Maybe because it was a Monday, a day he should've been working, he got a little defensive. Diane worked eighty-hour weeks, had slept at the office more often than she'd admit, and teased him ruthlessly about his casual lifestyle. "I wasn't expecting company."

"I did call," Diane said.

"I left my phone in the car," he said. "I don't like to risk it on the beach, let alone on a boat—"

"I called days ago. More than once. But let's move on. I decided it would be fun to surprise you. I wish I could've made it for your birthday, but I couldn't get away until today." She turned to Nicki. "I booked the ticket before I found out the second bedroom was occupied."

He translated Diane's implied question: *Has it recently become available because you'll be sharing his?*

"The sofa bed's pretty nice," he said. "My parents say so, anyway."

Diane laughed. "Your parents sleep in hammocks and tents with dirt floors all over the world," she said. "I can't compete with that. I'm a princess. You know that."

"All right," he said, clapping his hands together. He didn't know why he was in such a hurry. Nicki would be in her room, alone, without him—by request.

"I'll take the sofa," he said with a sigh. "You can have my—"

"Don't be silly," Diane said. "I got my own place. I'm right down the hall."

"Oh." He ran his hand through his hair. Something odd was going on, but his brain wasn't functioning at its best. Nicki had just tucked her hair behind her ear, which reminded him of how he'd licked, nibbled, and kissed that lobe just hours ago.

"You two probably want to catch up," Nicki said. What must she be thinking? "I'm wiped out. Time for me to crash. Thanks for your help today, Ansel. Nice to meet you, Diane. See you both tomorrow, I suppose." Then she waved at them both, as if they were a unit, and walked off to her room.

I suppose?

Diane kicked his bag off a chair and draped her sweater off the back of it, smiling at him over her shoulder. "How about some herbal tea?"

"Sure." Rubbing his jaw, he went to the cupboard for a mug. How much was he going to tell Diane? He wasn't a kiss-and-tell kind of guy, but he wasn't a sneak, either. Deciding he'd figure it out tomorrow, he said, "Did you really come just for my birthday?"

"Not just any birthday. You've been freaking out for months. How'd it go?"

"It wasn't so bad." He wondered if Nicki would be willing to go back to that waterfall and finish the drive.

"You've been dreading it all year," she said. "How could I let my best friend suffer all by himself?"

He filled Diane's mug with water and put it in the microwave. "I wasn't by myself."

Knowing him as well as she did, she read his look and smirked. "What'd you do?"

"Hana Highway."

"Again?"

"She's never been here before."

"Ansel to the rescue." She wagged her finger at him. "Hey, I got you something." She marched over to her laptop bag, took out a package wrapped in silver paper, and held it out to him with a confident smile.

He took the mug out of the microwave and dunked the tea bag into it before taking the present from her. "Another book?"

"Be quiet. Just open it."

"Your tea's ready."

Leaning against the counter, he tugged off the ribbon and tore apart the paper to reveal a best-selling book on executive mind control and world domination. A smooth-faced old man with gleaming eyes like laser beams was on the cover. Ansel looked up at her; she watched him eagerly. "Thanks," he said.

"To help you with your business," she said.

"Right. It looks great."

"It really helped me. I know it looks cheesy, but there's some really profound stuff in there. Promise me you'll read it." She poked him in the shoulder. "Promise."

Diane was great, of course, but she was at it again. What did she want him to do now? Apply to law school? Run for Congress? It was always something. "I don't promise you anything, you know that. You're too pushy."

Her smile tightened. "You love me and you know it."

"I do. I'd probably be stoned and pregnant without you," he said. "Like the day we met."

"That's better. Now where's that tea?" She got it and found a chair in the living room. "This unit's a lot smaller than I remember. You should upgrade, get your own place."

"I'll get right on that." He reached into his back pocket, pulled out his wallet. "Let's see… I've got about fifteen bucks. Guess I'll have to give up the ocean view." His dark, hot thoughts drifted to the cabana.

Worth every penny.

She reached over and slapped the book. "Read it. Imagine what you want and go for it."

What he wanted didn't involve vacation property. Unless Nicki was inside it, naked and aggressive again. "How long are you staying?" he asked.

"At least a week, maybe longer. Can you believe it? I haven't had a real vacation in years," she said. "And by the way, you really should act happier about seeing me."

"Sorry," he said. "Long day." He took the couch next to her. Diane had been one of the first friends he'd made after he'd left his fraternity—the morning after he'd almost slept with "Mickey"—and as overwhelming as she could be, he'd always liked her. Their brief fling had been comically awkward, two complete sex acts in as many weeks, but they'd recovered. Now she treated him like a brother, which was a familiar relationship for him, and over the years he'd appreciated her loyalty. His family's money didn't impress her, since she was driven to amass her own, and he never got the feeling she wanted anything from him but himself.

"I hope you had a decent birthday." She smiled at him over the rim of her mug. "You were nice to me on mine. I wanted to return the favor."

He frowned. "I didn't do anything."

"You did." She sipped.

"What?"

"You got me chocolate."

"I do that every year," he said.

"Well, I like it."

"I do the same for Rachel." He flinched. "Shoot, I forgot this year. I better overnight her something from Belgium." He got out his phone and pulled up his favorite online chocolate supplier in the browser. Giving chocolate to women was like giving hundred dollar bills to criminals. Always the right gesture.

There's an idea.

Diane caught him staring at the wall of Nicki's bedroom as he wondered if she liked dark or milk. And would nuts be too provocative?

"Well, I am wiped out," she said, getting to her feet. "I'd hoped to get here in time to take you to dinner, but let's make it brunch, all right? There's a place in Lahaina that got written up in the *Times*."

He didn't register what Diane had said until she was pulling open the front door. "I'll come by at ten," she said. "You should probably wear a suit jacket. No tie, it's the islands, but it never hurts to look good. And invite your roommate. I'm curious to talk to her."

It was an old joke that his mother and Diane had a few personality traits in common. He didn't usually put up a fight, but he could when he needed to. Jumping up to catch her at the front door, he said, "No, just us." He could save Nicki that discomfort, at least. "And it'll have to be later, more like one. I have plans in the morning."

"Really?"

"Yep."

"All right, see you then." She started to walk away, then turned suddenly and kissed him on the cheek. "Happy Birthday, Ansel. Your life is just beginning."

Nicki moved away from her bedroom door, where she'd been listening to Ansel's conversation with his BFF on the other side.

Not her proudest moment, eavesdropping like that, but at least she'd managed to overcome the temptation until just a few minutes before Diane had left.

Just us?

She ran a hand through her tangled hair.

Your life is just beginning?

It had been a very long, exhausting day. She'd overcome her deepest fears to save a boy from drowning and then made wild love in a luxurious tropical cabana.

Just thinking about it made her skin tingle.

In fact, if she hadn't freaked out, they'd still be there right now. Diane would be knocking fruitlessly on the condo door, waiting, waiting, and waiting some more.

An unfamiliar feeling came over Nicki. She'd had what—whom—another woman wanted.

But did she really have him? Maybe she should find him right now and climb in bed with him to stake her claim.

Just us, he'd told Diane. He'd made a date with her.

No, Nicki thought, getting out her pajamas. She'd spend the night alone. If he hopped into bed with Diane tonight, he wasn't a claim worth staking.

Chapter 21

Around midnight, Ansel gave up trying to sleep. He pulled on shorts and went down to the lobby before he did something stupid. Nicki's room was quiet. She'd closed the door. He got the message.

Downstairs, he found a padded wicker armchair under a palm behind the fountain and called Brand.

His friend picked up on the fifth ring. "Ansel?" he croaked.

"Oh, did I wake you?"

"I'm still in Chicago. Do you realize what time it is here?" Brand let out a noisy sigh. "God, I'd just fallen asleep, too."

Justice was sweet. Ansel put his feet up on an ottoman. "I need some advice."

"Don't do it."

"Don't do what?" Ansel asked.

"Whatever it is."

"What if I was talking about the property you want to buy, and I was thinking maybe you were right?"

"Actually, I'd just decided to cave on that," Brand said.

"Really?"

"I asked around. Apparently, it's not just the tourists who

like to look at the ocean. Stupid to buy a property on the beach that faces the wrong way."

Shoot. The afternoon with Nicki had reminded him how nice it was to have buckets of surplus cash lying around. If he put up his share for the oceanfront unit, he'd have just enough savings to live on for the rest of the year. "On the other hand," Ansel said, "it's a lot more money up front. Money we don't necessarily have."

Brand cursed under his breath. Ansel could hear a bed creaking, footsteps, a door banging, then the sound of pee striking a toilet bowl. "Couldn't this wait until the morning?"

"Now you know how I feel."

The line went dead.

If his ruthless friend hadn't woken him up so many times, he might've let him sleep. But that was so very much not the case. He pressed Brand's number again.

"There's something else," Ansel said when he answered.

"I'm turning off my phone," Brand said. "You only call me this late when you're about to get laid."

"Hey." Ansel looked around to make sure he was alone. "If that were true, I would've called you yesterday."

Brand groaned. "And now you want to gloat."

"I don't know what I want."

"All right. What's her name?"

"That's a funny story right there," Ansel said.

"Do you realize what time it is here?"

"Buy me a watch. For my birthday."

"Sounds like you need a calendar." Brand's voice was muffled, perhaps by a pillow.

"Can't you pretend to listen to me for a second?"

"Dude, I'm tired. I had dinner with a guy who spent two hours trying to sell me a thousand stainless steel commercial kitchen sinks. For you. I assured him your friend Jordan was unlikely to be expanding at that level for quite some time, but he had me pinned in a corner and refused to believe it."

"Maybe he found you attractive. You've got that scar on your chin. Very sexy."

"Shut up."

"Seriously, I need your help," Ansel said.

"I've been helping you all day."

Time to pull out the ace. "Diane is here." There. Brand wouldn't hang up on him now. He hated Diane the way an ex-smoker hated cigarettes. One night had ruined him for life, Brand liked to say.

"'Here,' where?"

"Here in Maui," Ansel replied. "At the resort."

"Why?"

"She's visiting me."

"Just happened to be in the neighborhood?"

"She wanted to surprise me. In honor of my birthday. Unlike some people, I might add."

"*I* sent you something."

"Your assistant sent an email. Very thoughtful. No wonder the restaurant men love you so much. All that sensitivity so close to the surface is hard to resist."

"At least it was on time," Brand said. "How long is she staying?"

"I'm not sure. A while, I think."

"What about her job?"

"I didn't ask."

"Don't you think it's strange she would show up on a weekday?" Brand sounded fully awake now. "When's the last time she took a vacation?"

"It's been a while."

"Five years," Brand said.

"So, she was overdue."

"Yeah," Brand said. Then his voice dropped. "Is *she* the woman you slept with?"

Ansel recoiled. "Of course not!"

There was a long pause. Brand's tone returned to normal. "Then who's the lucky lady?"

"A friend of Rachel's. I've been sharing the condo with her."

"Since when?"

"Didn't I tell you about that? Rachel gave her the family condo for the summer. I'm not really supposed to be here. So, we had to share."

"And then you had sex with her."

"It's more complicated than that."

"You strain my imagination," Brand said.

"Turns out… we knew each other in college." He cleared his throat. "Once."

"Christ on a cracker."

"We didn't actually sleep together, but when you're eighteen… I've never forgotten her."

"Except it sounds like you kind of did," Brand said. "What's her name?"

"Mickey. I mean, Nicki."

"True love, is it?"

"Shut up."

"My advice? Keep your dick in your pants for once. Especially around Diane."

Ansel laughed softly. "You poor loser. Still have a thing for her, don't you?"

"Tell Jenny I'm on board with the new property," he said. "I'll call the mortgage broker about adjusting the loan." Then the line went dead.

Nicki got out a loaf of white bread, two eggs, a carton of milk, sugar, and looked around the cupboard for vanilla, without which the French toast would taste terrible, but all she could find was a bottle of peppermint extract.

Even with a full night's sleep, she was a below-average cook; with two hours spread over eight, she dropped to the bottom fifth percentile of the cooking population.

There were only three items she had mastered, one for each mealtime: French toast for breakfast, grilled cheese for lunch, and pizza for dinner. Obviously, there was some flexibility there with lunch and dinner, but she kept it simple to maximize success. She was like that one guy you knew who could play one simplified Scott Joplin song on the piano but nothing else.

"There's no vanilla," she muttered. And there wasn't enough bread for Diane if she showed up.

Of course she would show up. The woman would probably arrive in lingerie and heels.

Just friends.

Oh, men. So clueless. So, so clueless.

How long had Diane been in love with him? How many times had she shown up like this when Ansel was with another woman?

Nicki almost felt guilty. She knew what it felt like to love a friend, and Ansel obviously had no idea about Diane's feelings, or he'd show a little sensitivity. He'd probably already told her about their hookup yesterday, and now Diane was going into red alert mode. She was going to style that perfect bob of hers until it shone like a Roman battle helmet.

Nicki put on her running shoes, shoved a pair of twenties in her pocket, and ran out to buy some pastries from the shop downstairs. It wasn't until she was handing over the cash and waiting for her pennies in change before she realized she'd taken the elevator.

Well, that was something. To celebrate, she ate a chunk of banana bread on the way back up—silently daring the elevator to break as she chewed—and was pulling out the rest of the piece when the door opened.

"Good morning!" Diane said.

She was jogging in place as she waited for the elevator. She wasn't wearing lingerie, but the jogging bra and stretchy shorts were skimpier than Nicki's bikini.

"Hi," Nicki said, mouth full, stepping off the elevator with the pastry box in her arms. "It's a beautiful day for a run." No reason she couldn't be friendly.

"I hate it, actually, but it must be done." Diane reached inside and hit a button that froze the elevator in place. "Oh, I can smell that from here. Banana bread?"

Nicki nodded, waiting for Diane to moan about her weight, her inability to eat. She was the kind of woman whose abs had abs. Or maybe those bumps were her small intestines. Not much covering the organs down there.

"Save me a piece?" Diane asked.

"Really? Sure."

"Hide it from Ansel. He'll eat mine, even if you tell him it's for me. Cover it with a napkin and put it somewhere he won't look."

Nicki couldn't help but laugh. "Okay. I promise."

"I could get my own, of course, but I don't have my wallet on me, and I'm lazy." Diane jogged into the elevator and hit the button. "Thanks!"

The doors closed between them; Nicki returned to the condo, wondering if she'd be able to stop herself from liking Diane. It would be easier not to. No matter what happened with Ansel.

Pastry box in her arms, she unlocked the door and pushed it in with her knee.

"Diane?" Ansel asked.

She froze. "No, it's me."

He came around the corner, hair mussed, bottled water in his hand, shirtless. When he saw the box, he let out a breath. "Hi."

"Hi." He looked like something that should be inside a pastry box. His chest hair was like chocolate and vanilla sprinkles. "I was getting breakfast," she said.

"I thought you'd left."

She went into the kitchen and put the box on the counter. Maybe she'd had only a few hours of sleep, but she suddenly felt wide awake. "Left in what way?"

"In a scary way."

She felt a pang of unease. "Without a suitcase? Or all of my clothes?" Was he suggesting she had a reason to take off?

"I figured you weren't naked or anything," he said, "just that you'd gone out and didn't plan on coming back anytime soon."

Maybe she'd been too relaxed about his gal pal showing up. "I saw Diane at the elevator." She scanned his face for guilt or deceit but found neither.

He simply nodded and put the water down. "She tried to get me to run with her. I thought she'd come back for another shot." Then he met her eyes, holding them with a suggestive smile. "You know I'm not much of a runner."

She felt desire blast through her body like a backdraft in a burning skyscraper. "You're okay," she said in a low voice.

"Okay?" He approached, never dropping her gaze. His bare toes bumped hers inside their flip-flops. He tilted his head back and smiled that lopsided grin at her.

"Yeah. You're okay," she said.

He slid a hand behind her neck. "How about you?" he asked softly. "Are you okay?"

"I'm great." As her heart began pounding, his fingers tangled in her hair. "Fantastic," she added in a whisper.

His other hand settled at her waist, lightly stroking the band of bare skin under her shirt. "I agree." Then he leaned closer and dragged his lips across her cheek. His breath was hot on her mouth, where he lingered. "Are you still feeling like you'd like to be alone?"

Her hands trembled so violently, she wouldn't have been able to write her name. "The way an antelope would like to be alone," she admitted, closing her eyes. She didn't know why it was so different from yesterday, why she would be afraid now and not then.

"But antelopes are herding animals," he said, moving his mouth to her throat. He licked the hollow where her pulse skittered at the surface.

"Says the cheetah." But he smelled like a man, like a fantasy. She tunneled her hands through his hair and let out a ragged sigh.

"Meow." He opened his mouth and bit the side of her neck.

She moaned. *Oh, God.* Desire melted the fear, erasing the awkward hours between when he'd pulled away from her, sleepy and satisfied—and now.

She rubbed her body against his, searching for his mouth with hers, and in a hot second he was pushing her up against the back of the front door, hands everywhere, no more joking.

"Nicki," he gasped against her mouth. He lifted her shirt above her bra, rough and fast, as he drove his tongue into her mouth. "You're… killing me."

She could do this; she could have fun without thinking herself into a panic attack. A bout of hyperventilation was proof she was doing the right thing. Just like swimming, bridges, flying, and elevators, sex was an everyday activity she needed to master. Like therapy. Not just once. Constant, consistent exposure was key.

Every day, every hour, every minute, every second…

He fell to his knees, hooked his fingers over the waistband of her shorts, and yanked them down to her ankles. The door was firm and smooth under her spine, holding her up when her own legs would've failed her. He didn't start where he'd gone yesterday, which had been perfectly perfect, but at her calves. As he lightly kissed her navel, his fingertips stroked the backs of her knees, tickling their way upward, spiraling over the flesh of her thighs. Then his hands were under the thin fabric, capturing her bottom, pulling her to his face.

He pleasured her without ever taking off her underwear. Through the nylon, rubbing and licking, which she would've sworn was impossible, but his mouth and fingers were everywhere, using the barrier to tease and push her higher, up, over.

After she came, she slid down to the floor as if she'd been shot. Blasted in the heart, the head, she sat in a daze.

It was at that moment that Diane rang the bell, knocking at the same time. "Okay, guys, I admit it," she called out. "I'm lazy. I want my banana bread now."

Nicki could feel the door vibrate under Diane's knuckles. Nicki's gaze met Ansel's, checking again for any doubt in his face but finding nothing but frustration. Sitting back on his heels, he hung his head and clutched his knees. Blood flow had resumed to Nicki's brain, so she was the one to stand up first, pulling her underwear and shorts over her hips as she moved.

Diane knocked again. "I know you're eating mine, Ansel."

Choking down a laugh, he staggered to his feet. "Not yours," he mumbled, palming his fly. "I need a minute. Just a minute." Then he strode off to his room while Nicki did a quick check that no culturally inappropriate body parts were on display before opening the door.

"Hey, sorry," Nicki said. "I was in the bathroom."

Diane walked in, eyes scanning the living room, the hallway, the kitchen. "He's hiding like a dog, isn't he?" But then she seemed to see the unopened box on the kitchen counter, and her smile froze. For a moment, she didn't move. She must've been running for a few minutes, at least, because every inch of her toned body was shiny with sweat, like a fitness model sprayed with water for a photo shoot.

Nicki walked past her and took out a few plates, pride at war with sympathy. "I'll give you the biggest piece."

Diane still hadn't moved. Nicki felt her watching her as she went to the sink. It had occurred to her that she should wash her hands. She lathered for the full length of the birthday song, as they taught in school, then dried her hands on a fresh towel. As she lifted the box lid, Ansel wandered in with a towel slung around his neck.

"Hey, Diane," he said. "That was fast."

Diane responded in a cheerful voice. "I ran into Nicki at the elevator carrying banana bread. I only made it a mile before I had to run back."

"She didn't think I'd be able to stop you from eating all of it," Nicki said. The double entendre caught in her throat, and she had to turn and grimace at the wall instead of breaking down with nervous laughter.

"Listen, Diane…" Ansel began. "Nicki and I—"

"Had plans for breakfast," Diane finished. "Obviously. But I came all this way, so you can share. I'll take mine to go." She punched him in the shoulder, smiling so broadly her back molars were visible. And then holding it there as if a bungee cord were wrapped around the back of her head, hooked into each corner of her mouth.

"No, don't go," Nicki said. The welcoming, reassuring skills she'd honed from years of teaching kicked in. "Let me get you a plate. You can tell me about your job. Ansel says you've got a great career, but he didn't say what—"

"It doesn't matter," Diane said. "It's all the same, isn't it? Corporations that take your youth, all your dreams and energy, until what passion you had on your first day on the job has been squeezed out of you like shit out of a toad." She was still smiling, but her eyes were haunted.

"Jeez, Diane, what happened?" Ansel asked.

"Excuse me," Nicki said, "but I think I should leave you two alone so you can catch up. Time for me to take a shower anyway, start my day. You know."

"But your breakfast—" Diane said.

Nicki was already at her bedroom door. "I'm fine, I ate in the elevator. But thanks." Then she was inside, leaning against the door, just like before.

She'd just had the best morning of her life. She could afford to share Ansel with his unlucky, unhappy friend.

Chapter 22

$\mathcal{A}$nsel watched Nicki disappear into her bedroom.
Again.

Watching her lose it like that, head falling back against the door…

Fifteen feet away. She was only right there on the other side of the wall, so close…

"I lost my job," Diane said behind him. Banana bread muffled her words.

He spun around. She looked serious. "What?"

She took his piece of banana bread from him and shoved it into her mouth. "It's no big deal."

"Did you say you lost your job?"

"I knew you'd overreact."

This from a woman who had more books on career planning than a college job placement office.

"That wasn't overreacting," he said, clutching his skull and stretching his face into *The Scream* expression. "Oh my God! You're going to die!"

She rolled her eyes. "Thanks."

"*That* was overreacting," he said.

After a sigh, she opened the fridge. "Do you have any unsweetened organic coconut water?"

"No, because I'm not—" *A yuppie poser*, he was going to say, before he saw her face: red, splotchy cheeks, lips sucked in between her teeth, eyes staring straight ahead. "Are you crying?"

She slammed the fridge door and turned away. "Jet lag. I didn't sleep well last night. You know how I get if I'm sleep deprived. Stupid, emotional. Stupid." She wiped her eyes with the back of her wrist.

"Talk to me." He remembered how Brand had asked why she was taking a vacation. And yet he, her best friend, had been too obtuse to question her.

"Usual story. We—well, not we anymore—got bought out. New people shut us down."

"And they just dumped everyone?"

She nodded. "We were redundant."

"That's disgusting."

"It's just business." She lifted her head, breathing deep. "You can't expect an intelligent corporation to pay a hundred people to do the same thing as another hundred people."

"People aren't interchangeable like widgets," he said.

Smiling pityingly at him, she patted his arm. "Sure they are."

"I thought you knew better than that," he said. "At least about yourself. Since when did you get humble?"

"Just being realistic."

"You think you're no better than anybody else?" he asked. "You? Diane Gambau, power human?"

"Maybe I'm tired of trying to be perfect."

"We all have our crosses to bear," he said.

"I'm ready to find some meaning in my life." She combed her hair with her fingers and then frowned at a loose strand she'd pulled out. "I'm glad I got laid off. It made me realize I was spinning my wheels, just a hamster in a cage, going nowhere." Her voice caught.

He looked for tears, alarmed at the thought of Diane without a steady income. Entirely self-made, oldest daughter of a single mom who still worked on commission at a discount furniture chain, Diane was insufferable if any hint of poverty was snapping at her heels.

Why had she flown out to see him if she'd just lost her job? "This trip," he said. "Taking the time, the money…"

"I don't want to talk about this anymore." She turned to him, chin raised. "It was just a job. I'm here to see you and have a nice time, and that's what I'm going to do. Today, we'll have an early lunch and tour the island. Rent a board, get a drink, be irresponsible for once."

His worry deepened. That didn't sound like the Diane he knew. "Let me pay for the condo. I don't know exactly how much this place costs, but…"

"You've got less money than I do now, and I've already paid for it, and I am *not* going to talk about this anymore."

He knew that tone. She was freaking out but refused to admit it. "I'm not broke."

"You are for a while. Look, Ansel—you want to do something for me, spend the day with me. Put on something decent, and let's pretend we're young again."

"We are young."

"You know what I mean." She walked to the front door. "I'll be ready in twenty minutes. We can take my car. I've already made reservations for lunch. Okay? Great."

<hr>

THEY DIDN'T GET BACK to the condo until after seven that evening. Diane was drunk; Ansel was sober but exhausted. Late night, bad sleep, early morning. And all he could think about was: *what's Nicki doing right now, and how can I do it with her?*

Slumped in the corner of the elevator, Diane stared at the ceiling, singing a pop song in perfect pitch with a smile on her face. She was barefoot and dangled one sandal from each index finger. Her black sundress had slipped off one shoulder, exposing a lacy gray bra strap.

He'd seen her this wasted a few times before, usually after a bad breakup, but during those times she hadn't been so *cheerful.* All day today she'd been laughing and telling jokes, the first to run out into the sand when they got to the beach, the last to want to leave when the rain started.

And of course she'd had to order everything on the menu that had an umbrella stuck into it, which, at a tourist bar in Maui, included even the broccoli.

Ansel wanted to get her safely tucked in bed as soon as possible so he could get back to Nicki. When they reached their floor, he banged on the door open button impatiently.

"You already slept with her, didn't you?"

He spun around to find Diane standing right behind him. She was petite, only a few inches over five feet, which contributed to her presently excessive blood alcohol level, and he had to press his chin to his chest to look her in the eye. She edged closer. "I thought you said you were going to fly solo for a while," she added.

He stepped out of the elevator and held out an arm for her. He'd been waiting for her to ask about Nicki, but she never had. Now was definitely not the time. "Let's get you in bed."

"Not with you," she said, scowling the way drunk people do to prove how sober they really are.

He paused near the stairwell. "Nope. All by yourself."

"Because you want to be with *her.*"

He was glad they were alone. This was just Diane being possessive, the way a child would be of her favorite toy—

nothing more. "No," he said slowly, "because you and I are friends."

"I like friends." She sighed.

"I like friends, too."

"I have lots of friends," she added.

"That's good."

"You're not like them, though." She leaned one shoulder against the wall and gazed up at him.

He blanked. Could he possibly be wrong about her? She'd never hinted, not once, that she wanted to sleep with him. Even in college, it had been his idea to have sex; afterward, she'd been so unimpressed with him, she'd refused to see him under any circumstances for a few weeks. Only after he'd promised he wouldn't try to have sex with her ever again did their friendship resume. His ego had taken six months to recover.

"I'm not like them, that's true," he said to her now, trying to lighten it up. "I'm better. That's what you mean. I'm the most awesome."

She nodded. "I think we should get married."

Chapter 23

"Oh my God," Ansel said under his breath. He took Diane's arm and tried to haul her around the corner to their hallway. "You need to sleep this off ASAP." Get married? What had they put in that lava flow?

She wouldn't move. Her barefoot toes gripped the tile. "Alone?"

"I don't know who else you know in Maui, but I won't be there," he replied. "And you don't want me to be."

She tilted her head back and looked down her nose at him, frowning the drunk frown again. "It might help you sleep better. Your insomnia really gets out of hand, Ansel. I wish you'd see a specialist."

That was the Diane he knew and loved.

As a *friend*.

"One thing that helps," he said, pulling out his phone, "is keeping to a schedule. Boy, it's late. I should be hitting the hay right about now." He flashed the time at her, pretended to yawn, then followed it up with an even larger real one.

"Yeah," she said, yawning too. "It's the middle of the night in California." She yawned again and slumped against him.

Then she did let him guide her around the corner, no more talk of marriage.

She was drunk, that's all.

God, he hoped so.

Because he kept a wary eye on her as they started walking again, he didn't recognize the man in the hallway until they were about ten feet away.

Leaning against the wall between both of their doors, cell phone in one hand, suitcase at his feet, Brand Henry Warren looked up at them and scowled. "Where the hell have you been?"

HER NEXT BLOG post would have to skirt the real issues, Nicki decided. What she wanted to write was: *Sex is great, you should try it, the end.* Instead, she wrote about wet suits and the importance of mastering the dead man's float.

Her heart wasn't in it. Would anyone notice? Who read this stuff, anyway? Fellow anxiety sufferers or just random bored people on the Internet? She didn't allow comments on her page, for her own sanity—she didn't need strangers to tell her she was nuts—but sometimes she thought she wasn't helping anyone, just setting herself up as comic relief. A bad example to soothe the insecure.

While she typed the last word—which described the moment of triumph when she returned to the boat, not when the water pitcher fell to the floor and she took off her clothes— she heard the condo's front door creak open and slam shut.

Finally. It was 9:43 p.m. Distracted by the thought of him, she'd been trying to write a single blog post for two hours.

He tapped on the door. "Nicki?"

Her lungs emptied and shut down.

"Nicki?"

Reboot. Inhale. "Yeah?" She tried to sound casually interrupted, not in the midst of erotically-charged cardiac arrest. "You can open the door." Because God knew her legs weren't ready to support her weight.

He peeked in. "I'm sorry."

"For what?"

"For disappearing all day. Diane had a bit of an emergency. Since she came all this way…"

"I figured."

"Look, I was about to make a drink. Would you like one?"

The look on his face was grimmer than she'd ever seen him. She sat up taller. "Are you all right?"

"Not really," he said.

She got off the bed, readjusting her satin robe. She was glad she'd gone shopping before her trip, otherwise she'd be wearing her dad's forty-year-old college sweatshirt and her oldest pair of XL granny panties. "Diane?" she asked.

He leaned against the doorway and tilted his head back. "Yeah, that too."

"Tell me about it while you make the drinks."

He sighed. "Okay."

In the kitchen, he got out a carton of juice from the fridge while she climbed on a stool across from him at the breakfast counter. The blender was already out, its lid off, sitting next to a bunch of speckled bananas. He got out other cans and bottles from the cupboards, two hurricane glasses, a box of paper umbrellas, and dumped ice and various liquids into the blender without measuring. He looked like a tourist's favorite bartender.

"I just offered my room to Diane," he said, right before he stabbed the blender on at the jet blast level.

Her worst fears surfaced like fart bubbles in a bathtub. When the blender stopped, she said, "Oh."

"She lost her job." He rubbed his face, eyes closed. "That's really bad."

"Yeah." She'd used up what verbal skills she had that night on her writing.

"She won't take it, though. She wants her own place. Even with Brand showing up and insisting on taking her second bedroom."

"What?"

"My partner."

"I know who he is. I mean, why is he here?"

"Brand Henry Warren has decided I'm incapable of making big manly business decisions without him holding my hand." He poured the frothy drink into two glasses. "And he's out for revenge."

She accepted the glass he held out and tried to focus. "He's that mad just because you don't want the same building he wants?" He'd mentioned the properties when they'd driven back from Wailea.

"Not revenge on me. On Diane." He unfurled a paper umbrella and impaled a small wedge of pineapple before dunking it in her glass.

After a sip, she admitted, "I'm confused."

"He's still bitter about a fling they flung a few years ago."

"Ah."

"He's taking her second bedroom. She refused to take mine. So I left."

"Maybe she wants him to be there," Nicki said.

"I don't think so. She was just too drunk to argue." As he stirred his drink with a long spoon, his voice fell. "We'll find out tomorrow when she sobers up."

He looked unhappy again. She took a longer sip, wondering what to say. It was sweet, more of a smoothie than a drink. "Is there any alcohol in this?"

"Oh. No. Sorry." He reached up into a cabinet and gazed up into it, his back to her. "What do you want?" His gray shirt pulled across his broad shoulders, making her hesitate for a moment.

She put her nose in her glass. "Whatever you're having."

"I'm having a virgin." There was a pause. Grabbing a bottle of rum, he turned, smiling faintly, and leaned against the counter. "How about you?"

Shivers tickled her spine. "I'm fine."

"Some people think they're too sweet."

The glass wasn't nearly big enough to hide her face in. "Not always."

Nodding, he put the pitcher in the sink. "Sadly true. They do have their own way of making you feel like crap the next morning."

She gulped down a rich, frothy mouthful. "But you get over it."

Another, longer pause. Staring at the counter, he took a drink and wiped the foam off of his lips with the back of his hand. "Not necessarily."

Her glass made a loud noise when she dropped it on the counter. "Oh, please. You didn't even recognize me."

"You dyed your hair." He pointed at her, serious now. "And you were wearing glasses."

"What are you, Lois Lane? Suddenly a pair of glasses is an impenetrable disguise?"

His frown turned into a sheepish laugh. He took another drink. "Good one."

"Thanks."

His gaze dropped to the opening of her robe. "I'd be over there right now ravishing you, but I'm tired and pissed off, and I thought you'd be better off without me."

"That's not it. My hair's down, so you didn't know who I was."

He laughed. Then they gazed at each other over the counter for a few hot seconds.

"I know who you are," he said in a low voice.

She slid off the stool. "Took you long enough." Then she took his hand and pulled him into her bedroom.

———

At 3:34 A.M., Ansel watched Nicki sleep, wishing he could do the same.

Diane was right: having a warm body next to him helped. But tonight, thinking about the woman who owned that warm body was keeping him awake.

He'd inherited insomnia from his maternal grandfather. His mom said it must've skipped a generation, since she and her sister never had any problems sleeping at any time whatsoever, but that their dad had always complained about sleeping troubles.

It wasn't usually this bad. The last time Ansel had had this many bad nights in a row was in college. But it wasn't getting bad grades that killed him then; it was giving up the partying. He'd given *that* up the night he'd almost slept with a girl—again—who was almost as drunk as he was. He'd left the fraternity a week later.

Mickey, he'd thought her name was.

He rubbed a strand of her hair between his fingers, tempted to wake her for more sex. Laughter. The sound of her voice.

Grandfather Jury hadn't only been an insomniac. His mom didn't like to talk about her childhood much, and with the arrogant optimism of his own happy existence, he hadn't thought much about it until she told him one morning, when he was just eighteen, that he'd better be careful. "You take after him in some ways," she'd told him. "Lots of good ways. But maybe not all good."

She went on to say a lot of nice things about Grandpa's intelligence and charm, but all he heard was the bad stuff. Even Ansel, with only photographs to go by, could see he was the spitting image of the old man—their build, the gray eyes. And this was the same man that, for as long as his mom could remember, had drunk himself to sleep. Every night. As her father got older, the nights and days became less distinct; family life deteriorated.

"So take care of yourself," his mom had said. Then, smiling, she assured him his fate was in his hands, nurture wasn't nature, and she trusted him to ask for help if he needed it. "Love you, study hard, see you at Thanksgiving."

Thanks, Mom.

So he didn't drink anymore. He didn't take medicine to knock him out, either; his mother's words had haunted him as much as sleep deprivation.

Eventually, around five, he left Nicki's bed and stepped out on the balcony to watch the sunrise. He waited until the sun was up completely before showering, getting dressed, and heading down the hall to call a surprise business meeting.

It took a couple of minutes of knocking on the brass pineapple before the door flew open. "What the hell?" Diane stood there with half of her hair pointing at San Francisco and the other half at Tokyo.

"Good morning," he said. "I'm here to see Brand."

"Why is he here? Answer me why a big important pain in the ass like him has to sleep in my condo?" she asked. "I don't even have a job."

"Can I come in?" Ansel asked.

"Fuck if I care." She buried her face in her hands and groaned. "Fuckity fuck, what did I drink last night?"

Brand appeared behind her, arms crossed over his chest.

He was already dressed, unfortunately; Ansel had been hoping for boxers and red eye. Maybe he could wake him up the next day, when his jet lag had worn off.

"You've got two bedrooms in this unit, Di," Brand said. "I was going to stay at the Westin, but this way I can keep an eye on my partner over there."

Ansel gave him a look that said, *you're so full of crap*. He wanted to keep an eye on somebody, all right.

"It's not just the bed or the bathroom, which is bad enough," Diane said. "He's breathing my air."

"Open a window," Brand said. "Besides, you said last night it was all right."

"I'm having second thoughts," Diane said.

"It's about time," Brand said in a low voice.

As Diane turned red, Ansel took her by the shoulders and moved her out of the way so he could step inside. "I'll protect you."

"Let's trade," Diane said. "You take him, I'll take Nicki."

"I like this unit better," Brand said. "The natural fabrics don't irritate my environmental sensitivities."

"You're about as sensitive to the environment as an oil executive," Ansel said.

"See? Get out," Diane said. "Tell Nicki I give great pedicures."

A pornographic lesbian daydream launched in Ansel's brain. "Uh…"

"He doesn't want her to move out," Brand said. "It would make it harder to have sex with her."

Diane went into the kitchen and took a liter of diet Coke out of the fridge. "You think I didn't know that?" She lifted the bottle to her lips.

"They go way back, you know," Brand said.

Ansel went over to him. "Shut up now."

Lowering the bottle, she said, "I thought she just showed up last week."

"He knew her in college," Brand said.

Diane turned to Ansel. "Why didn't you tell me?"

"Didn't come up."

"But he told *you* all about it?" she asked Brand.

"He tried to." Brand kicked back on the couch and put his hands behind his head. "That's how I found out you were here, though accidentally, since he called to talk about *her*."

The hurt on Diane's face made Ansel take a step backward. She hated to be the last to know anything. "Tell you what. I'm early. Much too early. I'll go out for some coffee, maybe a few breakfast pastries, fresh fruit, and by the time I come back, everyone will be happy and normal again."

"Since when is being happy normal for either one of us?" Diane muttered.

"I'll take the biggest coffee they've got, cream, no sugar," Brand said. "Something high protein to go with it, maybe a hard-boiled egg and some nuts if you can find them."

Ansel didn't really want to do any business. His goal, showing Brand he was up and working early—even earlier than Brand—had been accomplished. "Sure, no problem." He waved and ducked out into the hall before Diane could argue.

He only made it as far as the elevator before Brand caught up to him, a black messenger bag slung across his chest, and thumped him on the back. "Watch out for that one. She's got plans for you."

"You've never even met her," Ansel said.

"I mean Diane. She's not the type to spend her nest egg on a vacation," Brand said, "even if she hadn't just lost her only source of income."

"You think she wants in on the business deal?"

"No, Ansel," Brand said tightly. "She wants in on you."

The elevator arrived. It was already filled with a family

who had accidentally taken it up to the top floor on their way to the pool; Ansel had to stew for three long, angry minutes until they were walking into the foyer before he could reply.

He took Brand by the arm. "Hold on, you can't just say something like that and walk away."

"I'm not walking away, I'm walking with."

"Great, I choose a partner who had to go to both law school *and* business school," Ansel muttered.

"Why'd she get so drunk last night?"

"Those fruity drinks are stronger than they look."

"How many did she drink?"

Five and a half. At least. But Ansel said, "A few."

"She was trying to get up her courage. You didn't make it easy, having a new girlfriend right there in your condo. Has she met her yet?"

Ansel wondered if Brand was the one who'd been drinking. "Yes. They got along great."

"That's all part of her plan. Just you wait. I hope Mickey likes you enough to stick around once Diane gets going. She's your best bet for staying out of a bad marriage."

"Nicki," Ansel said.

Brand adjusted Ansel's collar, his face hardening. "Promise me. When Diane makes her move, think about what *you* want, not just what *she* wants, or thinks she wants," he said. "You have this bad habit of giving too much. Just this once, say no."

First Diane, now Brand. What the hell was the matter with them? "Listen," he said. "Diane and I will never, ever, have sex with each other again. We tried it. I know you want her, and I'm sorry she doesn't seem to feel the same way, but it has nothing, nothing, to do with me."

"Who said anything about sex? She just wants the other stuff. She's talked herself into believing that because you love each other, and you're getting old, why not?"

"She said this to you?"

"She didn't have to," Brand said.

"Yeah, she did. That's exactly what she'd have to do for me to believe it."

Brand put his hands on his hips. "You're having a midlife crisis of your own. Settling down with your best friend could seem like a logical next step."

"No," Ansel said.

"It could happen. If you had to marry me or Diane, which would you choose?"

"Is this your apocalyptic vision I'm hearing? Where will we be—an island in the South Pacific? The last remaining cubicle farm in North America as the land around us descends into preindustrial chaos?"

"You'd choose Diane," he said. "It's not that crazy."

"I'm heterosexual. I'd choose that lady over there before I chose you."

Brand glanced over his shoulder. A gaggle of tourists wandered around the potted plants, fountain, padded wicker furniture. "Which one?"

Ansel shrugged. "Doesn't matter. Any one of them. Because I'm not gay."

"You protest too much."

"I thought this was about you getting revenge for that nasty breakup of yours, but now I think you've got to be in love with her." Ansel whacked him on the arm. "Totally around the bend."

Brand didn't laugh. "Maybe I am."

Still wound up, Ansel took a few long seconds before he realized Brand was serious. He was always serious, but this was a different kind of serious.

This was serious in a *chick* kind of way.

"Huh," Ansel said and fell quiet.

"Yeah," Brand said.

"Wow."

"We going to get coffee or what? I'm half dead," Brand said.

They walked out to the front drive in silence. While they were waiting for the valet to get the car, Ansel struggled to think of something appropriate to say. Good luck? Tough break?

They got in the car. When they were on the road, halfway to the coffee shop, Ansel finally thought of something.

"I think I might be in love, too," he said.

Chapter 24

"**W**hat's the matter with her?" Brand asked.

"Excuse me?"

"Something must be the matter with her for you to be getting serious so fast. You have a thing for damaged women."

Ansel braked, nearly causing the car behind him to rear-end the family's vintage hybrid. He clutched the wheel, pulse racing. "What do you mean?"

"Come on. It's always something."

"I don't know what you're talking about." His sister teased him about it, but that didn't mean it was true. He signaled and turned off the road into a complex of shops and boutique hotels, where he parked.

He couldn't look Brand in the eye.

"What's the matter with her?" Brand repeated.

"It's not like that. She's not like..." Not like Anna or Yvonne. The two serious women from his twenties, each very different from the other except for the way they drained him. "She's a teacher. She's funny and smart. Very hot."

"Okay," Brand said. "Forget it."

"Damn it."

"Let's get the coffee." Brand opened the door.

"It's not like before," Ansel said. "She's not a mess."

"I'm sure she's very nice."

Except she *was* a bit of a mess. "She's not an addict. And she doesn't want me for my money."

"Great. We going in?"

"You're just humoring me. You don't believe it."

"I've never met her," Brand said, walking across the lot. "Think this place has anything without sugar in it? I'm trying to cut back. Not getting any younger, you know."

Ansel followed him into the café to the pastry case. He scowled at it without seeing anything. After Brand ordered a box of pineapple fritters, chocolate doughnuts, and banana bread—"they're for Diane"—Ansel looked at him and said, "She's afraid of things."

Brand handed his money to the young girl behind the counter.

"But she's working on it," Ansel said. "She was afraid of water but went snorkeling off a charter boat anyway." He wouldn't mention the stupid life jacket thing; he didn't think it would help his case.

Brand took a deep breath, not looking at him as he put his wallet in his back pocket. "You were there? Helping her?"

"Of course I was—no. This has nothing to do with me. She would've gone without my help."

"Okay," Brand said.

Ansel shoved his hands into his pockets. He didn't want Nicki because she needed his help. It wasn't like that.

"Aloha," the girl said. "What can I get you?"

Ansel stared at her. She had on more makeup than a mime. The beige stuff was caked on at least a quarter inch thick, and her eyelashes looked like tarantula legs. Why did teenagers wear so much makeup these days?

And when did he get so old he talked about teenagers like his father did?

"Coffee," he said. "Venti. You know, biggest you have."

He paid; they returned to the car. Ansel was grinding his molars. He didn't like Nicki *because* she was afraid of stuff. That would make him some creepy, pathetic guy who needed to feel superior because his ego was so weak. Or a guy who'd get off on seeing her overcome her fears and then move on to his next project.

Could Dad be right?

"I think Diane will like this," Brand said, patting the box in his lap. "Since she likes to eat so much."

"I'd like to see you tell her that."

"But she does."

"Add this algorithm into your code," Ansel said. "'If you tell a woman she eats a lot, then she will hate you.'"

"It's not like she's fat."

"You might want to trust me on this one."

Brand looked into the box. "Maybe we should drive down to Safeway for a fruit plate."

"Oh, no. You got her just what she wanted."

"You sure?"

Ansel glanced at him. Brand asking for advice? It had to be love.

Poor guy. Diane hated his guts. No amount of baked goods would fix that. "I'm sure."

"I'm trusting you, man."

"I know. Give her the box, but don't suggest she's going to snarf it all down by herself, even if she does," Ansel said. "And you should take one for yourself so she doesn't feel embarrassed to dig in."

"But... I'm off sugar for a while."

"Tell her that as you're stuffing her face. It'll make her sympathize with your lack of willpower."

Brand frowned at him. "I'm not sure I want to love somebody that irrational."

Ansel drove into the resort, feeling a kinship with Brand he'd never felt before. "I hear you, man," he said, patting him on the shoulder. "I hear you."

NICKI WAS SPRAWLING out on the living room sofa, wearing nothing but a robe and a coffee mug, when Ansel arrived with his friends. She scrambled to her feet, tightened the satin sash, and held out her hand.

"It's nice to meet you." She shook Brand's hand, trying not to stare. He had the bluest eyes she'd ever seen. The rest of him wasn't bad, either. He had dark movie star hair and a cleft chin and was one of those men who, against all odds, made pleated khakis sexy.

"Hope we're not too early," Diane said, making a beeline for the coffeepot in the kitchen. "Even though I know we are, since I'd be asleep if these two losers hadn't woken me up." She had bags under her eyes and still wore sweats and bunny slippers. She lifted the mug to her lips as soon as she poured it.

"Help yourself to the coffee." Ansel smiled at Diane, who was already gulping it down.

"I just brought you some coffee," Brand said.

Diane took another sip. "I needed more."

"Have as much as you like," Nicki said. "I can't handle any more caffeine today."

"I'm familiar with the concept," Diane said, "but must admit I've never experenced it for myself."

Brand turned to Nicki. "So, you and Ansel go way back, I hear?"

Nicki smiled politely, glancing at Ansel. "We met in college. He was visiting Rachel. I'm friends with her."

"Ah," Brand said, as if she'd illuminated a mystery. He didn't elaborate.

Nicki decided it was his turn to face the spotlight. "What brings you to Maui?"

Brand walked over to an armchair near the balcony and sat down. He faced Nicki, but his eyes kept darting to Diane, who'd climbed up on a stool at the breakfast counter. "When I heard Diane was here, I couldn't resist. She and I go way back, too."

"Unfortunately," Diane said, rotating on the seat with the mug at her lips.

"I didn't realize she'd just lost her job," Brand continued. "Maybe she'll have the time to show me around the island. I've never been here. Except on business."

"Sorry," Diane said. "Busy."

Brand smiled. "Aren't you always?"

Diane slid off the stool, went into the kitchen, and put her mug in the sink. "Nice seeing you again, Nicki. I've got to get going. Thanks for the coffee." With a wave, she walked out. The door banged behind her.

Brand stood. "I'd better go, too. I pushed our appointment with the electrical guy to the day after tomorrow," he told Ansel. "I'll send you an email with the new time."

"What electrical guy?" Ansel asked.

"We need better outlets in the break room. The ones there aren't up to code."

"Can't that wait until we close?"

Brand strode over to the door. "We have to line up all the labor now. These guys schedule months in advance." He nodded to Nicki as he pulled open the door. "Nice meeting you. I mean that sincerely." And then he was gone.

"Why's he glad to meet me?" Nicki asked Ansel. She had a funny feeling he meant it.

"Just being polite. He's never glad," Ansel said.

"I bet he'd be glad if Diane stuck her tongue in his mouth."

"I'm not sure glad's the word." Ansel came over, put an arm around her waist, and kissed his way across her face to her mouth. "Elated?" He licked her lower lip from corner to corner. "Ecstatic?"

"Think she ever will?"

"Never." He hauled her against him and kissed her hard.

Nicki didn't buy it. "She's letting him stay there."

"She's just being nice."

"Really?"

"Okay, maybe she's doing it as a favor to me. So you and I can be together." He untied the sash of her robe.

"That's quite a present, especially since she lost her job."

"I totally agree." One hand slipped between her legs, the other over her ass. His tongue slipped between her teeth and licked the inside of her mouth.

She pushed him against the wall, giving as good as she got, dropping another conversation that never had a chance as long as they were within ten miles of each other.

Chapter 25

The next day, Nicki woke up alone. She had to open her eyes to remember where she was. She brought her phone to her face to look up the time, date, and day of the week. Unlike the school year, when her life was doled out by the minute with bells, streams of students, parents, and principals. Then she couldn't even pee unless she added it to her schedule: between third and fourth period, and she had to jog, because the adult restrooms were on the other side of campus.

But that wasn't what her life was like today. Her phone told her it was Thursday, the twenty-eighth of June, just before nine. She was in Maui. She'd been sleeping with Ansel Jury-Jarski. He would be leaving soon but hadn't said when. Miles would be getting married in less than three weeks.

The phone didn't tell her all of that; she remembered it on her own. It did tell her another thing, though: Betty wanted her to call her.

She sank back into the messy bed and tapped Betty's green-haired snapshot in the corner of her screen. While it rang, she reminded herself to wash the sheets as soon as she got up.

Sleeping alone didn't put the same demands on the linens as what she and Ansel had been doing.

"Miles and Lucy think you're coming to the reception," Betty said when she picked up. "I was helping them order the food and drinks."

Nicki sat up. "No. I told him I couldn't make it. I can't afford the plane ticket back just for the day."

"He bought you a ticket," Betty said. "He had points on his credit card, he said."

Nicki jumped out of bed. "No."

"He really wants you there."

Two years earlier, Nicki had sat in the bleachers at the youth center clubhouse, just to watch Miles teach badminton to a dozen football players from the high school. Bouncing around the huge males, the birdie looked like a mosquito. The rackets seemed smaller than their hands. It had made her laugh so hard, she'd had to leave, and as she waited at the bus stop, she'd realized how hard she'd fallen for him. She'd decided at that moment that Miles was the only man for her.

A decision that was getting harder to comprehend. Miles was wonderful, of course, but he'd never once given her the kind of melting, hungry look he'd lavished on his fiancée; the kind of look that made you feel like the most beautiful woman on earth; the kind of look Ansel gave her when…

Whenever. These days, when *did*n't he look at her that way?

She dragged her thoughts back to Miles. "Why? Why would he want me there?"

"Don't get excited. Lucy's uncomfortable about the guest list. She wants to balance it out."

"I'm not excited, damn it. I'm angry. Why would he pressure me to humiliate myself like that?"

"He wouldn't if he thought that's how you felt about it. Be grateful he doesn't," Betty said.

"Why would he need me? He's got plenty of friends. Is

Lucy really that popular that he needs to pressure the unwilling to balance out *his* side?"

"Oh, Lucy only has a few friends. Small family. It's the adults they need. Right now the reception guest list has an average age of fifteen."

Nicki's heart pinched. She let out a breath. "He invited all the kids from the clubhouse."

"Yeah. Lucy even encouraged him. That's where they're throwing the party."

"So, he wants me to *chaperone*." Nicki ground out the word. "Because I'm a teacher, I bet. No wonder he wants to pay for my ticket. It's a commercial transaction."

"Don't get your panties in a twist—if you're wearing any, which I doubt, given what you've been up to, you floozie," Betty said. "He's a popular guy. He knows dozens of people who don't need airfare who'd come to the reception. He wants you because you're friends. Really close friends, remember?"

"I'm not going."

"What's your excuse going to be this time?"

"I'm too busy having sex with somebody who lo—" Nicki stopped herself.

"Hula? Rich dude does hula?"

Who loves me. No, no. Don't get stupid. This was just a fling. All they did was eat, swim, and have sex. A pleasurable enough lifestyle, but hardly the foundation for true love. "Who likes to have sex with me," she finished.

"I'm sure Miles would've liked to have sex with you, too, if he'd ever known you were interested."

"He was dating somebody else."

"And now he's marrying Lucy. You snooze, you—"

"I'm not going to his wedding."

"Not even I got invited to that. This is just the party. They're going to elope somewhere."

Nicki ran a hand through her hair. Of course she couldn't

go to a wedding; swimming in the pool had given her split ends. And her skin was peeling from the sun.

Elope? Somewhere?

"When?" Nicki asked.

"They're not saying. His friend the billionaire is threatening to crash it, no matter where it is."

"Then, for all we know, they've already gotten married," Nicki said. "Miles could already be married." She sat on the bed, staring at nothing.

"Could be."

"I'm over him." Nicki looked at her feet. The nail polish had chipped. The remaining red splotches made her toes look like a lawn mower had run over them.

"Then you can go to this thing without getting upset. Bring your roommate. I'm curious to see him." Betty cleared her throat. "And Jaynette would like to meet you."

Nicki managed a smile. "The breakup didn't work out?"

"She thinks I'm kidding. What do I have to do to convince her?"

"Tell her what you want," Nicki said. "If she dumps you, it's win-win."

"I'll tell them you'll think about it," Betty said.

"No."

Silence. Betty had hung up.

Damn.

Nicki bent over, put her elbows on her knees and her chin in her hands, and stared at a palm tree outside her balcony. They had palms in northern California, but they weren't like these. These made her feel like she was on the other side of the earth.

She couldn't go. She couldn't watch everyone celebrate Miles choosing somebody else. Why should she put herself through that?

"Nicki."

She looked up. Ansel stood between the sliding doors to the balcony. He had a sheet slung over his shoulders and a patio cushion under one arm.

"Hi." Smiling, she got to her feet. "I didn't know you were here."

He didn't move. "Who's Miles?"

ANSEL DIDN'T THINK of himself as a controlling guy. He'd never understood possessiveness; it didn't mesh with his naturally generous nature.

But when he'd heard Nicki talking—in a voice he'd never heard, angry and passionate—about another man, he'd wanted to rush into the room and demand an explanation.

Which he'd just done.

Nicki's smile disappeared. "You were listening?"

"I couldn't help it. You woke me up. I was sleeping right there." He pointed past the curtains to the balcony.

She looked past him, her face unusually blank. "Insomnia again?"

"Yeah." He noticed she wasn't answering his question. His stomach turned over. "Is he your ex? This Miles guy?"

"No, just a friend," she said. "He's getting married in a few weeks. I can't make the wedding."

He waited for her to say more.

"Just a friend?" he asked finally.

"Yes."

"You seemed pretty upset."

"My friend—the one I was just talking to, Betty—was giving me a hard time about not going."

He picked up her phone, where she'd left it on the nightstand. "You said you were over him. Those were your words."

She closed her eyes. Ducked her head.

"Just friends?" he repeated.

"We never touched each other."

It gave him a tight, uneasy feeling to realize he didn't know her at all. This woman he'd been sleeping with, a woman he'd met years ago, a friend of his sister's—she was still a stranger. "If you don't want to talk about it, just say so."

"I don't want to talk about it."

"Saw that coming."

She looked up and smiled faintly. "I'm sorry. Do you really want to know? It's kind of"—she paused—"embarrassing."

"Yeah, I'd like to know. I'm nosy that way." He walked over and sat on the bed next to her, patting his knees as if he were enjoying himself. "Tell me everything."

"There really isn't anything to tell."

"Which is why it's embarrassing," he said.

"Look," she said. And then didn't say anything else.

He was suddenly furious. How could he know so little about her? He'd just told Brand he was in love. He'd said it to himself. It was just him being ridiculous again—impulsively, blindly jumping off a cliff. "Was it recent, this thing that wasn't anything?"

"I haven't seen him in months. Maybe once since the school year started. We knew each other through work. He teaches an after-school sports program at a clubhouse he founded. Some of my students go there."

"Was there a time you saw him more often?"

She let out a long breath. "I suppose. All right, yes. We used to go to the movies, dinner, that sort of thing, maybe once or twice a month."

"But he never touched you."

"No, I told you. It wasn't like th—"

"Did you want him to?"

She stood and ran her hands through her hair, breathing too loudly. "I can't talk about this."

"He's getting married. Was that when—"

"Am I being indicted before the grand jury here? What's with all the questions?"

"That's it, isn't it? You stopped seeing him because he got engaged."

"Yes! Obviously! That's life."

He felt some slimy, unpleasant sensation come over him like a cape, tied around his throat, choking him. He thought it was anger, because she was lying to him about this guy and wouldn't admit it. Then he realized it was jealousy. He was flaming green with it.

"You were in love with him." He crossed his arms over his chest to stop himself from reaching out to her. This wasn't the time, but he felt the urge to confirm he could touch her. "Still are, it sounds like," he added.

She closed her eyes for a moment. Then she looked at him. "I thought he was perfect for me. It turned out he wasn't. I mean, obviously. I've moved on. I don't—"

She shook her head and walked past him to tidy up the bed.

He waited. "What?" he asked finally.

"I don't think about him anymore. I don't want to think about him. I've got a life to live." She punched the pillow into place, giving him a tight smile over her shoulder. "I'm here with you, aren't I?"

"Not by choice."

She stopped making the bed, turned, and stared at him. "Are you jealous?"

"What does he look like?" He was nuts. What was he doing? He wanted to stop but couldn't. He *had* to know everything about this guy.

"You're creeping me out. I have other male friends. I work with men. Are you going to demand to know about them?"

"Are you in love with any of them?"

She gave him a hard stare. "No."

"Then I don't care."

"Miles is no different. Maybe he was—all right, he was, I wanted more and it didn't happen—but now he's just some guy I know. A nice guy who's about to get married, and I probably won't see him much after that, because that's what happens, like it or not, when people find their"—she paused—"their soul mates. They tune out the rest of the world."

He wished he hadn't heard a word, not any of it. He wished he'd woken with the dawn and made breakfast and never fallen asleep on the balcony where he'd found out Nicki had a hole in her heart for somebody else. "Now I'm depressed," he said, and sat on the bed.

That seemed to make her feel better, even if it didn't do anything for him. Smiling, she plopped down next to him, put her arms around him, and buried her face in his neck. "I'm sorry you're depressed." She kissed him on the jaw as she stroked his chest.

"You seem cheerful," he said sourly. He didn't push her away, though.

"I'm flattered. I'm ashamed to admit it, but I am."

For a second, he was tempted to tell her about Diane's drunken proposal, just to even the score. He'd spent hours yesterday, and the day before, with Diane; wasn't Nicki even a little jealous? Most women found her intimidating, which was one reason her best friend was a man. His last girlfriend had hated her. "Best friends should be ugly," she'd said.

But he didn't want Nicki to be jealous; he wanted himself not to be. He pulled free from her arms and kisses and said, "The only way you'll convince me is if you go to the wedding."

She started to laugh before she realized he was serious. "I can't." Her voice shook the way it had before she'd driven over a bridge on the Hana Highway.

"You're scared," he said.

"Aren't I always?" She forced a laugh.

He got up and went out to the balcony. Paradise looked cheerful this morning. He wished it would rain.

"Ansel." She came up next to him, not touching him, just leaning against the railing inches away. "The wedding's in three weeks. I don't even know if you'll be here then. You said you wouldn't, but maybe your business will drag out and I, well, I wouldn't want to miss any of our time together."

That's nice, he told himself. *She wants to be with me.*

But they each lived in the same metropolitan region. They could see each other indefinitely, whenever, if they wanted to. He was assuming they would.

Apparently, she wasn't. And now he knew why.

"Maybe you're not in love with this guy," he said. "But you have to go, not just to convince me, but to convince yourself."

"I'm not going. It's just the reception, anyway. They'll probably elope."

"All the more reason," he said. "You don't have to sit through the ceremony, just the fun part afterward."

"It won't be fun."

The breath went out of him. What had he expected? A lie?

Maybe. Now he knew where he stood, what he was up against.

Was he willing to wait for her to get over somebody else?

He brushed his knuckles across her cheek. Meeting his gaze, she leaned into his touch, her expression softening.

Sure he was.

"If you want to use me sexually as part of the healing process," he said, "I just want you to know that it's okay with me."

Shooting him a sexy smile, she put an arm around his waist. "What would I do without you?"

"Drown?"

She tickled him in the ribs, grabbed his face, and kissed

him. Within seconds, they had to go back inside—never too early to start the healing—but there was desperation to the sex that hadn't been there before.

The entire time, he couldn't stop wondering if she was thinking about the other guy.

Chapter 26

*T*he next night, Nicki woke up only a few hours after she and Ansel had gone to bed. They'd retired early —right after dinner with Brand and Diane, who had come over with takeout sushi. All the busy nights had exhausted both of them, and as soon as they'd collapsed under the tangled sheets of Ansel's bed, they were asleep.

When she turned over in the dark and felt alone in his big bed, she sat up, patting the mattress—as if he'd shrunk to action figure size—then awoke completely. She got out of bed, pulling on a shirt and underwear she found tangled between the sheets, and walked over to the balcony.

The night was young; people at the pool lingered under tiki torches, and a few children were still splashing in the wading pool.

She turned on a reading light near the desk and pointed it at the balcony.

There he was. Curled up under a white sheet on the chaise, Ansel reminded her of her twelve-year-old Californian pharaohs in the middle of a class mummification demo.

He looked uncomfortable, like a man too tired to care his

head was at a right angle to his shoulders. His elbows and knees were bent, curled up into the air slightly, as though fending off an attack—or having just lost one.

She walked over and sat on a wicker ottoman next to him to watch him sleep, even though she was unable to see his face clearly in the shadows. Her fingers twitched to adjust his head. Surely he'd wake up with a stiff neck, sleeping like that.

She couldn't stop herself from watching him for a while, listening to the sounds of the ocean and the people below drifting up through the twinkling night.

Looking at him made her feel good—nothing complicated, just happy and alive. He had the cutest ears. They stuck out just enough to be interesting. He had a piercing but didn't wear an earring anymore; she wondered if he'd had a stud or a hoop, if it was gold or stainless steel. A diamond would look hot in that earlobe, very hot. She'd nibble on it with her teeth and make him squirm, blowing on it.

If he didn't have so much trouble sleeping, she would've woken him. She sat on her hands. Just watching him for a little longer wouldn't hurt.

"Ansel can't afford his own place, but you can. There's no reason for you to be here."

Nicki cocked her head. It sounded like Diane's voice, maybe from another balcony. Who else would be talking about Ansel? But Nicki must've heard her wrong. Ansel was rich.

"Speaking of reasons, why are you here again?" That sounded like Brand.

"Give me a refill, will you, penis brain?"

"My pleasure, sweetie plum," Brand said.

Nicki put a hand over her mouth, grinning. Should she go inside, give them some privacy?

Ansel snorted in his sleep, drawing her attention back to him. She sighed happily. He really was adorable. Maybe Brand

and Diane's loud voices would wake him up so she could drag him back to bed.

"I am not drunk," Diane said loudly. "The other night, okay, yes, I was drunk. I woke up the next morning with hair on my chest."

"I know you're exaggerating. I was there. I would've noticed. I studied you very carefully in that jogging swimsuit G-string thing you like to wear."

"You're disgusting," Diane said.

"You're beautiful."

"Shut up."

Low masculine laughter drifted over the balcony wall.

Oh, my. This sounds kind of personal. Reluctantly, she stood to go inside. Ansel *did* need his sleep.

"I really wish you'd leave," Diane said with a sigh.

"So, when are you going to pop the question? Although I suppose it's kind of awkward to propose marriage when his girlfriend is hanging around all the time," Brand said. "How many minutes have you managed to get him away from her?"

"She's not his girlfriend."

"Is that what you're telling yourself?"

"She's just a… thing. A fling."

"He thinks he's in love with her."

Nicki sucked in a breath, paralyzed where she stood on the other side of the balcony privacy screen, thoughts of going inside forgotten.

"You know how he is," Diane said. "He always says that."

"She's afraid of things. Lots of phobias."

"See? There you go. Ansel to the rescue. He's got to have a reason to gallop in on his white horse, carry off the damsel in distress. You know how he is."

Brand chuckled. "Yeah."

There was a long silence. Nicki pressed her back to the

balcony wall, heart racing, looking at Ansel for any sign that he'd heard.

Thinks he's in love with her. Damsel in distress. You know how he is.

Ansel didn't move.

She went up on tiptoes, straining to hear the next word, not caring anymore about the ethics of eavesdropping.

She finally heard Brand say, "You did not."

"I did. I wish I hadn't had so much to drink. He didn't think I was serious."

"That was right when I got here. Tuesday night."

"Yeah, your timing really sucks," she said.

There was another long pause. "He didn't mention it."

Nicki scowled at the balcony wall, which gave nothing away. *Didn't mention* what?

"He's not an asshole like you, that's why."

"I warned him yesterday, and he didn't say a word."

"Warned him. Thanks a lot," Diane said. "How could you know? I haven't said a word to anyone."

"Di, come on. You've been hinting for years. When we were dating, you flat-out told me you were going to marry him after you turned thirty if you couldn't find anybody else."

"I did not."

Brand snorted.

"Fine," she said. "Whatever. It's a good plan."

"You're having a midlife crisis. Just like Ansel. Except he's met somebody who might stop him from screwing up. She's good for him."

Feeling her face get warm, Nicki smiled, liking Ansel's taste in business partners.

"You're just saying that because she gets in my way," Diane said.

Brand's voice lowered. "The only person I want in your way is me, Di."

"Fat chance. I'm marrying Ansel."

Oh my God. Diane sounded like she believed it. Poor woman. Even if Brand was right, and Diane was just grasping at Ansel out of convenience, Nicki felt for her.

So why had her heart tumbled into her pelvis?

"He won't do it," Brand said.

"He loves me. He will."

"He loves you," Brand replied. "He won't."

"His father will forgive him if he gets married. He won't have to fake a living buying cheap office space in random places with you anymore. He'll be a credit-card-carrying Jury-Jarski again." Then Diane said something too quiet for Nicki to hear.

Silence stretched out between the balconies. Nicki realized she'd stopped breathing.

"I've always wanted to have children," Diane said. "I don't want his family's money. I know how to make money. But I—oh, leave me alone."

"I can't," Brand said bitterly. "I'm in love with you."

Nicki put a hand over her mouth.

She shouldn't be listening to this. This was none of her business.

But it *was* her business.

Her head spun with phrases out of context—proposal, children, love, money.

Ansel's father was mad at him about something?

"Brand, you can't mean it," Diane said.

"I think about you when I wake up, when I brush my teeth, when I call my accountant. I think about you when I'm stirring sugar into my coffee. I think about you when I'm supposed to be reading a book about other people, and I think about you whenever I see a beautiful woman with children that aren't ours."

Nicki sank down to the ottoman. Her hand, still pressed over her mouth, captured her sigh.

She knew she should go, but...

That was beautiful. If they'd wanted total privacy, they should've gone inside. Sound traveled far near water at night.

Her eyes fell on Ansel, still twisted at an odd angle as he slept, and her gooey feelings turned cold.

He hadn't told her. He hadn't told her anything about Diane proposing marriage, about family problems, about being broke.

Two thousand dollars for the cabana.

The restaurant. The groceries.

What else hadn't he shared? How much did she really know about him? Now Nicki was dying to know about his previous girlfriends.

Damsels in distress...

Her face felt hot. Is that why he liked her? Because she was pathetic?

She sat on the ottoman and watched him sleep, trying to understand how her happiness could've unraveled so easily.

WHEN ANSEL OPENED HIS EYES, he expected to see moonlight, stars, and palm trees, not Nicki's angry face.

"What's the matter?" He sat up, rubbing his neck, vowing to get a real mattress out here one day.

Nicki shook her head and disappeared inside. He didn't move at first, blinking away sleep, massaging his shoulder, but then she reappeared and waved for him to follow.

If she didn't look so upset, he'd be optimistic about her plans.

But she did look upset. He paused in the doorway, trying to shake off the nice dream he'd been having—about her.

It must be because he'd left the bed so early; he hadn't even given cuddling a fair shot. "I'm sorry," he said, slinging the sheet over his shoulder. "I knew I wasn't going to be able to sleep. Believe me when I say how much I wish I could. I can understand—"

"Close the door."

"What?"

She reached past him and jerked the balcony door shut. "I just overheard Brand and Diane talking on their balcony. I don't want the same to happen to us." She yanked the drapes over the glass.

He had a really bad feeling about this. "Brand and Diane?" He massaged his face, trying to wake up. What would make her so angry? Unfortunately, he could think of a few reasons. He wrapped the sheet around his waist.

"First of all," she said, "I admit I shouldn't have been listening. I didn't mean to at the beginning, and then, well, I just couldn't stop." She began pacing at the foot of his bed, staring at the floor. She was wearing one of his black T-shirts and a pair of white panties.

His body, accustomed to the gratification she could bring, hardened in response. He sank slowly into the desk chair, uncomfortable and pessimistic about anything good happening. "What did they say?"

"Why didn't you tell me Diane asked you to marry her?"

He blinked in surprise. He hadn't told Brand about it, so Diane must have brought it up on her own. "I didn't tell anyone about it, not just you."

"She said it was Tuesday, which means it was before you came down on me about Miles. Now who's the one hiding their feelings?"

"I wasn't hiding mine," he said, "I was hiding hers. She's a friend. She'd had too much to drink, she'd lost her job. I knew she didn't mean it."

"We slept together Tuesday night."

"I remember it fondly."

"A woman you love proposes to you, and you turn around and have sex with somebody else?"

He couldn't believe what he was hearing. "You wish I'd had sex with her instead?"

"This isn't happening." Her voice was heavy with despair as she sat on the edge of the bed.

"But nothing's happened. Nothing's changed. Not really."

"But it has," she said. "Brand said she's been planning this for a long time. Marrying you. She didn't deny it."

"You were eavesdropping from two balconies away," he said. "How can you be sure what she said?"

"I'm sure about that part."

"Well, I don't believe it. But let's forget that for a minute. Marrying Diane obviously isn't what *I* want, so why are you mad at me?"

She touched the lampshade on the wall sconce, adjusted it slightly. "There's more."

"More what?"

"More about you," she said.

If Brand and Diane were talking about him, his family and financial situation would've come up. Neither one of them thought he was handling it right.

He took a deep breath. "You found out I'm not rich anymore."

"They said something about your father."

"Yeah, he didn't like my life choices. He cut me off."

"When?"

"Last fall."

She shook her head, looking incredulous.

"It bothers you." It was a statement, not a question. Whether people wanted to admit it or not, money mattered. They liked him better because he had money. Why wouldn't they like him less without it?

"You should've told me," she said.

He crossed his legs, leaned back, and tried to hide how much it hurt to know she was the same as everybody else. "I'm glad I didn't. Maybe you wouldn't be here right now if I had."

Her mouth dropped open. "How can you say that?"

"What am I supposed to think? You're freaking out because you heard I'm not the rich guy you thought I was."

"I'm upset—*upset*—because you lied to me. You've intentionally made me think that money's no big deal, dropping two grand on a cabana so I could take a shower…"

He looked at his hands, entwined in his lap. "It was worth twice that."

There were a few long seconds of silence.

"Wow, I'm so flattered." Her voice dropped an octave. "Now I'm not only a prostitute, but an expensive one."

"Come on, you're overreacting. I didn't tell you everything, that's true. Neither did you. When you were going to tell me you were in love with another guy?" He stood. "A bit more relevant, don't you think? I didn't come down on you about that."

She shook her head. "I am not in love with Miles."

"Sure."

"I wouldn't have slept with you if I'd thought I was in love with another man," she said.

"Not even to help yourself get over him?"

"No."

"I wish I believed you."

"Yeah, me too." She turned away from him. Her shoulders were rigid under his shirt.

"This is why I didn't tell you," he said. "I was afraid you'd react just like this."

"You have a pretty low opinion of me," she said, turning. "But apparently, that's what you like. Women you can look down on."

"That is *not* true," he said. "I don't care what you think you heard."

"They laughed about it, both of them." She ran a hand through her hair. "You like to rescue damsels. I'm a damsel, I guess. Even though I didn't need rescuing, you obviously think I did."

"What I told Brand"—he clenched his teeth—"was that I *thought* I was in *love* with you." He looked down at himself, furious he wasn't wearing anything but a bed sheet. He couldn't put on his shirt because she was wearing it. She was also blocking his way to his closet.

Nicki didn't look surprised by his declaration. "Diane said, 'he always says that.' That's what they were laughing about."

"I don't care what either one of them said. I think it's pretty pathetic that you do."

"Pathetic," she said.

"Yes. It's just fear talking. You let it totally control you."

Her face hardened. "That's not fair. I heard what I heard. Don't twist it into something about me being crazy."

"You don't admit you have a fear problem?"

"Of course I admit it! But that's not what's going on here!"

"I feel what's going on between us," he said, "and I know what it's called. I'm not afraid to admit it."

"You're going too fast." She crossed her arms over her chest. "You don't know me well enough to love me."

"I was working on it." He pointed at her. "And so were you."

"Yeah, we've had lots of sex. It's great, but it's not love. You never talked to me, I never talked to you. Except about my phobias, which apparently you like."

"They're a pain in the ass, but I like you enough to overlook them."

Her face went blank. Then she looked down at the floor,

walked around the bed, and picked up her shorts. "I need to be alone," she said, pulling them on.

"Doesn't it mean anything to you? That I love you?"

Her voice was shaking. "You don't mean it. We barely know each other." She walked to the door. "You love everybody. You're just that kind of guy."

"And you're not that kind of girl?"

"Easy? Impulsive?" she asked. "No. And sometimes, that's a good thing. A very good thing." She strode out the door.

He moved to follow her, tripping over the comforter on the floor.

It's great, but it's not love.

He stumbled into the living room and caught his balance on the breakfast counter. He heard her bedroom door bang shut. Then the lock clicked.

This is how she reacts to the idea of me loving her.

He put a second hand on the counter, then his forehead. He stayed there for a minute, catching his breath, before going back to his room.

He felt too awful to feel anything at all.

Chapter 27

The next morning, Nicki crawled out of bed and immediately hauled her suitcase out of the closet.

She stared at it. *Here we go again.* When she'd landed in Hawaii, she hadn't expected to be on the verge of leaving it so frequently.

She couldn't, shouldn't run. With a deep breath, she shoved the empty suitcase back into the closet and began pacing around her bedroom.

She'd cried enough the night before; she was through with that. Part of her was ashamed about some of the things she'd done—eavesdropping, for one—but also for how she'd yelled at him when he said he loved her.

She was still angry about that. He insulted her with one breath and demanded she hand over her heart with the next. It wasn't irrational to be cautious about love. What did love mean to him, anyway—marriage? A few months of dating back in California? She had no idea, and she wouldn't call it *love* until she did.

She'd hurt him and been hurt, and that put her in an angry feedback loop, not sure whom to blame.

They had to talk. She got dressed and stuck her head out of her bedroom, listening for him. Not in any of the common areas.

It was only nine; maybe he'd gone back to sleep on the balcony and was still there. She got dressed and went to look for him.

No. Not on the balcony. Or in his bathroom.

She knocked on his bedroom door.

No answer. She knocked harder. "Ansel?"

She tested the doorknob; it turned, and she went in like a cop in a movie.

He wasn't in his bedroom, either.

She let out the breath she'd been holding. "Fine," she said to the empty room. "You went out. Okay."

But an hour later, after she'd taken a shower and put on the mermaid dress and made a pot of coffee, she started to get restless. What if he'd gone out for the day, and she was sitting there looking pretty, just passively waiting for him?

Brand and Diane might know.

Shoving aside her embarrassment, she walked out into the hall, strode over to their door, and knocked three times, hard. She commanded her cheeks to stay as pale as a starving vampire, even though she couldn't stop thinking about the things she'd overheard just hours earlier.

The door opened a crack. Diane's sleepy face appeared. "Nicki?"

"Sorry to bother you. I was looking for Ansel."

Diane closed her eyes. The crack in the door narrowed to a thin white line. "She's looking for Ansel," Nicki heard her say.

"He didn't say good-bye?" That was Brand's voice, muffled behind the door.

Nicki's pulse pounded in her ears. Her chest tightened. *Good-bye?*

She rapped on the door again. "Hello, still here."

It flew open. Diane stood there in a white bathrobe twice her size. Brand, similarly dressed, except the robe was snug, was right behind her. They looked flushed, glowing, happy, and ready to get back into bed. Nicki was too fixated on the words *he didn't say good-bye* to be happy for them, or relieved for herself to have Diane out of the way.

Ansel had taken himself out of the way. "Tell me," Nicki said, not moving.

Diane stepped aside. "Come in."

She shook her head. "Where'd he go?"

"You'd really better come in," Brand said.

Nicki's hands started to shake. She balled them into fists and walked slowly inside. "Did he get his own place?"

Diane glanced at Brand. "I didn't talk to him myself," she said.

"He's on a plane back to San Francisco," Brand said. "He called me from the airport."

Nicki's breath caught. "San Francisco?" She turned to Diane. "Seriously?"

With a sigh, Diane gave her a worried look. "He told us how you heard us on the balcony. Whatever you heard, please don't blame Ansel. It's totally my fault. And Brand. Brand's fault, too."

"Thanks," he said.

"He's on a plane back home, right now?" Nicki's back bumped against the front door.

"I'm sorry," Diane said.

"He was down in the lobby when the airport shuttle came," Brand said. "He said he felt like moving, so he got on it. Next thing he knew, he was in Kahului booking a flight. That's what he said."

"Because of me?" Nicki couldn't believe it. "Did you tell him about… about you two…" She made a vaguely romantic, hand waving gesture between them.

"I'm sure he'll be on the next flight back," Diane said.

Brand rubbed the back of his neck. "I don't think so."

Both women looked at him.

"He backed out of the real estate deal," Brand continued. "He said he needed to figure some things out. I told him not to buy a Ferrari, and he said he was doing the opposite—unloading his worldly possessions. I started to think he might join a throwback commune in Marin, the way he was talking."

"Here I thought *I* was nuts," Nicki said dully. She craved her beanbags. "Does he do this sort of thing often? Take off when he's upset?"

Neither of them spoke.

"He does, doesn't he?" Nicki asked.

Diane put her hand over her mouth and looked at the floor. Then she said, "Only once. But it was a totally different situation. He ended up in Seattle that time."

"Because of—something like this?" Nicki asked.

"Oh, no. Nothing like that." Diane looked at Brand. "A friend of his died in a skiing accident."

"Drew Probert," he said, shaking his head. "Great guy. Could make anybody laugh. Even me. The three of us used to play poker together. Drew and I would get wasted, and Ansel, sipping his diet Cokes, would still lose. On purpose, I assume. He knew Drew had tons of school loans."

"Ansel was in his car when he found out," Diane said. "He was supposed to meet me for pizza, but he got on 101 and didn't stop until he hit Canada." Diane was frowning at her. "Do you mind if I ask what you said to him last night?"

Nicki stared at her. This was *her* fault?

No. They'd just been having fun the way other people had fun when they were on vacation and found somebody to have fun with. There was no reason he should be running away as if she'd ruined his life because she wasn't ready to say—

"I only got here about three weeks ago," Nicki said.

"I understand," Diane said. "He got carried away again. He's never been the type to go slow."

"I have to go." Nicki turned and pulled the door open, not seeing anything but her fingers wrapped around the handle. Her legs were wooden, her body weightless.

Diane helped her with the door. "I really am sorry. We both are."

Nicki nodded at her and went back to her own place.

I'm not sorry, she thought.

Better now than later, when she might have been really stuck.

Carried away.

She just had to accept she'd been living in a dream world; they'd had a lovely time, a fantasy in paradise, and now the alarm clock had gone off.

Time to wake up.

It's strange how good I feel, Ansel thought as he sat in his favorite chair by the window in his apartment. It overlooked a shady corner of Glen Park in San Francisco, and smelled stale from his long absence, but he was glad he'd flown home the day before.

He hadn't felt this good in years. Great, actually. Great.

He was his own man. Nobody could tell him what to do. Nobody expected anything from him, nobody could. He was a grown man in his own apartment, drinking his own coffee out of his own mug.

He wasn't rich but he had the down payment for the oceanfront office building he wouldn't be buying, and little funds here and there from friends repaying him for old favors *he* had never called loans, but they had.

He'd do fine. She'd taken his heart and stomped on it, but

he'd survive. He saw the world more clearly now, like getting a terminal diagnosis and seeing what really mattered in life.

Making money wasn't ever going to make him happy. In spite of what he'd told himself months ago, he'd gone into business with Brand to impress his father. Not to become financially independent—like he'd fooled himself into believing—but in a last-ditch attempt to earn his father's respect.

He wasn't going to do that anymore. Even if his father never respected him, Ansel would respect himself. He'd continue to find value in his life—much like his mother did—through lending, helping, playing, living. He'd try to explain that to his father, but he wouldn't try to change himself to make the old man happy.

Kevin Jarski's sixtieth birthday party was in two weeks. Ansel wanted to be there. He'd even decided to help his mother with the arrangements.

He picked up the phone again and called Mel Jury's cell, not knowing where she was, not even which country.

"You're an angel!" his mother said after he'd made his offer. "It will mean so much to him!"

"No, it won't," he replied, "but that's okay."

"It'll mean a lot that you'll be there."

"I need to tell you something, Mom," he said. "You're not going to like it."

"Is that why you buttered me up first?"

"No. I was going to do that anyway."

She exhaled loudly. "All right. Let's hear it."

"Dad and I had a fight in September." He waited for her to tell him what she knew.

All she said was "Yes?"

"He wanted me to live my life differently than how I was living it. I told him to go to hell."

She breathed out again. He thought he could hear her lips pressing together.

"I didn't use those exact words," he continued, "but that was basically it. I told him I wouldn't draw from the family accounts anymore. I haven't."

"And you've run out of money and would like to make up?" Her voice was deceptively polite. It was the voice that used to send chills down his back.

"No. I don't need money. But I do need my father."

The line went quiet.

"Mom?"

Another loud exhale, this one from the diaphragm. "Oh, I'm so glad. This has been a horrible year, waiting for the two of you to pull yourselves together. Just horrible."

"Did you know?"

"Of course I knew, Ansel. Your father doesn't have a painful bowel movement without letting me know about it."

He laughed, relief flooding him. "I figured. That's why I called you."

"I'll get him on the phone. Just—"

"No. Not now. I'll talk to him at the party. He'll be happy to get away from everybody you invited and yell at me for a few minutes. That's my little present to him."

"I can't promise I won't jump the gun, Ansel. I don't keep secrets from him. He's my life partner. You'll understand someday."

"I doubt it," he said, sinking back into the chair. He had a moment of feeling very not good. "I'll set everything up with Jordan. You liked the food at the restaurant, right? Dad can have the party there?"

"It was very interesting. I'm willing to eat it again."

"Is that what you put in your Yelp review?" he asked. "That's kind of faint, as praise goes."

"It doesn't matter what I think. He had a line out the door. Are you sure he'll reserve the entire place just for us?"

"I'm sure."

They talked menus and timing. Then Ansel asked his mother something he'd wanted to do for a while but had been afraid of looking weak to his father.

"I'd like to go into business with you, Mom," he said firmly. He wanted to continue what he'd been doing with friends but on a formal, larger scale. "Saving the world."

She paused. "But that's what you have been doing, Ansel. Didn't you know that?"

Feeling his throat tighten, he repeated something about the menu before hanging up.

He sat in the chair and stared out the window at the park, the phone abandoned in his lap.

He was watching a man ride his bike with a small white dog on his chest in a baby carrier, thinking about Nicki, when his sister called.

He wasn't sure he wanted to talk to Rachel right then. She'd want to know everything. Everything. If she didn't know already, with her twin sister magic.

He hit the button. "Hi, Rache."

"I'm not getting married, and you're not going to say a word about it," she said.

He got up and walked into his kitchen. It was smaller than a suburban home's walk-in closet but wonderfully affordable.

"Okay," he said, relieved he'd escape from a conversation about his own love life.

Silence stretched between them. "Okay," she said. "Thanks."

"No problem."

"I'm actually packing right now," she said. "I hear I'll see you at Dad's birthday party."

Unless the tireless Melinda Jury had sent an email while she was on the phone with him, it was too soon for his sister to have gotten that news from their mother. "Where did you hear that?"

"Oh, you know."

"No," he said flatly. "I'd like to."

"Okay," she said with a sigh, "I talked to Brand an hour ago."

"Since when do you talk to Brand?"

"We don't talk every day or anything."

"But you barely know him. I didn't think you even liked him."

"I didn't used to, but then I got to know him last summer." She cleared her throat. "We went out for a little while."

"Went out where?" Then Ansel grimaced. "No way." Shaking his head, he took containers of yogurt and orange juice out of the fridge to make a smoothie. Liquefying products in a blender could be therapeutic.

"He was sweet."

"Sweet? Brand?"

"A real gentleman. But he was in love with somebody else."

"Thank God," he said. "I didn't realize how glad I'd be about that."

"They're worried about you. Well, Diane's worried. Brand's pissed."

He shoved a frozen banana into the blender. "Maybe I shouldn't have left like that. I was just about to get the car and go for a drive when the shuttle showed up. I'd assumed I'd turn around and go right back."

"You should. I'm afraid to call Nicki. My brother's being an asshole."

"When the plane was landing at SFO, I finally saw what everyone else had seen all along. Nicki was just looking for sex." He swallowed hard. "She doesn't want anything else from me." He banged the lid over the blender and punched the highest setting.

When he turned it off, Rachel sighed. "You don't know that."

"I'm just another challenge for her to cross off her bucket list. She'd been afraid of seeing me again after college, just like she was afraid of swimming or bridges or whatever. She built up a tolerance, got her fix, felt good about herself"—he yanked a bag of strawberries out of the freezer—"and it has nothing to do with me. She got what she needed."

"You haven't given her a chance."

"If I go back to Maui, we'll just get back in bed together and drag out the inevitable. Better to have a clean break now."

"I can't believe you're saying this. You didn't even talk to her."

"We talked. She ended the conversation. I'm happy to continue it, but not there. If she's interested in talking more, she can come find me in the real world."

"You're hurt and afraid and dumping all of this on her, instead of—"

"I told her I loved her. She told me to fuck off." He shoved an icy strawberry as big as a baby's fist into the blender. "It's not me who's afraid."

"Give me a break. You're terrified."

"Not anymore. I put myself out there—"

"And then ran away!"

He fired up the blender again and enjoyed the horrible noise. When it had pulverized the sugary mass into a rosy paste, he punched the off button. "She needs some time. I'm giving her time."

"Sounds like you're the one who wants time."

"Maybe I do."

"Can I tell her you want to see her when she gets back?"

"I'd tell you to mind your own business, but that's not going to happen." He pressed his thumb over the blender's ice crush button until Rachel yelled at him over the noise to cut it out.

He took off the lid and scowled into it. It would be a waste to pour it out, but his stomach was too tense to digest anything.

"By the way, I know you set us up," he said. "Believe me when I say I don't appreciate it."

"I'm sorry," Rachel said with a sigh. "I thought you two would really like each other."

"Yeah. We did. That was the problem."

Chapter 28

Two weeks later, on a Friday night in mid-July, Nicki pulled her laptop bag from under the seat in front of her and waited for the aisle to clear so she could get off the plane.

The other passengers looked happy, well-rested, and sun-kissed. She, however, was recovering from a bad burn after spending the day on a catamaran tour, and the skin on her shoulders was coming off in sheets. The flesh underneath was pink and tender, sensitive to the pressure of two bags slung across her body.

Her knees were still a little shaky from the landing as she walked off the plane, but she'd been writing through most of the trip and hadn't ordered a drink, popped a pill, or blown a gasket. She hadn't even squeezed the Phobic Phoebe stress ball that had finally arrived at the condo. The extras—Betty had sent two dozen—were in her suitcase insulating a hand-painted vase she'd purchased at an art show in Lahaina. The show had been one of the excursions she'd forced herself to make. She'd refused to mope in the condo.

He hadn't come back; he hadn't called. She'd relived the

fight in her mind over and over, concluding only that he'd wanted more than she could give. She wished he'd given her more time, and it galled her that he'd left like that.

The air inside the terminal was cold and humid, like a basement after a rainstorm. She found Betty waiting in the baggage claim; her green hair was now as purple as grape soda. On her, it looked more natural, almost black.

"Thanks for the ride," Nicki said. "Love the hair."

"I'm going through a conservative phase. Jaynette's driving around so we don't have to pay for parking," Betty said. "Is that all you brought?"

Nicki looked around for the right baggage carousel. "I checked a couple bags. Sorry, but I couldn't carry it all on."

"A couple? Just for the weekend?"

Nicki moved her laptop bag to the other shoulder, flinching at the sting of the strap tugging at raw flesh. "I'm not going back."

"But you've got three weeks to go! In Maui!"

"I've had enough." She didn't have anything else to prove to herself there.

"Damn, what a waste. I'll tell her to drive around again," Betty muttered, starting to text on her phone. "I wish Jaynette could get time off work. She and I could take your place. Fly out after the reception after chugging champagne."

"Sorry, it's already occupied." Brand and Diane had moved into the Jury-Jarski condo as a cost-saving measure. Diane was also taking Ansel's place in the real estate deal; although, because his abandoned possessions were still strewn all over his bedroom, they would be moving into the room Nicki had used.

"What's with the two backpacks?" Betty asked.

"Ansel forgot his computer."

Betty lowered her phone to gape at her. "You're his *mule*?"

"Gives me an excuse to talk to him."

"You already have an excuse to track him down and smack him upside the head," Betty said. "Talk to him then."

"I'm not angry anymore," Nicki said. "We both went a little crazy. Being away from home can do that to you. You forget who you are, do things you'd never do otherwise." Painful, pleasurable memories cascaded over her. She didn't know if she'd ever have such a comprehensively sensual experience again in her life. She didn't know if she'd survive one.

The first suitcase appeared on the carousel. Nicki maneuvered through the cluster of bodies and hauled it off the belt.

"That's exactly why you should've stayed there," Betty said, taking it from her. "Keep doing that stuff. The blog's on fire."

"I've got to talk to you about that. I've got some ideas about the future of Phobic Phoebe." The second bag came into view.

"You're going solo," Betty said. "I knew it. Blogs are too easy to set up these days. You don't need me."

"Not going solo. I thought I'd put all of the posts together in a book and self-publish them online. You and I would have to look into the copyright issues, get that all figured out before I do it." She'd needed something other than school and an empty apartment to come home to.

"What do I have to do with it?" Betty asked.

"It was your blog. You deserve a cut of the proceeds."

"What'd I do? Nag and complain, that's what."

"I couldn't have done it without you," Nicki said.

"You've brought me enough traffic to my blog to compensate me."

"That doesn't feel right," Nicki said.

"Look, if I lived my life to get rich, my parents wouldn't be so embarrassed in front of their friends." Betty pulled the handles up from each suitcase and started walking to the doors, dragging them behind her. "I do this for fun. Have your own fun."

"All right, I will." Nicki followed her out the automatic doors toward the taxis, buses, and cars. A cloud of cigarette smoke from the tobacco-toking corral near the door hit her in the face. Outside, the fog was cold and soupy, a typical July evening in the Bay Area. Jaynette had double-parked at the end of the curb and floored it when she saw them.

"How are things between you guys?" Nicki asked quickly, eyeing the approaching car.

Betty waved at Jaynette. "Not bad. She asked me if I'd consider meeting her father. He lives in Idaho, so I'm a little freaked. Not my target demo, you know?" She dragged the bag off the curb and knocked on the old hatchback's trunk. "Pop it, yogi!"

Jaynette was a yoga instructor. Not the best driver, if Nicki remembered correctly.

Her hands became clammy. As she hefted a suitcase into the hatch, she reminded herself that if she didn't survive the drive across the Bay Bridge, she wouldn't have to see Miles celebrate his marriage tomorrow.

Just sixteen hours. Ansel had been right; she wasn't over him. How could she be? She'd known Miles for years, loved him for most of it, and the thought of seeing him married to somebody else made her stomach twist like a string mop in a bucket.

How could she be angry with Ansel for leaving, given how she felt about somebody else?

She looked at her phone: 8:35 p.m. They would've eloped by now, if Betty's secret intel was correct.

The backseat of Jaynette's car smelled like lavender body spray in spite of the large black lab with a studded white leather collar sitting in the middle of it.

"Just shove Sir Chomp out of the way if he hogs the seat," Jaynette said. "Move it, Chomp. She's not in the mood for love."

So true, Nicki thought, wedging herself between the wall of bristly fur and the vinyl-upholstered door.

Married already. The party tomorrow was just to celebrate. She was going to smile and look ecstatic for their happiness, and he and everyone else, young and old, were going to believe it.

Jaynette peeled away from the curb, dodging between two city buses that didn't have room for her; the rear vehicle blasted its horn.

Nicki's hands started shaking violently. She clasped them together over her stomach. The backs of her arms felt as if she'd walked into a storage freezer—but it could be partly from the shock of being back in the Bay Area, not just the fear of being in a car being driven by a lunatic.

Miles was married. Ansel had never come back. She was still afraid of cars and bridges—though not water.

Sir Chomp, whose breath smelled like Parmesan cheese, licked her on the mouth.

She wasn't too proud to admit it helped her feel better.

FIVE O'CLOCK THE NEXT EVENING, using the rearview mirror in her car, Nicki applied a third coat of mascara, a second layer of lipstick, and the first handful of magnesium tablets, which she washed down with tepid chamomile tea in an insulated cup.

Miles's youth clubhouse was throbbing with pop music as if it were a high school dance. She got out of her car, adjusted her dress—it was a dark rose like an overripe watermelon; rather conservative, but it showed off her legs—and strode over to the doorway, where several kids in their early teens were walking in with their parents. They carried presents as if going to a birthday party.

School dance, kiddie party: not romantic. So far, so good. She could do this.

She'd ordered her own present for the happy couple the good old-fashioned way—through the Internet. Nothing said "personalized gift" like four out of the eight requested wine glasses, clicked on, checked out, shipped, and never seen.

So maybe she wasn't feeling very celebratory.

When she saw a boy half her age—this was possible now that she was old, she thought with a sigh—gawking at her legs, she tugged down her dress.

"You made it," Lucy said, holding out her hand as she greeted guests at the door. "Thank God. I don't know why I left Miles in charge of this. Just because he's the social butterfly, I thought, hey, who better to plan a party. The one time in my life I step back and let somebody else take over, and now I'm dancing to top forty with twelve-year-olds."

The bride's hair was swept up into a beautiful russet cloud sparkling with beads, braids, and ribbons. Her dress was sage green, clingy, shimmery, and low-cut, styled to show off a pair of killer heels. She looked like a wood nymph out on the town clubbing.

Nicki let out a sigh. "You look gorgeous."

"I'm just not into white. I tried. My friend—that's her over there, Fawn—she does this beauty thing for a living—"

Nicki saw a woman with fashion model proportions and long Barbie-blond hair surrounded by awestruck adolescent males, who lingered in a ring around her, standing about ten feet away, just staring.

"She wanted me to wear a gown at some point during this marriage process," Lucy continued, "no matter how often I told her I'd rather save my money for the honeymoon. Or a house. Dental work. Tampons. *Anything.* Spending thousands—actual dollars, the kind they have in banks—on a garment you wear once? No thanks. It's insane. It's a scam. I don't understand why women put up with it."

At thirty, Nicki was an expert on weddings, having watched most of her friends get hitched within the past few years. "It's even harder if you're my size. I'd get one second-hand, but not very many women are my height."

Lucy smiled up at her. She had to crane her head back like one of Nicki's smaller seventh graders. "I *so* know what you mean." She touched Nicki's arm and pointed into the clubhouse. "Get yourself a drink. Making do without the dress gave us an excellent booze budget. We got the good stuff—locked up from the kids—so ask Miles to fix you something."

The pool and foosball tables had been shoved against the walls, but the boys were using them anyway. There were a few young women, college-aged, who stood around smiling at Miles, taking pictures of him with their phones, laughing and talking. The rest of the guests were the usual array of suited men, women in floral dresses, and children chasing one another in their most uncomfortable clothes.

Nicki thanked Lucy, already starting to feel the pressure build in her chest. She hadn't let herself look at him yet; though of course she'd felt his presence the second she came through the door. Now she set her sights on the bar, where the largest man in the room, and in most rooms he entered, was pouring sodas into glasses for a few boys in their best hoodies, khakis, and sneakers. Nicki knew the brands well enough to know their outfits cost more than hers did.

As she approached him, her ankle, in unfamiliar heels, wobbled on a patch of worn carpeting. Her heart, like the music, throbbed at cardio training speed. She stretched a smile on her face and sought eye contact with the man she'd once assumed would be hers someday because he was kind and gentle, funny and intelligent, and towered over other men in every way.

He looked up and saw her. "Nicki! You made it!" He had a giddy smile on his face. "I didn't think you were coming! This is great. What can I get you? I've got a few bottles of good wine, red and white, I don't remember what they're called, but they're supposed to be good. Does that sound good? I can get them out if you want to look at the labels. Yeah. I should do that. These guys won't steal one, will you?" He smiled at the boys, who were pouring more soda into their cups.

Nicki stared at Miles. The sarcastic, subdued man she'd known was gone, killed by this cheerful, chatty bartender. Her grizzly bear had turned into a golden retriever.

She swallowed, thinking, after everything, she'd have trouble speaking. But then she said, "A glass of the white, please," and walked around the table to give him a hug. As tall as she was, he was almost half a foot taller, another selling point. But now, as she had to go up on tiptoes to kiss him on the cheek—which she did because it seemed appropriate, not tempting—she found his head's distance from hers to be inconvenient. "Congratulations," she added.

"Did you fly back just for this?" He bent down and tore the lid off a cardboard box. "Haven't you been in Cancun?"

He didn't even remember where she'd gone. Nicki scanned her heart for puncture wounds, finding none. "Maui," she said, laughing. "You didn't even get the right country."

She was *laughing*.

"I knew there was sand there," he said. "Sorry, I've been busy. Did you have fun?" He beamed at her, holding out a glass of red wine.

"Lots of fun." She smiled but didn't take the glass. "Dude, I asked for white. Would you like me to take over? You seem a little out of it."

"Hey, I got married. Did you hear?" He put her glass down before pouring another glass, also red. "I've got the ball and chain in the car. She lets me take it off to party."

She laughed again. "Nice of her."

He held out the second glass of red wine to her. "How was Mexico?"

"Funniest thing," she said. "They speak English now."

"All the American tourists," he said vaguely. He wasn't looking at her anymore but over her shoulder. "Lucy, look! Nicki made it!"

Lucy joined them with the tall blonde at her side. "Two glasses of the pinot for us, all right, hon?" Then she saw the two glasses of red, sitting untouched on the table. "Who are those for?"

"Nicki." He held them both out to her.

Nicki accepted them, biting her tongue. "Thanks, Miles. I was really thirsty. These will hit the spot."

"Need any help back there?" Lucy maneuvered around the table to wrap her arms around Miles's lower half. He bent down and kissed her.

The blonde chuckled. "Are those really both for you?" she asked Nicki, pointing at the glasses.

"No. He got distracted."

"I'll relieve you of one," the woman said, taking it from her. She had stunning cheekbones, luminous eyes, and the proportions one would expect if humans evolved on a planet with lesser gravity. She held out a hand. "I'm Fawn."

The model Betty had mentioned. "It's nice to finally meet you. I'm Nicki."

Her already big eyes grew enormous. "You're Phobic Phoebe!"

"Yup."

"You've been in Hawaii!"

Nicki smiled, glowing at the proof this gorgeous creature followed her blog, then flinching at the reminder of what she'd lost after she'd written her last post. Since Ansel had left her, she'd recycled a few extra essays she'd stored up in case of emergency; she hadn't been able to write anything new. "I'm flattered you remember," Nicki said.

"Of course I remember. I'm a fan. I even bought the stress balls."

Miles and Lucy were still kissing, partly because their young guests kept hitting their glasses of soda with whatever metal object they could find. The boys next to the table were drumming a two-liter bottle of Mountain Dew with plastic knives.

Just like the day in Hawaii when she put her face into the water, she looked at Miles as he kissed his beloved, who wasn't her, and forced herself to keep looking, even after his jaw moved to take her tongue into his mouth and her hand—which had limited access, given her height—twisted in his hair.

She didn't feel a damn thing. Slight amusement at the inappropriate display—the boys were hooting—and happiness for him, since he'd obviously found a nice woman, but nothing else.

It must be so much easier for them when they're horizontal, Nicki thought, watching Miles hunch over Lucy's petite frame. She put down the red wine. She and Ansel had a slight height difference that was notable only because she, the woman, was the taller one. All in all, they were perfectly matched, the way his hips fit against her pelvis, his mouth was right where she could reach it, his chest against hers—

They *had* been perfectly matched.

She needed a drink. "How about you and I take over the bar?" she asked Fawn. "These guys aren't up to it."

"I thought Betty was going to do it." Fawn looked around as she stepped behind the table, pushing aside Miles and Lucy, who laughed and went out to greet some other guests. "Where *is* that woman?"

"She's got purple hair now," Nicki said. "Blends in a little better." She joined Fawn and poured her own drink, downed it, and had another.

By the time Betty finally showed up to relieve them, Nicki was buzzed and introspective, no longer aware of Miles, the other guests, or much of anything. Music blasting in her ears, she wandered across the clubhouse, delayed a few times by former students, until she was outside gulping foggy, chilly air.

She weaved between the cars to her own and got inside. Pressure building in her chest, she found her phone in her bag under a jacket in the backseat and stared at the screen.

She'd plugged in his number that morning. The act had felt permanent, insanely optimistic; why would she need to record his number into her contacts if she called him only once?

Her head fell back against the seat. It wasn't the wine that made her dizzy. What if he didn't answer?

What if he did?

This was why she'd taken the laptop. It was an easy excuse, an icebreaker.

But when she'd taken it, she hadn't known what she knew right now. She'd wondered, but the myth of Miles had blinded her to the real, hard truth of it.

She loved Ansel. There wasn't any doubt. In her case, if she told her friends, "I love Ansel," they'd know it was true because she never, ever talked like that, not even with men she'd dated for over a year. It was always *care* or *want* or *desire*. Even with Miles, she'd called him *soul mate, partner, Thor.*

So she knew this was real.

Finger shaking over the glowing screen, she tapped Ansel's name.

Chapter 29

"Happy birthday, Dad." Ansel handed him the present he'd brought, a small, carefully wrapped package with a yellow bow.

Jordan had closed the restaurant for the night. Other than family, his mother had invited fifty people: her father's closest friends and forty-eight others.

"I wish you'd been able to talk her out of this," his father said.

"And miss the look on your face?" Rachel patted him on the shoulder. "Never. Open it up, Dad. Let's see what Ansel thinks you should be reading."

"How'd you know it was a book?" Ansel asked.

"What else would it be?" she replied. "Look at it."

Their father, looking trapped, glanced around the crowded restaurant before he pulled the bow and slipped out the book.

"*Power for the Hungry*?" He looked at Ansel from his chair in the corner, the seat closest the rear exit.

"I thought you might like it," Ansel said. "It's a how-to book on world domination."

His father set the book on the table and put his hand over

it, a faint smile on his lips. "Nice." He leaned back in the bench seat and lifted his drink.

Stomach tightening, Ansel glanced at Rachel. She nodded and walked away, greeting old friends of their mother's who wanted to talk about the mural over the front door. The rainbows and unicorns had been a huge hit with the post-irony crowd in the city.

"I talked to Mom," Ansel said, pulling up a chair. An abandoned popcorn-and-bok-choy spring roll lay half-eaten on a square plate on the table between them. "I suppose she told you."

"Your mom never tells me anything."

Ansel smiled. "Well, I've been thinking we should talk."

"Is this really the place, Anse? I don't know half of these people."

"We could go for a walk."

His father rolled his eyes. "In this neighborhood? You'd think your fifty grand could've paid for a hole in a nicer wall."

"It's San Francisco, not Truckee. Rent's expensive."

"Nothing wrong with Truckee. Great skiing." His father picked up his drink and drained it.

"You didn't used to be like this, Dad. You used to be just like Mom." Ansel looked down at the plate. "You know, happy."

"You don't think I'm happy?"

"No." Ansel poked the spring roll. It was a popular appetizer, though mostly for shock value. "And I think you're giving me a hard time because of it."

"Don't worry about me. You've got your own life to live." His father licked his lips, avoiding eye contact. "How's that going, by the way? You didn't have to drop off the face of the earth just because we had a little conversation."

Ansel managed to maintain a mild tone. "You didn't call me, either."

"I thought I was doing you a favor. You'd hit me up when you were ready." His father flashed a smile. "And here you are."

"Here I am." Ansel noticed the deep grooves on either side of his father's mouth, the worry lines above his brow. His dark brown hair was mostly gray now—thinning, but cut so short it was hard to tell. "I've figured a few things out. Not everything, but a few things."

"Your mother's been mad at me. She thinks I don't understand you."

"Do you think you do?" Ansel asked.

"I thought I did." He leaned back, sighing, and cast a glance at the crowd admiring Rachel's rainbow-and-unicorn mural.

Ansel tensed in the lengthening silence. He'd hoped his father would at least try to meet him halfway. "One thing I've figured out is that I'm never going to kill myself trying to get rich, just to make you happy."

Eyes snapping back to Ansel, his father said, "I never said I wanted you to—"

"You implied it. You wanted me to devote myself to something serious—"

"Which could be anything, even painting"—he pointed across the room— "unicorns."

"As if giving away money to people who have dreams isn't serious," Ansel finished. He leaned forward. "And now I know it is. I knew it before, but now I really know it."

His father pursed his lips and looked away.

Ansel put his hand over his wrist. It wasn't as big as he remembered, no bigger than his own.

"I made a spreadsheet," Ansel said. "You'll like it. Think of it as your real birthday present. It has lots of numbers on it. Hard data. I've gone back through all my files"—this was an exaggeration, since his files consisted of emails, scraps of paper in a shoe box, and online bank statements—"and compiled a summary of all the people and organizations, profit and non-profit, I've given money to in the past decade."

His father shook his head. "You've got the wrong idea—"

Ansel reached down and pulled out the manila folder he had in the messenger bag at his feet and slapped it on the table. "Read it." He jabbed his finger against the card stock. "Every penny accounted for. Well, mostly." He thought of all the forgotten bar tabs and restaurant checks he'd picked up over the years, which made him think of Nicki arguing about paying for the pizza, which made him pull open the folder and thrust the first page toward his dad. "Read it."

Kevin Jarski didn't take his eyes off his son's face. "I don't need to."

"Yes! Yes, you do! Do you know how long this took me to put together?" Ansel gave the folder a firm shove across the table and then picked up a water glass and looked into it, wondering whose it was. "Like I told you," he said, taking a sip, "I've been busy."

"I'm sixty years old."

"Happy birthday."

"I remember you and Rachel being born like it was yesterday." His father shrugged. "It's true. No other way to say it. I was a young man, I blinked, here I am."

"I know life goes quickly," Ansel said, assuming his father was trying to lecture him again about how he had to seize the day. He picked up the folder and waved it. "Just look at it. I've got thirty-five businesses—okay, some are just people, but they're just the kind of people you'd like, Dad, all serious and obsessive about something—"

His dad held up his hands, shaking his head, refusing to touch the folder. "You're not hearing me. Maybe it's my fault. Your mother says I should stick to email, give up on verbal communication altogether." He braced his palms on the table and leaned back. "I think it's been a rough year for both of us."

Ansel popped up to his feet. "Read it!" He shook the folder so roughly that pages slipped out and fell into the peanut sauce for the spring roll. "It's proof I'm not the loser you think I am. I'm not going to change, Dad, so you should read this. It'll help you feel better about me. " He picked up the paper and swiped at the sauce, blood pounding in his ears.

"Ansel." His father stood, reached across the table, and grabbed both of his arms. "I'm sorry."

"You don't have to be sorry—that's what I'm telling you. I just didn't see that everything I did *was* the same, *did* have a purpose, that having too much damn money didn't ruin me the way you think it did."

His father came around the table, still gripping his forearms, and gave him a shake. "Will you shut up?" He glanced over Ansel's shoulder, then back at him. "I'm trying to apologize."

Ansel looked behind him and saw his mother watching them hopefully.

He turned back to his father. "Let's talk in the kitchen. This needs to be between us."

His father grimaced. "All right." With a loud sigh, he slapped Ansel on the back and walked toward the kitchen. "Come on, then."

Jordan was blocking a young bald guy with tattoos on his neck trying to carry a plate of sandwiches to the dining room. "What the hell is that?"

The young guy, whose name Ansel recalled was Max, shot him and his father a pleading look. "She asked me."

"Who asked for what?" Jordan demanded. He peeled back the top piece of bread on one of the sandwiches, revealing tuna coated in glistening whiteness. He recoiled as if he'd found maggot-infested carrion. "Is that... *mayonnaise?*"

Standing at attention, the scandalous plate on display in his trembling hands, Max nodded once.

"Leave him alone," Ansel's father said, ushering Max past them out the swinging doors, out of Jordan's reach. "My wife's a force of nature—but has the palate of a second grader, unfortunately."

"Jordan, we need to borrow the kitchen for a minute," Ansel said. "We'll stay out of your way."

Jordan raised his empty hands, apparently still furious about the tuna salad. "No problem. I'm not needed here anyway," he said, striding out the back door to the alley.

"You'd think she'd learn how to eat more things, given all the traveling," his father began.

"Here, eight years ago," Ansel said, holding up the spreadsheet and pointing at the first line, "was the first little chunk of money I ever gave away. It's a job-training thing in Hayward, nothing fancy, but they needed a few computers—"

His father plucked the paper out of his hands and crushed it between his palms. "You don't have to justify anything to me."

Ansel gaped at his father's clenched fist. "I know it's your birthday, but don't you think that was a bit rude?"

"Ansel."

"I worked hard on that," Ansel said dully.

"Look at me."

Ansel finally processed what his father had said a minute earlier. He looked into his father's face. "That's not true. All you've ever wanted is for me to justify myself to you."

His father chewed on his lower lip, scowling. "I hate it when your mother is right, you know that?"

"She's always right."

"Maybe that's why I'm in such a bad mood all the time," his father said.

"Is that it?"

Kevin Jarski smiled. "No, that's not fair. It's my problem." He put an arm around Ansel and crushed him against his chest. "You're your mother's son, you know that?"

"She reminds me of it all the time."

"You're just like her. Giving, feeling, giving some more. I don't understand it. I couldn't keep up if I tried." His father whacked him on the back before embracing him. Compressed, Ansel's lungs strained for air.

"You're confusing me, Dad," he gasped.

His father relaxed his grip. "You should just keep doing what you're doing. If I'm jealous, it's my own stupid fault."

"Jealous of what?"

"Your mother has it too, that enthusiasm. When she inherited all that money, she didn't lose any of her drive. She just got more excited. More alive." His father released him completely and took a step back, his tone growing serious. "It's done the opposite for me. I realized, not long ago, that it was killing me. Not having to work. Not having to care."

"But you've always kept so busy—"

"Busy isn't enough. I need more," his father said. He crossed his arms over his chest. "I'm going back to school."

"What?"

"Engineering. Or chemistry. I have to relearn about six years' worth of mathematics before I can apply, but I've hired a tutor." He made a face. "Money's good for some things, no doubt about that."

"That's great."

"I won't need that book you got me. Or was that just a joke?"

"It was something Diane gave me," Ansel said. "I thought you'd like it more than I did."

"I've never wanted you to be like that. I've met assholes all over the world, just like that—why would I want you to be one of them?"

"You said—"

"I'm so sorry for what I said. I was talking to myself, not you. It's me who needs to commit to something," he said. "And that's what I'm going to do."

Ansel stared, absorbing the shift in his father's attitude. "Are you sure Mom didn't put you up to this?"

"Of course she did." His father looked at the crumpled ball of paper in his fist, a half-smile forming on his lips. "Thirty-five, huh?"

"At least."

Running his tongue along his lower lip, his father opened the ball of paper as if he were sectioning an orange. "You're proud of yourself."

"Yes."

He nodded. "That's what I wanted. I screwed up my messaging, but that's what I meant."

Ansel retrieved the paper and smoothed it out on the counter next to a stainless steel bowl half-filled with tuna salad. "Seven of the businesses not only survived, they've paid me back the original loan. Not that I called it a loan, but people are pretty cool if you give them a chance."

They discussed each one: what they did, who they were, why he cared. When they finished with the thirty-fifth, his father patted his hands on the wrinkled paper before walking away to the dining room. "We done? I want to tease your sister about those unicorns."

Chapter 30

When his father was out of sight, Ansel leaned against a counter and closed his eyes. That was good, but now that the conveniently distracting father issue was out of the way, his misery came over him at full blast.

Would she let him into the condo if he showed up in the morning?

He wouldn't, if he were her.

He had to try anyway.

Jordan came into the kitchen looking slightly less homicidal. He was washing his hands in the sink when Rachel joined them.

"Can I have my ride home now, Mr. Designated Driver?" she asked. "Mom's so happy about you and Dad that she said she'll survive if we make a run for it early. They're breaking out the karaoke."

Jordan looked up from the sink. "You mean they're leaving to go somewhere else to do karaoke," he said flatly.

Rachel shook her head. "Nope. They brought a machine with them." Laughing, she rolled her eyes at Jordan. "Don't worry. It's not like the cool kids will find out. It's a private party."

Ansel felt around in his jeans for his phone, wanting to know the time, but remembered his mother had confiscated it at the door. She had zero tolerance for phones that interrupted any actual living underway. Her children always handed them over like college kids turning in their keys at a kegger.

The first week he'd been back from Hawaii, Ansel had always had his phone with him—in the bathroom, at the gym, by his bed all night, always on and charged. Just in case Nicki had something to say, even to yell at him for leaving.

Jordan pointed at the dining room. "The walls are thin. People walking by will hear Joan Baez, and there goes my street cred, you know?"

"Embrace it with irony like you do everything else," Rachel said. She put a hand on Ansel's arm. "You coming? It's after eleven, and… hey, are you all right?"

"I'm coming." Ansel shoved the crumpled spreadsheet into a recycling bin. "Thanks, Jordan. Sorry about the mayo and the music. Spike the booze with Ambien if you have to."

"That will be great for business," Jordan said. "Especially after I've been sentenced to a few years in prison."

Ansel squeezed his shoulder and turned to his sister. "Just need to get my bag and shake down Mom for my phone."

Out in the dining room, Mel Jury was blessedly too busy singing into a large pink microphone to stop and chat. They retrieved their things, said their good-byes—their father asked if he could come with them, but they made him stay—and escaped into a blast of cold San Francisco air whistling through the narrow streets.

Since Rachel was living in London, she was sleeping on Ansel's couch during her stay. They hiked up a forty-five-degree angle side street to his car, got in, and drove to his place, not speaking a word.

He knew she was using her twin powers again, so he wasn't surprised when she asked, "Why don't you just fly out there and see the woman, you big dope?"

"You don't think it'll ruin her vacation?"

Rachel swatted him above his left ear. "Dumping her was much better."

"I didn't dump her. I practically *proposed*, for God's sake."

"Which was the perfect thing to do after knowing her for, like, two weeks."

"Three," he said. "And actually, we met years and years go."

"Which was so pivotal to your life, you didn't remember her face or her name."

"Shut up."

"You came on way too fast," Rachel said.

"Please shut up."

"You can't blame her for freaking out."

He shifted into first to make it to the peak of the hill they were climbing. She hadn't freaked out; *he* had. "I don't blame her for anything."

"Then—"

"I've already bought a ticket, all right? I'm flying out first thing in the morning."

Rachel exhaled. "Thank *God*. I won't blame her if she kicks you out on your ass."

He swallowed, fearing the inevitable. "Thanks."

She held up two matching cell phones. "We did it again. Same model, same color case."

He glanced over and smiled. They didn't have identical DNA, but they had odd moments of sharing identical taste.

On a street near his apartment, he parallel parked with inches to spare before taking his phone from her. As they trudged down another hill to his building, he powered it on— his mother always turned them off—and checked his messages.

When he heard Nicki's voice, he stopped in the middle of the sidewalk. Rachel, not noticing, continued on.

"Hey," Nicki said. There was a long pause. "It's me. Nicki. I don't know if you want to hear from me, and I don't care. I'm sitting in my car. I just saw Miles and his new wife, and I don't care about that either. Do you get it? I don't care. You were wrong. Wrong, wrong, wrong. Yes, I've had a few drinks, but that's not why I'm calling. I know I love you, and my love is much stronger than yours is even though it took me a while to figure it out—and I would never just run away without talking to you about it. Like you did. Everyone thinks I'm the coward, but I'm only afraid of stupid things. I think *you*'re stupid—"

With a beep, the message was cut off.

Rachel finally noticed he wasn't moving and turned to yell up the street at him. "What's the matter?"

He shook his head, frantically looking up the time of the call—7:45p.m.—and put it back to his ear.

Another message from Nicki.

"And I think your phone is stupid for cutting me off. Where was I? I'm sitting in my car. I have your laptop. Not with me, at my apartment." Loud sigh. "I can't go there now, though, because I have to sober up first. I only got in the car to call you, and you didn't even answer." There was a long pause, then a click.

Rachel was at his side. "What happened?"

He swallowed with difficulty. "Nicki was trying to reach me." He looked at his sister, lit up from one side by a lamp across the street. "Over four hours ago. I'm such an idiot. I never should've given Mom my phone. I'm thirty years old. What is my problem?"

"It makes her happy," Rachel said, "and you're a people pleaser."

"Fuck that. Nicki wanted to talk to me. Now she's pissed. Damn it!"

"Call her back, Einstein," Rachel said.

He was already listening to the third ring on her line, waiting for her to pick up. "Nicki, Nicki," he whispered.

"Want me to try on mine? Maybe she's screening her calls."

He ended the call and tried again as he started to march back to his car. "I'm going over there."

"Where?"

"Her apartment."

"It's kind of late," Rachel said.

"Don't remind me," he muttered.

Rachel pulled out her own phone. "I'll text you the address."

"I've already got it." Back in Hawaii, he'd asked Nicki for it. He got behind the wheel, blinking fast, hating himself for everything he'd ever done to risk this shot at happiness, and slammed the door.

Rachel ran after him and pulled it open. "You want me to come?"

"No, I have to do this myself." He revved the engine.

"Then can I have a key to your apartment? I'd rather not sleep on the street."

He put the car back in park and detached his keys. "Right," he said, handing them to her. "It's 3C, last one on the left—"

"I was there a few hours ago, bro. Good luck. Let me know if you need me to argue your case."

He waved, barely stopping himself from driving over his only twin sister in his desperation to get moving.

Chapter 31

*S*he heard the buzzer through several layers of consciousness, a pillow, her left arm, and what was left of three glasses of wine—and one of champagne—swimming in her bloodstream.

She'd had the sense to get a ride home from the wedding reception. Taxis, she'd told herself hours ago as she'd climbed out of the dented suburban cab, a station wagon from the 90s, existed for a reason. She'd have to retrieve her car in the morning.

The door buzzed again.

She got out of bed, confused but relatively sober. It must be late. Her mouth was parched and foul, as if she'd snacked on vomit before sucking on a blow dryer.

Maybe she'd imagined the buzzing. She used the toilet, brushed her teeth, and guzzled tap water for five long seconds before she heard it again.

She blinked at her own reflection in the mirror, more concerned about the mascara on her nose than whoever was ringing her bell.

Another buzz.

"Fine," she said, storming out of the bathroom to her door. She had a small apartment; crossing the living room took her four strides. She held down the white button on the intercom near the door. "Yes?"

"Nicki, it's me."

She took a step back, questioning her senses. She'd imagined his voice as she was climbing into bed, only to admit a moment later that it had been a neighbor's TV.

She held down the button. "Who?"

"Ansel."

Her heart began pounding so hard, she couldn't move. She swallowed but didn't know what to say. She'd expected a phone call, a grudging willingness to talk, not a home visit.

"I'm so sorry. Nicki? Please let me in. Hello?"

She needed time to figure out how she was going to approach this.

Now he wanted to see her? After weeks of silence, in the middle of the night?

She put her mouth near the mic. "Come back in the morning." A smile twitched at the corner of her mouth. In the four years she'd lived in the building, she'd always thought the intercom was a hassle; the price of living in a low-rent neighborhood near the freeway. Now she'd pay extra for it.

Thirty years old was late to learn you had a taste for revenge.

There was a long pause. So long, she started to regret her vengeful impulses. After counting to five in Japanese, she pressed the button again. "Ansel?"

He responded immediately. "I'll come back in the morning if you want me to. Or right now. Which would you prefer?"

Involuntarily, she smiled and put a hand on her chest.

She missed him so much.

All right, so her taste for revenge was a small one. He'd said he loved her. Maybe it was true.

She held down the other button to let him in.

He'd gotten her messages and come over in person. What had she said? She'd told him she was over Miles. She'd called him stupid…

She put her forehead against the door, waiting for him to climb the stairs and knock, which he did very gently, a tap so quiet she wouldn't have heard it if her head weren't pressed up against the wood.

And that thing about loving him.

She stepped back and opened it.

He was dressed in the usual monochromatic shades of charcoal but more formal than she'd ever seen him in Hawaii: slacks, button-down shirt, closed-toe shoes.

The sight of him sliced her right between the ribs and pinned her where she stood.

He returned her stare. He looked short of breath.

She stepped aside to let him in, then dead-bolted the door behind him with clumsy fingers.

He had said, with some evidence, that fear ruled her. But she had a spine when it mattered, and it mattered now.

"I love you," she said, putting her hands on her hips. She lifted her chin. "Is that why you're here?"

"I love you, too," he said. He took a step closer.

She let the words sink in, like butter into hot toast, before she responded. "You sure give up easily. You ran away at the first sign of trouble."

"I never meant to stay away so long. I have a ticket to fly to Kahului first thing in the morning."

She wasn't ready to let him see how much that meant. "Booked it as soon as you got my message?"

His face melted into a grin that made her breath catch. Shaking his head, he moved closer, about two feet away. "Booked it yesterday. I'm so nervous, I'm about to vomit, but you make me laugh anyway."

"I'm about to vomit because I drank too much."

His eyebrows went up. "Are you kidding?"

"Mostly." She combed her hair with her fingers. "I was celebrating a little too hard."

"I came as soon as I heard your messages. I've never driven so fast over the Bay Bridge as I did just now."

"Did your girlfriend mind you leaving her alone?"

He shook his head, the humor draining out of him. "There's nobody else. There's never been anybody like you."

"Oh," she whispered.

"You terrify me. Ever since I saw you floating off that boat and I realized I could lose you. Since you're the only one of you, you know?"

An unfamiliar joy washed over her. He was kind and funny, sexy, smart, everything she loved; she loved him, and he said things like that to her. "I'm sorry I scared you. If it hadn't been for that boy——"

"I know. You thought you had to do it, which is why I'm so afraid. You have these impulses that could kill you, and then who would I live with for the rest of my life?"

She stopped breathing.

"See?" He put his hands on either side of her face, capturing her. "You think you love me, but you're not ready for me. I'm impulsive, Nicki. I do things all the way. I dive right in. I'm stupid that way. I can't help it."

"Like leaving me?"

"Exactly. How could you ever forgive me for that? I never meant to stay away so long, but for each day that went by, I got more hopeless. I convinced myself you'd had a good time and you were done with me. I was just a substitute for a hot pool boy, nothing you'd want to bring home with you." He moved his mouth to her cheek, not kissing, just breathing. "Especially after you found out I was broke."

She drew back. "But if I wanted you just for sex, why did I

need you to be rich, too? If I was just going to chuck you over-board, so to speak, when I was done with you?"

He moved closer again. "You've got to understand, Nicki, until I met you, the money seemed to affect what most people thought of me. Not just women. Everybody."

"I think it affects what you think of yourself more," she said.

He rested his cheek against hers and pulled her close. "Yeah. I've been working on that."

His jaw was rough against hers. She put her arms around his waist. "I don't want you to be rich if it makes you unhappy."

"Being rich was fine. Trying to get there, not so much."

She smiled into his neck. "I like you right where you are."

"Yeah." His hands moved down her body, caressing, exploring. His voice lowered. "You scared the hell out of me when you said you didn't love me," he said quietly.

"I never said that."

"You couldn't say you did, though. That was enough."

She slid her hand down to his chest and felt his heart beating through the fabric. "I thought I was in love with you when we met. Way back when."

"But seeing me again cured you?"

"Getting to know the real you made it true," she said. Her body melted into his. She felt hot and charged, brilliant, happy, alive. "And I'm not afraid of this." She kissed him. "I want it all."

"I'll give you everything I have," he said.

"Same here."

"And if that's not enough," he added, dropping kisses along her throat, "I'll get more."

Deep anxieties, not the kind that had made her faint near swimming pools, but the more profound, existential type, stopped her from pulling him down to the couch and taking off his clothes just yet. "What if I'm not enough?" she asked him.

He caressed her hip. "Oh, you're perfect."

"I write for a blog about my phobias," she said. "I never told you about that."

"Sounds cool." His hand slipped under her shirt and fondled her breast.

"But as soon as I've tackled each one, I'm going to stop writing about it. I don't want to have any incentive to hold on to this way of thinking."

He ran his tongue along her lower lip. "Sensible."

"Ansel?"

He was sucking on her earlobe. "Mmm?"

"What if I cure myself?" she asked, closing her eyes. "I'm starting to believe it's possible."

"You will," he mumbled against her mouth, tilting his head to kiss her. "You're amazing."

She kissed him back, forgetting her worries for a minute and then pulling away as she remembered. It was too important to ignore, just the thing to sabotage this shared life they were starting. "Will you still want me if I do?"

"Want you if you do what?"

"If I get over the anxieties. If I'm not a mess."

"You've never been a mess, Nicki."

"Brand and Diane, even Rachel, say you like your women screwed up," she said, "but I'm not going to stay screwed up just to turn you on."

"Swear to God, I'm going to kill them," he muttered. "You, Nicki, are the least screwed-up woman I've ever known."

She stared at him. "How can you say that?"

"Who are you comparing yourself to?" He held her shoulders and looked into her face. "I've been with women who couldn't hold down a job or who relied on me for the cash to gamble or buy drugs."

"Wow. Really?"

"Feeling faint when you go over a bridge is a piece of cake compared to that."

"It can be a lot worse than that. I used to have days when I couldn't drive to work."

"And then what did you do?"

"I had to take the bus."

"Big tragedy," he said.

"I can't believe you're mocking my anxiety disorder." She let him squirm for a second before smiling. "I love it when you do that." She traced his jawline with her thumb.

"It seems better than freaking out with you."

She nodded. "Whenever other people take my fears seriously, it's like they're agreeing with me. Like I *should* be at full panic level."

"Speaking of panic, I'm starting to worry about getting you naked." He hooked his ankle behind hers and pulled her down with him to her overstuffed couch.

Before her pajamas came off, Nicki straddled him and pinned his shoulders to the cushions. "What were you going to do tomorrow when you got to Maui?"

His eyes were unfocused with passion. "What?"

"What were you going to say to me? Did you have a plan?"

"Of course I had a plan. I couldn't risk my life's happiness without having a plan," he said, caressing the small of her back.

His touch made her shiver with pleasure, but she continued. "Before you knew how I felt, what were you going to say?"

"You sure do talk a lot."

"I know how you men are. This might be the last time we ever have a decent conversation about our relationship," she said.

He turned his face away, groaning.

"Come on," she said. "Pretend you don't know I adore you

and want to spend the rest of my life with you, and I've just opened the door."

"Are you naked?"

"Nope. Lots of clothes."

"Good," he said. "Then I'd be able to concentrate, remember my notes from the plane."

"You have notes?"

"Not yet, since I wasn't on the plane, was I?"

She grinned, wriggling on top of him. "Okay. I'm standing there in my clothes. You remember your notes. What do you say?"

"Are you wearing that sexy green dress? Because then I might forget my notes."

She was feeling forgetful herself. His body felt so good beneath her…

"It was short," he said. "I was going to improvise the rest of it."

"Let's hear it. Don't be nervous. You already know how it's going to turn out."

He reached up and touched her face. "I need you."

"I can feel how much you need me," she said, rotating her hips. "Focus. What do you say?"

"That's it. That's what I say." He gazed up into her eyes. "I need you."

She sobered, struck by his serious tone. "I need you, too, Ansel."

"That's how you're different from the other women in my life. They needed me, never the other way around." He lifted himself up until his arms were around her waist and his face was close to hers. "I can't imagine life without you. That's what I was going to say. You don't have to love me. I just want to be with you. I need to have you in my life even if you aren't nearly as crazy about me as I am about you."

Her mouth was dry. "But I am. I love you like I've never loved anyone."

He paused. "Thank God," he said finally with a sigh, rolling over with her in his arms. "But really, as long as you'll let me stick around, I'm happy. Because I need you that bad."

She kissed him, gently at first, then desperately. Neither spoke for a long time. They were suddenly in a hurry to make up for the long, lost weeks, even though they knew they had a lifetime to do it.

Epilogue

They were married six months later in a beachside ceremony. It was the height of whale watching season, and the flash of giant tails rising out of the water interrupted the vows more than once.

Nicki, barefoot, wore a custom-made white silk sundress that danced around her long legs like butterfly wings. Ansel wore a tuxedo jacket with board shorts.

Brand and Diane were their honor attendants. Because of their devotion to their shared career in the real estate field, they had flown in for only the day, although they were in high spirits and laughed at all of Nicki's jokes. Their gift to the couple was an oceanfront office building with monthly rents twice that of the neighboring structure. Its maintenance costs were reduced by the solar panels on the roof.

Jordan was in charge of the guests' picnic bento boxes after the ceremony. As a dig to Melinda Jury, he'd packed her a box that contained one tuna salad sandwich with extra mayonnaise, an apple, a small package of cheese-flavored fish crackers, and a chilled carton of chocolate milk imprinted with a dancing cow princess. She laughed and ate every bite.

The father of the groom, wearing a three-piece suit and waterproof hiking sandals, offered a long, meandering toast about how he hoped his new daughter-in-law knew what a terrific, generous human being she'd married, and if she ever doubted it, to come by for dinner and he'd set her straight. Only Nicki's mother, who was touchy about that sort of thing, thought it was in poor taste.

At least twice at the reception, Rachel told everyone that she was responsible for the happy couple being together. Brand and Diane claimed the same thing. Betty knew they were all wrong, but she was too busy proposing to Jaynette—and then enjoying her response—to argue.

When the celebration was winding down, and the guests sat in the sand, watching whales have a party of their own, everyone agreed it was worth the cost of the trip halfway around the world.

It was at that moment, while they held hands on the outskirts of the celebration, that Nicki and Ansel shared a long meaningful look. They were supposed to leave a little later, after another round of drinks.

Ansel glanced at the parking lot. "Shall we?"

Nicki grinned. "Thought you'd never ask."

And so they made a run for it, muffling their laughter as they galloped across the hot sand to the old gas-electric hybrid, garishly decorated with paint and streamers, that waited for them.

"*Now* will you tell me where we're going?" she asked as she buckled her seat belt. He'd refused to tell her where they'd be spending the night, although she had a pretty good idea.

"It costs two thousand a night," he replied, "and has excellent privacy curtains."

As he peeled out into the road, she laughed, wondering when she'd ever been so happy. So completely, blindingly happy.

She was thirty-one, so—she counted back through the years—one, two, three…

Never. Yeah, never was about right.

<hr>

Don't miss the story of Miles
and Lucy

<hr>

Excerpt of
THE SUPERMODEL'S BEST FRIEND
Chapter 1

THIS WAS NOT IN THE plan, Lucy thought, staring at the handsome face on her phone. Her fiancé was supposed to be standing by her side, pen in hand, not using video smartphone technology to dump her from another state. *I don't love you enough to let you ruin the plan.*

"You must've known I had some doubts," Dan said, his voice as small as he was.

Lucy looked around the empty living room of the spacious three-bedroom California bungalow with original plank hardwoods and walnut built-ins. "You said you'd kill to have this house," she said, wondering if the real estate agent, laying out the pages for their revised offer on the granite breakfast counter in the kitchen, could hear them.

"It's a great house," he said, sighing. "A perfect house. But now I see that it would just tie us down, drag out the inevitable."

She blinked, not sure what she was hearing. "We've been planning this for almost five years."

He hesitated. "I met someone."

"When? This morning?"

Licking his lips, he said, "Why don't we talk later, after you've had a chance to calm down."

She frowned. "I'm hardly hysterical, Dan."

"Yeah, I noticed."

"You'd like me to be hysterical?"

"Forget it. Of course not. It makes everything easier."

She nodded, belatedly piecing together some clues he'd dropped over the past few months. "Your six-month assignment in Seattle wasn't the opportunity of a lifetime, then."

"Well…"

"Ah. A personal opportunity, you meant."

"I wanted to be sure. For both—for all of us."

"Very considerate of you," she said.

"Damn it, you don't have to be sarcastic."

"You're hardly in a position to tell me what to do. I'm the wounded party here, wouldn't you agree?"

"I think we'll both need some healing."

Lucy dropped the phone to her side and noticed that Robin, the real estate agent, had come up behind her. Her face was pale.

This was really going to screw over the older lady, the two of them walking away from the deal now. Robin needed a sale badly. Typical of Dan to think the world revolved around him.

Lucy lifted the phone. "We'll have to call the mortgage broker."

He jutted out his chin. "I already have."

"You told Inez the mortgage broker before you told me?"

"She kept after me to sign the latest thing. It didn't feel right to string her along anymore—" He stopped and cleared his throat. "Look, you're getting digitized. I think the connection is breaking up…"

"It didn't feel right to string *her* along?"

He sighed. "So much of our lives together is what you wanted. Not me. I felt… superfluous a lot of the time." He tilted the screen of his laptop so she was staring out the window of his suite at the Extended Stay America. It wasn't supposed to be sunny in Seattle. It looked sunny. She wondered if the new girlfriend was there, listening off-camera. Dan came back into view with a coffee cup at his lips.

In Berkeley, outside the house she wasn't going to have, the sky was as gray as lint. "Our relationship was always shaped by what you wanted. We talked about marriage years ago. I hoped to have my first child before I turned thirty. But you wanted to save up for the house first, so we did, even though that was third on my list."

"You and your lists. That's one thing I've learned from Brittany—how to trust my heart."

"Ah, so she's one of those." She took a deep breath and peered into the phone for a glimpse of her. "What else did the little ho say?"

Dan's mouth dropped open in shock.

"You wanted hysterical. This is my version."

He looked away, then back at the screen, his lips popping up and down like a broken garage door. "Brittany is not—" He shook his head and stared off to the side, made an apologetic face, then jerked his head.

So she had been there. "Thanks for making this such a private moment."

"I can't believe Brittany had to hear *you* call *her* a—a—I can't even say it."

"What? She's been sleeping with my boyfriend. For months, apparently.."

"Brittany has nothing to be ashamed of."

"Does she know about me?"

"Of course. She knows everything."

Lucy snorted. Her college advisor would've broken out in a rash to hear her insult a woman for exercising her sexual liberties, but to hell with it. She was under a lot of stress. "Ho."

Dan's eyes went wide as he leaned into his laptop camera. "She is completely innocent. Brittany's not in such a hurry to take her clothes off. Unlike *you*."

Lucy felt an odd snapping inside her, her last grip on reality disengaging from Dan's voice. "We lived together for five years. You think we should have waited until we were, what, forty?"

"It's not how long we waited, it's how *often* you wanted it. And how much you wanted to do it. I'm a man, Lucy, and I didn't need half as much sex as you did." Then he ran his hand over his eyes and said, "I'm sorry. I never intended to talk to you about this."

Her throat suddenly felt tight. She realized Robin the real estate agent was hanging on every word. "Did you talk to her about this? Brittany?"

His sheepish look grew sheepier; he leaned away from the camera. Faintly, she heard him say, "That's how we… how we knew we were perfect for each other. She was avoiding her boyfriend, and I… I was taking a break, too."

"And where was this? Her convent?"

"Lucy," Dan said, shaking his head, looking so *disappointed* in her.

Humiliation didn't feel right, so she tapped into the rage, breathed it like oxygen. "I'm just trying to get the full picture here. I deserve to know the details."

"Information isn't knowledge, Lucy," Dan said. "Knowing everything doesn't make you wise."

"And having a penis doesn't make you a man," Lucy said.

Robin snorted and patted her hard on the back. Lucy closed her eyes. *He didn't like having sex with me*, she thought. It's not like she had a he-harem of previous boyfriends to call up for rebuttals. She was thirty-four, but she'd started late.

Damn. It took him five years to propose. She didn't have another eight to work on someone new. There were houses to buy, retirement accounts to fund, ovaries to harvest.

She frowned at him. "You've really messed up my plans."

"Sometimes I think that's all I was to you, Lucy. Just part of your plans." He leaned back and put his hand over his heart. "I've learned that I need a partner who acts without analyzing everything to death. Someone more flexible."

Lucy glanced at Robin, but it was far too late for any privacy. Holding the phone up to her mouth, she said, enunciating each word, "One of my plans was for decent sex. I was flexible about giving up on that."

She drew back to see his reaction, but the window had gone black.

———

THE SUPERMODEL'S BEST FRIEND is available now in ebook and paperback!

Also by Gretchen Galway

SONOMA WITCHES (Paranormal Mystery)

Dead Witch on a Bridge (Sonoma Witches #1)

Hex at a House Party (Sonoma Witches #2)

A Spell to Die For (Sonoma Witches #3)

OAKLAND HILLS SERIES (Romance)

Love Handles (Oakland Hills #1)

This Time Next Door (Oakland Hills #2)

Not Quite Perfect (Oakland Hills #3)

This Changes Everything (Oakland Hills #4)

Quick Takes (Oakland Hills Stories Boxed Set)

Going For Broke (Oakland Hills #5)

Going Wild (Oakland Hills #6)

Oakland Hills Romantic Comedy Boxed Set (Books 1-3)

RESORT TO LOVE SERIES (Romance)

The Supermodel's Best Friend (Resort to Love #1) - Miles & Lucy

Diving In (Resort to Love #2) - Nicki & Ansel

About the Author

GRETCHEN GALWAY is a *USA Today* bestselling author who writes mystery, fantasy, and romance. Raised in the American Midwest, she now lives in in Sonoma County, California.

Sign up for her newsletter at www.gretchengalway.com and hear about new releases, sales, and goodies.

www.gretchengalway.com

www.ingramcontent.com/pod-product-compliance
Lightning Source LLC
Chambersburg PA
CBHW031314210726
48287CB00005B/1550